PASSION'S PERILS

Carter regarded me steadily. "What is it you find amusing, Miss Manning?" he asked.

Thinking the moment needed a little levity, I said brazenly, "I was wondering what sort of kisser you'd be." I was completely prepared for a prudish blush and relished the idea of distracting him with what he would consider shocking boldness. Instead, his eyes narrowed, and his mouth curved into a seductive smile that turned my stomach to jelly.

"You could find out," he offered in that voice, low and smooth as mulled wine.

I tried to make my next comment light but failed. "Just because you see me as some sort of harlot," I said in a very odd voice, "does not mean I am willing to experiment with you."

Carter's relentless gaze narrowed as he allowed himself a full, slow smile. "Then watch what you say, Shelby," he said, "lest you be taken at your word."

ELAINE FOX

TRAVELER

LOVE SPELL **NEW YORK CITY**

To my mother, Connie Carter, for her unconditional love and boundless generosity.

To my sisters, Jacquelyn V. M. Taylor and Elizabeth M. Harbison, for being my best friends.

To Pat Gagne (aka Dani Sinclair), for her valuable critiques and invaluable encouragement.

To Gary Potter, for sharing with me his beautiful language.

And to my late father, Jack McShulskis, for teaching me what a real hero is.

TRAVELER

Chapter One

An ominous growl rumbled through the cold night air. At the edge of the Civil War battlefield park, my normally goofy and affectionate border collie stared into the darkness with teeth bared and hackles raised. So strange was this posture for her that a tiny shaft of panic pierced my stomach.

She'd just rooted a tennis ball out of the bushes when she stopped, dropping the ball as if it were not the dog's equivalent of gold, and lowered herself to stealth position. With her face a mask of intensity, her eyes were pinned to a spot to my left. I nervously followed her gaze. There in the grass, not twenty feet away, sat a man. Only a moment before I would have sworn there was no one other than myself in the tiny park. The hairs on the back of my neck prickled as a chill crept up my spine.

He swayed a little and clasped his head in one hand, oblivious to me.

It occurred to me that he might be drunk, but that was

too odd. There were no bars nearby, and I'd never seen a street bum in Fredericksburg, the small Virginia town where I lived. It might have been someone left over from the battle reenactment that day, but the idea of that gathering leaving its patrons to pass out on the grass was ludicrous. Battle reenactments don't usually draw the college-age party-animal types. Not to mention that it was December 13, and the temperature had been in the twenties all day—weather not conducive to napping, no matter how drunk you got. Now, close to midnight, it had to be in the teens.

The man in the grass steadied himself and dropped his hand to his lap, studying his right palm and sliding the fingers together as if they were covered with something sticky. After a moment he wiped the hand on his pants and looked up, way up, to the huge overhanging branches of the oak tree and a bouncing red ski hat that dangled like a yarn flare from one of them.

The wind died down for the moment, but the clouds that had been gathering all day still blocked any light there might have been from the half moon. The dense, cumulus ceiling above gave me the feeling that the heavens themselves had bent low to watch us, cozying us in solitude.

Steve, the dog, stalked forward with a poise I had to admire and growled again, a little louder this time. At the sound of it the man swung his head toward her, caught sight of me in the process, and did a nearly comical double take that caused him to rock dizzily with the effort. His hand went to his temple again, where I could now see a nasty-looking wound, blood running down his cheek to his jaw.

I rose from my seat on the platform of the old Stevens well and the man jerked to his feet, stumbling and swaying. He looked much more alarmed than I thought a man of his size ought to when confronted with a lone female and her dog, though I must say the dog was putting on quite a show of protection. And, to be fair, of the three of us I was probably the only one who knew she would never follow through on the threat that low growl made.

"Steve," I called, giving my voice a touch of weary exasperation for the sake of the frightened fellow. "Steve, come here."

Steve glanced at me; then, head still lowered and hair on end, walked crabwise to me, keeping her steely gaze pinned on the man.

"Good heavens, Steve." I laughed, amazed and slightly amused by the new act. "Come here and give the guy a break."

The man had stopped, backed up against the fence that surrounded old Widow Stevens' grave, and glanced quickly back and forth between the dog and me. For his comfort I snapped on her leash.

"Are you all right?" I called, moving toward him. "You look hurt. Is that a cut on your head?"

The man watched me with stricken, horrified eyes, and I looked down to see what I was wearing. For me it was normal attire: jeans, dark green cowboy boots, and a down coat. My red hair had something of the Medusa look to it after the afternoon of wind, but surely that would not elicit horror in a man. At most I would have given him leave to be disgusted.

"You look a little disoriented," I said, finally getting close enough to see him clearly. "That's quite a bump you've got on your head. Maybe you've got a concussion. I can take you to a doctor, if you want." He wore the uniform of a Union soldier and, as we passed it, Steve sniffed at a pistol reproduction that lay in the grass where he had been sitting. "You must be a reenactor!" I deduced triumphantly. "Jeez, are you guys so authentic that you inflict actual wounds on each other?"

I was close enough now to see his horror replaced by

confusion—a deep, evidently terrifying confusion that caused him to study my whole form as I neared him and to watch my lips as I spoke. Most definitely concussion, I concluded. He needed to be taken to the emergency room.

As I got close, the light from a distant street lamp illuminated the side of his face. He was a handsome guy. Not really a man, I wouldn't say, because he looked to be about twenty-two, and I don't consider males to be men until they hit about fifty. He had to be around six feet tall and was broad across the chest in an athletic sort of way. He had thick, dark blond hair the color of wheat, not cornsilk, that was straight and hung lankily to the tops of his well-defined cheekbones in front and down to his collar in back. Though I could not distinguish their color, his eyes were clearly light because the street lamp seemed to glitter right through them. Yes, he was definitely good-looking.

Unable to resist this motivation, I offered to help. "Listen, my car's not far; why don't I run get it and take you to the emergency room? I really think you should see a doctor."

He didn't answer. His mouth opened as though he might speak, but then he shut it decisively. Steve sniffed at his pant leg and he glared down at her.

"Don't worry about her. She's all bluff." As the words left my mouth, I wondered about the wisdom of imparting this information to a man who was clearly fresh out of a fight and not behaving normally. "Were you mugged or something?"

Finally he spoke. Or croaked, rather. His voice was cracked and harsh. "Who are you?" He seemed stunned by the sound of his own voice, because he drew back his head a little, as if a spider had suddenly dropped to a spot right in front of his nose.

14

"I'm Shelby Manning," I announced, extending my hand confidently. "And the dog is Steve."

He looked at my hand as if I'd thrown out a dead fish. "And your name is . . . ?"

He glanced around himself; at the tree, the well, the historic Innis house, then back at me. He cleared his throat. "Carter Lindsey, Lieutenant, 114th Pennsylvania." He hesitated a moment, then reluctantly took my outstretched hand and shook it once. His hand was cold—icy—and callused, and it dropped mine quickly.

"Oh, well, okay," I said, nodding. It was my turn to glance around, down the street toward my house, then back at him. "Well, aside from all that, do you want me to help you to a doctor?"

He absently fingered the wound again. "Where am I?" he asked in a voice so soft I barely heard it.

I leaned in close and looked into his eyes. They appeared clear and alert to me. "You're in Fredericksburg, Virginia. On Sunken Road. There was a—um—a *thing* here today." I waved airily in the direction of the road and the hill rising beyond it. "A, you know, an enactment—of the battle. One hundred-thirty-fourth anniversary, I believe." I gestured to his uniform. "Marye's Heights? The Civil War?" I prompted.

"Yes!" he said urgently. "The secessionist war, Burnside, Lee. Where are they now?" He nearly took me by the shoulders but stopped himself at Steve's growl.

"Good Lord, Steve, sit!" It struck me that she might be taking the act a little far. But though I didn't want to scare the poor befuddled guy off, I felt comforted by her show of valor just the same. "I imagine they've all gone home," I said. "The thing ended about five o'clock. But you guys come from all over, right? Maybe you're staying at a hotel?"

He laughed at that, white teeth flashing in the dark, but he squelched it immediately. "The camp. Across the

15

river. Have we retreated then?'' He looked over his shoulder, then muttered to himself, ''Where did these houses come from?''

This conversation was not going in what I considered to be a productive direction, so I changed the subject. ''Come with me,'' I said firmly. ''You're not thinking clearly and I'm freezing. I'll get you some tea and clean up your face and then you can decide where you want to go.'' I moved to take his arm, but he jerked back.

''You can't take me to your home. You would be in danger! Unless—do we occupy the city?''

I pondered this odd statement for a moment. ''Well, I certainly do,'' I said finally. ''Come with me. You're not in any danger, except maybe of frostbite.''

He let me take his arm. We moved slowly toward the old Innis house, which had withstood the bloody battle 130 years ago to stand virtually unscathed now, and he looked at it with some relief. As soon as his feet hit the pavement he stopped, his eyes dropping to his feet. He knelt quickly and placed a palm on the asphalt, looking down the length of the paved street.

''How did they get it so smooth?'' he asked in an almost reverent tone.

I frowned and felt intense consternation coming on. ''Steamroller, I guess. Come on.''

He rose and followed me, keeping his eyes on the ground until we passed under the street lamp. At this he looked up, turning around to walk backwards as we passed it, until I took his other arm to guide him. He winced dramatically, and it was then I noticed the dark stain at his shoulder.

''Good God, what's happened here?'' I demanded, touching his sodden shirt with light fingers. I heard him suck in his breath as I touched the tender spot, but he did not flinch again. You really got beat up. We better get you out of here in case whoever it was comes back.

16

Do you still have your wallet?'' I was suddenly glad of Steve's theatrics.

He ignored this question and stood staring at the porch of a house across the street. "It's so bright here. Why is it so bright?''

He was getting worse. The concussion was obviously beginning to affect his vision. I needed to get him into my house before he passed out right here on the pavement and I had to knock on a stranger's door. "We're only a block away now. Come on.''

By the time I'd gotten him into the house Steve had decided that he was worthy of petting her. After I'd pushed him into a chair she sidled up beside him and shoved her nose under his palm. He rested a square, tanned hand on her head.

I flicked on the lights. In a surprising burst of motion, he ducked as if they might possibly come cascading out of the ceiling. I hesitated, watching his disorientation with concern. He gazed up at the light fixture, rapt. Definitely 911 material, I decided.

I picked up the phone receiver to call the hospital when a thought struck me. "Do you have any insurance?'' I asked. He looked at me blankly. "Health insurance?'' I prompted. "It's just that I've heard stories that if you don't have insurance they'll charge you for the ambulance and still not treat you when you get there.''

He looked at me shrewdly through heavy-lidded eyes, and I could see now that they were gray. Not dark or bluish, but a kind of soft, light, brushed gray, like a cat's fur. The color reminded me of an old cashmere sweater I'd gotten from my grandmother.

"I don't know what you mean,'' he said.

I decided to try a different tack. "Do you have a job? What do you do for a living?''

He looked relieved again and leaned back gingerly in the chair. That's not to say he was relaxed, by any means, but he seemed to understand the question at least. "I own a small farm. I'm a farmer." He thought about this for a second, then added, "And a teacher. I'm also a teacher."

"A teacher; that's good. Do you still have your wallet? Maybe you've got a card or something." I must have unconsciously touched my own pockets because his hands moved to his pants. He dipped a hand in one pocket and pulled out a tiny, flat leather box, what looked like a silver lighter, and a stub of a charcoal pencil. Out of his other pocket came some string, a button, and a bunch of what looked like old Civil War bullets except they were shiny, like they'd been plated in silver. He turned his hands over, palms up, in a helpless gesture.

"I haven't any money. I'm sorry," he said. His tone was dignified, quiet, and I noticed a soft flush stain those marvelous cheekbones.

I held the receiver to my chest for a minute, considering. "Well, let me take a look," I offered, hanging up. "Maybe if I clean you up a little you won't look so frightening."

His eyes snapped up to mine. "Do I frighten you?" he asked quickly. "I mean you no harm."

His expression of concern and remorse pricked surprisingly at my heart, and I felt myself get embarrassingly choked up. The poor guy had been so knocked around that he couldn't even remember where he was, let alone who he was, if he was not actually Carter Lindsey of the 114th Pennsylvania, and he was worried about me.

I looked into those heavy-lidded, pillow-soft eyes and shook my head. "No, you don't frighten me. I just want to get a little of this blood off you, that's all."

The facial wound was easy—at least it was easy to clean up. Whoever had inflicted it had had serious damage in mind, and the bruise was going to be a spectacular one. Carter flinched as I pulled away the hair that had stuck to the dried blood but only stared resolutely as I swabbed the broken skin with alcohol. I'm no nurse and I know alcohol is painful, but it was the only thing I had in the house that I knew was capable of disinfecting, other than the Mr. Clean I used on the floors.

It was when I got to the sore shoulder that I had my most serious doubts about tending to this stranger alone. The shirt had dried to the wound and the pain involved in removing it required more than the proud stoicism Mr. Lindsey had at hand. I retrieved a bottle of Jameson's whiskey from the cabinet.

He nodded grimly at the sight of it and quickly downed three shots, after which he examined the label on the bottle as if it were someone he knew but couldn't quite place. I figured this preoccupation was as close as I would get to anesthesia and added to the Jameson's a bottle of Mt. Gay rum, a bottle of Stoly's vodka, no doubt pilfered by my bartender-boyfriend Rory from one restaurant or another, and some seltzer.

I pulled back the damp, now purple, fabric of his shirt and shuddered nearly as violently as he did. Below the bloody material was a puncture wound the depth and violence of which I'd never before seen. Even the time in the fifth grade when Marty Goldsmith broke his leg and the bone stuck out paled in comparison to this bloody carnage. He looked like a steak someone had undercooked and had sliced open to tell.

"That's it," I declared, shaking my head. "I'm not dealing with this. No. No way. I can't."

Clear, compelling eyes froze me where I stood. "Please."

I shook my head again. "I can't. You need a doctor—"

"No," he growled in a voice that sent slivers of real fear down my spine. "No doctors," he added more calmly.

I took a deep breath. "But—"

Elaine Fox

"No!" He rose unsteadily to his feet. "I'll leave." He swallowed hard, his face pale as a corpse's, and nodded at me once. "Thank you for your help. I'm sorry to have disturbed your evening." He tried to turn toward the door, stumbled, and grabbed the table. The ripped fabric of his shirt gaped open to reveal the wound, bright red with fresh blood.

I felt my stomach heave and clapped a hand over my mouth, closing my eyes and turning partially away. For one horrifying moment I thought I might have to charge into the bathroom.

The owner of the gory spectacle clenched his teeth, reached for the Jameson's, and chugged heartily. After a second he looked at me and casually extended the bottle. I looked at it, then at him, and then followed suit, chugging as delicately as I could. Immediately, I feared I'd added gunpowder to the fire; my stomach clutched briefly in surprise at the fiery liquid, then settled down.

I met his eyes, feeling the whiskey stain my cheeks a hot pink. "Okay," I said, resigned. "Sit down."

He smiled and slowly lowered himself into the chair. "Thank you."

"Don't thank me yet," I muttered.

As I neared the bloody gash once again, I felt him looking at my violently shaking hands. "Steady now," he said in a subdued voice, at which I nearly laughed. *Physician, heal thyself,* he might as well have said.

I clenched my hands into tight fists to steady them, then unfurled my fingers to pluck at the shirt with as much confidence as I could muster. "I'm doing the best I can," I asserted, then echoed the phrase that kept battering the inside of my head: "I'm not a nurse."

Carter sat still, but I thought I saw the corners of his mouth lift slightly as he raised the bottle. "I'd guessed," he murmured and drank again.

I dropped my hands to my sides. Fine time for *him* to

be joking, I fumed. "I don't understand why you won't see a doctor," I said defensively. "I know enough about medicine to know that *that*," I splayed a palm in the direction of the wreckage, "should be stitched. And God only knows what's inside there. Were you shot or stabbed? And who in the world would do such a thing? What happened up there?" My voice rose over this discourse, and I felt an unfamiliar panic welling within me. Who was this person that he would sit calmly in an unknown woman's dining room, chugging whiskey and gritting his teeth, while a perfect stranger performed obviously inadequate medical techniques on his shoulder?

"Shot, I believe," he answered succinctly. "Perhaps a minie, though I'd gotten close enough for a fifty-eight."

"A Minnie?" I repeated dumbly. An absurd picture of a mouse with a slingshot entered my head.

He nodded. "It was when I came to after the battle that I got clubbed in the head. Didn't want to deal with a live body, I imagine. Damned yellow reb," he spat, then added to me with a serious expression, "begging your pardon."

"You were shot and then struck when you woke up? And whoever it was left you there like that? Don't tell me this was part of your—your *thing* today." What *did* they call those things? Battles? Reenactments? "I thought everyone shot blanks and had rubber bayonets or something."

He pressed a hand to his wound and looked at me strangely. Then he looked down at his palm as he pulled it from his shoulder. "I think you ought to bandage it, please. It's starting to bleed again." His speech had thickened, and I knew at once that I had made a dreadful mistake in trying to help him myself. This was serious bleeding; people died from that.

"*I'm* not going to do a thing to it!" My voice inched its way up the octaves toward hysteria. A dead guy in my dining room dressed like a Union soldier and reeking of whiskey was all I needed to convince my family that I really was crazy. "I'm taking you to the hospital," I announced. "You've obviously taken a knock on the head. Once they fix you up they'll find your wallet and your insurance and your family and friends, and everything will be fine."

Carter's head, which had begun to sag somewhat, drew up with surprising speed. *"No."* His fist crashed to the table, rattling the napkin holder and threatening to topple the salt and pepper shakers. I jumped, every muscle in my body tensing. Wounded or not, this man could do some damage if he wanted to. *"No hospital.* I told you I *will not go."* He gritted his teeth and said slowly, with an effort, "I'll die there sooner than here. Besides—they'll want to take it off—the arm. You fix it. Please. You can do it."

I had unconsciously stepped back a short way at the threatening tone. The idea of helping a deranged man with a bullet wound was suddenly so completely insane that I wondered what had possessed me to bring him here. I imagined people reading about my death in the morning paper thinking, *Well, she brought him to her house; how stupid can you get?*

He gazed at my fear through those heavy-lidded eyes and repeated in a more gentle tone, "You can do it."

I flung my hands out to the sides, trying to convey outrage rather than the fear I actually felt. "What are you talking about?" I blustered. "I can't do it! I don't know anything about injuries like this. I don't know if you realize it, but you're spewing blood like a friggin' geyser, and for all I know you've got severed muscles, or torn ligaments, or whatever else you can get when someone shoots a hole in you like that! Not to mention the threat of infection and blood poisoning. Can you even move your arm now?"

He closed his eyes, thick flaxen lashes brushing his cheeks. "Thank you for not instilling hysteria in the patient," he said weakly. He took a deep breath. "Please. Just do it."

Just do it, I thought. An unbidden vision emerged of Michael Jordan in the Nike commercial, executing a swirling, slow-motion lay-up. I doubted Nike had anything like this in mind when they brainstormed the slogan, and I wondered briefly, if they had, what sort of shoes they'd have recommended. Not green cowboy boots, I was fairly certain.

Rather than doing as he asked, I grabbed a clean dish towel and pressed it to his shoulder. "Hold this here, tightly," I instructed, then swung around him to the phone. He eyed me through his lashes as I sat at the telephone table and looked up a number in my address book. His breathing was ragged but steady, and though I had the feeling he was on the verge of passing out, I was not sure if it was from the alcohol or from loss of blood.

Jerry answered on the fourth ring. "Oh, thank God you're home," I breathed into the receiver. "It's Shelby, and I really need your help. What are you doing? Can you come over?"

"I'm fine, Shel, and how are you?" Jerry answered with a laugh. "What do you think I was doing at twelve-thirty in the morning?"

"I know you weren't sleeping; you sound too wide-awake. But I'm sorry, anyway. It's just that I've got a real medical emergency here and I don't know who else to call."

Jerry's voice was dry. "Nine-one-one?"

Carter watched me with an expression that spoke of doubting my sanity, which struck me as ironic, considering he'd just told me he'd been shot by a "yellow reb." I could almost see the thoughts churning in his eyes, as if he debated the wisdom of staying here against risking his life out in the elements.

"Well, I thought of that, but it's kind of a strange situation." I tried to reflect on what was so strange about it and could come up with nothing other than the fact that the guy might be crazy. My willingness to humor his wish not to go to a hospital was due more to a feeling I had about him than any real belief that the hospital wouldn't take him. I seemed to be able to feel his panic at the very idea of a hospital, as if I was afraid of it too, and I shared his reluctance to go as though I knew they might do something awful to him—though what that might be I could not fathom. The most awful thing they were likely to do was give him a psychological examination, which wasn't a bad idea. It's not everyone who goes to a Civil War reenactment only to wake up with a real bullet wound and the conviction that he's an actual member of the Union army.

Jerry's voice interrupted my reverie. "Shelby, I'm a podiatrist, remember? Have you stubbed your toe or something?"

I sighed in exasperation. Why was communication so cumbersome? I felt as if I ought to be able to just beam him an image of the situation rather than having to put the whole thing into words. "It's not *me,* Jerry."

"Who then, some stray without insurance?" Jerry asked resignedly.

"In a way that's part of it. But he's sitting here bleeding on my carpet, and I think you'd better be quick." I watched as Carter's head lolled to the side.

Jerry's voice suddenly became serious. "Who's bleeding on your carpet? It's not Rory, is it? Or James? Is James there?"

I shook my head frantically as Carter's body began to drift, and I moved to cup the side of his face in my hand. Maybe if I held his head up he wouldn't slide out of the chair completely. "No, no, it's some guy. I found him on Sunken Road and I think he's been shot. He's just fainted!"

Jerry finally took the cue. "I'll be right over. And for God's sake, call an ambulance!"

I tossed the receiver toward the phone, heard it clatter to the floor, and knelt next to the unconscious body. Mr. Lindsey apparently did not feel the need to keep his body where I held his face, and his heavy shoulders crumpled toward my chest. I pulled him sideways toward me. He was incredibly heavy for someone who wasn't fat, and as used as I was to manipulating Rory's unconscious body, smelling similarly of whiskey if not blood, I found myself floundering under the unexpected bulk of him.

Once I had him stretched out on the floor I gingerly began to unbutton his shirt. He was better off unconscious, I decided, and so I was careful not to jostle him too much. When I had the shirt open and the cloth pressed to the wound, I examined the muscular chest for any signs of streaking. I remembered my mother's admonition that streaks from an injury indicated blood poisoning, but I could not for the life of me remember how or why we had found ourselves in such a conversation, not to mention why she, a Washington, DC, socialite, would know anything at all about it.

There were no streaks, but there was an odd assortment of scars. He had one that went from the middle of his left rib cage straight around the ribs to his back. Then there was another, newer one that ran the length of his chest from nipple to navel. Then, down near where his pants began, there was what looked to be a nasty burn about the size of a nickel and several millimeters deep. Only one of them had been stitched—the newest one— and it looked as though the sewing had been done with a knitting needle and yarn. Well, not quite, but it was not the neat, careful stitching I had on my appendix scar.

After what seemed an eternity I heard Jerry burst unceremoniously through the front door.

"Shel?" he shouted.

"In here," I called, leaning forward to see him through the dining-room doorway.

His ginger hair was pushed up against the side of his head, as if he really had been in bed, and I felt momentary guilt for calling him. But the alternative—having a man die on my cerulean blue carpet—was out of the question.

He carried a little black bag, just like the doctors in old movies, and he opened it as he knelt down next to Carter in a graceful move that any self-respecting ballerina of stout form might envy. I wondered what a foot doctor would carry in a little black bag—emergency moleskin?

"Did you call an ambulance?" he asked in a business-like tone.

I flushed. "He didn't want one. I don't think he has insurance."

Jerry glared at me.

"He was quite insistent," I said a trifle testily.

Jerry felt Carter's neck for a pulse, then dug through the bag and looked in his eyes with the tiny flashlight he found inside it. "He's not likely to put up a fight now," he said. His fingers gently probed the wreckage of the man's shoulder. "Call them, or I will. This man has a bullet wound that needs to be treated in a hospital. Not to mention the fact that the police should know about it. How did you get him here?"

"He walked; he was conscious for a while. In fact, I didn't notice the shoulder wound at first."

"Did he tell you what happened?"

"Well, not exactly." I rose to go to the telephone. "He seemed to think there was an actual battle up on Sunken Road today."

Jerry sat back with his hand on Carter's neck again.

"The bump on the head could account for the delusion. But his pulse is relatively steady." It was then Jerry noticed the man's clothes. "Hmm. A Union officer, looks like."

"Think they'll treat him?" I asked wryly.

Jerry filled a syringe with a clear liquid and gave me a sidelong glance. "Not if you don't call them."

I gave the dispatcher the information and prayed Carter would not awaken before the paramedics arrived. I could still feel the chill that had swept over me when he'd told me he wouldn't go to a hospital. I'm not a timid person, but I'd felt a strong instinctual response to obey that growled order. And, thinking about it now, I had to revise my initial impression of his age; the cold fury and strength of his determination was of a caliber one couldn't reach at the age of twenty-two. At that moment he had looked far older, and wiser, than anyone I knew.

The paramedics got him safely to the ambulance, and Jerry took his leave of us.

"He's in good hands now," he said, pulling up the collar of his coat against the chilling wind. "I really don't think you need to go with them. They'll call you if you want to know how he's doing."

"No," I said thoughtfully. "I feel like I ought to go. I'll just wait until a doctor looks at him and then I'll come home."

Jerry shook his head. "Yeah; I know you, Shelby. But this isn't one of your strays. Wounded people are a lot like wounded animals—unpredictable. Don't get yourself in too deep."

"What's that supposed to mean?" I asked indignantly.

Jerry smiled. "Just that you're too much of a caretaker. Let the professionals handle this one. He'll be all right."

"He's going to the hospital, Jerry. What else do you want?"

"Nothing," he said. He started walking to his car.

"Let me know what happens. And who he turns out to be."

I glanced at Carter's pale face as he lay in the brightly lit ambulance. "I will. And thank you, Jerry," I called. "Thanks for coming so quickly."

"No problem. Any excuse to leave a warm bed, you know." He grinned and waved good-bye.

I followed the ambulance in my car and arrived at the hospital in time to see them wheel Carter in without his waking and causing a scene. I felt it only fair to warn them that they might be dealing with something of a live wire when he awoke, but they merely nodded at my revelations and hustled him through some swinging steel doors, away from me.

I gave the nurse on duty the only information I knew: that the man thought his name was Lieutenant Carter Lindsey of the 114th Pennsylvania and that he believed himself to have been shot by a "damned yellow reb." They looked at me as if I were the nutty one and shuffled me off to an orange vinyl waiting room.

I'm not sure how long it was—at least a couple of hours—before a crisp, white-coated doctor summoned me from the waiting room. He steered me into his office and sat me across the desk from himself.

He was an average-looking man of about forty with thinning brown hair and small brown eyes. A stethoscope hung from his neck like a broken leash and he had a silver pen clipped neatly to his pocket. As if on cue, he slipped the pen from his pocket and directed it toward the clipboard he held.

"I'm Dr. Blake. I have a few questions I'd like to ask you about the patient, uh," he read the name off the clipboard, "Mr. Lindsey. But first, your name is . . . ?"

"Shelby Manning."

"Very good. Miss Manning, are you a friend of the patient's?" His expression was one of sincere concern, giving the brown eyes some depth and making him look like a small woodland creature, something out of Disney. I liked him and was glad of it. Carter would need someone with some compassion if he came back to consciousness as confused as he'd left it.

"No. I only just met him tonight. I found him up on Sunken Road."

"Was there anyone else there?"

I shook my head and pushed an unruly mass of curls away from my face. "Just my dog. We'd been walking up there for almost an hour before I even noticed him. Is he going to be all right?" I suddenly had the disturbing thought that the doctor was going to ask me if I knew who his next of kin was.

The doctor nodded slowly, straightening the blotter on his desk and setting the clipboard neatly upon it: the finicky squirrel, setting things "just so" for the winter. "He'll be fine. He was lucky. The bullet missed the bone; and that sort of bullet could have shattered it."

His tone was unmistakable. "What sort of bullet?"

He cleared his throat and looked at me squarely. "Miss Manning, the reason I'm curious is that he was shot with a soft lead fifty-eight caliber bullet, at a low muzzle velocity." He tried to share an incredulous look with me, but I could only muster one of blank confusion. "In other words, he was shot by a Civil War–era bullet from a Civil War–era gun. Those guys apparently weren't playing games up there today—at least some of them weren't."

I'm sure at this point my expression rivaled his. "But that's incredible. Why would someone do such a thing? And how?"

The doctor shook his head, looking very solemn. "My guess is that amid all the noise and commotion whoever it was thought their real shot would not be detected among the blanks. As it turned out, they were right. But the gun that they used, a working Civil War musket— that's pretty distinctive.''

Unfortunately I had to disagree. "Is it really? Those reenactors are fanatics for authenticity, I've heard. They've probably all got them.''

"I don't know. In any case, a bullet like that, had it hit either the shoulder joint, or the collar bone, would have rendered that arm virtually useless. As it is he'll just have a nasty scar.''

"To go with the set," I murmured.

Dr. Blake sat forward. "That's another cause for curiosity. At least one of those scars on his chest is fairly recent. And from the looks of it he received no professional treatment. I think there's sufficient evidence just from the marks on his body that someone means that boy some harm.''

Unable to sit still any longer, and wishing the sudden curling of my stomach would abate, I rose and walked to the window. "What about his head? How do you suppose that happened?''

The doctor sighed heavily, looking at me beneath raised eyebrows and shaking his head some more. "Acute cranial contusion. Someone intended to finish the job. Perhaps they thought if they knocked him unconscious he would lie there long enough to bleed to death. It's a damn good thing you happened along.''

I nodded vaguely. Again I pictured the spot where Carter had lain—the spot that I was sure had been vacant moments before. If he had been there all along surely Steve would have noticed him when we'd first arrived. After all, we'd passed that spot when we'd come, and by a much closer margin than Steve was when she'd noticed him after rooting through the bushes.

"Could you tell—'' I hesitated. "Do you have any idea how long he might have lain there before we did find him?''

The doctor frowned. "Hours, I'd think," he said. "He'd lost a lot of blood, but the wound was already starting to close. It doesn't take long, you know, before the body begins to try to heal itself. It's an amazing thing, the body. The more you learn about it, the more fascinating it becomes."

Not wanting to deny the man his expression of job fulfillment, but unwilling to leave the subject at hand, I broke into his reverie. "I'd like to leave my phone number, if you don't mind, and have someone call me when he comes to. If he's in the same state of delusion after waking up, he could panic. And though he doesn't really know me, he might recognize me from tonight." I felt a kind of kinship with the man whose blood lined my fingernails. I envisioned again the fear and confusion, masked by determination, that had stood out so clearly in his eyes.

The pen flashed again from the white pocket. "Of course. It's good for us to have a contact, as well, in case he doesn't remember who he is."

I turned to look at him. "And if he doesn't? He didn't even seem to know what I meant when I asked him about insurance. Will you still be able to treat him?"

Dr. Blake squirmed almost visibly. "It's an unfortunate thing," he began. "Much as I detest the system, it's a fact of life. He'll be under financial obligation for the surgery, the anesthesiologist, the attending nurses, drugs, equipment usage, paraphernalia such as bandages, and so on. My fee—well, we could negotiate on that, but the hospital—you understand, they have an obligation to stay in business."

"I see," I said coldly. "So he'll have to leave if he awakens without knowledge of his identity. Regardless of the fact that, in that case, he'll be most in need of help."

Dr. Blake studied the clipboard in front of him. "The

injury should heal now without incident.''

I expelled an exasperated breath.

His eyes turned back to me and he had the decency to look somewhat abashed. ''The hospital does have some funds set aside for indigents, which we might be able to apply to his bill,'' he said cautiously, ''but we'd have to be very certain he has no other means before those would be available. As far as discovering his true identity, I'll check around for a psychologist who might be willing to negotiate his fee, as well. But this is all jumping the gun.''

''So to speak.'' I couldn't resist.

He smiled dryly. ''But he could well remember everything upon waking. He had a concussion, but not a severe one. Did he have any personal effects on him when you found him?''

''Nothing to give a clue to his identity. Just little bits of string, a cigarette lighter; umm, some bullets—you know, the kind they sell downtown, but very shiny. No wallet.'' I suddenly remembered the gun, lying in the grass. ''Oh, I almost forgot! He had a pistol; one of those reproductions. We left it in the grass in the park. I'll go back and get it.''

Dr. Blake cleared his throat. ''With all due respect for your good intentions, I wouldn't go near that park again tonight. Whoever did this could come back looking for our man. Don't worry; I have to relay all this information to the police anyway. I'm sure they'll uncover something. They'll probably go to the scene to investigate.''

This was most likely true, but something inside me wanted a look at that gun. The feeling in my stomach was not simply fear at the fact that a human being had been brutalized right in my neighborhood, but also a sinking feeling of dread that this mystery would not be unraveled so easily. Carter Lindsey had not been deluded,

I was suddenly sure. He had merely been confused by my incomprehension.

I thrust the thought away as Dr. Blake rose.

"In the meantime," the doctor said purposefully as he walked me to the door, "Mr. Lindsey had better be plenty careful once he gets out of here."

"Well, surely you'll give him instructions or medicine or something!" I protested, scandalized, stopping in my tracks. "Or is common decency only covered under insurance these days?"

He took my arm and patted it with compassion. "Of course I will. I'm not an ogre. But what I meant is far more serious: It seems obvious to me that somebody wants Carter Lindsey dead."

Chapter Two

I arrived home to find Rory pacing the floor like a caged animal. From where I stood, removing my gloves in the darkened living room, I could see him slink, with all the sinew of a leopard, along the perimeter of the brightly lit dining room, telephone clutched between shoulder and ear while his hands bent my address book in half, forward and back, forward and back.

I dropped my keys on the coffee table and he stopped dead, eyes snapping to meet mine. All six-foot, three-inches of him was a coiled spring of irritation.

"Here she is. I'll talk to you later," I heard him murmur into the phone. Then I heard him place it back in the cradle with a murderously accurate *crack.*

I entered the dining room hoping to pass right through it to the kitchen for some tea, but it was not to be. He grabbed my arm and spun me to face him, his grip biting even through my coat.

"Where the hell have you been?" he demanded, ice

blue eyes slicing their way to mine from a chalk white face. His dark hair had been raked repeatedly back from his forehead so that it now waved uncontrollably. I had never seen him so angry, and I had to admit I found it somewhat attractive. So used was I to his lazy grin and flirtatious mannerisms that this man before me with such deadly purpose was a stranger.

"At the hospital," I said, shaking his hand off my arm and removing my coat.

"I know," he growled. "I just talked to Jerry. What the hell were you thinking? That guy could have been dangerous! He could have had a gun, or a knife."

"Actually, he did have a gun," I said, suddenly remembering my desire to find it before the police did. "But we left it in the park."

He glared at me incredulously. Then his hand played further havoc with his hair as he turned away to resume his pacing. "I come home to find the house empty, Steve stuck like glue to the front door, and *this*," he stopped and pointed with statesmanlike righteousness to the floor, "lying here unexplained like some sort of *flag* of disaster." He was pointing to a large bloody stain on the pale blue of my carpet.

I glanced down with him, wondering what on earth would remove a stain of such dramatic proportions. "You seem to know the whole story now, Rory. What's the problem?" I asked mildly.

At this, the formerly white face suffused with red, and I thought for a moment that he might actually blow steam out his ears. "The problem? I'll tell you what the problem is, I—I—" He held his hands in front of him helplessly, as if I'd asked him to explain what purpose they served. "God, Shelby, I thought you'd been killed or something." His voice was quiet and he swallowed hard, looking back up at me.

I softened immediately. "I'm sorry," I said, taking his

hands. "I guess I didn't think about how it would look."
I glanced down at the carpet. The bloody dish towel lay
discarded near the wall. "It does look pretty gruesome,
I suppose."

Rory took me in his arms and squeezed so hard, I
couldn't inhale for a second. I snaked my arms around
his waist. "I'm sorry," I said again. It always shocked
me when people worried about things—particularly
me—to the point that they convinced themselves some
calamity had occurred. I feared it might be a moral failing
on my part that I never, ever, considered disaster a possibility when confronted with confusion or the unknown.

Rory smelled familiarly of smoke and alcohol, the latter being mostly on his clothes and shoes, but somewhat
on his breath. He loosened his hold and looked down at
me, the cold blue of his eyes now warming with relief.
"You gave me such a scare, Shel. It really surprised
me." He grinned balefully. "I guess I always thought I'd
react better in a crisis."

I glanced down at the carpet again, and at Steve, who
hovered around our ankles. "I suppose the evidence did
point to foul play," I agreed. "How did you think to call
Jerry?"

He kissed the top of my head and released me, leaning
back against the table. "Well, he wasn't the first person
I thought of. In fact, you might want to give your parents
a call. And Sylvie. And Janey. And you might have had
to call James, but I couldn't find the goddamned relay
number." He laughed ruefully, shaking his head.

"That's just as well." James was my brother, who is
deaf. In order to get a hold of him, Rory would have had
to call a special number to get an operator with a TTY
(a keyboard attached to a modem), who would then type
Rory's words to James and read James's typing to Rory.
I was glad Rory couldn't find the number, or James
would have been in his car careening down here from

Washington at top speed. "So Jerry told you the whole story?"

As I ambled into the kitchen and placed the kettle on to boil, I thought idly of the cup of tea I'd planned to make for Carter to fix him up after a gunshot wound and an acute cranial contusion.

"He told me you found some nut up on Sunken Road who'd been shot. He said the guy thought there'd actually been a battle up there today." He shook his head as he leaned on the doorjamb, his arms crossed. "Leave it to you, Shel, to find the last surviving Union soldier."

I pictured Carter Lindsey's face, the gray eyes trying futilely to mask a great deal of confusion and pain. "He was really—interesting," I explained inadequately. "He had a nasty bump on his head, which the doctor said accounted for his delusion, but he seemed very—" I searched for the right word—"vulnerable. Not out of it or irrational at all; just confused."

Rory watched me spoon some loose tea into the tea ball, then arrange the tiny chain attached to it over the side of the mug and twice around the handle. "You felt sorry for him," he stated.

"No. Well, yes, obviously; but that wasn't the reason I helped him. I felt drawn to him, as if I were the only person who could help him. It was weird." I opened the cabinet to pull out a box of Milk Bones. Steve's ears pricked at the hollow cardboard sound, and she floated unobtrusively into the kitchen, past Rory. "In fact, I left my number with the doctor, in case he doesn't remember who he is when he wakes up." I handed the bone to Steve, who backed expertly out the door with it.

The water in the kettle hissed suddenly, the way all water does when it begins its ascent to a boil, as if all the molecules at once had broken into a dance. Was there some agreed moment, I often wondered, when the heat reached a certain point, that they all decided to move?

I felt Rory's arms wind around me from behind, pulling my body to conform to his. He bent his head to my shoulder and nuzzled my neck, warm hands cupping my breasts. I hadn't realized how tired I was until that moment, when I could rest my head back against him and absorb his warmth.

"Please, don't ever do that again," he whispered.

I closed my eyes. "Do what?"

"Leave the house with a bloodstain on the floor, a bunch of strange artifacts strewn on top of the table, and a neurotic dog trying to dig her way out of your front hall."

I laughed. I'd forgotten about the strange and meager contents of Carter Lindsey's pockets, left on the table. "Steve was doing what?"

Rory's hands found their way under my sweater and now caressed my skin. "Nothing. I promised her I wouldn't tell," he said into my hair. He had to back slightly away after that to get the curls out of his mouth.

I poured my tea, not offering him any, as I knew he hated the stuff, not to mention the production I usually made out of making it. But tonight was different. I didn't have the energy to break out the tea cozy and tray. I was almost wholly preoccupied with what poor Carter was going to feel when he woke up. Suppose he still didn't know who he was? Would he create a scene? Had the doctor believed me when I told him he might get overly agitated?

"Come to bed," Rory urged, taking my arm.

I stopped by the refrigerator. "I just need some cream. Anyway, Rory, how was I to know you'd be coming here tonight? It's not like you ever give me any warning."

He sighed heavily. "Let's not get into this now," he said, dropping my arm.

I stopped at the long-suffering tone he employed and glared at him. "I'm not *getting into* anything. I've just

38

been feeling guilty for leaving you in the dark about this whole thing, and I don't think I should. Should I have stopped en route to taking a dying man to the hospital to write a note just in case you decided to show up to-night?''

He gave me a tired look. "I was just worried, that's all.''

I concentrated on the swirl of cream in my tea, watching as it disappeared into the whirlpool created by my spoon.

"Come on," he said cajolingly. "We're both exhausted. We don't do well with these middle-of-the-night conversations. Let's just go to bed. By the way, Jerry's going to be calling at five-thirty. Just to remind us, he said, of the hour he gets up every morning.''

This brought a reluctant chuckle from me. "Poor Jerry. He was bummed when I called him. What time did you get him?''

"That was him when you came in," Rory said, with a small, devilish grin. I glanced at the clock: 3:30.

I laughed again, imagining Jerry's tolerant irritation with us. He was one of my best friends, though we could not have been more different, and frequently we each felt the need to impose our own specialized brand of absurdity on the other's life. I had no doubt that he would call. "We'd better unplug the phone." I flipped off the dining-room light and snapped my fingers for Steve to follow. Her head appeared as if by magic beneath my palm.

Rory preceded us through the dining room, then stopped to lock the front door. I admired the cut of his jeans as he walked. He had a studied poise that was rarely shaken, and a casual grace that back in high school I had tried to imitate, finally concluding that it was a male thing. But his poise had been shaken tonight. He'd been scared, and badly. And it was over me.

I slid into his embrace as he turned from the door.

"Thank you," I said. His arms tightened automatically. After years of habit our bodies seemed naturally to gravitate to each other. "Thank you for worrying about me."

He laid his cheek on the top of my head and sighed. "I didn't like it, Shel."

I smiled, knowing it was the truth. "I won't make you do it very often. I promise."

"All right, then." He turned me around and sent me up the stairs with a swat on the behind. "Get upstairs and prepare to apologize properly."

"Hah!" I scoffed, ascending with dignity. "It's you who'll be tending to me, Mr. Feagan. I've done my share of favors for the evening."

His hearty laugh bounded up the stairs ahead of us. "I'm sure you've a few favors left for the needy."

Apparently I did have a few favors left for the needy, though not of the sort that Rory had received. The hospital called me at the bookstore the next evening, just as I was getting ready to call them, and informed me that they could not, in good conscience, keep Mr. Lindsey past the following morning, knowing that he had no insurance.

"Really, it's for his own good," the nurse on the other end of the line said in a voice that made me sure she had no lips and a hunchback. "He'll still be financially responsible for the care he receives, and the longer he stays, the more debt he will accrue."

I tapped a pencil on the counter in irritation. "I don't suppose you took into consideration that it's hard to collect from a dead man?"

I heard a prim sniff. "Mr. Lindsey is sufficiently out of the woods to recover at home. In fact, most patients recover more quickly at home."

"That's all well and good," I seethed, "except that I have no idea where his home is and, apparently, neither

40

does he." She had already informed me that Carter's mental state had not improved after his bout with anesthesia, and implied, though she probably did not realize it, that his agitation was part of the reason he was being released.

"Be that as it may, the doctor believes he will fare better outside the confines of the hospital. I was given your name to call. If you don't want to take responsibility for him, I will not bother you further," the nurse intoned. "Shall we expect you to pick him up, or shall we summon a cab for him?"

I took a deep breath and counted to ten. I deplored this kind of rule book bureaucracy. "I'll come get him," I gritted. "But if he dies at my house, I'm holding you, Nurse Ratched, personally responsible."

I heard the shuffling of papers. "He'll be ready at nine," she spat. "If we don't see you by then, he'll leave in a cab. Good-bye." She hung up.

"God!" I breathed in fury. "Why do people like that go into service positions? You'd think a basic love of humanity would prompt you to want to heal people."

Sylvie, who was shelving books a few feet away, turned her bobbed head to me. "They kicking him out?" she asked. I had, after Rory's frantic call to her looking for me, felt obligated to explain the whole situation to her. Perpetually single and desperately looking, she had viewed the situation from a romantically advantageous point of view. "It sounds *perfect!*" she'd cooed. "He can be made into anyone you want!"

But after being away from him for a day, I'd reassessed my motivation to help the stranger. Try as I might, I could not summon the irrational need I'd felt to protect him. I must admit, Rory's objections weighed heavily against further involvement as well. Putting voice to all of my most buried fears, he had succeeded in convincing me that to have taken an unknown man into my house in such a condition was nothing short of lunacy. He could have attacked me. He could have escaped from a mental institution. He knew where I lived now and could, conceivably, be planning to seek me out again.

However, when faced with the alternative of having the poor soul released onto the streets—streets he seemed completely unprepared to face—a modicum of the old protective instinct flared. It seemed I was actually to *take responsibility* for the guy, as Nurse Blowhard had said.

"Yes, they're kicking him out," I finally answered Sylvie. "I'm such a pushover. And Rory will kill me." This last thought, however, did more to reconcile me to the matter than to cause concern over it—a feeling I did not pause to analyze.

Sylvie wheeled the cart to a shelf closer to the register where I stood. "If you need any help, I'd be happy to come by sometime," she offered.

I eyed her with a half smile. "You want him?"

She rolled her eyes. "Yeah, I'll just stick him in my parents' room. There's plenty of room *between* them in that king-size bed."

I laughed. "Actually, help would be great," I admitted. "I don't know much about tending wounded people, though I expect they'll give me some instructions." I remembered Dr. Blake's assertion that he would do just that. *I'm not an ogre,* he'd said; though anyone who would turn out of the hospital a person who'd been shot came dangerously close to landing under that heading in my book.

"When are you going to pick him up?" Sylvie asked. "Do you want me to come?"

"No, thanks. They said he'll be ready tomorrow at nine. And he's probably confused enough as it is. I imagine he's been pretty bombarded by strangers at the hospital." I shuffled some Visa receipts into the little black cubbyhole designed for them. "I can get him home, I

42

think, but I may need to stay with him a while. Can you manage things here tomorrow morning alone?''

''Sure,'' Sylvie said, though her disappointment was evident.

''Maybe after lunch we can trade places and you can sit with him.'' I remembered the feral glint in his eye when he'd told me he wouldn't go to the hospital. ''But we'll have to see about that. I just hope he's a little more reconciled to things now.'' For some reason I'd been able to remember only the threatening moments of last night since daylight. Of the confused and helpless soul I'd thought I'd seen I remembered very little.

The bell on the door jingled and both of us looked up. Business had been pretty brisk all day, what with Christmas coming, but today had been so cold that the crowds had slacked off considerably after dark. Most people found refuge in the malls on nights like this.

Jerry's brown head appeared behind a bookcase—he was a little on the short side, about five-foot-five—and not long afterward his stocky body also came into view.

I smiled at the sight of his cold-pinkened cheeks and ruddy red nose. ''You've either been walking a long way or drinking heavily,'' I teased. ''Thanks for not calling this morning.''

Jerry shushed up to the register in his fat down coat like a child in a snowsuit. ''I did call this morning,'' he frowned. ''No one answered.''

I leaned toward him on the counter. ''Must have been a wrong number,'' I said, remembering the distant wail of the telephone as I'd snuggled closer to Rory's warm body. ''Lucky for you they were heavy sleepers.''

Jerry nodded, accepting the lies with narrowed eyes and pursed, half-smiling lips. ''I came to make sure you were still alive. I was a little surprised you weren't home by the time Rory called last night.''

''Well, thanks for calling earlier,'' I smirked, idly

straightening a pile of books waiting to be shelved. "I could have been dead all day and you'd only be finding out now."

"Rory told me when you got home. I just wondered what took you so long. What happened? To the guy—the soldier, I mean?"

I pushed up my sleeves. "I stayed at the hospital until they patched him up—just to make sure he hadn't expired or anything—and then I came home. Then I massaged Rory back into a jellied calm and went to bed. The doctor said the guy would make it and would probably know who he was when he woke up."

"And did he?"

Sylvie laughed sarcastically from behind a nearby bookshelf. Jerry glanced backwards, then back at me.

I shrugged. "When he woke he knew that he was Carter Lindsey of the 114th Pennsylvania and that the world had somehow gone nuts. The nurse told me they'd had to redress his shoulder three times because he kept busting it open trying to get himself dressed and out of there. They called me tonight to come get him tomorrow."

Jerry frowned and shook his head. "I don't think that's a good idea, Shel."

I sighed. "Well, what else am I supposed to do? The nurse said they'd stick him in a cab if I didn't come. Can you imagine what that would do to the poor guy?"

"Might spark his memory of real life," Jerry said dryly.

I shook my head. "I feel kind of responsible for him, having found him and all."

Jerry's eyebrows rose and his mouth quirked into that triangular grin that so reminded me of the misfit elf in "Rudolph the Red-nosed Reindeer." "You feel *responsible?*"

"Yes. Yes, I do," I said. "The hospital has said they think he'll fare better in a home," I paraphrased, "and I feel, since he's already a little familiar with mine, that it would be best for him to come to my house.''

''Actually,'' Jerry said, ''the hospital probably would have kept him themselves if they hadn't had a contact. Most hospitals have contingency funds for situations like this.''

That took a little of the wind from my sails. ''I have no intention of fobbing the poor soul off on some beleaguered social worker when I am perfectly capable of helping him. How hard could it be to figure out who he is? *Someone's* got to be looking for him.''

Jerry sniffed. ''Maybe, maybe not.''

''Well *I* would be, if he belonged to *me*,'' I said, realizing as the words left my lips how much I meant it.

The following morning threatened snow, which always excited me. My breath frosted in the morning air as I revved up the motor in my trusty Mazda. Truth was, I was invigorated by the upcoming adventure. All fear of the unknown man had vanished with the darkness of night, to be replaced by an eager acceptance of the challenge of helping him.

I shifted into gear and inched forward. The old car always felt as if it were forcing gum through its pistons for the first ten minutes of driving in cold weather. Defroster howling and radio blaring, I made my way slowly up Kenmore Avenue toward the hospital. By the time I got there the heat had just begun to show itself.

''May I help you?'' a pert pink candy striper inquired of me as I reached the desk.

I glanced around the lobby, wondering if I needed to go to a different floor or something—someplace less perky, a Serious Injury Ward, perhaps, or possibly a pick-up/delivery area. ''I'm here to pick up a patient. His name is Carter Lindsey.''

At this the plump girl's little brown eyes shone, and I

could have sworn I saw a slight flush rise to her cheeks. "Oh, Mr. Lindsey. Yes, he's ready. Just a moment."

With a coy, half-hidden smile, she turned and disappeared. *Making a conquest or two,* I thought. *How healthy.*

Fifteen minutes later, she led him out by one arm, his other arm held in a sling. He was dressed again in his Union blue, now clean, with the ripped shoulder neatly stitched. He looked much heartier—and bigger—than I remembered. His cheeks held a healthy glow and his eyes, though still lazy-lidded, were clear and alert, even relaxed enough to show mild surprise upon seeing me.

I approached him with my hand out. "You're looking much better," I said with a broad smile. "Shelby Manning; remember?"

His answering smile was slow and slight but sincere. "I remember you well, Miss Manning. Thank you for coming to get me." His voice was smooth, like a rich cognac, not the raspy growl of two nights ago. He took my hand solidly and shook it once.

"Oh, well . . ." I waved the thanks away and turned to the mini-nurse. "Did the doctor leave any instructions?"

Carter held out a fistful of prescription-sized papers. "I've got them. And I thank you for your concern, but it's nothing I can't handle."

Blushing, I nodded. I'd been thinking of him, and treating him, like a helpless child, I realized. "Oh. All right. So, let's get you to the car." I busied myself digging the keys out of my purse.

"Now you let us know how you're doing," the little nurse said prettily. "We like to keep track of our patients and make sure everything heals up properly."

Like hell, I thought sourly. If that was the case, I would not be here and Carter Lindsey would be getting the medical care he required; though I had to admit he looked quite self-sufficient now that his eyes weren't rolling back in his head.

Carter, to my intense surprise, was planting a brief kiss on the back of nursekin's hand when I looked up from the frantic foray into my purse. "Thank you, Miss Paula, for being so kind. I'll not forget it," he said in a cultured, genteel voice.

Miss Paula clutched her hand when he released it and giggled. "It's just my job, sir."

"Come on," I said brusquely. "I haven't got all day. I've got to get back to work."

Carter followed me obediently to the parking lot, where he looked about himself with a curiosity I could feel was barely held in check. I myself was looking about with a good deal of curiosity as well, as I could not for the life of me remember where I'd parked the car.

After a few minutes of the two of us standing in the middle of a sea of automobiles, gawking dumbly, Carter asked, "What are we looking for? What are all of these?"

He started to walk across one of the aisles when I grabbed his arm. Someone in a large black Lincoln sped by, far too fast, on his way to the exit. Carter jumped in exaggerated surprise and glared after the offending vehicle. He stared back at me and raised an arm to point after the car, speechless.

"I know, another jerk in a big car," I commiserated, and bit the nail of my thumb. "Mine's a red one. Kind of a faded, orange-red. A Mazda." I put a palm to my forehead as if to shield my eyes from the sun, though the sky was banked with clouds.

He dropped his outstretched hand and stared after the Lincoln. "A mahhhzdah," he murmured beside me, then gazed in the same direction I did. From the way he said it, I wondered what exactly he was picturing.

"There it is!" I exclaimed upon pulling from the masses the bent antenna and faded red roof of my small car. He followed me to the car, and even around to the driver's side, where I inserted my key.

"A Mazda," I heard him say again, this time with considerably less relish, as he assessed the sorry-looking piece of machinery. Though I loved my car dearly, it held fewer obvious charms than the shiny, new models around it, even to the untrained eye, I supposed, giving his delusion the benefit of a very small doubt.

"Yeah, well, it runs," I muttered, opening the door. It looked for a moment as if he was going to slide in beside me until he caught sight of the bucket seats and walked uncertainly to the other side. I unlocked the door and opened it from the inside, thrusting it out toward him, where it neatly clipped him in the thigh. He grunted and got in.

The look of wonder on his face when he sat was comical. But when I burst out laughing he quickly masked his expression and stopped a slight bouncing he'd begun on the seat.

"What?" he demanded, eyebrows creased and fist clasped tightly around the prescriptions.

I leaned over and pulled the papers from his hand. "The pharmacist has to be able to read these," I said, taking them and setting them on the dashboard. "You see? The car may not look like much on the outside, but it's not bad inside."

I turned the key in the ignition, which let loose a torrent of sound and fury. Between the noise of the engine starting, the defroster blowing, and the radio blasting, Carter thrust himself back into the seat as if in the grip of several G-forces. He clutched the edges with both hands for dear life as the sling sprang from his arm and dangled uselessly.

I smiled wanly, quickly flipped off the defroster, and turned down the radio. "Sorry." I shrugged apologetically. He glowered at me, his face slowly regaining its natural color as I eased the car into reverse.

Chapter Three

Carter sat stiff as a ramrod and white as a priest in a bordello for most of the way home, regardless of the fact that I drove like an arthritic grandmother to keep him from having heart palpitations. White-knuckled and stiff-jawed, he spoke not at all and only eyed the radio with suspicion the one or two times he was able to tear his eyes from the road.

It wasn't until I'd crept to the curb in front of my house and pulled the emergency brake that he finally relaxed. As I gathered my canvas carryall and purse, I felt the tension ease from his body, and he leaned forward to examine the radio buttons. The car was off now, so I turned the key far enough that the music resumed.

He pushed a button, and bluegrass music emerged. I saw his eyebrows rise slightly. He punched another button, and the Stones ground out of the speakers. His brow furrowed and he looked at me. "Is that music?"

I laughed slightly. "It's rock and roll. Yes, music."

"Rocking roll?"

I nodded.

"Where does it come from?" He ran a finger around the edges of the tape deck, poking one finger through the empty casette door.

"Air waves. Radio frequencies. It's very complex," I said, wishing I knew something about the workings of things. Although, I reminded myself, for all I knew, this guy installed car radios for a living. In fact, it was likely that somewhere in his head he knew a lot more than I did about all the things he seemed to be so fascinated with. On the heels of that thought I pondered what I'd do if I found out the whole thing was some elaborate joke. If we hadn't been in my own car, I might have even been tempted to look for the hidden camera. But, of course, that was ridiculous. Who could fake a gunshot wound?

I pulled out the key and opened my door.

Carter straightened as the music disappeared, gave the deck one last glance, and turned to the door. First he pushed. Then he gripped the armrest and turned the window handle. Finally he pulled the door handle and the door sprang open. If he really was deluded into thinking he was from the Civil War, whether because of amnesia or some other phenomenon, I liked the way he handled his confusion. He approached things in silence and asked only after considering them for some time from his own point of view. This was intriguing to me, as I have on many occasions noticed that most people react to confusion with hostility.

He rose from the car seat with an agility, an efficiency of movement, that I admired. I supposed that it came with strength, or courage, for he did nothing timidly.

After I unlocked the door he preceded me, at my wave, into the house, where he was summarily barraged with affection from Steve. Twisting like a snake someone gripped from behind, she curled around him, whipping his legs with her tail. It was one of the things I hated about having a female dog: She ignored me completely when there was a man in the room.

Carter bent down to pet her, scrubbing her heartily behind the ears, until he realized I was stuck in the doorway behind him. He continued into the house.

Steve gave me a cursory hello when I entered, a cold nose to the palm, then rushed off after Carter. "Hussy," I muttered, following them both.

Carter went directly to the dining room at the rear of the small house, where he at once flipped the switch and watched with unconcealed fascination as the lights sprang to life. Steve, always in the same mood as whoever she was with, looked up obligingly at the light as well, standing as still with rapture as he.

Carter turned to me, eyes slightly narrowed, obviously fighting the dazzling effect of bright lights. "Gas?" he asked doubtfully.

I shook my head. "Electric."

"Electric," he pronounced. "Yes. Like lightning." He turned back to the light.

"Yes, exactly. But don't ask me any more about it because I don't know. I was never much good at science." I dropped my bags on the couch and moved past him to the refrigerator. "Are you hungry? Did they give you any food this morning?"

I heard a muffled sound behind me, reminiscent of a scoff but much more subtle. "I think so. Something that looked like eggs and tasted like chalk." He ran his hand assessingly down the oak molding around the kitchen door. "And a yellow drink." He stood in the doorway, and I could not help but compare his broad but trim figure to the bulkier vision of Rory standing in that same spot two nights before. Rory was not fat, though perhaps he had gotten a little soft around the middle from overindulgence on the job, but he did not have the lean, carved grace that Carter possessed.

I opened the refrigerator, embarrassed to see such a meager selection. Milk—though only enough to cover the bottom of the plastic container—pickles, cream, cottage cheese, three or four doughnuts in a box with a plastic window in the lid, and every condiment imaginable. I must confess I am something of a condiment queen. Food with accessories is one of my favorite things.

But at this particular moment there was not much material for a decent meal. On the tip of my tongue was the suggestion that I go pick up some carry-out, when the realization struck me again that this person was a perfect stranger, and it would not be wise to leave him alone in my house. Who's to say that he wouldn't clean me out of house and home while I was gone? Rory's admonishment about Carter's possible ulterior motives sprang back into my head, and with it the knowledge that Rory would be livid to find this man here.

But what really bothered me was the fact that I had to keep reminding myself of these things. Contrary to everyone else's fears, I had an overwhelming, perhaps irrational feeling that Carter Lindsey was not capable of theft or deception. And that he was everything he said he was.

I'd order a pizza, I decided. That way I wouldn't have to leave the house. A complete food, tomato sauce and cheese, vegetable and protein . . . An unhealthy meal couldn't really kill a person who was recovering from a gunshot, could it?

Well, pizza it would have to be. Without realizing he had bent over me from behind to study the refrigerator's interior, I straightened with resolve, coming smack up into his rock-hard chest and bumping the top of my head on what I supposed was his chin. His good hand closed on my elbow to keep us both from ending up on the floor, but I jumped away from him in surprise. He stumbled back, grunting as the chopping counter caught him in the small of the back, and I fell forward onto the racks of the open refrigerator. The door fell open to crack against the doorjamb.

"What in God's name are you doing?" I demanded shrilly.

His face flushed crimson and he moved around the counter to back up farther. "Nothing! I—I was looking for the ice," he said. His eyes glanced at me, then away, then back at me.

I slammed the door with a rattling thud. "Well, you could have asked me for ice! It's not in there." I motioned to the lower half of the split door.

He gave me an uncomprehending look. "How does it stay cold?"

Between Rory's threatening ideas of murder and mayhem, Jerry's warnings of pain-warped patients, and my own latent fears of molestation by a stranger, I was a little impatient with this feigned or real nineteenth-century bumpkinism. "What difference does it make?! For the love of God! You've been *shot;* someone's trying to *kill* you. You don't know who you *are.* Don't you think there are a little more important things to think about than goddamned *appliances?!*"

Carter's face had returned to its normal color, but his posture had straightened defensively. His eyes had shed their normally wary demeanor and now drilled me with intensity. "I know who I am," he said quietly. "And I told you how I was shot."

I looked at him helplessly. "You're confused. You have to be. Don't you see how crazy it is?"

His breathing was controlled but still showed his anger. "Yes, I *am* confused. I'm more confused than I've ever been in my life. But I *know* who I am," he said very deliberately. "And I know how I was shot."

I shook my head, not relinquishing his gaze. "Let me just ask you straight: What year do you think it is?"

He leaned back with a thump of disgust on the wall behind him, his eyes were heavy-lidded with condescension. "It's 1996."

I looked at him in surprise. Was it all a *gag?*

"But when I was shot," he continued, "three days ago, it was 1862."

I couldn't help it; my mouth snapped shut and I rolled my eyes.

Carter's fist came down on the counter with enough force to rattle the pots and pans in the cabinets. My eyes flew open. "I don't care if you don't believe it!" he exploded, his body tensed like a cat about to pounce. "I don't believe it either. But for pity's sake, give me a chance; give me some time to adjust! I was shot in the year 1862, and when I woke you were there. The world was somehow different, just off, odd. You brought me here, to this house, with you, and the next thing I knew I was in a world that looked *nothing* like my own! All white and silver—all hard edges—and—and *cold.* I thought you'd sent me to a madhouse." He glanced wildly about the room, not looking at anything. "People came and went, poked at me and asked questions I didn't understand. Then they looked at me as if I was stupid— a dumb animal who could not be responsible even for itself." He stopped to try to control his rising voice. His good hand clenched and unclenched by his side. He was the picture of a war within. After a moment he continued, "I know this is odd for you too. And it's right good of you to take me in. I know you've had misgivings." I watched the muscles in his jaw work between sentences. "But I just need—" He sighed desperately, helplessly, his shoulders slumping. "I don't—I don't have anywhere else to go." He averted his eyes at this admission. "And I don't understand what's happening."

I felt my throat constrict as I watched him battle for control. His chest rose and fell rapidly, and his eyes blinked quickly, as if to keep tears from falling. I wanted to go to him, to touch him, to comfort him, but he was so defensively self-composed that I was sure he would shy away.

"Let me make you some tea," I said finally. He didn't move. "Really. I've got some chamomile tea, and maybe we could talk. You know, just talk. I'd like to know more."

He remained stationary, so I took him by the arm to lead him to the table. As I'd suspected, he disengaged himself from my grasp and seated himself. "I'm all right," he said firmly, if quietly.

"Well, just sit there for a minute." I moved swiftly back to the kitchen to put the kettle on. Given the situation, I decided that the full tea treatment was required. The tray, the crocheted doily, the blue-and-white-flowered Victorian teapot, the china cups, the linen napkins, the real cream, everything I could think of went onto that tray, including a couple of the doughnuts.

When I emerged with all of this shining splendor Carter was sitting at the table with his head in his good hand. The fresh bandage at his temple gaped slightly, and I could see part of the blue-black bruise and split skin beneath. He looked up when I set down the tray and gazed at it, a small, solemn smile winning the battle to appear on his lips.

"At least there are some things still familiar," he said, leaning back stiffly in the chair. He flexed his bad shoulder slowly, wincing as he circled it back, then forward.

I studied his drawn face, his eyes where the wheat-colored lashes brushed his cheeks, the mouth pulled down at the corners.

"Are you married?" I asked, glancing at his left hand, where it lay docilely in the sling. He wore no ring.

He was surprised by the question. "Yes. To Meg—uh, Margaret Gilley. Lindsey."

I found this stumbling charming. "Newlyweds?" I asked.

He frowned. "No."

I poured the tea, looking expectantly at him, hoping he might elaborate. He didn't.

I sipped my tea. "You must miss her terribly."

His eyes met mine and held them for a moment. "Are you married?" he asked.

"No."

"Any beaux?"

I smiled at the quaint word. "Yes. One."

"What's his name?"

"Rory—Robert Feagan."

He blew quietly on his steaming tea. "You'll marry him?"

I squirmed at the question. "Okay, I can see where this sort of grilling is uncomfortable."

He smiled, a respectful, knowing smile, and inclined his head.

"We can talk about more general things, though I've never been much good at small talk." I placed two doughnuts on two plates and placed one in front of him. "Where are you from?"

"Bucks County, Pennsylvania. Near Philadelphia."

"You have a farm there?" I encouraged.

He bit into the doughnut and nodded. Then he set it back down, brushing the crumbs from his fingers onto the plate. "A small one. Mostly corn, but some beans as well. A small vegetable patch for the kitchen."

This had to conclude the topic of farming; I didn't know enough to even formulate another question about it. It struck me again how hopelessly ill-equipped I was to deal with someone who thought he was from the past. (Not that anyone could really be said to be *equipped* to

56

deal with someone who thought he was from the past.) My life was ordinary in the present day, with a good working knowledge of the technologies I employed and a complete ignorance of the way they came into being. I couldn't even stretch my imagination far enough to guess what life might have been like 130 years ago; which things he might be able to understand now and which would shock his disoriented frame of reference.

"Do I look familiar to you?" he asked suddenly.

I looked at him in surprise. "No. Not really." The poor fellow was grasping at straws if he thought I might actually know who he was and have forgotten somehow.

He studied me intently. "You look familiar to me," he said, eyes narrowed and head cocked slightly to one side. "A little."

"Do I?" I meticulously pushed the crumbs on the table in front of me into a small pile, picked them up, and dropped them onto my plate. "Well, I have a theory about that. I believe that there are only so many faces to go around, and occasionally you run into one that has been repeated. That's why you always run into people who look familiar, but you can't figure out where you might have met them." I refilled my cup. I could feel the chamomile beginning to send its massaging fingers of relaxation through my veins. "That happens to me all the time."

I glanced up to see him smiling at me, one eyebrow raised.

"What?" I asked.

He shrugged. "I've never heard that theory before," he said dryly. He poured some more tea into his cup. He drank it plain, I'd noticed; a man without appreciation for food with accessories. "Do your parents live here?" he asked.

I refilled my own cup. "No." I wondered what might have given him that impression.

He looked surprised. "You live here alone?"

"Well . . ." I looked down with some disgust at Steve, who lay curled in an obsequious ball at Carter's feet.

"Aside from the dog," he amended.

"It's my house, yes."

He digested this slowly. "Have you never been married?"

"No, I haven't. I bought this house myself. And I have a business in town. I sell books."

This brought a look of admiration to his face. "You've done all that yourself?"

I felt a flush of pride I hadn't experienced in a long time for the accomplishments. "Yes, I have. It's not going gangbusters or anything, but I can support myself and a small part-time staff."

I noticed him shift uncomfortably in the chair and realized that I had not yet filled the handful of prescriptions the doctor had issued.

"Are you in pain?" I asked anxiously. "God, I'm sorry. Do you think some aspirin would help?"

Carter picked up his tea again. "I'm all right. My shoulder just feels as if it's stiffening up some."

I grabbed my purse from the back of the chair next to me and pulled out the prescriptions I had stuffed into it when we'd gotten out of the car. They were, of course, written in that illegible doctors' code, but I hoped there was a painkiller among them. "I need to get these filled for you," I said, forgetting about the worry of leaving him alone in the house. I think I was incapable of mistrusting someone with whom I had shared tea. "Are you going to be all right here alone?"

He looked up at me anxiously. "Are you going to the apothecary?"

I smiled. He was consistent. "Well, in a way. We call them pharmacists now." If there *was* a hidden camera somewhere, they were going to get a hoot out of me. I was actually starting to enjoy humoring his delusion.

Carter nodded, committing it to memory, it seemed. "I'd be obliged if you could pick up some willow bark tea," he said solemnly.

"Willow bark . . . ?" I must have looked as bewildered as I felt at the request because he elaborated.

"For pain. It's not extreme, but if they've got any . . ." He let the sentence hang, presumably not wanting to elaborate on the need. He was not the type who liked admitting to pain; I could tell.

"Oh, they've got something better for pain than tea," I said.

He stood when I did, and I noticed, perhaps for the first time, his solid, black leather boots and the heavy, coarse material of his pants and shirt. "We've got to get you something more comfortable to wear too," I said thoughtfully. He couldn't possibly relax, let alone sleep, in that rig. "Come with me," I commanded.

We trudged up the stairs, Carter's step heavy enough to cause the pictures on the stairwell wall to quiver silently. I led him into the guest room. "You can sleep in here," I said. "It's the guest room. And the bathroom's right at the end of the hall." I left the room for my walk-in closet and returned with a pair of Rory's sweat pants and one of his sweatshirts. "You can put these on in the meantime. They'll be a lot more comfortable than what you've got on."

He took the black blob of material from me and held up the sweat pants with one hand, the sweatshirt dropping to the floor. "I think Rory's a little bigger than you around the hips, but those should fit. They're elastic," I explained, thinking that perhaps this was something they wouldn't have had in the time he thought he was from.

His lips twitched as he pulled at the waistband, holding one side gingerly with his weak hand. "So I see."

I flushed. So much for trying to explain the obvious.

"Anyway, I shouldn't be long. The drug store's only a couple of miles away. Do you need anything else before I go? Oh, and you'll find towels and shaving stuff in the bathroom closet."

"All right." If he didn't know what a bathroom was, he wasn't asking. And I wasn't about to launch into an explanation of it only to be smirked at again by those assessing eyes.

I looked at him playing with the fabric a little, then turned to go. "Then I'll see you in a few."

He didn't answer and barely looked up as I left; he just stood in the middle of the room, looking around at the furniture.

When I returned he was standing at the sink in the kitchen, playing with the faucet. I could hear the water rush on, then off, and then on again as I entered.

His hair, neatly brushed, looked thick and rich against the black sweatshirt, and his shoulders looked even broader out of the torn and wrinkled shirt of his uniform.

Steve, I suppose having tired of Carter's explorations, greeted me warmly.

I was unexpectedly relieved to see Carter, not realizing until that moment that I'd unconsciously feared Rory had been right and I would come home to a ransacked house.

"I'm glad you're there," I called to him. "Get yourself a glass of water; I've got your medicine here."

I saw him turn, and then someone knocked on the door. Reversing my route, I plodded back and opened it. Standing on the porch, looking unnecessarily large and intimidating, were two policemen. One of them, the shorter one, held Carter's pistol.

I feared for a moment that they'd come to arrest us for some unknown crime, filled with the same automatic guilt that causes me to immediately hit the brake whenever I see a squad car on the road, whether I've been speeding or not.

"Hello." I beamed a charming smile at them. "Can I help you?"

I saw my neighbor stop on her way to her car across the street. She watched with unconcealed, no doubt self-righteous curiosity.

"Are you Miss Shelby Manning?" the taller of the two asked.

I nodded, stepping back from the door. "Yes, come on in."

They single-filed through the door. "We're looking for—"

Carter emerged from the dining room with a glass of water. "Ah—you must be Mr. Lindsey?" the tall policeman asked.

"I am," he replied, with such relief that I realized he must have thought someone had recognized him at last.

"The hospital gave us your address," the policeman continued, looking at Carter. "We found this up on Sunken Road. They said it was yours."

A blank mask descended on Carter's face, but not before I had caught a glimpse of near-fatal disappointment. His head dropped a fraction, barely perceptibly, but I noticed it.

He moved forward stiffly. "Yes. It's mine." He reached out a hand and took it. I'd half expected them to snatch it back, demanding to know why it wasn't registered, when I realized that I had begun to think like someone who believed the outlandish story of Carter's appearing from the past. Of course the gun would be registered. This man could not really be from 1862; he'd merely lost his memory—or his mind.

"Did you happen to research the registration on that gun?" I asked pleasantly. "I only ask because Mr. Lindsey is suffering from a temporary bout of amnesia and can't remember where he lives. Was there anything . . . ?''

The policeman bowed his head politely. "We would have, ma'am, but these old guns can't be registered. In fact, I'd put that somewhere real safe because it's still loaded.''

"Loaded!" I repeated. "Well, let's unload it, shall we? I'd rather not have a live firearm in the house, if it's all the same to you.''

The policeman smiled and glanced at his partner, who smiled back. "Oh it's all the same to me, all right. But these old guns, once they're loaded, there's only one way to unload 'em.''

"And how is that?" I asked practically.

Carter's voice came from behind me, sounding like a command. "Shoot them.''

I jumped. *Good God, was he planning to kill them?* He was a crazed murderer after all! Rory would be so happy. I turned to glare at him, expecting to see the weapon pointed at the policemen. "What?''

Carter cradled the gun in his good hand. The policemen chuckled. "That's right, ma'am," the tall one said. "Once they're loaded, the only way to unload 'em is to shoot 'em.''

For the first time Carter seemed to be smiling sincerely, if not broadly, and his eyes glinted beneath his lashes.

I heaved a sigh. "So you're just returning this loaded pistol that you've found in the park to this man who has just left the hospital?''

The policemen eyed each other uncertainly, the short one shifting his weight from one foot to the other. "Dr. Blake told us you said it was his. He told us it was there, where you said it was. It's not yours, sir?''

"It's mine," Carter said with certainty.

The policemen nodded with satisfaction at each other. Mutt and Jeff. "Well then, that's all we need," the tall one said. They both turned to the door.

"Thank you, gentlemen," Carter said.

The tall one waved a hand over his head. "No problem, no problem," he replied. "Just don't like to have those things lying around, you know."

I followed them out to the front porch, closing the front door behind me. "Wait a minute," I halted them somewhat indignantly. They turned in unison halfway down the stoop. "Did Dr. Blake tell you it was all right to give this man a gun?"

The tall one's brow furrowed in consternation. "He said it belonged to him."

"What I mean is," I said with considerably more patience than I felt, "that this man is suffering from a delusion that he was wounded during the Civil War. I'm not sure it's wise that he have a loaded gun."

The two men shared another uncomfortable look. "I suggest you talk to Dr. Blake about that, ma'am." I noticed that the short one never spoke. What was he? I wondered. Ornamental? Just there to share irritating looks with the tall one?

I could hardly believe they had stopped by simply to drop off a gun and leave. "Are you trying to tell me that there's nothing illegal about a man having a loaded gun in a public park?" I asked, though it was not my intention to have Carter arrested.

"As long as it's not concealed, ma'am, he's allowed to carry a loaded gun anywhere he pleases." The tall one hiked up his pants to punctuate this statement of The Law.

They could have knocked me over with a feather. "You're joking."

He shook his head solemnly. "No, ma'am. It's his right under the law."

I stared at them, flabbergasted. "How comforting," I

said. They turned again to leave, but I stopped them once more.

"Excuse me, but isn't there some sort of investigation of this incident going on? Don't you want to question us?" Did these guys know anything about crime-solving? Didn't they even watch TV?

The tall one turned slowly this time, exasperation evident in the movement. "Mr. Lindsey was questioned in the hospital, as was the attending physician. You were not present for the shooting, were you?"

I tried to look haughtily at them from my perch atop the stoop and failed. "Well, no."

"Then that's probably why our investigative team hasn't questioned you. If you have some information, I suggest you call them."

I shoved my hands in my pockets. "Won't they call us? Won't they let us know how it's going?"

"Of course, Miss Manning." It was obvious he considered himself the soul of patience. "They'll keep you informed about how it's going. But I'll be honest with you; until Mr. Lindsey recovers his memory, we have very few clues to work with."

Just the fact that he was shot by a fifty-eight caliber lead bullet that came out of a Civil War musket. "Fine," I said curtly. "Thank you."

They folded themselves in unison into the squad car and left, the car uttering a powerfully low growl as it cruised off. I turned back to the house to find Carter standing at the screen door.

He looked at me thoughtfully, and I thought for a moment that he might be angry about my illegal-gun-in-a-public-park question. But he merely opened the door for me.

I eyed the gun in his hand and gave it a wide berth as I entered. "Here's your medicine," I said vaguely, trying to regain my equilibrium as I picked up the prescription

bags from the couch. Tetracycline, a cream called Beta-
dine, and something called Lorcet Plus, which I took to
be a painkiller.

Carter placed the gun on the side table and picked up
the glass of water he had deposited there.

"One of these every four hours," I said numbly, handing
him the pain pill. "One of these three times a day." I
handed him the antibiotic. "And there's some cream here.
I'll put some on next time we change the bandage."

I sat down heavily in a chair, wondering what to do
with this man and his gun. Somehow the gun made it all
seem more real, more threatening. Whereas before I was
willing to take it all as an unusual adventure, the gun
weighted everything down to depressing reality. Maybe
it was just fatigue, I thought, rubbing my hands across
my face.

"Where would you like me to put it?" Carter asked.

I opened my eyes.

"The pistol," he added. Something outside of me
noted that he looked very good in Rory's old sweats.

"I don't know. Someplace where I don't have to look
at it."

"Shall I keep it in my room, or would that make you
nervous?" he asked. His face was calm, concerned even,
and I felt my mood lighten a little.

Realizing that he would be able to get to this gun no
matter where I told him to put it, I said significantly,
"You do what you think is best with it."

He smiled at me gently. "Don't worry, Miss Manning.
You'll never see this gun pointed at you." His eyes were
laughing, an effect I most definitely liked on him.

I felt my lips turn up slightly in return, though I
couldn't help giving them a cynical twist. "Well, that's
something, I guess."

Chapter Four

Sleeping is one of my fortes. Not only is it something I enjoy, but I've always had the ability to sleep through virtually anything. But that evening I awoke from a pretty heavy sleep to hear voices downstairs. My house being old, it has an open vent between floors for heat from the wood stove downstairs to drift through, and sounds travel up just as easily. I thought that perhaps Rory had come in and turned on the television—until I heard Steve's low growl.

I sprang out of bed, envisioning armed, stocking-faced men in my living room, and stood paralyzed where I'd landed. Shaking with adrenaline, I slipped a pair of sweat pants on under my T-shirt and crept to the door. Silence answered my straining ears.

I eased open the door to see the downstairs hall light on. Not very clever if they were burglars, I thought, as some of my anxiety evaporated. It had to be Rory.

Squinting against the brightness, I moved to the top of

the stairs. The scene that greeted my light-bruised eyes was enough to dilate them fully and send an extra shot of adrenaline pounding through my veins.

Carter stood at the foot of the stairs with his good arm around Rory's neck and the other holding the long Civil War pistol to Rory's temple. I careened down the stairs.

"Carter! For God's sake!" I missed the bottom step, landed on the hall floor with a considerable thump, and grabbed Carter's pistol-wielding hand.

Carter's grip relaxed as he turned to me, and Rory stumbled away with a gasped expletive, raking his hand through his hair and glaring at Carter as if he planned to disembowel him on the spot the second he found out what the devil was going on. Steve cowered away from Rory's lunging body, tail tucked neatly between her legs.

Carter turned bland eyes on me. "You know him?" He gently uncocked the pistol.

My heart was racing as if I'd just run a mile. "Yes, I know him. Good Lord, would you have shot him if I hadn't?"

Carter set down the gun on the hall table. "Not immediately."

"Shelby," Rory growled in a voice barely under control, "who the hell is this *idiot* and why is he wearing my clothes?"

I turned uneasily to him. "Well, you remember the other night—"

His eyes shot heavenward. "Holy shit," he breathed. "This is that nut who thinks he's a soldier. Isn't it?"

I glanced at Carter to see how he was taking that. He didn't reach for the pistol, so we were doing better than I'd feared.

"Isn't it!" Rory yelled. He pulled both hands through his hair this time and turned away, walking into the living room. His body was stiff with anger and he whirled again to face us after only a few steps. "What the *hell* do you

think you're doing taking this lunatic in off the streets? I thought we talked about this. I thought he was in the hospital. Have you completely flipped, Shelby?''

I felt my insides quiver upon becoming the object of this barely controlled anger, and with that feeling all memory of my rationale in bringing Carter home departed.

''I felt sort of—responsible,'' I offered weakly. ''He seemed harmless enough.''

Carter issued a brief snort at this comment and leaned against the banister, his arms crossed.

Rory's eyes rolled and he nodded exaggeratedly. ''Yeah, oh yeah, he's pretty fucking harmless, Shel. He only threatened to blow my goddamned head off in your front hall.''

Not knowing what to do in the face of this Schwartz-eneggeresque barrage, I turned my anger on Carter. ''What did you think you were doing? Do intruders in the nineteenth century come armed with *keys,* for God's sake?''

Carter raised his eyebrows at me and gave me a one-shouldered shrug. ''I thought I'd make sure.''

This, actually, made a little bit of sense to me. After all, he had no idea who Rory was, and no reason to believe that a man would enter the house of a single woman at three in the morning and be welcome.

I turned back to Rory. ''You know, he had no way of knowing . . .''

He gaped at me, started to say something, then shook his head and gaped at me again. ''I—*huh,''* he scoffed and turned away. ''You know, I used to tell people that this nutcake act of yours was just a front, but I don't know, Shel. I think you might just be as screwy as you seem to everyone else.'' He paced back and forth in front of us.

I felt myself flush at this accusation and glanced at

Carter from the corner of my eye. He regarded Rory stiffly, a calculating intensity in his gray eyes.

"Maybe if you didn't just pop in at all hours of the night," I said with what force I could muster, "maybe if I saw you in the daytime every now and again, you'd have met Carter and avoided this whole stupid scene."

Rory stopped his agitated pacing. "I can't believe that you take a perfect stranger into your house, he pulls a gun on me, and I get blamed for being here. That is really rich, Shelby." He started to brush past me, but I grabbed his arm.

"Rory, wait," I said. Carter straightened from his leaning pose as we all found ourselves within three feet of each other. "I'm sorry. It must have been shocking for you. It's just that I had no idea—that is, I hadn't warned him—about you—oh, anyway, let me at least introduce you. This is Carter Lindsey. Carter, Rory Feagan." I stepped back to allow them room to shake hands.

Carter extended his cordially enough, but Rory simply gave the hand a withering look. "Are you going to keep this psycho here after he just tried to kill me? Are we all supposed to just go merrily on to bed after this? I should have him arrested!"

"Actually," I said thoughtfully, remembering the tall policeman of that afternoon, "it's not illegal for him to carry a loaded weapon. As long as it's not concealed."

Rory stalked to the door.

"Rory, please don't go," I said, and he stopped, hand on the knob. "They were going to stick him in a cab. Can you imagine? A guy with amnesia? What was I supposed to do? He's got nowhere else to go. And Dr. Blake seemed to think it was all right that he come here." Actually, I hadn't asked Dr. Blake, but that wasn't something Rory needed to know.

At this point, tiring, I suppose, of hearing himself talked about like a stray dog, Carter stepped forward.

"Mr. Feagan," he said in a voice that was low but commanded attention, "I apologize for frightening you. I was under the mistaken impression that you meant Miss Manning harm, and she has been kind to me."

Rory's eyes were lit with something unreadable, but they looked more alert than I'd seen them at this hour of the morning in a long time.

I grabbed at the excuse. "Exactly! How unsafe could I be if he was trying to *protect* me? Please, let's just get over this. I hate misunderstandings."

I saw the wheels turning in Rory's head, cranking on the gratification of walking out against the inconvenience of driving all the way home. Finally he dropped his hand from the knob and gazed at me, shaking his head. "I'm really tired. We can talk about this in the morning." Rory shot an angry parting glance at Carter and mounted the stairs to my room.

A long sigh escaped me.

"He stays here?" Carter's dry voice roused me. I turned.

"Yes. He's the guy—the beau—I told you about. He works as a bartender, so he frequently shows up late. I guess I should have told you more about him."

Carter shrugged and turned to the stairs. I stared after him, wondering if the judgment I'd seen in his eyes was real or just my paranoia.

How was it that I'd turned out to be the villain in all of this? Why was I apologizing to everyone? I suppose things were going along just *fine* before I turned up. "Good night," I said testily.

Carter turned soberly back to me and said, "Good night, Miss Manning. Sleep well."

I felt my hands bunch into fists at my sides. "You know," I halted him again, "this isn't all that unusual."

He turned back again. "What isn't?" But his expression was not questioning, not the way I knew it was when he was really confused.

I struggled for words that would justify without subtly incriminating. "This. Rory, me—you know," I said vaguely but with great energy.

He smiled politely, though the gesture didn't reach his eyes. "Things have not changed overmuch."

"I've known him since high school," I continued absurdly.

His brow furrowed. Not wishing to involve myself in a discussion about the twentieth-century American educational system, I threw up my hands and turned away. "It's none of your business anyway," I said over my shoulder.

"I know that," he said, a slight emphasis on the *I*.

I whirled to face him. "Then why are you giving me that judgmental look?" I demanded.

He held up his hands innocently.

"You were," I said. "It was *not* my imagination." Who was I arguing with? Myself?

He looked at me with a genuine smile this time. "Aren't you tired?"

"Yes! Yes, I'm tired. That's why I'm rambling on like this," I said, definitely disgusted with myself. "Go on, go to bed. I'm irrational."

I headed for the kitchen. Tea. Chamomile. Relaxation. I was becoming a tea junkie, I thought irrelevantly. I heard him saunter in behind me as I slammed the kettle onto the burner and cranked up the heat.

"Shelby," he said, in a low voice that made me acutely aware that it was the first time he'd used my first name. "I have no grounds to judge you."

I scoffed. "That doesn't stop most people."

He leaned against the doorframe. "Why would it matter if I were judging you?" he continued, taking me by surprise.

71

Why *would* it matter? I didn't care what most people thought; what made him different? Because even knowing that his mind was in a different place, if not a different time, did not quell the surge of embarrassment I'd felt at his *correct* assumption about Rory's presence. What could that signify?

I felt myself blush. "I don't know. I don't do well being woken up in the middle of the night." I reached to the stack of Celestial Seasonings tea boxes on the shelf next to his face. I could feel his eyes on me, and his nearness sent an unexpected, though not unpleasant, shiver along my spine.

"Would you like some tea?" I asked sullenly.

He smiled again, this time with real amusement. "No, thank you. I'll not lose my life over a cup of tea, if you don't mind."

I was slow to catch his meaning. "Lose your life?"

His eyes traced a path to the bedroom upstairs. "I've the feeling your Mr. Feagan would not take kindly to my lingering down here with you. And after all," he motioned toward the sweat clothes he wore, "I do owe him something."

That brought a laugh to my lips and I pushed the heavy curls of my hair behind me as I leaned against the counter. "I thought I'd made it clear that there would be no bullets flying in my house. At least not tonight."

"You were most clear about it, yes." He straightened. "In any case, I'll bid you good night, Miss Manning. And sleep well," he said again, this time with just the ghost of a smile in his eyes.

Rory was livid when I finally made it upstairs. He sat bolt upright in bed, turning the pages of a home improvement magazine without casting so much as a glance at what was printed on them.

"What the hell were you doing, explaining our lives

to him? Who the hell is he, anyway?'' he demanded.

I was rapidly losing my patience for suffering outraged abuse, though I mentally kicked myself for having that whole conversation with Carter right below the heat vent. ''I'm sure I'm not qualified to answer that question, if he's not.''

Rory tossed the magazine onto the bedside table, from which it slid onto the floor with a soft slurping sound. He leaned his head back against the wall. ''I really don't understand you sometimes, Shelby. The guy was wandering around downstairs with a loaded gun when I came in. How do you know he wasn't on his way up here?''

There was no way I was relaxed enough to attempt sleep, so I began to fold clothes from a basket of laundry that sat on the floor. Besides, it was very hard to argue with someone sprawled next to you in bed. ''Well, for one thing, he had the gun in his room, so he was probably not on his way '*up here*' to kill me; unless he wanted to get a glass of milk before he did it.''

''My point is the same. If he had it in his room, what was he doing with it downstairs?'' It was a good point, I thought, mentally marking one up for Rory. ''You know nothing about this guy. But you've taken him in, literally off the street, and brought him home to live with you, a single woman. Does that make any sense?''

I pulled a shirt out of the basket and shook the wrinkles from it. After grabbing a hanger from the small closet behind me, I turned to him. ''Fine. Would you like him to come live with you?'' Rory lived in a tiny efficiency apartment that was rarely clean enough for anyone to find the floor. And the main reason he showed up here so often, I was convinced, was that his refrigerator was perpetually empty and the furnace perpetually broken.

''Yeah! Sure! Let's ship him out! He can stay there and I'll stay here.'' His expression dared me to disagree.

''Oh, right, Rory. The poor guy has amnesia. He thinks

he's from the Civil War. He was terrified in the car this morning. How do you think he'd do in that rat trap of yours? Not to mention that he wouldn't be able to get anywhere from there without a car." I stuffed a handful of underpants in a dresser drawer. And besides, I couldn't add out loud, for some reason I thought Carter needed me. His speech about the harsh unfamiliarity of the hospital had tugged so strongly at my sympathies that I was not about to turn him out into the cold world alone again.

Rory snorted. "Good; he can sit there until he remembers where he lives. Maybe he needs a little negative reinforcement." He sat petulantly staring at the curtained window. "You know, you read about people who never get their memory back. Suppose he doesn't ever remember? What then? He'll live here forever?"

I'd nearly finished the laundry when I realized that this basket had been the one full of dirty clothes. Swearing silently, I began pulling the clothes back out of drawers and off hangers and throwing them back into the basket. "*No,* he won't live here forever. We can cross that bridge when we come to it. I'll be in touch with Dr. Blake, too, to see what can be done to help him remember."

There was a moment of silence as Rory watched me. "What are you doing?"

I whipped the shirt from the hanger and threw it in the basket. "I forgot that these were dirty clothes," I said irritably. "Look, I don't want to argue about this. He hasn't even tried to hurt me—"

Rory sat forward. "But that's just *it.* If he's mentally unbalanced you won't know when it will happen."

"Or *if.*" I leaned against the dresser, arms crossed.

He pointed a knowledgeable finger at me. "Or if, but that won't help you sleep at night, will it?"

"The only trouble I'm having sleeping at night is because of you, Rory. Carter could have wandered around all night with that loaded gun and I'd have been blissfully unaware of it if you hadn't shown up.''

His lips thinned with the effort to stay calm. ''Oh, okay. So it *is* my fault. We're back to that.''

I sighed. ''The only thing we're back to is that it's late and I don't want to be awake anymore.'' I moved to my side of the bed and sat down. ''Let me just ask you this, though: If Carter had been a woman, would you be making this fuss?''

Rory scoffed and punched his pillow to lay back against it. ''You think I'm jealous? Is that it?''

I shot him a look. ''Yes, I do.'' I slid under the covers and curled onto my side, facing him. ''Think about it, Rory. The guy's afraid. He really is. I could see it in his eyes. Don't you think it's up to people to help other people in trouble? I mean, if we all continue on this path of 'looking out for number one,' we'll be in real trouble. We'll closet ourselves away in our houses, hoping that trouble won't befall us, because if it does, we'll be on our own. No one will help us. Is that what you want for the human race?''

I'd coaxed a reluctant smile out of him. ''I hate it when you start talking like this. Baffling me with bullshit.''

I let that veiled insult go and closed my eyes, turning my back to him. ''Good night, Rory.''

He curled against my back, and I could smell the smoke and sweat that clung to his skin. ''Hit the lights, Shel,'' he said quietly.

Business was booming. Christmas was a week away, and it seemed everyone had suddenly thought of books. This was a good thing, of course, but dealing with people in the throes of Christmas shopping while making do with two or three hours of sleep was something of a challenge. Both Sylvie and Janey, another part-timer, were working full-time for the Christmas rush, and the three of us were shelving and re-shelving madly.

The after-work rush was finally starting to subside, and Janey had just left, when Sylvie joined me behind the counter.

"Check out the history section," she breathed low. "*Gorgeous, gorgeous* male. I've completely cleaned up women's studies just watching him."

I chuckled. Sylvie's eagle eye when it came to men was astounding at times. She would spot a man two blocks down and across the street and follow him for the afternoon to find out where he lived. She was relentless. "And he's still there? What are you doing back here?"

She sighed. "It's a selfless act of generosity. He's so good-looking, I couldn't absorb it all myself. I had to share it."

I sorted through the Visa and MasterCard receipts, separating out the ones for American Express. "Tell him to buy something. I'll consider him much better looking if he has money in his hand."

Sylvie leaned forward in an effort to catch a glimpse of him through the shelves between us and history. "Really, Shelby, you've got to look. Just go straighten up business. Or here—" She grabbed a copy of *Advise and Consent* from the "hold" shelf and thrust it at me. "Shelve this."

I was about to remind her that if she wanted to get out of there by seven o'clock, she'd better let me finish the accounting, when her swiftly indrawn breath announced the approach of the stranger.

Lieutenant Carter Lindsey appeared before us, carrying a book. He still wore the black sweat clothes, but he had donned his black leather boots and an old leather bomber jacket of Rory's that had been hanging in the hall. I had to admit he looked stunning. His already broad shoulders were accentuated by the old jacket, as were his slim hips and muscular legs in the black sweat pants. Personally, I would have pitched the boots for an old pair of running shoes, but the effect could not have been more arresting.

"Well, well, Lieutenant Lindsey," I greeted him, unable to quell the smile that spread across my face. "What are you doing out of your sickbed?" Even the sling was gone.

The smile I received in return nearly turned my knees to jelly. I had not yet experienced the full impact of an uninhibited smile on his face, and the effect was breathtaking. He was one of those people whose faces are transformed by a smile. Gone for the duration of it was the expression of wary confusion and insecurity, replaced by a sparkling good humor. There was even a bit of mischief dancing in his clear gray eyes. I felt myself attempt to speak, but the words did not come.

"Miss Mannning," he replied. "Had I remained in that bed I would surely have died—of boredom."

I felt, more than saw, Sylvie's goggle-eyed look of amazement as the object of her obsession addressed me in a familiar way.

"How long have you been here?" I asked.

He glanced with amusement at Sylvie. "Quite some time. You've the finest library of books I have ever seen," he said seriously, opening the book he held on the counter between us. It was a thick volume of the history of agriculture, complete with full-color photographs and line drawings. "The fineness of the tintypes. The paper . . ." He ran his fingers lightly, reverently, across the pages.

I smiled as I watched him. "Would you like that book?"

He looked up at me sharply. "You know I can't," he said quickly. "I only meant to look. I didn't mean to imply—"

"Don't be silly." I waved away his objection. "I'll give it to you at cost. When you find your family you can pay me back."

He gazed down at the book. "No, thank you," he said firmly.

His hands, so gentle on the cover, made me want to do something for him. I flipped open the front cover. It was a hardback book, and a little on the expensive side, but I could give it to him for forty percent off. I pulled the calculator from under a pile of receipts. "It would only be sixteen dollars with the discount," I said temptingly.

His eyes, big as saucers, lifted slowly from my fingers on the calculator to my face with an expression of stupefaction. "*Sixteen dollars?*" he repeated.

"Well, it's twenty-six full price," I said a little hesitantly.

He removed his hands from the counter and put them by his sides. Looking down at the book in horror, he said quietly, "Thank you. No."

Wishing to diffuse the suddenly uncomfortable silence, I turned to Sylvie. "Let me introduce you to one of my co-workers. Sylvie Stratton, this is Carter Lindsey."

Carter composed himself quickly and glanced up at Sylvie, who had stood watching the whole proceeding. I had told her the story of Carter Lindsey, and she now seemed torn between disappointment that her Gorgeous Male had turned out to be my crazy man and fascination that the crazy man had turned out to be such a gorgeous male.

"Very nice to meet you," she said. Then, for the first time since I'd known her, she had the floor and had nothing to say. She clammed up, tongue-tied.

Carter gave her a half bow. "Miss Stratton."

Silence descended again. "How are you feeling?" I asked. "Do the pain pills help?"

He looked self-consciously at Sylvie, then back at me. "I'm fine." But he straightened his stiff shoulder unconsciously.

"You've remembered to take the other medicine?" I pressed. "And the cream—you used the cream when you changed the bandage?" What a mother hen I was becoming.

Carter took the book in his hands and ignored my questions. "I shall return this." He walked back toward the history section.

I turned to Sylvie. "Tally these receipts, will you?" I ignored her expression, including her significantly raised eyebrows and coy smile. "I'll be right back."

I followed Carter through the maze of shelves to the history section, along the wall. He placed the book in the empty spot from which he'd obviously pulled it, and I wondered what had brought him here, downtown, to the store. Though my house wasn't far, if you didn't know where to look for the store, you could wander for quite some time up and down the shop-lined streets.

"Did you see these?" I asked genially, stopping at the gardening section. I pulled from the shelf a beautiful, coffee-table-sized book full of landscaping plans, pictures, and literature.

He didn't take the book from me but stood very close and looked over my shoulder. I was intensely aware of his presence, of the smoky leather smell of Rory's old jacket and the warmth emanating from his body. I pulled my hair around my left shoulder to give him a better view. The pages turned with a thick rustling sound that testified to the book's quality. I glanced at him out of the corner of my eye and saw deep concentration in his eyes and posture. I studied his profile, strong and straight, until his eyes slanted toward me. I realized too late that I'd been staring, not turning the pages.

Sylvie, whom I'd heard with half an ear shuffling through the shelves to lock the front door, picked that moment to turn off the lights, and we were plunged into darkness. I could almost feel my pupils dilating in the sudden blackness. The safety lights took a moment to flicker on, and in the midst of their lightning flashes I could see that his eyes were on mine, undistracted by the warm-up of the battery-powered lights.

My breath caught in my throat. The intensity of his eyes froze me where I stood. I felt his hand cup my elbow, and though my mind told me to pull away, my feet stayed rooted to the spot. The safety lights snapped on, casting a dim greenish glow on everything. Still, his eyes held mine.

"I know you," he said intently. His voice was hushed in the weird green atmosphere. "Don't you know me?"

For a second I had the thought that some mystical re-incarnation thing had occurred and he'd come to me across the years from a past life. Why was it, then, that I didn't remember him? He wasn't even remotely familiar to me.

"Do you want me to make the deposit?" Sylvie's voice was shrill in the silence and made us both jump. "I've cashed out. We balanced within three dollars and something." She appeared from around the women's studies table. Carter and I were now a discreet distance apart.

"Great, great," I said. "Sure, if you don't mind making the deposit. That would be a help."

She smiled brightly at Carter. "It was nice to meet you," she said pertly. "Are you guys going out or something tonight?"

I glanced uncomfortably at Carter. "Carter just stopped by to see the place." I looked back at her. "I'll see you at ten tomorrow, right?"

Sylvie nodded. "Yeah, sure. Ten o'clock. Plenty of time to sleep late in the morning. Maybe I'll head for the Grill tonight. If you guys want to join me . . . ?"

I answered hastily. "No, thanks. Maybe another night. I've got Christmas shopping to do."

"Family getting tired of books?" she asked with a smile. She was never going to leave, I decided.

"Yes, in fact."

Carter stepped from behind me. "It was a pleasure to meet you, Miss Stratton."

"Oh! Yes, you too. Maybe we can go out another night," she said again, holding out her hand. Carter took it. For a moment I thought he might kiss it, as he had the little nurse's, and I braced myself to catch Sylvie's swoon. She didn't allow him the opportunity, however, as she took his hand in both of hers and leaned close. "You know, I had a friend who had amnesia once, and it didn't last very long. Enjoy it! It's probably the last time in your life you'll be really free of responsibility."

Enjoy it, she said. Sylvie was the only person I knew who would advise someone to enjoy such a calamity.

Carter smiled politely, extricating his hand. "Thank you for your concern, miss," he said. "Good night."

Sylvie glanced from one of us to the other, her small, sharp eyes picking up more than I wanted them to. "Okay. Good night, then," she said with a quick toss of her bobbed head. "See you in the morning, Shelby."

I couldn't tell for sure, but I thought I heard a note of warning in her voice; then again, my paranoia was a powerful thing. Though Sylvie and I had worked together for over a year, and I trusted her with moderate responsibilities in the store, she and I weren't what one would consider real friends. For one thing, she was fairly young—about twenty—and still tended to enjoy activities that I, at twenty-seven, felt I had outgrown. We rarely saw each other outside of work, though, due to our talkative natures, we knew a lot about each other's private lives.

I heard the bell jingle as she left through the front door, and I moved decisively away from Carter to bolt it behind her. From there I went back to the cash register at the back of the store to be sure Sylvie had taken all the receipts. Everything looked to be in order.

"I'm sorry if I made you uncomfortable." Carter's voice floated to me as he emerged from the shelves.

I reached under the register and retrieved my purse. "No, you didn't make me uncomfortable," I lied. At least he hadn't for the reasons he might have thought.

He approached the counter and leaned against it. "I suppose you remind me strongly of someone I met recently." He laughed lightly at that and added, "A hundred and thirty years ago."

Intrigued, I asked, "Who do I remind you of?" Perhaps it was some ancestor of mine. As if, I kicked myself, the whole outrageous tale could possibly be believed.

He shook his head. "It's not that important. I'm not even sure of her name."

I nodded mutely, wondering what I was to do with him now. I really did have shopping to do. And I was afraid that if I brought him with me, the distraction would prove too much. On the other hand, he could use a few things himself, like more comfortable shoes and perhaps a pair of jeans. The allure of distraction won out.

"I have some shopping to do. Do you want to come with me?" I asked, starting for the door. He fell into step beside me.

A slow smile turned up the corners of his mouth. "As it happens, I am not busy this evening. I would be happy to join you."

I laughed up at him and saw the expression in his eyes soften dangerously. My own eyes snapped forward. This might be more distraction than I could handle, I thought, expelling a deep sigh.

Chapter Five

I have to admit, I took some pleasure in the unadulterated awe I saw on Carter's face as we traversed the Spotsylvania mall. It wasn't even a fancy mall, like the ones closer to Washington, that made even seasoned shoppers feel as if they might have wandered accidentally into Shangri-la.

By this time I couldn't say if I actually believed Carter's bizarre assertion that he was from the past, or if I was just tired of having to remind myself that he was crazy; in any case, I'd decided to simply go with the flow of his beliefs. And in doing so I found myself really enjoying his amazement. The whole way to the mall he had studied the movement of my feet on the car pedals, the way the left one lifted to depress the clutch at an exact moment and the right one shifted between brake and accelerator. He made me feel as if driving a car was some wonderful accomplishment, an affirmation that could work wonders on one's self-esteem if practiced daily.

He also watched my way with the salespeople and my familiarity with the sheer abundance he saw contained in the little shopping center. My use of a credit card astounded—and delighted—him. He laughed out loud as one of the salesgirls accepted it, good naturedly pointing out that any shopkeeper worth his salt wouldn't accept such a flimsy promise of payment in exchange for valuable goods. I noticed that the girl ran my card through the approval machine twice after that.

By the time we reached The Gap Carter was thoroughly burdened by my shopping bags, so I directed him to ask the salesman at the register if we could stow them behind the counter.

"If you're so wealthy," Carter stated when he returned empty-handed, "surely you could afford a manservant or two."

I laughed at that. "There's a thought. But wealthy I'm not. This may look like a ridiculous amount of stuff," I admitted, "but it's par for the course for a lot of people. Christmas is a time when most people exceed their budgets, and I'm no exception."

He frowned at a tall stack of yellow shaker-knit sweaters. "But the things you've bought—the expense— surely most people would do better to make their own gifts."

My eyes scanned the racks full of clothing. "I'm sure they would," I agreed. "If anyone had the time. Or the talent." I headed toward the back of the store, where the men's jeans were laid out in stacks on shelves that stretched to the ceiling. "But now we're going to concentrate on you." I nabbed a passing pony-tailed salesgirl. "Excuse me. We need some jeans. Could you help us?"

"Sure!" She smiled brightly. "What size do you need?"

I eyed Carter critically from the waist down, not an unpleasant task. "What do you think?" I mentally compared him to Rory, who, at six-two and 190 pounds, wore a thirty-five waist and a thirty-four inseam. "Thirty-two, thirty-three waist? And maybe . . . maybe a thirty-three inseam?"

The salesgirl obviously enjoyed the study of Carter's physique as much as I had. "Okay, we'll try that. Sir, what color would you like? Jet, sand, plum, hunter, natural, or, of course, blue? Stone-washed, acid-washed, straight-leg, boot-leg, button-fly, zipper, relaxed cut, loose fit, or regular?"

Carter stared at the woman as if she'd just recited the Lord's Prayer in pig Latin, then turned helpless eyes on me. Unable to resist clothing a man exactly the way I wanted to see him, I chose for him. "Stone-washed blue, uh, straight leg, button fly, regular," I announced. I'd never realized how many opinions I had about jeans.

The girl rushed off to do my bidding. A manservant, I thought idly, would not be such a bad thing to have.

Carter watched the girl's progress from one shelf to the next. "I'll pay you back," he said.

I smiled at him. "No, I don't want you to. Merry Christmas."

His gray eyes lit briefly on me. "I thank you," he said solemnly, "but I cannot let you buy me such a gift. It's too extravagant."

"Don't be silly. I want to do it. And it's not that much." I smiled. "I'll just give them that little plastic card. It's painless."

He studied me for a moment. "Don't you have to honor your debts? Isn't it like a promissory note?"

I scowled and held up a white v-necked tennis sweater against him. "You sound like my mother," I said. "I pay them. I always pay off my credit cards. Now keep quiet or I'll buy you this sweater, too." He grinned, and the effect was dazzling with the sweater.

"I'll pay you back," he said again. "I mean it." His tone was not worth arguing with. And anyway, where would he get the money? If it assuaged his ego to think he would pay me back, fine. I wasn't going to worry about it.

The girl returned and led him to a dressing room. At his questioning glance, I urged him inside. "Try them on," I said. "Make sure they're comfortable before we buy them." As he disappeared into the tiny room, I called, "And come out before you take them off. I want to see them."

The salesgirl stood next to me as Carter, presumably, undressed. Interrupting the enjoyable progress my imagination was making with this idea, she asked companionably, "Is he your boyfriend?"

For some reason the image of him in the bookstore after closing, his face illuminated by the unearthly green glow of the safety lights, popped into my head at the question, his gray eyes translucent in the light determinedly fixed on my face. I had thought he was going to kiss me.

I shook my head. "He's just a friend."

She nodded with a small smile. "He's cute. I'd snap him up if I were you."

"Would you?" I asked, smugly wondering what this apparently sane girl would think if she knew he got up regularly at night to pee in the backyard. For some reason he couldn't remember the bathroom in the middle of the night, a habit that endeared him to Steve, at any rate. "You're welcome to try," I added, wondering what Carter would do on a date.

The girl's smile broadened. "Send him back in sometime."

Carter stepped out of the dressing room a little uncertainly, but he smiled when his eyes found me. The jeans were the right length and fit well up the thigh.

"How do they feel?" I asked.

"They feel good," he said. He looked down the length of himself, nodding. "Very soft." His palms splayed along his thighs.

"That's the stone washing," the salesgirl said, circling him with a critical eye. "They look pretty good. How are they in the waist?" She slipped a hand beneath the sweatshirt and hooked a finger into a belt loop, pulling gently. Carter sprang away from her as if she'd grabbed him in the crotch.

The girl flushed crimson. "I'm sorry. I'm just so used to fitting these things for people—I'm sorry."

Carter's face was almost as red as hers as he concentrated on the waistband. "It's all right. They feel fine, fine."

I enjoyed the girl's discomfiture. It's not often a woman of the Nineties gets put in her place by a modest male. The fact that I myself was a woman of the Nineties did nothing to dispel my amusement.

"They looked a little loose in the waist," I said, helping the poor embarrassed girl out. "Maybe he should try a thirty-two."

She shot me a grateful look and returned quickly to the shelves.

Carter fiddled with the waistband some more. "People here are awfully familiar," he said sullenly.

I leaned against a display rack. "I suppose that's true," I said slyly. "And she'd like to be a good bit more familiar with you."

He looked up quickly, then developed a slow smile. "Well, I'm glad to know the reliable course of women's gossip hasn't dissipated with the years." His smirk needled me.

"I was not gossiping!" I exclaimed.

He leaned against the mirror. "What were you doing?"

"I was answering her questions."

He cocked his head at me, his eyes clearly amused. "So she was gossiping—not you."

He was teasing me, I could tell, but it was a point that needed clarification. I stated imperiously, "I was *disseminating information.* Women do that just as men do. Is there anything wrong with that?"

He shrugged slightly. The girl returned and handed him the thirty-twos. Turning back to the dressing room, he shot me a guileless look over his shoulder. "There's nothing wrong with gossip," he said.

When he emerged a minute later I pounced. "You know, women actually have changed quite a bit," I said, overcoming the temporary distraction of the perfect fit of the jeans. "And a comment like that about women and gossip could get you into some serious trouble."

Carter studied himself in the mirror. "Do these meet with your approval?" He smiled at my image in the mirror.

They most certainly did. "My point is," I continued, "that there are people called feminists who would eat you alive for a statement like that. This is important, Carter. This is basic advice on survival in the Nineties."

The salesgirl had moved off to help someone else. Carter raised his sweatshirt to pull at the belt loop as she had done. He raised questioning eyebrows to me.

"Much better," I said, looking away from the portion of flat, muscled stomach visible beneath the sweatshirt. "You can no longer generalize about women. We do as we please now."

I heard a sarcastic laugh and glared at him. He said dryly, "You've always done as you've pleased."

"Well, now we vote. We smoke. We work. We divorce. We choose to have children out of wedlock. We support ourselves.'' *We've come a long way, baby.*

He regarded me now with open dismay. ''And women consider this a better life?''

I hesitated. ''Women consider it freedom.''

The salesgirl popped back up again, having deposited her other customers into dressing rooms. ''Those are perfect!''

I turned to her and swung my purse up onto my shoulder. ''Yes. We'll take them,'' I said. ''Can he wear them out?''

''Of course!'' The salesgirl beamed. ''I'll just put his other things in a bag.'' She followed Carter into the dressing room. I entertained myself by imagining her trying something a little more direct than yanking his belt loop once she had him in such a confined space. That would teach Carter Lindsey not to assume things about modern women.

I paid for the pants while they collected Carter's clothes. When he joined me at the counter he looked quizzically at a piece of paper in his hand as the salesgirl drifted away.

We walked out into the mall and he handed me the slip of paper. ''What does this mean?'' he asked.

I glanced down. In my palm was a paper with ''Lisa 234–7253'' written on it. I started to laugh and handed it back to him.

''What does it mean?'' he insisted.

Smiling, I eyed him for a moment. He was good; no slipping into twentieth-century habits for him.

''It's her name and phone number,'' I chuckled. Really, of all the things she could have done in that little room, this was the mildest.

''Phone number?'' He nearly walked into a cement trash bin but sidestepped it at the last minute.

I shot him another look out of the corner of my eye;

then, deciding once again to humor him, looked around us. "There." I pointed to a pay phone and proceeded to explain the basic workings of the telephone. "So, that girl wants you to ask her out on a date."

I handed the paper back to him. He continued to study it as we walked. I steered him clear of a baby stroller.

"A date," he repeated. "You mean she wants me to court her."

"That's right. Didn't you do any courting before you became an old married man?" I teased.

Carter's cheeks pinkened. "Not really. Meg and I have known each other since we were children. Our area was not what you would consider very populated." His eyes swept the hordes of Christmas shoppers around us.

I watched his fingers fold the slip of paper and remembered the way he'd bowed so debonairly over the little nurse's hand. He hadn't exactly seemed unused to seduction then.

I slanted him a suspicious look. "You act like someone who's had his fair share of feminine attention."

To my surprise, he flushed even more deeply. "Well, after I joined the army . . ." He let the sentence trail off.

"No!" I said in exaggerated disbelief. "Did serious and sincere Carter Lindsey cheat on his wife?" I cackled heartily.

He glared at me, raising his head to look down from his full, impressive height. "I most certainly did not," he stated disdainfully.

Unintimidated, I supplied, "Though not for want of opportunity, hmm?"

His heavy-lidded eyes viewed me with cool condescension. "I'd appreciate it if you kept your assumptions about my morality to yourself. As I do mine about yours," he added pointedly.

This caught me off guard, and I was surprised by the sting I felt. I stopped dead in my tracks. "I *knew* it!" I said. "I thought you had 'no grounds to judge me,' Carter. What happened to all of that?" I shook my head and marched away before he could answer. He caught up to me, slowed considerably by the heavy bags in his hands, while I continued. "You know, I really hate that. You're perfectly tolerant and polite on the outside, but inside you're as judgmental as everyone else!"

He scoffed. "No more so than you."

I stopped again. "I was not judging. I was *teasing*. There's a difference!" I turned away and continued toward the door. Behind me, I heard the rustling of my bags against his legs.

He caught me at the door, my bag skittering to the floor as his hand grabbed my arm. "*If you please, madam!*" He turned me to him, his eyes flashing anger. "Kindly stop running away," he gritted. He took a deep breath. "Now. I am not familiar with your humor. Forgive me if I attacked you injudiciously."

I absorbed this reluctant apology with all of the sincerity with which it was offered. "As opposed to attacking me judiciously, I suppose. Look, you've a right to your opinions. I told you that before. I'd just appreciate it if you kept them to yourself."

I started to pick up the bag he'd dropped. A stream of exiting shoppers stepped between and around us. "Please," he said more calmly, bending to help me.

I snatched the bag away from him. "No, don't. I don't need your help. You need mine, remember?"

He stood, then, bristling. "I apologize," he said firmly. "At least let me help you when I can." He held out his hand for the bag.

My conscience pricked me at his obviously wounded pride, but he had wounded mine as well. "You know, Carter, I would have expected a lot of things from you, but moral censure is not one of them. If you have a problem with me, then perhaps we'd better clear it up right now." Though I spoke in a perfectly calm and rational manner, I couldn't believe the tension I felt as I awaited his opinion of me.

He looked around us at the mall people who inevitably collect by the doors. A few of them watched us in their boredom while waiting for whatever it was they waited for.

"We should talk about this privately," he said.

I felt my face begin to flush. "Is what you have to say so awful?"

He sighed in exasperation. "I have nothing awful to say, but I have no desire to continue to be entertainment for the masses."

He said this so scornfully that a few of the watching heads turned swiftly away. But a few of them didn't.

I considered telling him that I had no desire to hear what he had to say, but it would have been a lie. Besides, I was starting to think that a beer might be just the thing over which to discuss my immorality.

"All right. Come on then," I said decisively, leaving the mall with my head held high and an irritated soldier in tow.

We arrived at my favorite pub in town, miraculously finding a parking place right across the street. Carter gazed raptly at the historic inn as he got out of the car. It was a beautiful old building, particularly as it was now, completely restored, festooned in Christmas garlands, and lit by floodlights.

"I know this place," he said quietly, looking up and down the street. "I've been to this house."

I watched him with an odd feeling creeping up my spine. We crossed the street and I made for the side entrance and the stairs down to the pub. He walked slowly behind me, pausing now and then to study the building from every angle revealed by our path.

I wanted to continue on without him, but his rapt expression held me hostage. He stopped near the walk to the side entrance, his gaze fastened on the house across the street, and I heard him laugh.

"What is it?" I asked, reaching him.

He turned a soul-shattering smile on me. "Mackey's Folly!" he beamed. "Who would've thought it?" he asked the air, turning back to the house. "Other than old Mackey himself, of course."

"Mackey's folly?" I asked, bewildered.

He put his hands in the pockets of the bomber jacket, and I could see his shoulders shaking with subdued laughter. He turned back to me. "That means this has to be old Miss Lomax's house. I should have known immediately. It doesn't look that different." He said it as if I'd tried to argue the point with him.

I looked up at the inn. "Okay," I said. It did look old-timey, with its Christmas decorations and meticulously restored whitewash.

"Robert Mackey," Carter said, taking my arm and turning me to the house across the street, "built this house back around 1815 or 1820; I can't remember exactly when. It was before I was born. But it broke him. He put every cent he had into the thing, and then had nothing else. They called it 'Mackey's Folly.' People laughed at him, called him a fool, but look—here it stands." His smile was one of genuine delight. "God, I love it when bankers are wrong."

I smiled at that. We'd stopped on the sidewalk, looking across the street at the house. "And old Miss Lomax," Carter continued, turning us back to the inn, "called it right. She said a man doesn't need anything else if he has his own home. She said that when he built it, and again when she had this one built for herself. And here they both are, still standing. Truth to tell, they look better than I remember them."

Our breath frosted in the cold night air. "You knew

this Miss Lomax?'' I asked, intrigued. If nothing else, the guy was a good storyteller.

His eyes scanned the facades, concentrating for the moment on the upper windows. ''When I was young. I came here a lot when I was a child. My mother's people were from Fredericksburg. You see, I'm related to the Carters of Virginia; maybe you know the family name.'' He thought for a moment. ''Or maybe not. Maybe they're all gone now.''

Shivering, I clapped my mittened hands together to warm them. ''No, I've heard of them. I know they were quite a prominent family in Virginia.''

He turned his face to me. ''I don't suppose you know if there are any left.''

I shook my head. ''Sorry, no. But I'm sure we can find out.'' That gave me an idea. There was no reason, if I were to humor Carter and his outrageous story about his identity, that I couldn't find some kind of genealogical chart that might tell me more about Carter Lindsey—if he actually existed.

''Anyway,'' he said briskly, shaking off his thoughts, ''Miss Lomax would occasionally have me over for supper. Then I'd weed her garden and trim the grass. Nice old biddy. She loved my mother. Always talked about how much they missed her back home. Couldn't believe she'd up and married a *Yankee.*'' He smiled. ''The way she said it, you'd think my mother'd married a mule.''

I watched the wistful smile and faraway look in his eyes fade as he recalled where he was. For a moment he looked embarrassed and glanced away from me.

I ran my hands along my sleeves. ''Come on. Let's go inside; it's freezing out here,'' I said. ''It sounds like there's an interesting story about your parents and I'd like to hear it.''

He didn't look at me but turned straight ahead. I watched the burden of his predicament descend again on him. "No. Not really." He took a deep breath and looked up at the sky, thick with stars in the cold, clear night. "You go on in," he said. "I'll be in in a minute."

My instinct was to stay with him. Aside from my fascination with the stories he told, I felt an unwilling connection to him, to his sadness. But my feet were freezing and my eyes kept tearing up from the occasional cold breeze.

"I'll stay. I'll wait for you," I said.

He turned a wan smile on me. "No, you're cold. I'll be in soon. Don't worry." He took my arm and turned me to the door. With a slight, good-natured push, he said, "Go on. I'm just going to look at the garden. I'll be right in."

I went reluctantly. But the blast of warm, fire-scented air that hit me when I entered the pub drove away any thoughts I might have harbored of staying outside with him. I could feel my cold skin tighten and tingle with the heat.

I had already sat and ordered two beers by the time he entered. I could see him as he scanned the room for me and was struck anew by the attention he attracted. What was it about him? He was good-looking, certainly, but that didn't explain why the men eyed him so speculatively, as if he was a force to be respected.

There was an air of composure about him, a reserve that spoke of strength, but I did not think it could be perceived by those who had not even met him. Maybe people had a natural affinity for time-travelers from the past, I mused. I certainly had seemed to, considering the fact that I had taken him to my house as a perfect stranger. A waitress stopped to inquire if she could help him, but he spotted me and shook his head.

The pub was small, several rooms in the basement of the old house connected by a bar. Its brick walls were painted a dark green, which gave it a very intimate air, but the back room boasted French doors that opened out onto a sunken patio. A musician with an acoustic guitar had set up his equipment in one corner.

Carter pulled out a chair and sat gracefully.

"I've ordered you a beer," I said.

He gave me an inscrutable look. "I wish you hadn't."

I was startled. "Don't you drink beer?"

He sighed heavily. "Must we go through this again? I haven't any money, Shelby." He looked pained at the admission. "I do not wish to take any more from you than I already have. Please, don't humble me further."

"I'm not humbling you," I protested, then smiled slyly. "You can trim my grass and weed the garden. Would that make you feel better?"

He shook his head, a wry smile on his lips. "You jest."

"No, I'm serious. My yard is in desperate need of attention." I watched as his face took on a reluctantly interested expression. "I can barely get myself to cut the grass. And there are dead branches on all the trees. Really, it would be a great help. We'll call it even for room and board. How's that?" I couldn't have cared less about the yard. As far as I was concerned, it could grow to a jungle, as long as I had a place in which to let Steve run around. But the idea seemed to take hold in Carter's mind.

"I could do that," he said thoughtfully. "I'm a good gardener."

"Great!" I enthused. "Then it's settled. What a *relief!* I've been looking for a good gardener for just—*months.*" The dubious expression on Carter's face told me I might have gone too far. "In any case," I hastened to change the subject, "tell me more—"

He leaned toward me across the table and pinned me with a glare, his hand closing on my forearm. "Don't patronize me, Shelby. I don't want pity," he said

96

roughly. "I can work, and work hard. I take advantage of no one."

I pulled back involuntarily. "I know you don't," I said. "I'm not patronizing you."

He leaned back in his chair and took a calming breath, his eyes drilling a hole in my face.

My gaze shifted to his mouth because I was unable to meet the hardness and veiled humiliation in those eyes, where not half an hour ago there had been warm good humor.

"I'm sorry if I offended you, Carter. It's just that I don't want you to feel bad about staying with me." I looked back up into his eyes. "And I really would like you to take care of the place."

He seemed to be considering this skeptically, so I smiled and lay my hands on the table. "That's it. That's all. The fact is, I want you to stay." I felt my cheeks flaming at the admission, but my own embarrassment seemed to be the only way to banish his.

I'd coaxed a small smile into his eyes and his lips curved gently. "All right," he said quietly. "Thank you. Your garden will testify to my gratitude."

"Great." I grinned idiotically. "That's great."

Again I turned my abashed gaze to his mouth; the look in his eyes caused my breath to come too quickly. His lips, sensuously firm and well formed, had relaxed, the corners tilted up slightly. I felt a sudden desire to kiss them. I wondered what sort of kisser he would be—soft and skilled, or wet and sloppy? Against my efforts to the contrary, I felt a smile tug at my lips. My gaze flicked up to his.

He regarded me steadily. "What is it you find amusing, Miss Manning?" he asked.

Thinking the moment needed a little levity, I said brazenly, "I was wondering what sort of kisser you'd be." I was completely prepared for a prudish blush and relished the idea of distracting him with what he would consider shocking boldness. Instead, his eyes narrowed, and his mouth curved into a seductive smile that turned my stomach to jelly.

"You could find out," he offered in that voice, low and smooth as mulled wine.

My mouth fell open silently and my breath caught in my throat. My previously jellied stomach clenched into a fist of apprehension. I had never been attracted to a man more than Rory in my life, and this feeling unnerved me.

Before I would have expired from lack of air, the waitress arrived with our beers, allowing me to look away from Carter's compelling gaze and actually take a deep breath.

I tried to make my next comment light but failed. "Just because you see me as some sort of harlot," I said in a very odd voice, "does not mean I am willing to experiment with you."

Carter's relentless gaze narrowed as he allowed himself a full, slow smile. "Then watch what you say, Shelby," he said, "lest you be taken at your word."

I bristled at the chiding tone. "I just wanted to shake that damn reserve of yours," I exclaimed, flinging up a hand and nearly slapping a passing waitress. "Sometimes you frustrate the hell out of me."

He raised his beer to me and cocked an eyebrow. "Likewise."

I looked at him sternly for a moment, then had to laugh. I raised my own beer. Our glasses touched with a muted *clink,* and we sipped in unison. Carter looked down at the contents of the glass after swallowing.

"Bass Ale," I supplied. "Do you like it?"

He nodded. "Extremely smooth."

The guitarist began to tune his instrument, and Carter jumped at the sound as it came over the speakers. He turned to watch the man. "It's uncommon loud," he said over his shoulder to me.

"Speakers," I murmured, though he wasn't listening. He sat enraptured as the man began to play, a classical tune for guitar that segued into *Somewhere Over the Rainbow* from *The Wizard of Oz*. I reflected on the fact that it could have been worse for Carter; he could have found himself transported to a land full of midgets and witches.

Carter turned back to me anxiously. "Do you think he would let me try it?"

I shrugged. "Maybe. Ask him during one of his breaks."

Carter nodded and continued to concentrate on the music. I watched the couple next to us, sitting in the flickering glow of the candle on the table. They were holding hands and talking, heads close together in a very intimate way. They had to be in their twenties, I imagined, but still seemed quite young. They kissed, once, twice, then resumed their talking. I watched as one of the man's hands gently released the woman's and snaked around her shoulders to bury itself in her long blond hair.

He reminded me of some kind of salesman, in his cheap suit and tall, blow-dried hair. He pulled her close and kissed her again, a long, deep kiss, his hand massaging her hair. He pulled back and they talked some more, very close. I could see the wet sheen on the woman's painted lips.

The pub was a dark, private place, but this display made even me a little uncomfortable. They kissed again, intimately, and then the man's other hand began to make its way up her forearm, squeezing and petting. I wondered where it would stop and watched in a sort of morbid fascination.

Carter turned back from the music to me and his beer. "It's amazing music," he said.

I pried my eyes from the sensuality on display just over his shoulder. It was doing nothing to help stem my unwilling attraction to Carter. "Do you play the guitar?" I asked conversationally.

He shrugged. "I used to. Back . . . in simpler times. Before the war."

I leaned forward, elbows on the table, and looked him in the eye. "You were going to tell me something," I said. "Before, in the mall. You—" I searched for a word, "disapprove of me. Isn't that right?"

He frowned. "I don't disapprove of you."

"Yes, you do," I insisted.

He shook his head. "No. I don't *understand* you, certainly, but it has nothing to do with disapproval." His hands cupped his beer, turning it on the green-checked tablecloth. "I think you're unusual," he said finally.

I rolled my eyes. Why was it I never received regular compliments from men? Just a bemused sort of interest.

"Exceptional," he amended then. "Perhaps because of that I think you're due more than you settle for."

I knew people frequently called mentally retarded children "exceptional," and I wondered about Carter's interpretation of the word. Was it a compliment? Or was he concerned about some sort of inherent strangeness I might possess? I had to know. "What do you mean?"

He didn't answer immediately, but studied his own square fingertips where they lay around the sweating pilsner glass. "The Irishman—what's his name?"

"Rory."

"He takes advantage of you."

I sighed and shook my head. My gaze flicked to the couple behind Carter, who now gripped each other with a fervor of gravitational proportions. "I told you, it's normal now for men and women to—"

Carter shook his head as well, cutting off my explanation with one look. "That's not what I mean. Apart from your modern-day—*arrangement*—he doesn't give you what you want. He doesn't give you what you deserve."

I narrowed my eyes and smiled. I knew the quaint picture he had in mind. "What is it you think I deserve? A half dozen kids and a man who brings home the bacon?"

He didn't return my smile. "I think you deserve passion, Shelby, a soul-altering passion," he said, leaning forward. His eyes engulfed me with an all-seeing intensity. "I think you long for a real love, a complete love—one with bones and teeth, not just caresses and pretty words. I think your soul cries for kinship, for knowledge and the unknown, for comfort as well as challenge. You believe an uncertain person like Rory is what you need. But what you *deserve* is a lifetime of dedication, of exhilaration and abandon, of storm and seizure." He stopped and gazed deep into my eyes. "I think you're leading the wrong life, Shelby. And that man is helping you do it."

I couldn't think of another man on this earth who could have said such a thing at all, let alone have said it and looked so damned intensely masculine at the same time. I sat breathless at the words and the torrent of emotion they evoked in me.

It's flattering to have someone try to figure you out. There's a certain amount of natural gratification in someone telling you they understand what you need and deserve. But to have someone look into your soul and voice things you've been afraid to put into words, for someone to pinpoint exactly the elusive feelings you've both longed for and feared, *that* is something altogether more intimidating. And my response to it, contrary to what I might have thought it would be, was a nearly overwhelming impulse to flee. It was as if he'd caught me walking naked outside—it wouldn't matter if he told me he admired my body; I would still be naked in public.

I stood abruptly and grabbed my purse. Carter looked up in surprise, his thick hair falling back from his face.

"Excuse me. I'll be right back," I said in a tight voice, and turned to head for the ladies' room.

I made it into the small white brick room and heaved a deep, shaky breath. What had unnerved me so? Perhaps it was the fact that it was Carter the invalid, the lost soul, the confused and wounded soldier, who'd looked so easily into my eyes and seen so clearly what was wrong with me. I was supposed to be the capable one, the sane one, the one from the twentieth century, for God's sake; and here he had come along and in three days exposed secret desires that I'd so jealously guarded that even I had trouble seeing them.

Outside the door the music continued, meshed with the low sounds of babble and the clink of dishes and glassware against silverware.

I gazed at myself in the mirror, my fingers automatically feeling through my purse for a brush. I pulled it out and dragged it through the thick waves of my dark red hair. My eyes were wide, green, and thoroughly unimpressed with my loss of composure. I should have stayed, my mind lectured; and perhaps smiled mysteriously. *Is that what you think?* I should have murmured. Or, *how intriguing.* Instead I'd bolted like a deer shocked at finding cars on the highway. What a fool I was.

I brushed some glaze across my lips and pinched my cheeks, thinking with just a shred of humor that I looked as if I'd just seen a ghost. Only the ghost was not the 150-year-old man I sat with; the ghost was within me.

Someone knocked at the door. I shoved the paraphernalia back into my purse and turned to leave. Stopping to take one last breath before opening the door, I noticed in the brick wall one of those old iron rings that people had used to tether horses. Had this basement been a stable at some point? I remembered Carter's statement that he knew this house, had even been here before, and I touched the ring cautiously. Had he been in this spot? Had he touched this very ring, threaded a worn strip of leather through it, fingered it in an idle moment, over a hundred years ago? I could feel the dents of the hand-wrought metalwork in the smooth black surface.

The knocking sounded again. I dropped the ring and opened the door, pushing the disquieting feeling away from me. Of course he hadn't.

"Sorry." I smiled at the blond girl waiting outside the door. Her eyes were clouded with drink and her lipstick was smeared. It was the girl from the table next to us, the thoroughly kissed one. Squelching the urge to smirk and mutter "Get a room," I merely passed her with a tolerant smile.

When I reentered the barroom the table was empty. I glanced around and quickly found Carter, his tall back to me, conversing with the musician. Between the worn sweatshirt, blue jeans, and the longish cut of his dark blond hair, he could have been any interested fan as he took the guitar the musician extended to him.

I saw the white flash of his teeth as he accepted it. He held it by the neck, examining the curved, polished body and the point where the plugs connected, then settled it, after some manipulation of the wires, comfortably against his torso. At first he simply ran his fingers along the strings; then leaned toward the musician and apparently asked a question about them, because the man bent toward his guitar case and handed him a package of unused strings.

Carter read the package carefully as the man spoke, then nodded and handed them back. He raised a booted foot to rest it on the bottom rung of the musician's stool as his fingers plucked out a few random, clear notes. He lifted his head at the amplified sound, his eyes on the ceiling, listening.

I could tell from the comfort of his stance and the shape of his fingers on the neck that he had some experience with the instrument, an impression that was justified in the next instant when his fingers gained momentum and a pure, mournful tune arose from them.

I sat at the table and glanced briefly at the lone man at the table next to me. He caught my eye and gave me a flirtatious wink as he straightened his jacket. I scowled at him.

Carter's tune gained in volume, the minor key rising and falling with an emotion that was almost tangible. I'd never heard the song before and I watched his downcast eyes as he played. The thick flaxen lashes that brushed his cheeks were visible even from where I sat. He was either concentrating on the strings or had his eyes closed, but his face was relaxed, completely absorbed in the music. I wondered what feelings the sad tune evoked in him and why he'd decided to play that song. *Homesick,* was my first thought. Then, *he misses his wife.* I was unprepared for the sadness that idea produced in me and swallowed back the lump that grew in my throat.

Had she gotten word he was dead? Did he worry that she had? She was home in Pennsylvania, I guessed, with all of his things, his clothes, his books, his letters. Did she go through them, touch them, hoping to touch him? Did she imagine his spirit was near, watching her?

The sad futility of that last thought was enough to bring my choked-back tears to the surface. I felt my eyes well.

How ridiculous, I thought, to be crying for a woman who probably didn't even exist. Or perhaps she existed, but not in 1862, not in a farmhouse in Bucks County, awaiting word of a husband who'd gone off to war. But as I dried my eyes discreetly with a cocktail napkin, I could not reconcile the strong and steady Carter Lindsey with a yuppy housewife in the suburbs of Philadelphia, awaiting word of her husband, the reenactor. In fact, the very thought of Carter Lindsey as a reenactor was, for some reason, not acceptable.

The song ended and the room was filled with polite, even enthusiastic applause. Carter looked chagrined by the attention but smiled and bowed his head. He carefully handed the instrument back to the musician and bowed ever so slightly in thanks. The guitarist smiled easily and held up his hand. *No problem*, I could read on his lips. Then he leaned forward and said something to Carter. Then he pulled the microphone to his mouth and said, "That was Carter Lindsey, ladies and gentlemen. Let's give him another hand."

Carter held up his hands in protest and genuine embarrassment, shaking his head as the people applauded again. He returned through the clapping hands to our table.

"That was beautiful," I said to him. "What was that song?"

Carter took a long swallow of his beer, then rubbed his palms on his pants legs. He sighed. "Nothing, really. Something I made up not long ago. Before the Dunker church battle, I think it was." His eyes did not meet mine. "He has an interesting instrument. The strings are not silk or catgut, but some kind of wire." He lifted his left hand and rubbed his fingers together. "A bit painful to play, but it has a beautiful sound."

I watched his uneasiness, wondering where it stemmed from, now that the applause had ended. "It was the song that was beautiful," I said again.

He looked up at me then, and we gazed at each other for a minute. "I'm sorry to have pried," he said. "Before, I mean. It's easy to feel as if you're seeing everything objectively when you're in a position like mine. But I don't know you well, and I haven't the right to presume. I apologize."

I swallowed hard and tried to look unconcerned. "Apology accepted, of course," I said. "You've every right to your opinions . . . as I said."

He smiled and shook his head. "But not to voice them as fact. I know there's much about me you don't put voice to, and I'm sure I appreciate it."

I smiled at that. "I've nothing insulting in my head about you."

His eyebrows raised and he rested his elbows on the table. "Oh? I've noticed you've never said out loud that you thought me insane. Nor have you ever mentioned the possibility of mental instability or—Lord preserve us— *witchcraft.*" With that word he narrowed his eyes at me. After a second he continued, "No dogcarts to Bedlam have pulled up in front of the house, nor have I yet caught you rolling your eyes at any of my perhaps ridiculous questions. You must think me mad, and I thank you for not saying so."

I flushed at that. "What am I? An open book?" I protested with a laugh, hoping to deflect more accurate mind-reading on his part with some weak humor.

"No," he said. "These are simply thoughts I know I would have, if presented with a similar situation. You don't believe me, I know. I don't know how you could. But I appreciate your forebearance. I want you to know that."

I looked at his hand where it lay on the table. Without analyzing the impulse, I placed my own on top of it, spreading his fingers flat on the surface and lacing mine between them. There was a moment of tension before he squeezed my fingers back.

"I don't know if I can," I said, "but I want to help you." And it was true—I did want to help him. But he was wrong about one thing, I realized as we sat there, hands clasped. I did believe him. Maybe it was because I *wanted* to believe him, but at that moment I was convinced.

Chapter Six

That night, after we got home, I offered to help Carter rebandage his shoulder. He was due to get the stitches out the next day, and I was curious to see how the wound was healing. He wore nothing beneath Rory's old sweatshirt, and as he pulled it over his head, I couldn't help watching the display of sinewy muscle along his back.

The wound looked pretty good to my unschooled eye, the skin around it healthy and firm, not pink or puffy. And he hadn't even winced as he'd pulled the old tape and gauze from his skin. The bullet had entered just above the collarbone, in that firm, muscled area that most people like to have massaged, but it had not exited, so the skin of his back was unmarred.

I took the tube of cream from the prescription bag, where Carter unfailingly replaced it after each application, and unscrewed the cap. Surprisingly, the cream was a bright fluorescent orange. I squeezed a couple of inches of it onto my finger and moved in front of him where he sat on a dining-room chair. When I glanced up from the tube I found him watching me. A feeling of self-consciousness crept over me. Other than the first time I'd cleaned the wound, the night I'd found him, I hadn't touched him, and to do so now, as he watched me so closely, was cause for unexpected discomfort.

I rubbed the cream between my icy fingers in a vain attempt to warm it. "I hope this doesn't hurt," I said, studying my now carrot-colored fingers.

His powder gray eyes were calm, lazy-lidded, as he said, "It's not very sensitive anymore."

I touched my fingers gently to the wound, the initial contact causing a static shock between us. "Oh! Sorry," I said with a nervous laugh, though I had jumped at the spark and he had not. I felt my breath grow shallow as I pressed softly on the torn skin and hard plastic thread of the stitches. Frowning in concentration, I asked, "You're sure I'm not hurting you?" It seemed nothing was going to deflect his eyes from my pinkening face, and I couldn't for the life of me understand, or control, the giddy tightening of my stomach.

"You're not hurting me," he said quietly.

Some objective observer inside my head noted that Carter's breathing was a little faster than normal too as he sat motionless beneath my fingers, but that could well have been explained by the fact that my cold fingers were probing the wrecked skin of a gunshot wound. My only excuse was the unnerving effect of that steady gaze.

I had to press harder than I thought was comfortable in order to work in the cream, and the warmth of his skin seeped through the slickness into mine. His chest where I lay my other hand to steady myself was muscular and firm, the skin hot to my cold fingers.

Before I was tempted to continue down his chest with the stuff, I stepped back from my handiwork and wiped my fingers on a napkin. "There," I said, turning to the pile of adhesive tape, gauze, and scissors I'd gathered before the unveiling. "Now for a clean bandage, and you'll be all set for tomorrow morning."

His brows raised. "Tomorrow morning?"

"Yes, don't you remember?" I moved behind him to gain a better angle for taping and to avoid those calm, unswerving eyes. "The doctor will remove the stitches; then all you'll have to do is—" I cut myself off. I'd almost said "remember where you live," but knowing how the idea of amnesia irritated him, I stopped myself in time.

He didn't seem to notice. "So I must go back to the hospital," he stated.

I shook my head. "No, this time we can go to his office. It's not far and will only take a minute. I don't see any evidence of infection, so there shouldn't be a problem."

His wheat-colored hair fell in thick layers and hung nearly to his shoulders, except for the shortened locks in front, which he kept brushed straight back from his face. It was beautiful hair, I noticed not for the first time, a dark burnished gold with each strand slightly lighter or darker than the last, a hundred different colors up close to create an overall shining depth. The color of fall leaves, I mused, or polished oak. I wanted to touch it, to see if it felt as rich as it looked, but I battled down the impulse. If the feel of his warm, solid skin was enough to cause me heart palpitations, touching his hair would probably kill me.

I placed the square of gauze over the injury and held it as I taped the edges. I scrupulously avoided touching his skin again, as if some irresistible avalanche of tactile temptation would descend embarrassingly upon me if I did.

He raised his head and shook his hair back out of his face as I finished, turning in the chair to thank me. Afraid he would see the thoughts in my eyes, I quickly began to clean up the bandaging paraphernalia.

"You're welcome. I think it looks pretty good. The doctor should give you a clean bill of health," I murmured.

He nodded and pulled the sweatshirt back over his head. "Then it'll just be up to me," he said, rising.

It was the very thought that had entered my head: that the doctors had done all they could for him and now all that was left was to find his home. For him to *remember* his home. Or something. I shook my head at my confusion. It would have been so much simpler if he just didn't remember—if he could admit that he couldn't remember. But for him to be so sure he did remember, and that he had actually been transported from the past—that was what made it so confusing, along with the fact that he was so damn convincing about it that in unguarded moments he had me believing it as well.

I put the bandages back in the bathroom medicine cabinet and wandered into the living room behind him. He sat in the chair by the woodstove, peering into the fire.

The saddest part of his odd belief was the hopelessness of it, I thought, sitting across from him on the couch. To be transported in time by some unknown force was a scarier and more intangible cause of displacement than any amnesia would have been. If it was true, practically the only course open to him was to wander aimlessly in the hope of finding the rabbit hole to 1862 that he had fallen through to get here. And, in keeping with that hope, the poor fellow had gone walking every day, presumably in search of his home, and himself.

"Have you gone back up to Sunken Road?" I asked. There was always the possibility of it being some sort of Bermuda Triangle for time travelers up there, as if he could step on the same spot where he had appeared to me and be magically transported back to the past.

"Yes," he answered flatly. "It's odd...." His eyes stared into the flames, and I could see the pupils shrink to pinpoints.

"What's odd?" I prompted.

He shook his head. "It's very peaceful up there. Quiet and calming." He frowned. "The battle ... There was such carnage."

I picked up a pillow and placed it on my lap, my fingers playing idly with the fringe. "I find it peaceful too. That's why I walk up there so often. I used to think it was strange that I found a battlefield so soothing. But now I think maybe it's because a given area can take only so much hostility, and once that's worked out of it, all that's left is the peace."

Rory would have chuckled or rolled his eyes at another one of my cosmic theories, but Carter did neither. He just turned his head to gaze out of the window into the darkness. From where I sat I could just see a portion of his face and the tips of his lashes glowing blond from the light of the fire. His voice was solemn and deep. "Then that place ought to be peaceful for a long, long time to come."

He turned back to the fire and rested his head in his hands, expelling a deep breath. He rubbed his hands over his face, letting the open palms rest on his eyes for a moment. Then he straightened, lowering his hands and looking at me intently.

His voice held a tense note as he began. "Shelby, I must return. There's so much ..." He gripped the arms of the chair as if he might rip them right off with his bare hands. "The farm, my land ... my *wife*. I don't know how, and I don't expect you to figure it out, but I *must* return. Every day I find myself trying ..." He let the words hang, his expression thoughtful, his eyes unseeing. "I feel so—but I can't—I can't—" He closed his eyes and pressed his lips shut in frustration. "There's something going on here that I can't figure out. Not just my being here, but something . . . within myself.'' His grip on the chair arms relaxed and he turned deep, liquid eyes to me. "I'm interesting to you. And God knows you and everything here are interesting to me. But I can't pretend to myself that I'm just some poor soul who's lost his mind. I know better. I have responsibilities.''

I regarded his anxiety with pity. "Of course you have. And we'll find your home. This can't last forever.''

He scoffed at my tone. "Can't it?'' he asked aggressively. "Have you ever heard of this happening before?''

I looked away from his penetrating eyes. "There must be case studies,'' I sputtered. "Surely someone, somewhere, knows about things like this.''

"You speak of amnesia, Shelby,'' he said with an oddly compassionate smile. "Which may be common enough—especially *lately*,'' he added half to himself, with a quick shake of his head. "But I know, in a way that you can't, *what's* happened here, if not how.''

"Okay,'' I nodded slowly. Further agitation on that topic would surely lead nowhere. "But what about the *why?* You say you know the 'what,' and we can't figure out the 'how.' But whatever happened to you must have happened for a reason. Don't you think? I mean, what could be the point of it all? What's the point of you showing up here, a hundred and thirty years into the future, if the only thing you do is struggle to go back? Maybe there's something you're supposed to learn here.'' His gaze became focused on me, interested. "Maybe some aspect of modern technology started with you back then, and the only way you could do it was to learn about it here. Maybe you do something really spectacular because of your experience here.''

He nodded his head. His hands released the chair arms and one of them came up to stroke his jaw. "Maybe I've been looking for the wrong thing. I've been looking for escape, for deliverance. Perhaps I should . . ." His foot tapped the floor. "Perhaps I should be looking for answers. I should be studying. I should concentrate on learning." He looked up at me as if a great weight had lifted from his shoulders. "Perhaps you're right. Maybe I was brought here to take something back."

"Or maybe you become a prophet of some sort. You will know the future," I said excitedly. This could actually be fun, thinking about time travel. "You could alter the course of history." The truth of that statement struck me at that moment with great force. "The Civil War—the War Between the States—was one of the bloodiest ever fought. Maybe there's something you could learn here to lessen the bloodshed." My mind raced with possibilities. Libraries were full of studies and analyses of every major battle and inconsequential skirmish of the Civil War. Carter could discover something that, if known to a general at the time, would alter the future of the war. How many times had I read that if this general had only known that another general was weak, or uncertain, or not there, the war would have ended far sooner than it had? How many theories had there been on the subject of opportunities missed?

I looked up from my enthusiastic imaginings to see Carter regarding me with an intense, inscrutable expression. "What?" I asked. "What's the matter?"

His eyes did not leave mine, and he sat still enough to be holding his breath. "Someone once told me that it did no one any good to know all there was to know. That knowledge could cause more trauma than ignorance. But I need to know." He took a deep breath, eyes flickering in the firelight. "I was afraid to ask," he said quietly, "but I've seen a strange flag, though a similar one, flying on buildings in town. I need to know if it was all worth it, if we were right. Has the Union survived? Did we win?"

Consumed by the tortured expression in his eyes, I echoed dumbly, "Win?" His pain was evident, but curiosity and fear held equal sway in those articulate eyes. "You mean the North?" Had he been less emotionally involved with the question, he would have thought me an idiot. But the expression on his face was so moving that for a moment the questions were lost on me. I couldn't imagine having so much of myself invested in a political dispute.

His voice was low, hoarse. "Tell me we didn't die for nothing."

I felt my stomach curl and my heart slow with the weight of what it must be like to die for a cause. Or, if not die, to see your friends and family, comrades in arms, mown down like blades of grass by the sickle of physical combat. It was all there on his face, and in his words. And all of my conviction of the night before, the surety I'd felt that he was exactly who he claimed to be—that he was a misplaced soul, a reluctant time traveler—all of it came rushing back to me. The empathy I felt for his pain and displacement was almost more than I could bear.

I nodded slowly. "You won," I said. "The North won."

His eyes closed. I could see his jaw muscles tense, and then he let out a long, slow breath.

"The United States is fifty states now. That's why the flag looks different. And there are no slaves anymore. You won," I said. "It took you four years to do it, but you won."

If I'd expected him to thank God, or rejoice in exultation, I was disappointed. What he did was lean back in the chair and stare at the ceiling.

The firelight played on his features, making dark hollows of his eyes and cheeks. I had a sudden grotesque image of his body lying dead on the battlefield, hollow-eyed and staring, until I saw his lips curl into a smile of sorts.

"It's all just history to you, isn't it? It's not real. I'm not real. Do the issues even matter anymore? Are they important?" He raised his head, bringing life back to his eyes and banishing the horrible image I'd seen.

I raised my eyebrows cynically. "Well," I said, "some areas of the South still hate the North, and the Yankees. But, yes, to most of us it *is* history. Important, God yes, but history."

He shook his head lightly. "It's just as well, I suppose. I don't recall the blood of the Revolution, but its importance is paramount, particularly in the current struggle. In the War Between the States, that is."

I nodded again. I was scrupulously apolitical. But at that moment I found myself wishing I believed in something as completely as Carter obviously believed in the Union. I would not relish the idea of having that belief tested under fire, but I could only admire the kind of strength it took to make a decision like that. But then, Carter's strength wasn't something I ever found myself questioning.

The next day I stopped on the way home from work to buy some film. My plan was to take a picture of Carter and have it published in both the local and the Philadelphia newspaper. This, coupled with a short description, would accompany a post office box address where anyone with clues to or knowledge of Carter's identity could write.

I wasn't sure if this was an effective way to track someone down or not, but I could think of nothing better. And I figured I owed it to rationality to give the practical a try, even though the more I spoke to him, the more certain I became that Carter Lindsey wasn't crazy at all. The fact that it was the same thing I would do to help a stray dog made me sorry for him, though. It had to be humiliating to be treated like a lost child, as if he was incapable of accurately identifying himself.

When I entered the house after work it was already dark outside, but inside it was cozy and warm, gently lit by the glow of candles. The woodstove was stoked and the radio was tuned to a classical station. The tantalizing smell of frying onions hung in the air.

I threw my bags on the couch and hung my coat on a peg in the hall. I'd also stopped by the mall to pick up some Fruit of the Looms for Carter, but I decided to hold off giving them to him until I could think of a tactful way of broaching the subject, as well as conjure up some project he could do to "pay" for them.

I left the stuff on the couch and wandered into the kitchen. Carter stood before the stove, his back to me. Steve lay in the kitchen doorway, nose in the air, brown eyes intent on Carter's back.

"Smells great," I said, announcing myself. Steve jumped up at my voice and greeted me with a wet tongue, leaning against my thigh as I massaged her ribs.

Carter whirled to face me. A broad smile swept across his features. "Hello! I hope you don't mind . . . ?" he said with a short wave of his hand toward the stove.

I peered past him into the pan of sweating, butter-soaked onions. "Mind? Are you kidding?" I looked around the counter at the half-used stick of butter, the opened carton of milk, the onion skin in the sink, bread crumbs scattered about the cutting board, and celery tops pushed against the backsplash. "Are you finding everything okay?"

He smiled ruefully, and I wondered what sort of mishaps had occurred to produce this scene of culinary excess. "Finding things was not the problem," he said. "Almost everything I needed was labeled." He gestured toward the stick of butter, the carton of milk, and the plastic wrapper of the chicken I'd had in the freezer. "Took me some time to soften up the chicken, though." He frowned and gingerly picked up the wrapper with two fingers. "I wasn't supposed to leave this on, was I? It looked more like a chicken without it." His face was as serious as they come, but his eyes could not contain his humor.

"You did the right thing," I said and opened the oven door. The warm smell of roasting chicken blasted me in the face. My stomach growled. "It looks perfect," I enthused, rising. "Where did you learn how to cook? I would have thought your wife would have taken care of all that."

I immediately regretted mentioning her. Carter's face closed up and he turned away from me to the pan of onions. Stirring them, somewhat fiercely I thought, he said simply, "I enjoy cooking."

Why did I always put my foot in it just when it seemed he was really starting to loosen up? Trying to change the subject as quickly as possible, I picked the first topic that came to mind. "So, what did you think of this?" I asked, patting the electric stove with one hand. "Did you have any trouble figuring out how it works?"

He threw me an unreadable look. "It's pretty self-explanatory," he said.

I looked down at the dials, with HIGH, MED, LOW, and BAKE, BROIL, CLEAN, and OFF clearly printed on them. Pretty self-explanatory, I had to admit. He was never amazed when I thought he should be.

"I imagine it beats the hell out of cooking on a wood stove," I muttered.

He lifted the lid on another pot, from which steam billowed. "Actually," he mused, "the last meal I cooked was in Baltimore, on a stove that used gas. I think I preferred it." He poked a fork into the bubbling contents of the pot.

I was about to reply when the phone rang. Saved by the bell, I thought. I walked briskly to the phone and lifted the receiver to hear the telltale bleeps of James's TTY, the teletype machine for the deaf. I pulled my own TTY out from under the phone book and placed the receiver in the modem. James's words streamed across the display after my initial "Hello."

"Finally!" he said. "I tried to get you all last night. Where were you?"

"I was out with Carter Lindsey. Did Mother tell you about him?"

This was followed by a stream of *O*s and *H*s: OOOOOHHHHHHH. If he could have spoken it would have been an exaggerated, sarcastic word. Mother had apparently told him of my adventure with the misplaced soldier, and he was anxious to meet him. He asked me if I planned to bring Carter to Christmas with the family, and I was struck anew that Carter's whole future was a giant, looming question mark. Christmas was only a week away, but who knew whether he would be here even then?

I was thankful that we'd gotten off the subject of Carter when I felt him come up beside me. James was typing something about getting together on Christmas Eve, and I glanced up. Carter had that now familiar crease between his brows as he studied the display. James had typed GA (go ahead) twice before I noticed that he had finished, so I quickly typed back that Christmas Eve sounded good, and that we'd both be there. Carter watched in fascination as my fingers flew across the keys.

After James and I had signed off Carter cautiously punched one or two of the keys. "You're very skilled at that," he said as I hung up the phone. He turned to look at the receiver in the cradle. "I thought you could speak into it."

I smiled wryly. No explanation was ever complete;

there was always some extenuating circumstance to muddy up the waters. "You can. And most people do. But that was my brother, who is deaf. This is a special machine so he can use the phone."

Carter looked at me with compassion. "Your brother is deaf?" I nodded. "I'm sorry," he said sincerely. "It must be hard on your family."

I laughed at his overwrought expression. "Don't feel sorry for us," I said. "James is about the most self-sufficient person I know. He teaches at Gallaudet, a university for the deaf. And he's a photographer. He doesn't even consider himself handicapped, and frankly neither do I."

Carter looked unconvinced. I turned off the TTY and pushed it back under the phone book. "In any case," I continued, "I've told him we'd go to his house Christmas Eve." At his chagrined expression I added, "That is, unless you have other plans."

He gave a small smile at my attempt at levity. "None that I know of," he said. "But then, my secretary has been remiss in informing me of travel plans lately."

I laughed, relieved. So his sense of humor hadn't deserted him after all.

"Your brother's a teacher," he said. "And he's deaf."

"That's right. He teaches photography."

"Photography," he said thoughtfully. "It's a complex procedure, I understand. Meg had one done, of herself, when I left for the army, for me to carry with me."

I nodded. "I would like to have seen it," I said tentatively. "Was she pretty?"

His eyes flicked to mine with a stricken expression, which he quickly masked. "Yes. She's pretty," he said bleakly, looking critically into the distance, as if seeing her in his mind's eye.

I leaned toward him, my forearms on the table. It was a risk; every other time I'd brought her up, he'd closed up like a book. But I thought it might help him to talk about her. "Tell me about her," I said softly.

He leaned back in his chair and regarded me thoughtfully. "She's not as pretty as you are, but she's more delicate, fragile-looking." He issued the compliment in such a way as to rob it of any gratification it might have given me. He might as well have said she was not quite as stout as the pear tree outside. But a compliment was a compliment, after all.

"Delicacy in a woman is highly prized in my day," he continued. "Delicacy of feature and coloring, that is, not necessarily of body proportions. Many of our beauties are quite plump." He smiled and met my eyes. "Not like you. Or your friend Sylvie. I've noticed young women here are rather thin."

"Maybe they just look skinnier because they're not trussed up in a dozen petticoats and whatnot," I offered. If he had indeed been sent here to learn something, it would do no one any harm to offer some fashion advice. It would have to benefit my ancestresses to be rid of all that rigmarole.

This time, however, Carter flushed. "That's a point. There isn't much hidden these days." His eyes skimmed over my long, clingy sweater and black leggings. I felt my breath shorten again.

I rose and walked to the far wall. "Here's one of James's photos," I said, pulling down a matted, wood-framed photo of Steve. The black-and-white photo was an extreme close-up, with the light coming from the side, so that her eyes seemed to be illuminated by a light of their own. The white streak down her otherwise black face was nearly as white as the background, creating an eerily feral, almost abstract look to the grinning face.

I handed him the frame. "Yes, I've noticed this. The quality is exceptional," he said.

"And the prints in the upstairs hall are his as well. The color ones."

"I wondered about those," he said, nodding. "They seemed too fine to be paintings, but I've never seen anything like it before. They're beautiful."

He handed me back the picture and I replaced it on the wall.

"How old are you?" Carter asked in the ensuing silence.

I turned. "Twenty-seven."

His eyes widened in surprise. "Really?"

I smiled. "I'll take that as a compliment. Why? How old are you?" I'd wondered for a while. When I'd first met him he'd looked very young, but ever since that first night his composure and intelligence had had me convinced that he wasn't nearly as young as I'd first imagined.

"Twenty-five," he said. "I would have thought you were quite a bit younger than myself. And how old is your friend Sylvie?"

I felt a pang of—what?—jealousy?—at his curiosity about her. "She's a bit younger. Twenty, I think."

"She seemed younger than that to me."

"Yeah, well, people age better now, maybe." I glanced up and caught the flash of his grin. "Well, not you, I mean. I thought you were younger, actually, at first. Then maybe older. But you look good, you know."

Thankfully, there came a knock on the front door. This was not unusual; I made it a policy to encourage people to stop by my house anytime. I'd moved to a small town for precisely that reason—the feeling of community. I didn't even own a television these days, because I hated the way it sucked up time. I preferred conversation and books.

Steve jumped up and trotted to the door, id tags jingling. She stopped a foot from the door and stared at the knob.

Carter glanced up at me, "Are you expecting someone?" He rose to go back into the kitchen.

"Not really," I said, walking through the living room. I hadn't noticed earlier, but now I saw a large stack of freshly split logs on the hearth. Carter must have cut up the dead tree out back. It had fallen last year, and Rory had been promising for months that he was going to split it himself, as soon as he had the time and the money to rent the log-splitter.

I opened the door to find a grinning Jerry on my doorstep.

"Jerry!" I greeted enthusiastically, stepping back to allow him to enter. "What brings you out on this chilly night?" Steve wound herself up with her tail and twined around his legs.

He bent to pet her. "Just seeing how you're doing," he said. "I was out, down at the Grapevine, and things were a little slow, so I thought I'd drop by." He lowered his voice. "Is he still here?" he asked conspiratorially.

This poor excuse for blatant curiosity amused me. I leaned toward him and gave him a mysterious look. "Yes," I said dramatically. "He's in there. I think he's got a knife. What do you think we should do?"

Jerry's eyes widened and he straightened abruptly. "What's he doing?" he croaked in a whisper.

I turned my head slowly to the left, and then to the right. "He's—" I grabbed the dog and covered her ears—"*he's cooking dinner.*"

Jerry looked at me uncertainly for another minute; then heard a pot clang against the metal sink. His body relaxed and he frowned at me. "Dammit, Shel. Who is it really? Rory?" He started for the dining room.

As if on cue Carter emerged from the kitchen, wielding a large knife. Jerry's face, which I couldn't see, must have shown his alarm because whatever expression it wore stopped Carter dead in his tracks. He looked at Jerry with concern.

The laughter welling up inside of me was squelched when Jerry stopped and immediately backed up, treading heavily on my foot. He sprang away from me, slammed into the doorjamb, and knocked the breath out of himself.

Carter came to him swiftly and grabbed his arm, presumably to keep him from falling, but Jerry had other expectations. He jerked his arm away and stumbled backwards.

"Are you all right?" Carter asked, bewildered, stepping back. He carried the knife at his side.

Laughter came bubbling out of me.

"*For God's sake, Shelby,*" Jerry breathed at me.

My eyes teared with the laughter. Carter looked at me as if I had gone suddenly insane, causing me to laugh even harder.

Carter shook his head and looked at Jerry. "She's been nipping at the bottle all evening," he deadpanned. "At her age she doesn't handle it well at all."

Jerry looked at Carter as if he were a talking horse. Then he straightened and coughed once or twice in embarrassment. Finally I controlled myself and introduced them. Carter transferred the knife to his left hand and the two shook hands.

"Actually, Jerry met you the same night I did," I told Carter. "He's a doctor, so I called him after you passed out here. He helped clean your shoulder that first night."

Carter looked at him with polite interest. "Then I have reason to thank you, sir. I've met with more kindness than even I knew about. I've prepared some supper. If it meets with Shelby's approval, would you stay and join us?" Carter gazed at me questioningly.

"Of course, Jerry. Stay for supper," I said with a smile, amused again at his expression of disbelief. Not only was the soldier still here, I could read on his face, but he was making himself quite at home too.

"Well, I, uh—Jerry stammered.

I put my arm through his. "Come on, Jer. You know you want to. Let's let Mr. Lindsey here show us how *real* old-fashioned cooking tastes."

Carter slanted me a cynical look and said, "Yes. I'll just go check the kill to be sure it's no longer twitching. Do you prefer yours skinned or natural, sir?"

Jerry paled, then blushed crimson as laughter overwhelmed me again.

Chapter Seven

Jerry warmed up over dinner. He ceased to regard Carter as a deranged phantom to be treated with caution, and his curiosity began to take over. Without succumbing to any sort of belief in Carter's predicament, I was sure, Jerry took the idea of his time travel as a remote improbability to be humored and began to ask questions.

He leaned over his plate, drumstick in hand, and asked Carter in a probing voice, "So, how does it feel to be a hundred years into the future? Do things seem familiar, or is it all completely alien?"

Carter's eyes flicked briefly to mine, then back to Jerry. "Human nature doesn't seem to have changed much," he replied.

Jerry sat back to mull over his response, then laughed as he got the joke. "Well," he drawled, "you have to admit it's a curious situation. I'm not trying to get personal or anything. I just wondered—does anything look the way it used to?"

125

Carter regarded him thoughtfully and picked up his wineglass, an absurdly delicate thing in his strong hand. He gazed into its ruby depths. "I suppose," he began, "more things are familiar than not. But it's easy to lose track of that beside the enormity of what's unfamiliar. It's hard to realize how emotions are tied to a man's world until you take it from him." He looked again at Jerry, who nodded in understanding. "Then again," he smiled, "I have already begun to feel more at ease here than I would have thought possible initially. Perhaps I'm more adaptable than I realized."

Jerry took a large bite of the chicken in his hand. Chewing, he asked, "What's the oddest thing you've seen here yet—the thing that most amazed you?"

"Do you mean by way of inventions?"

Jerry nodded.

"The cars were pretty astonishing at first," Carter said, "but now they seem like a natural progression from the train." He thought further, cutting his meat and sliding a piece into the gravy on his plate. "The electricity—or rather, the number of things powered by electricity—is surprising. The brightness of the lights. The refrigerator . . ." He shook his head. "To create cold where there is none is incredible. The radio—music, beautiful music, from the air—a wonderful thing. The knife," he turned to me with a smile and a short wave toward the kitchen, "the chopper, what did you call it?"

"A food processor," I supplied.

"Yes. The food processor." He laughed. "*That's* a handy device."

"What about the phone?" Jerry asked, watching Carter in fascination.

"The telephone? Yes, that's impressive. But not so very far a cry from the telegraph. It was only a matter of time before someone figured out how to transmit voices on the lines."

I smiled as I saw Jerry struggling with the same frustration I'd felt when I'd expected Carter to be amazed by something and he hadn't been.

Carter finished his meal and pushed his plate away, leaning back with the wineglass in his hand. "But more interesting than the innovations," he continued, spinning the glass in his fingers, "are the social changes. Women," he turned an ironic look on me, "have changed quite a bit. Or at least their situation in life has. I believe I like them better this way."

I narrowed my eyes. "And what way is that?"

"Independent," he said. "Not that I haven't known many women with independent spirits. But here, now that they're allowed to exercise that independence and live according to it," he shook his head, "it's a wonderful thing to see." His eyes stayed on me with a look of admiration in them that made a very warm feeling creep up my spine.

I felt a blush color my cheeks as I saw Jerry glance from one to the other of us, and I broke our gaze. "Well, there aren't many women who wouldn't agree with you there," I said. "We fought long and hard to get where we are, to get the respect that we have." I wasn't a feminist by any stretch of the imagination. In fact, I rarely even thought about feminism. As far as I knew, I had never been the victim of discrimination; but in comparing what I'd had the right to achieve, without any real struggle, to the life that women in Carter's time were forced to lead, I found myself feeling truly thankful for those militant women who had fought for me.

"Women always had respect," Carter stated. "It was opportunity they lacked."

"And why was that?" I asked. "Perhaps because men had no respect for their abilities?"

Carter laughed shortly and inclined his head to me.

"Perhaps," he said. "Perhaps you're right. It is not

something I have thought much about until . . . recently.''

Jerry, impatient with such philosophizing, redirected the conversation. ''Tell me more about the differences,'' he demanded. ''I'm curious—what about airplanes?''

''Airplanes?'' Carter repeated, eyebrows raised, looking at me.

I hadn't thought about them. Being so far from a major airport, Fredericksburg didn't have nearly the air traffic that Washington, fifty miles north, had.

''I guess he hasn't seen one yet,'' I said to Jerry; then I turned back to Carter. ''Planes, in the sky—you know, flying.''

Carter's expression became confused. ''You mean like birds? A kind of man-made bird?''

''Yes. Huge machines to carry people across the country—or the world,'' Jerry interjected, excited by his ability to impart such stunning news. ''Like cars in the sky.''

Carter's expression was doubtful.

''Surely you've heard them,'' Jerry added. ''They're really noisy.''

''It is loud here,'' Carter admitted. ''Between the cars and the radios, all the machinery constantly in use . . . but I don't recall seeing something in the sky.''

''I'll take you to the airport,'' I offered, and then thought uncomfortably of the parking lot near National Airport, where many people parked at night to watch the planes take off, and to neck. I felt a blush creep into my cheeks again. ''When we go to my parents' house—it's near there—we can go during the day sometime.''

Jerry didn't notice my discomfiture. ''And the television, Shelby. God, living this Spartan lifestyle here with you, he hasn't seen many of the best modern conveniences.''

''The best?'' I repeated. ''Surely that's open to interpretation. After all, I do have a food processor.''

''Central heating,'' Jerry continued, undaunted. ''Air

conditioning. Microwaves. VCRs. Computers. God, the list is endless.'' Jerry shook his head and grinned at me. ''It's amazing, isn't it?''

I couldn't hold back a brief laugh. ''*I* think so. Should I take this to mean you're beginning to believe Carter's story?''

Jerry looked disconcerted and had begun to sputter something about hypothetical situations and curiosity when we heard the front door open. Steve jumped up from her place under the table and slithered between my chair and the leg of the table to get to the door. From my seat I could just see through the doorway to the front door.

''Hey, Stevie.'' I was surprised to hear Rory's indulgent voice and see his large body emerge from the darkness outside. It seemed like forever since I'd last seen him, when in reality it had only been a few days, and I felt an unpleasant anticipation in the pit of my stomach at the sight of him. Then, bothered by that involuntary response, I forced a smile to my face and rose.

''It's Rory,'' I said to Carter and Jerry, in a voice that was more nervous than happy. I left the dining room to greet him.

''Fancy meeting you here,'' I said, approaching him. ''And at such an early hour,'' I added, glancing at my watch.

He carried a brown paper bag that smelled of Chinese food. A feeling of trepidation rose again in my chest.

''Shelby Manning!'' he said expansively. ''What in tarnation are you doing here?''

His smile was broad, enticing, and his blue eyes glittered in the dim light. It was the first I'd seen of this mood in a while, and I knew it was bound to die a horrible death the moment he saw Carter. As I neared him, he took me by the waist with his free hand and planted a solid kiss on my lips. ''Missed ya, babe,'' he said with laughing eyes. "And I brought you some sustenance," he continued, moving through the living room to the dining room.

The moment he crossed the threshold I could feel the tension envelope his body, like a sheet dropped from the ceiling to cover him.

"Dr. Gardner," he greeted Jerry with a nod. "What a cozy party." He walked stiffly into the kitchen to place the bag of Chinese food on the counter. He gazed levelly at Carter. "And you're still here, I see," he said caustically.

I felt embarrassed for Rory at that moment, embarrassed for all of us, that civility was such an optional thing in our society.

Carter did not answer—assuming, I guess, that Rory's hostility was unanswerable.

I pulled out my chair and sat down. "Have a seat, Rory. Have some dinner with us and *relax.*"

Jerry rose and moved to the sideboard. "Let me pour you some wine. It's pretty good stuff. I bought it." He laughed into the tense silence and poured the wine, even though Rory hadn't answered.

Rory took the glass from Jerry and eyed Carter thoughtfully. Then, apparently making some kind of decision, he sat down across from him in the only available chair. Idly, he picked up a piece of chicken with his fingers and chewed it slowly. He glanced at me and said, "Good," with a curt nod.

I hesitated to tell him I hadn't cooked it. Then, feeling stupid for wanting to lie about such a simple thing, I said, "Carter made it."

Rory shot me an angry look, as if I'd lied just to irritate him. I shrugged and sipped my wine. He leaned back in his chair and said nothing, sitting at the table like a great frowning Buddha.

Jerry and I tried to get the conversation back on track,

but Carter would no longer participate, so we gave up. Eventually I got up to clear the table and Rory moved into the living room with his wine. From the kitchen I could hear the door to the woodstove open, and then the *clunk* and *whoosh* of the fire as he threw another log on it. I cringed inwardly and braced myself. Sure enough, Rory soon stalked back into the dining room.

"Where did those logs come from?" he demanded, standing so that he could confront me and glare at Carter simultaneously.

I turned from the steaming water, my rubber-gloved hands covered with soapsuds, and looked at him in dismay. "From the tree out back that has been lying there killing the grass for three months while you procrastinated. Carter split it."

Rory stared at me. "Yesterday," he ground out, "I made arrangements to rent the log-splitter this weekend."

I looked at him in exaggerated horror. Water dripped from my rubber gloves to my feet. "Oh my God, no," I said dramatically. "Where are we going to get another dead tree now?"

He breathed tensely for a moment, and I could almost see a cord of anger inside him twist tighter and tighter. He came toward me in the kitchen, out of view of Jerry and Carter. "You're just having a grand old time, aren't you, Shelby? This is getting pretty chummy," he said in a low, insinuating voice.

"What does that mean?"

He stood very close to me and looked down from his imposing height. "How long is he staying?"

I stepped back, turning off the water, and leaned against the counter. "Rory," I said softly, so Carter wouldn't overhear us, "we've talked about this before. Just the other day. He's a sick man." I felt a guilty pang at saying this, but I knew it was the only explanation Rory might buy. "He doesn't know where else to go. I don't know when he's leaving, and I'm not particularly worried about it. He's been a help. And I thought it was nice that he cut the wood." I could hear Jerry and Carter talking in muted tones in the other room.

Rory scrutinized my expression coldly. "Is he still in the guest room?"

My mouth dropped open and I felt as if he'd kicked me in the stomach. "Where else would he be?" I hissed, furious. "Just because there's a male in the house doesn't mean I'm going to jump into bed with him."

My display of rage did nothing to faze him. "Not because *he* doesn't want it, I can guarantee you that," he growled. "I can tell by the way he looks at you. Makes me want to deck him."

I felt a reluctant tingle of excitement at his assessment of Carter's feelings but quickly shoved it away. "Don't be ridiculous," I snapped. "Honestly, you're like a rooster in a henhouse. What're you going to do, keep pecking at him until he runs away?"

"Tell me you wouldn't be mad at me if I took in some crazy woman who claimed to be a *time traveler.*" He emphasized the words sarcastically, moving his fingers upward through the air like some sort of spooky magician. "Someone from the Donner party who looked at me as if I were a God-damned steak."

I couldn't help laughing at that. "Do you know how ridiculous you sound?" I began to pluck off the rubber gloves one finger at a time. "Carter is not crazy. And besides, he's as worried about taking advantage of me as you are, though not in the same way. We've already discussed it. He's going to work for his room and board."

Rory crossed his arms. "Don't tell me—he's going to be your butler."

I smirked. "Close. My gardener."

Rory's laugh was an incredulous snort. "Your *gardener?* That's—that's—" He laughed harshly again and rolled his eyes. "You need a gardener, Shelby, like Don King needs a toupee. This is starting to seem like one of those stupid sitcom plots! 'What happens when a wacky single girl takes in a time-traveling soldier from the Civil War?' " He gave me a wide-eyed, cynical, clownish smile. " 'Stay tuned!' "

I threw the rubber gloves into the sink, where they landed with a wet *thwop*. "What is it you're worried about? Do you think he's going to rob me? Rape me? What?"

"I'll tell you what I'm worried about," he said, raking a hand through his hair and leaning toward me. "I'll tell you exactly what." He pointed an accusatory finger at me. "I want to know what it is about this guy that's got you worked up into this maternal good samaritan care-taking lather. What's produced this blind trust and loyalty to a guy you don't know from Adam? I know what it is. And I think you do too."

His blazing blue eyes pinned me where I stood. Was it true? Was it only because Carter was a charming, good-looking man that I felt this desire to help him? I didn't have time to consider the idea further because at that moment Carter entered the kitchen. Both Rory and I turned startled gazes on him.

He cleared his throat. "Shelby, it's easy to see that my presence in your house is causing a problem." He glanced at Rory. "I apologize for any misgivings I have produced in you." Rory watched him suspiciously, but Carter turned back to me. "Your friend Jerry has invited me to stay at his house, and I think it best that I accept."

"No!" The word burst from me before I had a chance to stop it. Both men turned surprised looks on me. "I mean, it's silly that you have to uproot yourself because of a juvenile case of jealousy. Everything's fine. Isn't that right, Rory?" I turned seething eyes on him.

Carter continued. "No, I think it's apparent that my

133

presence has brought out uncomfortable insecurities, and I don't wish to cause any more problems.''

Rory straightened at these words and looked at Carter haughtily. ''I am not at all *insecure* because of you. I'm just worried about Shelby's safety.''

There was a small, barely discernible smile on Carter's lips. ''I think there's more to it than that, Mr. Feagan. If I'd had any desire to steal from her, or compromise her, I could well have done it before now, don't you think? At this point I think it's obvious your concerns are territorial. I can respect that. So I shall remove my presence if you find it threatening.''

Rory's face reddened at this and he sputtered briefly. ''I—that's—what an ego! I don't give a damn where you stay. I don't feel the least bit *threatened* by you.'' He flung his hands out to his sides in angry exasperation. ''You're *insane,* for God's sake. What woman would find that attractive?''

''Nevertheless, it is probably in your best interests that I stay with Jerry,'' Carter said calmly. ''Isn't that right?''

''What are you trying to say?'' Rory demanded. ''That I might lose what's mine if you stay here? Is that what you're saying?''

''Absolutely not,'' Carter replied, the soul of patience. ''I merely want to relieve you of your concerns. I have no wish to take your place here.''

''Take my place?'' Rory repeated, incredulous. ''You think you have the ability to take my place?''

Carter shook his head. ''I only meant that you seemed upset over my chopping the wood. If that was to be your job, I sincerely apologize. If I were to stay I would be wary of inadvertently usurping your position again.''

Rory threw back his head with a groan. ''This is ridiculous. I don't care where you stay. Stay here, if that's what you want. In fact, I *insist* that you stay here. You have nothing to do with me. I was just—I was concerned for Shelby. That's all."

"He's been a perfect gentleman," I interjected quickly. "And he doesn't need your permission to stay here."

Carter looked back at Rory as the ball reentered his court and shrugged as if that was all there was to say. I nearly smiled at the masterful way he'd pulled it off.

"If you insist, then of course I shall stay," Carter said, looking at the ground humbly and shaking his head. "I thank you for your forebearance."

Rory snorted and looked at me with an angrily bewildered expression, then turned his perplexed gaze on Carter. Finally he shook his head and turned away. "I hope you're adequately insured," he muttered to me.

Two days later, I stood on the front porch as darkness descended, waiting for Carter to show up. I guessed he'd gone out walking and hadn't returned, but the fact that this was the first time I'd arrived home to an empty house had me worried. Had he finally found that window to the past and fallen through it to 1862? The anxiety this idea produced in me was unnerving, though I masked it by thinking of a myriad of other reasons he could be late returning.

I watched a streak of orange and purple be devoured by the encroachment of thick, cast-iron gray clouds just above the western horizon. They were predicting snow tonight—quite a lot of it—and though I knew it never came down fast enough to actually trap a lone walker on the street, I worried that Carter would somehow be hampered or hurt by the onset of such cold.

I hugged my arms to my stomach as I gazed up and down the street in search of him. A chilling gust of air swept by and agitated the wind chimes. Low and friendly in the summer, they now echoed hollowly in the cold. I shivered and rubbed my arms.

What if he didn't come back? my mind demanded. What if he disappeared from my life as quickly as he'd come into it? Was this whole bizarre situation going to be nothing more than a strange blip on the screen of my life? It would be the eternal, unanswered question: a befuddled amnesiac or a soul truly lost in time? And there was always the possibility that he was some nut playing a sick joke—or a criminal with an ulterior motive. Should I check the silver drawer? I wondered.

The wind lifted my hair and blew it across my face. I raised my arms to pull it back, tying it into a knot at the base of my neck.

The street remained empty as the clouds obliterated the setting sun, plunging the world into a rapidly darkening twilight. Lights glowed from the windows of the houses. Across the street I could see old Mr. Williams sitting in his worn brown armchair, reading the newspaper. He and Mrs. Williams had recently celebrated their forty-eighth wedding anniversary, I remembered as I looked at him. Forty-eight years.

The wind gusted again so I turned back to the door, feeling the emptiness of the house yawn to greet me. I thought about cooking something for dinner, but the idea of cooking enough for two only to have Carter not show, depressed me more than anything. If he showed, I would take him out for dinner, I decided, if he'd let me. Someplace nice. He hadn't experienced a restaurant yet—only bars. I decided not to think about what that said about me.

On a whim, I went upstairs to his bedroom. Steve fell in behind me, unwilling to let me go anywhere without her. It was strange of her, this clinginess. Perhaps she felt the void as keenly as I did.

I pushed open the door to his room gently, as if I might have missed him napping on the bed on my first search of the house, but the room was empty. Steve walked into the middle of it and sniffed the air. Her tail swayed slightly, then drooped.

The bed was neatly made, my guest room knickknacks all in place. I opened the closet and felt a profound relief when I saw his Union blue uniform hanging there neatly. I went to the bedside table and opened the drawer. Inside were the shiny bullets, the lighter, the button, the string, essentially all of the items he'd had in his pockets when he'd arrived, including the odd leather box. I pulled this last from the drawer.

It opened on a hinge to reveal a glass, sepia-toned picture of a woman. His wife, of course. Her stern, translucent eyes stared out at me, and I imagined I saw an accusation in them. For what? For my having him when she could not? For somehow stealing him from her? Of course the idea was ludicrous, but for some reason I felt as if I *had* stolen him from her.

She was blond, it looked like, with a sweet, soft mouth that looked out of place with the hard eyes and determined brow. Her white dress had a ruffled bodice and a high collar that daintily framed cheeks that were round and firm. If it weren't for those eyes, she would have looked cherubic, and so young as to be almost childlike.

I traced a fingernail along the line of her jaw. Did he touch this picture as I did, but with love and sadness that they were not together? Did he miss the soft feel of her skin, instead of the cold glass of the picture? The thought was incongruous. She looked tough, I thought. Though her features were fragile, her expression was stern, forceful.

"She looks like a bitch," I said to Steve, who sniffed at it and licked my fingers. "No offense," I added to her.

What could their life together have been like? In trying to imagine it I felt a possessiveness toward him almost in defiance of those steely eyes that stared blankly from the tintype. A possessiveness and an angry loss. Did she have him back now?

I snapped the box shut and gazed up at the ceiling. What sort of relationship could he have had with her? I wondered. Did they laugh as much as we did? Did he challenge her the way he challenged me—with words and wit and charm? Was she kind to him? Did she love him? Really love him, with all the passion and strength her heart could muster? Because he deserved that.

I lay back on the bed and grabbed his pillow to my chest, sniffing the sheets deeply. They only smelled clean, and slightly like the soap I had bought for the guest shower.

I pictured Carter's face. The high cheekbones under the soft gray eyes, the oak-blond hair and the dark stubble of his beard. I envisioned the way he moved, strong and sure, with no extraneous motion, no nervous fidgeting. If he'd been born in my time he'd have been an athlete, a soccer or tennis player. He'd move with an agile grace, a quick snapping accuracy, and walk with a masculine swagger in those hard legs and slim hips. Or he might have been an executive, in a tailored suit and crisp white shirt, managing meetings and chatting arrogantly on his car phone.

But he was a farmer. He split wood precisely and turned the soil with tireless surety. He reined a plow horse with strength and planted seedlings with tender care. He taught school with a slate and chalk. He was so real, I wanted to touch him, hold him in my hand. But he was so enigmatic that he could be gone now forever.

I don't know how long I lay there, but it was quite a while. By the time I got up and carefully straightened the bed I was convinced that I'd never see him again.

It was dark, snow was falling, and the fire in the wood-stove had burned down to embers, casting the house into a chilly gloom.

I went downstairs with Steve following at my heels, her nails clicking quietly on the uncarpeted stairs. Picking up a log to throw into the stove, I paused to consider the smoothly cut edges. How long had Rory procrastinated about cutting up that old tree? Only to be angry after Carter had done it and saved him the trouble.

I held the log to my chest, heedless of the sharp slivers and bark that stabbed my skin through my shirt. An overwhelming sense of loneliness consumed me. He was gone. My adventure with the unknown was over, and all I'd done was argue with myself over the sanity of my own actions, never bothering to actually help him. Oh sure, I'd fed him and bought him some jeans; I'd done all the easy material things that only required the signing of a credit slip. Why hadn't I listened to him more? Why hadn't I seriously investigated his claim, his *belief* in who he was? I knew he wasn't crazy; why had I continuously treated him as if I thought he was?

I threw the log into the fire and felt a lump rise in my throat. The thought of turning from the fire to face the empty room suddenly felt more than I could bear. Was it just that he had provided a welcome relief from the boring self-searching I had engaged in for the last several months? Was it that his presence had masked the underlying unhappiness I'd felt with my own inertia? Or was it that his presence had truly been a balm to my spirit, a comforting foundation for the crumbling edifice of my life?

Was I just to go merrily onward now as I always had—without him?

I felt a tear travel down my cheek, stinging the skin as I stood before the fire. It was impossible. He'd changed my life somehow. I no longer wanted to look at things the same way. When he was there everything had been wonderful, magical. The simplest activities had taken on a fascinating appeal. I didn't want to give that up.

I'd wanted to teach him how to drive. I'd wanted to show him the airport, the subway, the museums of Washington. I'd wanted him to meet James and my parents, and I'd wanted to spend Christmas with him.

At the thought of Christmas, tears welled and fell freely down my cheeks, and an unbearable feeling of isolation descended on me.

Steve jumped as the storm door opened, and then the front doorknob rattled. I swiped furiously at my eyes, pushing away the tears until it hurt my face. What in the world would Rory think if he found me shedding tears in a darkened house? He would know exactly why, and he would despise me for it.

I heard him enter the hall and hit the light switch, at which point I turned swiftly, though as nonchalantly as possible, to face him.

Carter stood squinting in the light of the hallway, peering at me in the darkness of the living room. Relief washed over me, sweeping all my emotions to the surface of my very readable face.

He stopped midway in unzipping his jacket and stared at me. "What's the matter?" His voice was soft in the darkness, full of concern.

I felt the mortifying tears welling up again and looked away from him. "Nothing. I—nothing," I said, but my voice quavered.

He came slowly toward me. "Shelby?" Again the soft voice. I took a deep breath.

His hand reached out and pushed my hair behind my shoulder. He dipped his head to look into my face. "Is everything all right?"

I covered my eyes with my hands and took another deep breath. "Yes," I squeaked. "Everything's fine. I just—I thought you'd gone for good. And now I'm just so—*relieved.*" I looked up at him with bleary eyes and attempted a ridiculous smile.

Carter's expression softened even as he frowned. His hand, which had swept back my hair, now took my forearm in a light grip. His thumb rubbed gently on my skin. He watched me thoughtfully for a moment. Then, "I found a job," he said quietly.

A job! He meant to stay! I laughed through my tears of relief. "That's—that's great, Carter. That's really great." My voice was weak, but a smile took control of my lips, and I could not meet his eyes, so full of emotion were they.

"Shelby," he said, in a voice low and intense, "this is dangerous."

I looked up at him then, unsure of his meaning and not wanting to misunderstand. His eyes glittered in the firelight as I felt the pull of his hand on my forearm.

I resisted, frightened. "I don't know, Carter," I said, confused.

He shook his head. "I don't either," he replied, and pulled me toward him.

Chapter Eight

A thousand protests shot through my head as our eyes locked, his strangely alive in the firelight, mine blurred by unshed tears. *He could be gone tomorrow as easily as I thought he'd gone today. He could actually be crazy, as Rory thinks. He could be claimed by someone answering the ad I placed. He could just be missing his wife.*

I felt my body go rigid as his other hand took my upper arm in a firm but gentle grip. "You're afraid of me," he murmured, his voice incredulous.

My breath came quick and shallow. "In a way," I whispered. I couldn't take my eyes from his face. His hands on my arms felt warm, exhilarating, and I didn't want him to let go.

His brows drew together as he searched my face. "I would never hurt you," he said; then his eyes dropped, as if he knew the futility of speaking words like those.

I smiled grimly. "Not intentionally, no. I know that."

His hands slid slowly down my arms, his expression unutterably sad. "I'm sorry. This was wrong of me."

But as his hands slid down my forearms to my hands I grabbed them, squeezing the rough, work-hardened palms in my soft ones. I clasped them together at my stomach, as if I could somehow draw him inside me, and I looked at him penetratingly. "Are you lonely, Carter?" I asked softly. "Do you miss your home? This must all be so strange and awful for you." I couldn't bring myself to ask if he missed her. *Meg.*

He didn't reply, but his eyes told it all. Pained to their depths and layered with frustration, they asked of me a million questions and told me they expected no answers.

I moved quickly before I could change my mind. My hands released his and I stepped forward, wrapping my arms around his waist. He hesitated a second before his arms went round my shoulders and pulled me so tightly against him that I could not for a moment draw breath.

His chest was broad and his back strong, but it was the way our bodies fit together that made it so sinfully gratifying. Our hearts beat against each other as our torsos melded. It was a hug I'd offered, solace and comfort; but what I got in return was a charge of the soul. I could feel his cheek where he laid it against my head and felt as if I'd been rescued from drowning and given life-sustaining breath through the contact of our bodies. His hands held me as if he might pick me up 'and place me on a shelf in his heart. Something stirred deep inside me.

I pulled back. He was slow to release me and, though I already missed the warmth of his body against mine, I stepped away from him. He looked at me with an unknowable expression.

"I think I'd better go upstairs now," I said self-consciously, my eyes darting back and forth from my hands clasped before me to his face above me. "I'm glad you're back. I'm sorry to have—I—I'm sorry," I finished lamely, though what I was sorry for I wasn't sure. Perhaps for leading him into an awkward encounter, perhaps for putting a stop to it. But I was certainly sorry for having to leave his arms, and that was the very reason I did. After all, he was married and I—well, I was *involved*.

"You can tell me about the job in the morning," I said as I reached the stairs. It was early and I would miss dinner, but I knew if I stayed near him my resolve would leave me.

He turned partly away from the fire, affording me only the silhouette of his profile as he concentrated on the jacket's zipper. His hair fell forward to half cover his face. "Yes," he said flatly.

I ascended the stairs, lonelier than I'd been in years. Lonelier, perhaps, than Carter Lindsey, for I knew I could never have what I'd so secretly wanted from that first instant he'd taken my arm.

The following morning I woke early; or rather, I rose early, for sleep had eluded me most of the night. I pulled on my heavy terry-cloth robe and thick slippers and padded downstairs to stoke the fire.

When I reached the living room I saw immediately that Carter was up and had already fed the fire. Moving through the dining room, I saw him in the kitchen, standing before the stove with a cup in his hand, the paper and string tail of a tea bag hanging from it. It was ironic—he couldn't understand why I insisted on the old-fashioned loose tea when there was such convenience available. Carter Lindsey, born in 1837, longed for the newfangled, while Shelby Manning, born in 1969, couldn't be rid of enough of it.

He turned when he heard me finger the newspaper that lay open on the table.

"Good morning," he said neutrally. "Shall I make you some tea?"

I searched his face and posture for a clue as to what he was thinking. "Thank you. Yes."

He moved stiffly, I thought, his back straight and proud. With great care he took another cup from the cabinet and placed it on the counter; then, from the shelf behind him, he took the loose Earl Grey tea and tea ball. What an extraordinary man he was. He knew which kind of tea I preferred at each time of the day—no small task in my tea-laden house. Most men I knew couldn't tell me what color my eyes were, let alone what kind of tea I drank.

His movements, as usual, were quiet and sure. His care with my cheap plates and cups was no less than had they been Royal Doulton. I sighed as I watched him.

"So tell me about this job," I said cheerily. "How did you find it? And what are you doing?"

I could hear the soft chink of metal against glass as Carter poured the steaming water over the tea ball, then a hiss as he turned the kettle to his own mug. He turned with the two cups and sat across from me at the table.

"Shelby," he said, and I knew that what he was about to say would have nothing to do with the job. "I want to talk about last night."

I began to wave my hand. "There's no need—"

Carter quelled me with a look. "You were afraid of me, and that's the last thing I want. I won't touch you again. I give you my word."

If he'd meant to make me feel better, he hadn't. In fact, I felt a door slam somewhere in my heart upon hearing his words. But it was better this way, I reasoned. So we're attracted to each other; so what? So one day he remembers who he is, or where his wife is, or he drops through the ground into another life, and then where would I be? Alone, that's where.

But when I looked into his face as he apologized for—for *nothing,* really—and I saw that expression that was so closed and proud, yet so sincere, my resolve almost left me.

I cupped my hands around the steaming mug. "Carter, it wasn't you I was afraid of last night," I said to the mug. "It was me, my reaction. When you didn't come home yesterday and I thought you'd left, I was—surprised by my feelings." I looked up into his face, into the dove-gray eyes that watched me silently. I forced myself to keep going. "But it's an impossible situation. I have . . ." What did I have? Rory? Perhaps. I had part of him anyway. But I had a life, a future, that did not include a married man. "You need to find your wife," I said bluntly. With those words the open, watchful expression on his face closed up. He looked away and took a deep breath.

"Of course," he said brusquely. Then he stood and carried his mug to the kitchen. I could hear the liquid splash into the sink. When he returned his eyes were cold and his lips held an odd, half-cynical twist. "I'll have to tell you about my wife sometime," he said cryptically and strode past me to the living room. "Not that it would change anything."

I stood, teacup in hand, and followed him into the next room.

"I shall be with a Mr. Malone at a place called Green Way Landscaping," he said, donning the leather coat. "He said he could use someone who knows about winter pruning and plant protection."

"Great," I had time to murmur before he opened the front door.

"I'll be back about six," he said, then paused. "And don't worry; I plan to buy a new coat with my first week's pay."

I shook my head. "I'm not worried about it."

He looked at me, then gave me a dry smile. "Well, see you later."

" 'Bye," I said quietly. He turned and pulled the door shut behind him. I shivered in the cloud of cold air that reached me.

Despite the awkwardness between Carter and myself, I felt my spirits lifting as I left the house and walked the ten blocks to the shop. The snow that had threatened had mostly missed us, and we'd only gotten enough to whiten the grass. Now the sky was blue and the air crisp with the cold. I squinted into the brightness.

At least he was still here, I found myself thinking. We were tense, we were battling something invisible between us, but at least he was still here. Just knowing he would be there to go home to made me feel optimistic. About what, I wasn't sure.

As I headed down Kenmore, I decided to cross through the reservoir park and head up Princess Anne Street. It was a longer route, but I was early and in the mood to walk. The frozen grass crunched under my booted feet and my breath frosted in the air.

I passed a house with a mailbox shaped like a birdhouse, the name LAWRENCE painted across the bottom. I wondered if there were any Lindseys in town and was struck by the thought that I had not even done the simplest thing to ascertain Carter's identity, and that was to look up his name in the phone book. I vowed to do it the moment I got to the store.

As I trudged up the hill past the Blacksmith restaurant, my eyes fell on the big old house Carter had called Mackey's Folly. I wondered if it was true about the house, and how I could find out. As I came even with it, I turned to look at the Kenmore Inn, wherein lay the pub I had taken Carter to. Out front, a woman was sprinkling salt on the steps.

"Good morning," I called as I approached.

She looked up and smiled, a pretty woman somewhere in her mid-fifties with soft brown hair, wearing a classic beige coat over what appeared to be a flannel nightgown. "Good morning. How are you today?"

"I'm fine." I stopped before the stoop and looked up at her. Shoving my hands deep in my coat pockets, I asked, "I was wondering if you know anything about the history of that house over there." I dragged out one of my gloved hands and pointed across the street.

She put a hand on her hip and gazed at the house. "It was built before this one, I know. And that side was added on in the twenties." She motioned to the right-hand side and shook her head. "But I can't recall much more about it, really. All I know is that the main part of the house was built in the early eighteen hundreds, a few years before this one." She turned her eyes to the front porch on which she stood.

From the expression on her face as she looked at the inn I could tell that she loved the old house. "What about this house?" I asked. "Does it have an interesting history?" What was it Carter had said about this place?

The woman smiled. "This house was built for a maiden lady in about 1824. Lomax, I think her name was. She supposedly had some beautiful gardens round back, but that was a long while ago. They're all gone now; such a shame. That's the only thing this old place is missing, in my opinion." She shook her head again. "But it's a wonderful old house. I just love it." She patted a prideful hand against a porch column. "Would you like to see the upstairs?" she offered. Upstairs was a bed-and-breakfast and a formal dining room, a restaurant in which I had not yet had the pleasure of dining because it was considerably out of my price range.

"I would love to," I said sincerely, "but I'm on my way to work now. Maybe some other time?"

We agreed that I would stop by sometime to see the inside, and I continued on to work. Lomax, I thought as I cut down an alley. That could have been the name Carter'd mentioned, but I couldn't remember. I'd ask him tonight.

I walked gingerly down the ice-slicked alley, noticing on my right what looked like a barely used back door to an apartment house with the words EXIT ONLY spray-painted in fluorescent orange on it. I wondered what had prompted such a dramatic announcement of the fact.

On the left was a small brick row house that had a tiny window with a neon hand in it that I'd noticed often. A sign that hung limply from the window sill below it was partially hidden by a dumpster, so that all I could see were the words PALM READING. I'd passed this house many times before, never stopping to find out what the rest of the sign said; but since I was early today because of my sleepless night I stepped around the dumpster to read the rest: PALM READING, $5, MADAM ERIKA.

I had always wondered about the little window and the woman I sometimes saw come out of the door. She was tiny and gnarled, like a gnome, or the way I pictured the witch from "Hansel and Gretel," and she made me nervous in an odd way. She seemed mystical enough to actually be able to read the future in a hand. I wondered what my palm would have to look like to indicate the arrival of a visitor from the past. Or what Carter's would look like, I thought with sudden, real interest. Maybe he would have some special, historic aura or something that would tell a psychic he was from another time. The idea took root in my mind as I gazed at the neon hand.

Suppose we were to go to this psychic and she were to confirm, somehow, that he was from the 1800s? Would she be able to advise him how to get back to the past? Was this kind of magic a reality to some people?

My imagination was just getting started when I heard

the door to the apartment house open behind me.

"I'll call you," a familiar voice said. I turned and peered around the dumpster to see Rory in the doorway, facing a blond girl who wore an oversized shirt and very little else. I felt my stomach drop at the sight. "Thanks for letting me crash here," he said, and for the moment my worst fears were mollified. Perhaps he'd only stayed there to avoid the drive home. Now that Carter was staying in my house, he might be uncomfortable coming to me.

But my immediate suspicions were confirmed a moment later when, after a few inaudible words from the girl, she reached up and pulled him toward her by the shirt. He kissed her, letting his hand slide up her rib cage to cup a breast through her shirt before pulling away from what looked like a very wet kiss. He laughed, and I felt my heart twist as I pictured those blue eyes crinkling to look at her with that same warm amusement with which he looked at me.

"I'll call you. I promise," I heard him say again, between chuckles. The girl's hand was doing something to his chest, and he struggled gently away, laughing.

I felt as if I might throw up. Rory turned away, broad shoulders at a jaunty angle, and tucked in his shirt. His hair was mussed as he shrugged into his coat. I felt my stomach roil upward. This wasn't happening. I'd always known Rory was a flirt, but I'd never suspected him of cheating. Actually, to be perfectly honest, I'd never even let myself think about it. The opportunities were too endless. People naturally gravitated to bartenders, especially pretty young women to handsome, dynamic men like Rory. But that's as far as he'd take it . . . or so I had always thought.

Tumbling upon these thoughts was the realization that this was probably not the first time. I never knew where Rory was. He had friends all over the city. Frankly, I didn't usually think about where he was when he wasn't with me. He'd always show up every couple of days, and that was fine. That was just the way our relationship was. But I'd thought we had an understanding. I had thought he at least wouldn't *sleep* with other women.

I leaned back against the dumpster as Rory strode casually away from me toward the street, out of sight. Bile rose to the back of my throat and humiliation stung my face red. I doubled over, my arms around my stomach, and closed my eyes.

And *he* had accused *me* of infidelity when he'd asked if Carter was still sleeping in the guest room! What self-righteous anger he'd mustered then! Angry tears burned my eyes. Maybe he'd been so sure about my actions because it was just the thing *he* would do if he found himself with a good-looking woman in the next room night and day; he would sleep with her. Naturally.

What a fool I'd been! Just now, with that girl, he'd been so casual, as if he weren't struggling with any sort of guilt or commitment anxiety. Even the expression on his face as he'd strode briskly off had registered no concern whatsoever. I felt my breakfast leave my stomach and bent my head beside the dumpster to wretch.

Empty and sweating, I rose, passing a hand over my forehead and eyes.

"Are you all right?" a harsh, reedy, strongly accented voice called.

I opened my eyes to see the little gypsy woman standing on the cement steps outside her door, peering down at me. A chill passed over me at her unexpected presence.

"I'm sorry," I said, straightening slowly from where I'd leaned against the dumpster. "I suddenly felt ill. I'm very sorry." I bent toward the ground and picked up my purse, which I had dropped.

"Come up here," the little voice commanded. It sounded like a Russian or Czechoslovakian accent, and it made her seem very formidable. Her iron gray hair was tightly curled, as if it had just been freed from rollers, and her bent little body was covered by an ornate silk robe of a dark blue and maroon paisley design. Her eyes, which from where I stood could have been either brown or gray, were piercingly clear and looked at me angrily. She frightened me.

"I'm sorry. I'll clean it up," I said weakly, appalled at her interference and wanting to get away. But I was unable to turn away from her insistent stare.

"Come up here," she directed. A crooked twig of a finger beckoned me forward and pointed to the stair landing.

Reluctantly, I gathered my coat around me and stepped up the icy stairs. When I reached the top one my left foot slid from the step below and I stumbled. She grabbed my arm and steadied me with a surprisingly firm grip.

"I knew you were here," she stated, pushing me to a standing position. "You disturbed my reading."

"I'm sorry."

She opened the door and went inside, still talking. I had no choice but to follow. "Then the Hanged Man showed up and I knew he was not for me."

Great. The hanged man, I supposed, was looking for me.

She turned and pointed the bony finger at me again. "You have a pervasive angst," she said.

"I'm terribly sorry," I said again, this time a little indignantly.

She didn't seem to notice. "I am Madam Erika," she said imperiously, pronouncing the name *Ereeka*, as we entered an ordinary-looking laundry room.

Then we emerged into what must have been the principal room for her business, a dark, creepy place with a real chandelier. The floor was painted black, with a gold circle that surrounded a black lacquered table in the middle of the room. The walls were a dark purple, and all the lamps were draped with a filmy red material. Oriental rugs hung from the walls and covered doors. In each of the two far corners was a plump, well-worn armchair with a reading lamp next to it, and next to the door we had just entered stood an ornately carved sideboard.

The place smelled of incense and laundry soap. I looked at the cards on the black tabletop. Tarot, of course.

"You've suffered a shock," the woman said. "I could feel it." She sat at the table and motioned me to take another chair. Next to her place at the table was a mug with cartoon dinosaurs on it, a strange burst of normality in the witchy room. "You were just a small presence at first," she continued, scooping up the cards and shuffling them. "Then you burst into flame." She looked up and gave me a twisted smile. "I wanted to see what you looked like."

I sat uneasily, watching the gnarled hands skillfully shuffle the deck. I wondered what time it was, but I was more curious what this woman planned to do with me. "What do I look like?" I asked.

She began counting out cards and putting them back on the bottom of the deck. Her gray-brown eyes snapped up to mine. "You look like a flame," she said, nodding. The fingers of one hand reached out to my hair and took a long curl between them, rubbing the strands back and forth. "Flame," she smiled and nodded. Her eyes looked slightly insane. "You're a very beautiful woman."

It was hard to take this as a compliment from a woman who looked as if she'd just materialized from a toadstool. But I smiled back genially and thought again about leaving.

She placed the cards on the table and slid them across to me. "Shuffle until you feel their warmth, then cut three times," she commanded, her eyes shrewd and lucid again.

I took the cards in my chilly hands and shuffled, thinking they'd never feel warm as the shock of seeing Rory had drained the blood from every limb in my body. I tried to block from my mind the image of his hand on the girl's breast, but I couldn't. Instead I saw up close, in my mind's eye, the small crescent scar on the back of his hand surrounded by the white cotton of the girl's shirt.

I quickly cut the cards and looked at the gypsy woman, swallowing hard over the lump in my throat. She picked them up carefully and turned one over. The weird pointed smile returned.

"Cups, yes, I knew. The knight." She nodded. She turned over another card, murmured, "Death," and then turned over what I immediately recognized as a hanged man.

I laughed bleakly, feeling tears sting my eyes. *Perfect.* Death, a hanged man, and some cups. I guessed I'd probably drink myself to death after killing Rory. But Madam *Ereeka* was smiling.

"You are emotional, intuitive. *Cups.*" She nodded. "You like to be happy."

"Doesn't everyone?"

She ignored this and continued. "But there is an oppressive presence. Here. The Death card. Don't fear it. It is a positive card." She looked me in the eye. "Women should never fear the death card; they must see the dawn in it. You shall be rid of this ugly presence and this," she tapped a frail fingernail on a card, "the Hanged Man, tells you that. You have had this *click*, this mental turnabout. That is why you burst into flame just now. Isn't that right?" She drilled me with her eyes. This was not a rhetorical question.

I had to think hard about what she was asking. Had I

burst into flame? Could I? It seemed appealing just then. Or was it the mental turnabout, the click, that she asked about? I thought about Rory, his deception, my naive assumptions about our relationship. "It was a little louder than a *click*," I said finally, wryly, "but yes, I suppose so."

The little woman cackled gaily at my words and turned over another card. Then another and she *oooh*ed when another came up. "The King of Wands," she said. "A good one, an honest one." The she frowned. "The Tower. Things will be tough. A revolution is coming. Watch out and keep calm, so you will overcome all of these obstacles. You will be like the Chariot then."

I pictured Ben Hur careening out of control on a Roman stone road.

Madam Erika placed her hands in her lap and regarded the cards for a moment more. "Yes, you have some trials in your life now. You must be wise and strong. You must decide for everyone, your past and your future. You can control what is to come." She closed her eyes and raised her hands. I wondered if this were the grand finale. "Go now and do what is right. Take the path of the goddess."

I rolled my eyes.

"Go now. Go on," she continued, her hands rising ever higher.

Confused, I stood and rummaged through my purse for my wallet. She hadn't even looked at my palm.

Her eyes snapped open and pinned me where I stood, elbow deep in my bag. "No money," she said, hands still over her head. She looked a little like a spider monkey. "I do this for you because of your angst. It was a warm-up for me." She smiled. "Go have a nice day."

Have a nice day? I thanked her and left through the laundry room. Would anything ever get the image of that little woman with her arms raised out of my head? I was even able to smile about it, until I saw the EXIT ONLY door across the alley and my stomach plummeted again.

Rory with another woman. Death, the Hanged Man, the King of Wands. What a bizarre way to start a morning.

Chapter Nine

Work was a blur. Janey was working instead of Sylvie, and I was heartily glad of it. If I'd had to sit through a day of Sylvie's chatter on top of all my turbulent thoughts, I would have lost my mind.

Periodically I was able to lose myself in something I was doing, either checking in a new shipment of books, or reading *Publishers Weekly* or one of the various book reviews to which I subscribed. But inevitably the image of Rory's hand on that strange girl's breast and his head bent to hers in that lavish kiss came floating back to my consciousness and my stomach would hit the floor all over again.

What was I going to do? I wondered all day. *Should I confront him, or wait to see if he tells me? How can I even see him, look him in the traitorous, two-timing face?* If he had walked in the store that day, I am sure I would have shattered into a thousand tiny pieces before him on the floor. I had never realized until that awful, fateful morning how deeply I'd depended on Rory as a foundation in my life. And though I had never actively sought marriage, I had assumed in a sometimes pleasant, sometimes unpleasant, way that we would marry. After all, we'd been together since high school. I'd barely known anyone else.

But apart from all that, it wasn't anger I felt for him—not a deep anger anyway—or even hurt. My biggest emotion was shock, a profound, mind-boggling shock. The unexpectedness of it was where the cruelty lay. It was as if something had happened to me that was so far from the plan, so weird and inconceivable, that it changed everything about the way I saw life. This strange event could not possibly have happened without meaning that the world was really a place that I had never seen before. It was as if I'd suddenly found out my parents had never existed.

And throughout all of this turmoil, the only thought that saved me from complete despair was the fact that Carter, with his knowing gray eyes and sincere, steady presence would be at home when I got there, like a beacon to a sinking ship. His presence kept me from thinking my life had absolutely no meaning.

The day dragged on and the rush of Christmas shoppers kept us hopping, creating the unpleasant sensation of running frantically all day on a clock that would not move.

When at last the day did end, and Janey packed up her things and went home, I was reluctant to leave the shop. I sat at the desk in my little upstairs office and stared at the door.

How could I ever trust Rory again? How could anything ever be the same again? It couldn't. My relationship with Rory was over, and that was the last thing on earth I was prepared to deal with. Even the appearance of Carter, a stranger claiming to be from the past, was less of an upheaval in my life than this was. I caught myself thinking, *why couldn't I have just gone to work the same old way this morning?* But that was ridiculous. I'd have just been a dupe that much longer.

Then I told myself I was being unfair, that maybe it had been a mistake, and Rory was sorry. That maybe it was Rory's way of reacting to Carter. But it wasn't true. Somewhere inside me I knew this had not been the first time he'd cheated on me. So many little details that had passed me by before came to me now with Rory's infidelity as their reason: articles of clothing he'd thought he'd left at my house that were not there, evenings when I could not get him on the phone even though I knew he wasn't working, times he'd said he'd be by after work and he never showed . . . I'd been given the last piece to the puzzle and the picture was now clear. He'd been sleeping around for years.

I lay my head on my desk and tried to cry but couldn't. I was empty inside, dry. It was as if he'd ripped out my heart and never put it back. I felt nothing. Complete, desolate nothingness.

I tried to analyze why I didn't want to go home, when just a few hours before I'd thought Carter's presence would be the one thing to save me, and realized that it was because he saw too much. He was too perceptive. I wouldn't be able to hide it from him. He would take one look at my face and know that something was drastically wrong.

Then I would have to explain; I'd have to voice all those horrible words and make it all real, and I just didn't think I could face it. Carter had been right about Rory. All those veiled comments he'd made about my relationship with Rory, about him being undependable and not what I needed—he'd been right. And he'd seen it immediately.

Vaguely, through the noise of my own thoughts, I

heard a knocking downstairs. I lifted my head and listened. It came again. Someone was definitely knocking on the glass of the front doors. I rose slowly and walked down the creaking wood stairs. Even from the back of the store I could tell it was Carter from the angle of his shoulders as he leaned against the door and the glow of his hair from the street lamp. In spite of all my warring emotions I felt a smile tug at my lips at the sight of him.

He flashed a grin at me when I emerged from the stairwell and stepped back from the door as I opened it.

"I saw the lights," he said. "I hoped you'd be here." His expression was far lighter than it had been this morning, and his eyes fairly danced.

I felt a lump grow in my throat. He was so beautiful, it hurt to look at him. Carter would not in a million years do what Rory had done. No casual liaisons, no lying. Even what had happened last night between us, the embrace and whatever it might have become, would not have been like the sleazy game I'd seen played out this morning in back of that apartment house.

I should have done it, I thought then, looking at Carter. I should have taken all I could get from him last night, before he disappeared and I wouldn't have the chance. But I didn't, or he hadn't. And for a moment I hated both Rory and Meg Lindsey.

"How was your first day of work?" I asked with forced cheerfulness.

"Great," he said. "You know, it was the first time since I got here that I felt I knew what I was doing."

And it showed, I thought. The confidence emanating from him was palpable.

"That's why I'm here." He took me by the arm and led me toward the back of the store. "Come on, get your coat and bag; I'm going to take you out. Got paid today." He patted his jacket pocket with pride.

I laughed at his ebullience. "Okay, okay. Where are you taking me?"

"Right down the street. A place I passed on the way here. Come on, put your coat on."

I pulled on my jacket and ran upstairs for my purse. In the little office I paused for a moment at the scene of my despair, then, consciously leaving my "pervasive angst" on my desk like a pile of paperwork, I quickly extinguished the lights and ran back downstairs. Maybe this was just what I needed—diversion. And if Carter Lindsey wasn't diversion from just about any man on the planet, I didn't know what else would be.

I locked up the store and we headed down Caroline Street. Carter pulled my hand through his arm and smiled down at me. I felt my stomach flutter at the easy comfort of the gesture.

"So how was your day?" he asked me, quietly mimicking the tone that I frequently used to ask him the same question.

I smiled at the subtlety. "It wasn't very good. Pretty hectic," I said, as honestly as I could.

He gave me a sidelong glance. "I would think that a busy day at your own shop would be a good thing. You don't look very happy about it."

I glanced away. "Well, you know how customers can be—demanding and rude. Especially just before Christmas. How was *your* day?" I forced a light expression on my face and looked up at him.

His lips curved into a smile. "My day was quite good, thank you," he said, slowing to open the door to the Windsor Tap Room. He stepped back and motioned me to enter before him.

Though it was dark outside, the dimness of the dark-paneled room took a minute to adjust to. The place was pretty crowded for a Tuesday. The front dining room was nearly full, so I guessed the small bar in the back must be, too, since that was the room that usually filled up first. Christmas shoppers, I guessed, warming up from the cold.

We took a table by a bow window in front that had just been vacated and waited for the busboy to clear it.

"So, tell me about it," I said. "How did you find this job and what are you doing?"

The busboy arrived and cleared the table. Then Carter leaned forward and rested his weight on his elbows. "It's nothing very interesting. I was just walking and I came across a rather large establishment selling plants and trees. Green Way Landscaping, the sign said, and there was another sign in the window that said 'Help Wanted.' "

"Green Way; wait a minute," I stopped him. "Is that the one up near route 17? Across the bridge?"

Carter nodded.

"But that's miles from here! You walked all the way up there?" I protested.

He laughed a bit at my attitude. "It's not more than a few miles."

I rolled my eyes. "Yes, miles!" I laughed. I barely ran two miles when I forced myself outside for exercise and almost never walked more than three, considering myself quite the walker at that. Green Way, I was sure, was farther away than that.

Carter shook his head. "At any rate, I struck up a conversation with Mr. Malone, who runs the place, and he offered to hire me. Simple as that."

"What in the world does a landscaping company do in the winter?"

Carter picked up and eyed a drink menu in a plastic tabletop frame, then placed it back on the table. "It's deceptive, I know. Mr. Malone wants to begin to advertise to cure people of just that notion, that plants are dead in the winter. It's easy to think there's nothing to be done to a bare winter yard, but it isn't so.''

The waiter arrived and took our orders: a beer for me and a brandy for Carter. It was interesting; I'd always ordered him beer, or offered him beer at home, assuming him to be like every other twenty-something person I knew. But now, on his own dime, I discovered that he preferred brandy. How much else did I not know about this man because of my twentieth-century assumptions?

''So, are you being paid well?'' I asked, as discreetly as I thought possible. I hoped good old Mr. Malone was paying him a decent wage. It would be awful if Carter were to be shocked and embarrassed when the bill came; those brandies probably cost four dollars apiece. Considering how he'd reacted to the cost of a book and some jeans, he'd more than likely be stunned at the price of a nip of brandy.

Carter eyed me for a moment with a sort of wary amusement. ''Satisfactorily,'' he answered with a short nod.

It was obvious I was not to ask further.

He straightened as the waiter placed a large brandy snifter before him and a beer bottle and a glass in front of me.

''Thank you,'' he murmured to the waiter, palming the snifter in one large hand. He lifted it to me in salute. ''To you, Miss Manning. Thank you for all of your help,'' he said.

I smiled. ''And to you for yours,'' I replied, thinking he didn't know the half of what he'd given me. Just the ability to sit here and smile after the events of this morning was a gift the proportions of which he'd never know.

He swirled the liquid in the glass with just the smallest motion and watched the way it clung to the sides. Then he sipped the fiery brew, his heavy-lidded eyes glowing with appreciation.

''That's better,'' he said with a deep exhalation, then

added softly, "Now, tell me what sort of day would put that sad expression in your eyes."

At his words the pain reared up inside me, the same way forgotten tears spring to life when a child with a skinned knee sees its mother. I wanted to tell Carter my feelings, to confide in him, but I couldn't. For some reason I didn't want him to know of Rory's perfidy, or my humiliation.

"Oh, you know . . ." I waved my hand in dismissal, looking out over the dimly lit dining room. "Just one of those days."

Carter took the hint. "Just a lot of inconsiderate people," he said with a smile in his eyes.

I laughed wryly. "Yes. Inconsiderate people."

"What sort of books did these demanding, rude people buy?" he asked conversationally.

I spun my beer glass before me on the table, watching the sudsy bubbles spin like soap in a wash cycle. "A lot of books about faraway places," I answered with a laugh. "I guess that's the truth about rude people; they're just unhappy with their own lot and coveting another's."

Carter nodded. "Very astute of you, Miss Manning. I think you're absolutely right."

We talked on about various topics, Carter always curious about me and my life but brushing aside questions about his own. But though he was reticent on the subject of himself, what he did say was always in keeping with his assertion of having come from the past. There seemed to be nothing I could say that would cause him to remember something modern, nothing to force him to indicate that he suffered from a delusion instead of a cosmic phenomenon.

After a while I excused myself to go to the ladies' room. I had had several beers and was feeling significantly better about things when I stepped through the narrow hall that separated the front dining room from the back bar. The restrooms were just off this hall.

Before entering I stepped into the back bar to see how crowded it was. The ambience in the back was always nicer than the front because there was a working fireplace that people gathered around on nights like this one. Sure enough, the room was packed. Just as I was about to turn away from the scene to reenter the hallway to the bathroom, I spotted Rory behind the bar. The moment I saw him my stomach dropped like a lead weight. This was the problem with his being a freelance bartender; I never knew where he would show up.

He stood, leaning his elbows on the bar, and faced a woman who sat on the other side. One of his hands held one of hers limply to his lips. He was smiling and teasing her about something; I could tell from the expression on his face. The blue eyes were crinkled into a smile and he looked at her through his dark lashes in a sultry, seductive way I knew well. My glance fell on the woman. Hot adrenaline snaked through my veins as I recognized the blond from this morning.

I turned abruptly and ran smack into a busboy with a rack of clean glasses. He managed to hold on to them but bumped into the wall with a loud clattering of glass against metal. I pushed past him to the front room. The blood rushed in my ears like the noise of a waterfall. The normal restaurant sounds of voices and silverware against plates became a roar as I rushed away from the scene.

I had just neared our table and Carter had just looked up in surprise at my hasty return, when Rory grabbed me by the elbow and turned me to face him.

"Shelby, what on earth is the matter with you?" he demanded. "Didn't you hear me calling you?"

I took a deep, shaky breath. "No, I didn't," I said through bloodless lips. My face felt paralyzed with rage as I looked at his guileless expression.

"How long have you been here?" he asked.

I tried to still the quaking of my limbs. "Why? Are you afraid I might have seen something I shouldn't?" I asked stiffly.

He frowned. "What are you talking about? I just wanted to know. Why don't you come sit in the bar?"

"Wouldn't that cramp your style?" I asked acidly. This time he managed to notice I was angry. "I wouldn't want to upset your little blond friend's evening."

Rory rolled his eyes and I nearly punched him. "She's just a barfly, Shel. I was talking to her, that's all; a little harmless flirtation."

"With your lips all over her hand."

Rory chuckled indulgently. "Don't go getting jealous on me now, Shelby. Anything for a good tip, you know." He glanced at Carter with an uncomfortable back-me-up, male-bonding kind of look.

I seethed with the desire to shove my fist down his patronizing throat. "And how well did she tip you this morning?" I hissed.

Rory's eyes narrowed, but he didn't miss a beat. "This morning? What are you talking about?"

"I saw you. I saw you with her this morning in that alley, you ass. Your paws all over her—" I felt a lump consume my throat and blood burn my face.

He assumed an outraged expression. "Were you following me?" he demanded.

I laughed harshly in disbelief and forced myself to turn away and grab my purse and coat. But Rory swung me back. "Were you?"

"No!" I said indignantly, and loudly enough that a few heads turned our way. "But apparently I should have been. How many other girls have you slept with that I didn't know about, Rory?"

Rory blanched, and Carter rose from his seat as the noise in the room lessened noticeably at my rising volume.

"Let's go outside," Carter said in a quietly commanding tone. I saw him give Rory a cold stare that brooked no argument.

"I'm working," Rory said back.

I punched my arms into my coat sleeves and swung my purse onto my shoulder. "Yes, and you'd better get back to her."

"We'll talk about this later," Rory told me.

I stopped at the door. "No, we won't," I said with a glare that I felt could burn holes through lead. "I know what happened last night and that's all I need to know. I never want to see your lying, hypocritical face again."

Carter opened the door and I stalked out. Rory followed.

"Shelby, I don't know what you think you saw—" he began.

I whirled on him. "I'll tell you what I think I saw," I said. "I think I saw you leaving an apartment house downtown this morning at about seven-thirty. I think I saw a girl, with very little on, choking you with her tongue. And I think I saw your hand in her shirt while you promised to call her. *That's* what I think I saw, Rory. What do *you* think you *did?*"

Rory raked his hand through his hair and shook his head. "Shelby," he said. I stood before him breathing my anger out toward his face in white frosted clouds. "I can explain."

I raised my eyebrows and said nothing.

Rory glanced uncomfortably toward Carter, who leaned against a wall a few feet away. Rory rubbed his hands together in the cold.

"Go on, Rory, explain," I said. "This is your last chance, because after this I'm going home and changing all the locks on the house."

Rory sighed in exasperation. "Don't you think there's a better time and place for this?" He shivered lightly.

"Just tell me this, Rory," I said. "Did you, or did you not, sleep with that bimbo last night?"

Rory looked heavenward. "Yes, I *slept* with her, but—"

"Did you *have sex* with her?" I demanded. He wasn't going to weasel out of this with semantics.

"You know, Shelby, this all strikes me as pretty ironic considering you've had *this* guy," he flung an irate hand toward Carter, "sleeping in your house for two weeks. How do you think that makes me feel?"

I glared at him in amazement. "I don't care how it makes you feel, Rory. Carter's been in the *guest room,* remember? I don't have to sleep with everyone *I* meet."

Rory nodded with great sarcasm. "And how do I know that? How do I know you're not taking him to bed every night, just the two of you alone in that house?"

"Because I just told you, that's how. Are you going to tell me you didn't have sex with that girl last night?"

Rory gave me a withering glare. I felt my knees go weak with the anger in it. "You don't trust me," he said. It was the first moment that doubt crept into my mind. His eyes glittered angrily, meeting mine squarely.

"Apparently not," I said. Could I have possibly been wrong? He was so thoroughly angry, and I thought I could see in his eyes the betrayal he felt at my suspicion.

Rory shook his head and turned partly away with a short laugh. "After all these years, Shelby. You'd think we would know each other better than this after all these years." He glanced back at me, his eyes a liquid blue, looking toward me but seeing something else, perhaps a time when we trusted one another, a time when I wouldn't have questioned him this way.

Out of the corner of my eye I saw Carter stiffen, straightening up from his casual lean against the building.

Rory turned back and approached me. His hands took my upper arms in a light, warm grip. "Shelby, you know how I feel about you. How could you think anyone could mean as much to me?''

I felt confusion weaken my anger. ''That doesn't answer my question, Rory.'' I looked up at him and felt tears sting my eyes. ''Did you make love to her?''

His dark hair had fallen against his brow and the expression in his eyes was enough to melt ice. ''No,'' he said softly. ''No, I didn't. I wouldn't do that.''

''But what about this morning? You slept there, right?''

Rory's smile was warm, consoling. ''Yes, because I didn't want to drive home. And, to be honest, I was a little angry at you because of him.'' He jerked his head in Carter's direction. ''She offered me her floor.''

''And that was just a kiss of gratitude I saw this morning?''

Slight color pinkened Rory's cheeks; was it just from the cold? ''Well, you know. . . . She'd wanted more and I felt, you know, I couldn't just insult her. It was just a kiss.''

''Just a kiss and a thank-you grope for good measure?''

Rory's face stiffened. ''It didn't mean anything.''

I didn't believe him. I saw again his hand ride up that girl's rib cage to squeeze her breast with a familiarity that could only come from having known the whole body intimately. ''You're lying,'' I said, seeing him with sudden, perfect clarity. ''You not only slept with her, now you're lying about it. You're a whore, Rory. How big of a tip did you expect she'd leave you tonight? More than last night?''

Rory's grip tightened on my arms. ''Shelby . . .''

''Let go of me, you lying dog. You've made a mockery of this whole relationship *after all these years,*'' I mimicked cruelly.

His fingers dug into my arms and he shook me. "Shelby!"

"How many other women have there been, Rory? How many barflies have you found yourself in bed with when you just weren't in the mood for me?" Tears rolled over my lashes and down my face, and my mouth twisted with the words that wouldn't stop. "How many times have you lied this smoothly to me after some sleazy night with a cheap lay?"

Carter came up behind me. "Shelby, let's go," he said quietly.

Rory's hands tensed again on my arms. "You stay out of this, Lindsey. This is between Shelby and me."

Raw emotion bubbled up inside me, and I couldn't control the sobs that broke from me.

"Enough is enough," Carter said, pulling me from Rory's grasp.

I turned and buried my sobbing face into Carter's chest. I felt his arms close protectively around me.

"This doesn't concern you," I heard Rory say between gritted teeth. "Shelby, look at me," he ordered.

I turned my face to him, tear-streaked and puffy. "The truth, Rory—just tell me the truth about that girl. Surely you can do that."

His jaw clenched and unclenched. "All right," he said finally. "I slept with her. But I can explain why."

My eyes narrowed and a coldness descended in my gut. "And how many others?"

His hand raked through his hair again. "None, I swear," he said, too quickly.

I shook my head at him with disgust. "Bastard."

I pulled myself from Carter's arms and walked away. I heard Rory start to follow and then Carter's calm voice. "Leave it be."

I glanced behind me in time to see Rory's fist move with lightning speed. He caught Carter squarely in the jaw with a right that would have sent a lesser man to his knees. Carter's head snapped to the side, but he didn't stumble.

"Rory!" I yelled in complete amazement, running back toward the two of them.

Carter moved his head back slowly, gazed at Rory for a minute, and began to turn away. My own hands balled into fists at my sides as I stopped. Carter's eyes met mine, and I was shocked by the cold fury I saw in them.

"Go on home with him, then, Shelby," Rory's voice taunted. "You're not so lily-white yourself. You can't tell me there's nothing going on between you."

At that Carter stopped in his tracks. Then, with a natural grace borne of coiled rage, he swung back around, planted his feet, and sent Rory to the ground with one well-placed punch to the jaw.

Chapter Ten

I stood frozen as Rory crumpled to the pavement. He
landed with a loud *whuff* and lay deathly still for a long
moment before he lifted himself heavily onto one elbow.
I was intensely relieved to see him move; as far as I was
concerned, there had been enough force behind that blow
to have killed him. He shook his head a couple of times
and blinked his eyes, as if to regain his bearings.

Paralyzed by the scene, I could only look from one to
the other of them in bewildered silence. I would have
thought I'd have been more immune to this kind of physical violence after being raised on television and movies.
But though only two punches had been thrown, the very
real sound of flesh meeting angry flesh was far more
disturbing than any prerecorded blows.

Carter unconsciously rubbed his fist as he stood watching Rory.

"You *take* too much," he said quietly to the dazed
man below him.

Rory rubbed a hand along his jaw. "I should kill you," he snarled, but he made no move to rise.

Carter turned and walked slowly back to me. There was a red welt along his jaw and his lips were pressed in an angry line. He stopped before me, his eyes hard, uncompromising.

"Do what you want, Shelby," he said. "But make sure it's what *you* want." Then he brushed past me.

I turned and watched him walk down the sidewalk, hands in his coat pockets, his stride long and composed. I thought about the look on his face when he'd come to pick me up at the store, his lighthearted confidence after a day of work and a day's pay. His pleasure at being able to take me out had been genuine, the first of its kind I'd seen in him.

I looked back at Rory, who had stood up and now watched me watching Carter. His handsome face, with those quick eyes and sensuous mouth, so dear to me for so long, now struck me as blatantly dishonest. His expression was thoughtful, slightly calculating, and wary of my next move.

With a blast of music and warm smoky air, a waitress burst from the front door of the bar. "There you are! We've been looking all over for you! Are you working or not?" she demanded of Rory.

Rory shot her an irritated look. A bruise was already developing on his jaw. "I'll be right in," he said shortly.

The waitress looked from one to the other of us and shrugged. "Well, you'd better hurry. Richard is *pissed*." She disappeared back inside.

Rory cleared his throat. "I'm sorry about Rachel," he said.

I felt my stomach knot again. "Who's that? The blond?"

He took a deep breath and nodded. "It's just that guy, that Lindsey, he really *gets* to me." His anger rose again with the words. His hands clenched into fists as he spoke.

I shook my head. "Don't blame this on Carter."

"Why not?" Rory boomed. "He's the reason I didn't go to your house last night." He thrust his hands out to me, palms up, in an aggressively supplicating way. "It was revenge! I was jealous. And even if you're not sleeping with him, the amount of time you spend together—you see him more than you see me."

I snorted in disbelief. "Come on, Rory. Whose fault is that? You pop in and out of my life whenever you damn well please. If you had wanted to see me more, you would have. It just never occurred to you until Carter came along."

Rory obstinately pressed his lips together and shook his head.

"Rory, last night meant nothing to you. I know that. And the next girl will probably mean nothing to you either. But it means a hell of a lot to me, and you've known that all along. You just didn't care."

He shifted his weight and pushed his hands into his tight jeans pockets. "What the hell is all that supposed to mean?" he asked angrily.

I gazed at him for a moment, anger at his stupid false bravado and his selfish pride welling up inside me. "It means," I began slowly, "that if I could have, it would have been me throwing that punch just now. It's over with us, Rory. I can see now what I couldn't—or wouldn't—see for years. You're a liar. I don't *ever* want to see you again." I turned on my heel and walked steadily away.

Behind me I heard the door burst open again and the waitress's voice: "Rory, are you coming or not?"

I broke into a run, slowly at first, then quickening my pace. My hair slapped the back of my coat as my feet moved faster, the cold air chilling my ears and freezing my lungs. It felt good to move, to flee, to leave Rory behind. I didn't run for fear he would catch me; I knew he wouldn't follow me. I ran for myself, to make the physical statement of departure, to burn into my muscles and lungs the distance between us.

I caught up with Carter near the train station. He turned at the sound of my running feet on the sidewalk. I stopped in front of him, breathing heavily. The freezing air burned my throat and my cheeks stung with cold and drying tears.

"I'm sorry," I exhaled. "I'm sorry he ruined our evening." My coat squeaked quietly against itself as my chest heaved up and down.

Carter's face was impassive, his stance relaxed. "You caught him with another woman," he said.

I nodded. "Yes."

Carter studied me, then raised a hand from his pocket and rubbed his thumb down my tear-streaked face, his fingers lightly cupping my cheek. I squeezed my eyes shut and pressed my cheek into his palm, feeling tears drip through my lashes.

"I'm sorry," I said again, though I didn't know why.

I opened my eyes and Carter shook his head. His fingers tightened slightly on my cheek, then slid to my neck and buried themselves in my hair. He stepped forward, his other hand emerging from his pocket and pulling our bodies close.

I heard a train in the distance, its whistle signaling the station of its imminent arrival. Cars hummed past us on Lafayette Boulevard and the wind blew around us, not daring to come between our closely joined bodies.

Above me, Carter's eyes were compelling, and I was breathless now only in part because of my run. "I'm glad of it, Shelby," he said, a rueful half smile on his lips. "God help me, but I'm glad he's done it."

Then his lips descended on mine. I inhaled sharply,

involuntarily, as his mouth brushed mine, once, twice, before his tongue traced my lips.

My hands lifted of their own volition and grasped the sides of his coat, pulling him closer. As if taking the movement for permission, his mouth closed roughly on mine and my lips opened beneath his. My heart rose to my throat as our tongues met, impatiently tangling in a whirlwind of pent-up emotion.

His kiss was aggressive, his arms powerful, and something inside me met his strength with equal force. It was a meeting of spirits that seemed to recognize each other, spirits that combined into a tempest of desire.

My heart pumped wildly in my chest as the train thundered into the station, bells clanging and lights flashing. Beneath us, the ground shuddered.

He pulled me closer, making me feel tiny and powerless, yet protected and cherished. I raised my arms to his neck and held his head in my hands, my fingers buried in hair that was as soft as it was thick.

The night air frosted around us and our breathing became ragged and fierce. The kiss deepened. Never had I felt such a tornado of emotion and desire. I wanted my body to melt into his, my mind and being to become one with the intense, vital spirit that lurked in his eyes.

Just when I thought the exhilaration might consume me he pulled back. My breath came out in rapid gasps. He kept his eyes closed for a moment, as if to regain control, the thick flaxen lashes brushing his cheeks, and then he opened them. The heavy-lidded gaze burned with every emotion I felt churning inside myself, making me feel I could dive right into their depths, never to resurface.

He said nothing but watched me with an inscrutable intensity, his own breathing rapid.

"Carter," I whispered, every ounce of desire I possessed charging the word. I felt my own gaze trapped in his, as if our souls had transferred something at the contact.

He leaned forward slowly and kissed me again, soundly, then rested his forehead against mine. I closed my eyes, inhaling the scent of him, the warm, clean, masculine essence of him mingled with the leather of his coat and the cotton of his shirt.

His hands found my waist and squeezed with some sort of tempered frustration, lifting me off my feet. Then he lowered me gently and his arms slid round me again.

I clung to his shoulders, my cheek against his chest. "Promise me you won't leave me," I whispered. "I'm so afraid you'll go back."

His arms tightened and he exhaled. "I know," he said softly. "I know you're afraid." His head turned and he kissed my forehead. His hand rubbed my back through my coat.

I felt tears sting my eyes again. Was he thinking of her, of his wife?

"I don't want to leave you, Shelby," he said then, quietly.

I laughed, a sound that was half a sob. "Good," I said with a smile. "That's good."

"There's someplace we have to go," I said to Carter as we walked back to the house.

His hand held mine in the pocket of his coat. "Where's that?"

I glanced at him out of the corner of my eye. "You might think it's a little strange, but I think it could help us. Rather, *she* could help us."

He looked at me as we walked. "She?"

"A strange little woman I met. Madam Erika." I nearly laughed as I said the name, it sounded so dramatic. "She's a psychic. And I think, as weird as everything has been, maybe she could help us sort things out. She

seemed to know a lot about me the last time I saw her.''
I frowned, remembering her statements about my pervasive angst and the oppressive relationship in my life.
Were those the sort of things psychics said that applied
to everyone? For everyone else's sake, I hoped not.

Carter's thumb rubbed the back of my hand in his
pocket. "What's a psychic?"

I searched for a similar term that might have been used
a 150 years ago. "A witch, I guess." He stopped, drew
back, and gave me a disturbed look. "Well, not really a
witch. More like a seer, or a prophet, of sorts. Someone
who's in touch with spirituality."

"How do you know she's a witch?" he asked.

"She's *not* a witch," I corrected, wondering how on
earth to describe something as nebulous as the feeling I
had about the woman. "She's more like—oh, I don't
know." He was looking at me so strangely, I felt com-
pelled to add, "Of course there are no such things as
witches, but—there's just something about her . . ."

He cocked his head and looked at me with narrowed
eyes. "You don't believe in witches?"

What was he getting at? "No, of course not. Well," I
reconsidered, "I suppose anything's possible—"

"So you don't consider yourself a witch, for exam-
ple."

The statement took me by such surprise, I burst out
laughing. "*Me?* A witch? *You're* the one who traveled
through time!"

A smiled tugged at his lips, then a reluctant chuckle
escaped him.

"What is it? Why did you ask me that?" I asked,
bemused.

He shook his head, laughing a bit more to himself, and
started walking again.

"Nothing, no reason." He had relaxed again. "So
we're to see this woman, this person with a crystal ball,

perhaps?'' I could hear the smile still in his voice. ''This person who can tell us our future, or maybe our past? Who can look into our hands and tell us how long we shall live and how many children we'll have?''

The idea of us having children at all filled me with a flush of pleasure. Suppose she did see that sort of future for us? Would I allow myself to hope that he'd stay? Would I ever be able to relax about his coming home night after night, without suffering the anxiety I'd felt the night he'd been late?

''I don't know about that,'' I said. ''I just thought maybe she'd be able to see something that might give us a clue as to why you're here.'' *And if you're really here from another time,* I did not add. Sometimes I found myself wishing he *were* crazy. At least that way I wouldn't have to worry about him disappearing somewhere I couldn't follow, back to some other time.

Carter's voice was casually skeptical. ''You think she'll be able to divine God's will? A gypsy?''

''Why not? God doesn't speak to gypsies?'' One of my favorite topics of debate was the convenient way different people's gods approved and disapproved of the very things they themselves admired and deplored. But I hesitated to get into that with someone who was most likely raised in a more devout environment than I had been. ''Who's to say that odd things aren't possibly happening to other people as well as you? Maybe she's seen it before. Maybe she knows how it happened.''

''Maybe she'll tell me how to go back,'' he said, without looking at me.

I stepped over a puddle and said, as casually as possible, ''Or how not to.''

I felt him turn to me, but I didn't return the look. ''And anyway,'' I continued, ''it was kind of fun having her tell me about my future, even though I didn't really understand a lot of it.''

"What did she say about it?"

I tried to remember. "Something about chariots and hanged men. Didn't sound great to me, but she seemed to think it was positive."

"Chariots and hanged men," he murmured. "Maybe you've done a little traveling through time yourself."

I chuckled at that. "No, she seemed to think those were things I could achieve."

Carter laughed. "Then I shall have to watch my step. I didn't come through a war to be hanged by a woman." He thought a moment. "At least I hope I didn't."

I regarded him sourly. "Keep with these subtly disparaging comments about women and you'll be hanged by more than one."

He chuckled under his breath. "You oughtn't leave that nerve so exposed," he said with a smile. "The temptation to toy with it is sometimes more than I can resist."

We walked on. "So will you go with me?" I asked.

"I don't know," he drawled. "You think she'll be able to tell I'm nearly a hundred and sixty years old?" Sarcasm laced his voice. "It's not something I'd like bandied about."

I shot him a dry look. "For one who claims to have traveled through time, you're not giving this idea much of a chance." Immediately upon my words I felt him tense.

"What? What did I say?" I asked quickly. I could see a muscle work in his jaw.

He said nothing for a minute, then drew in a thin breath. "You still don't believe me," he said with barely suppressed emotion. "You think I am deranged." He stopped and turned to me, loosing our hands into the cold air. "Or you think I'm a liar."

"That's not true!" I protested. "I *know* you're not lying—"

His lips twisted. "But I could be deranged."

"Carter, no!" I was unsure what to say next. He could be mistaken, confused, deluded . . . all of those things would be unacceptable to him, and for some reason I didn't want to convince him of my doubt.

He stood seething for a moment; then he grabbed my hand. "Come with me," he said.

"Where are we going?" I asked in moderate alarm. The determined look on his face told me I'd hit an exposed nerve myself, but not one I could gloss over with a well-placed joke.

We traipsed past my house and up the street to Spotswood. From there we cut through an empty lot and up two more blocks to Sunken Road. We were both puffing after the silent, hasty walk to the battlefield, and he didn't stop until we were at the Widow Stevens's well, the very place I'd been sitting the night I'd found him.

He nearly flung my hand at me as he sat me on the deck of the well and turned away, searching the ground for something. He strode several yards away before turning back to me, pausing to look up at the stars.

"It was about here, wasn't it?" he demanded in a tight voice.

"What?" I asked, knowing what he asked but confused by his actions.

"That night." He shoved one hand in his jeans pocket and pointed the other at the spot on the ground. "This is where I was."

I nodded. "That's right."

He paced over to me and pinned me with a steely glare. "I want to tell you something, Shelby. I want to tell you how it was. I want to tell you what it was like to hear the roar of nearly two hundred cannon and the small but threatening whine of shot and shell sailing past my head." As he spoke his hands moved to illustrate, his anger etched in the short, choppy movements. "It was our third day of fighting, the third day of smoke and noise and blood, the third day of wondering what Burnside wanted of us and what Lee expected." He gazed up at the hill beyond the stone wall. "You've no idea the tension that accompanies uncertainty until you know that death rests with the wrong decision. And to have no control over the decision is something else again."

I watched as his eyes glazed over with memory, no longer seeing the mature oak behind me, the carefully maintained lawn, the restored stone wall. The tormented expression on his face told me he saw something completely different than the peaceful little park at the end of Mercer Street.

He stalked several paces to my right and circled a spot, looking down at the grass. "Peterson lay here," he said in an eerily low voice. "His blood was spilling onto the broken, brown earth. There was far too much of it to allow for any life to remain in his body." Carter shook his head solemnly. "He was a friend of mine. We'd come through second Bull Run together. And Fair Oaks. He'd just received a letter from his wife. . . . " His eyes clouded. "Not much news," he reflected softly, "just the goings on of the town. . . . "

He looked up again, this time to Marye's Heights and the university president's house. Only it was Confederate artillery he saw, I was sure, and not the stately, manicured mansion on the hill. "Some said it was murder, not warfare, to send us onto this plain," he continued. "Wave after wave of us, until it became difficult to walk for all the fallen bodies. You could see holes form in our ranks as the rebel shells fell, sweeping away lives as if clearing the dinner table of crumbs." His head shook, his haunted eyes dropping to stare vacantly at the ground.

"I was hit toward the end of the fighting and, God help me, I was glad—glad I would die and be spared the memory of that hideous day. But instead of death, or even unconsciousness, I lay relentlessly awake as night fell, listening to the appalling, inhuman moans that rose around me like the vapors of hell. It was like an orchestra of warped voices heralding death.

"Men begged for water, for help, for death, hopelessly. Some delirious voices spoke—dreamily—lovingly—to people who weren't there. Others merely ground their teeth and moaned. And all the while the temperature dropped and a stiff wind blew over and past us."

He took a deep breath and shoved his previously animated hands into his pockets. He bent back his head and gazed at the stars. "I'd lost consciousness and come to several times; but the last time I awakened I thought sure that death was near. I remember lying on my back, looking at a nearby sapling and wondering if I would ever see it grow to maturity, or if instead my blood would nourish the earth where it grew—and no more. Then, beyond the tips of its uppermost branches, I became aware of a fire blazing in the heavens—the likes of which I'd never seen. A meteoric display hovering over the field—it was magical."

"The Northern Lights," I murmured. I remembered then, reading about how one of the only times the Northern Lights had been visible so far south was the evening of that battle. The South had taken the appearance as a heavenly sign of their victory . . . while the North had buried their dead by its light.

"Yes," Carter said, nodding. His eyes focused lucidly on me for the first time since his recital had begun. "And as I stared at the display—in absolute terror and wonder—I felt a sort of shift. Not physical, not to begin with, though it was from outside of me that I felt it. But a kind of awareness came to me, a difference in the air, the light, the silence. Then I felt the ground move slightly beneath me, the way sand shifts beneath a bare foot, and I knew that I didn't lie on the hard, bloody earth of the plain

183

any longer. And above me swayed the thick, strong branches of a full-grown tree. So I sat up . . . and I saw you."

I shivered under the cold night sky. Carter's expression was profound, consuming. I felt myself drawn to my feet. In his eyes I could see the haunted remains of the soldier who had trod the broken bodies of his comrades to fulfill a destiny. In his stance I could imagine the sheer physical bravery it had taken to move one foot in front of the other while harbingers of death whistled and whined past him, plucking souls from the living on both sides of him.

As I neared him I saw the tears that clung to his lashes and streaked his face. I saw before me a man who had lived with a memory he'd sought death to avoid. I saw in him the strength of a survivor mingled with the weakness of fear and horror. But it was his strength that had won, both on that day and now, both in war and in trauma. How had he possibly survived that kind of nightmare, only to be transported to another, perhaps more terrifying, time?

"I wanted it, Shelby," he said then, as if reading my mind. "I wanted to be as far away from that scene as the fates could possibly allow. I begged for it, prayed for it, offered to sell my soul for it. If there was a God in heaven, or a Satan in hell, I wanted deliverance from that scene of torture. And whether I willed it, or whether it was conferred upon me from a higher being—I *thank God* that I'm here, with every second of every day that I draw breath."

Chapter Eleven

The idea that Carter wanted to be here, actually enjoyed being here, was one that hadn't occurred to me before. I guess I had assumed that any sort of displacement would naturally be negative. But when juxtaposed with living through a barbarously bloody war, after seeing nearly everyone you knew or became close to blown away, frequently while they stood beside you, I could see where traveling into a future bereft of such sadness would hold great appeal.

The hope that I felt when he told me this, however, was frightening. How could I have come to want him to stay so badly in such a short time? And the fact that he was glad he was here did not necessarily mean he wanted to stay. What about his feelings for the life and the people—namely, his wife—that he'd left behind? How could he be happy having just disappeared from all who might have loved him back then? And what made me think he even had the choice to stay or to leave?

I knew that Carter wasn't the sort of man to provoke casual dalliances with women, nor was he the type to cheat on a wife. Was it something between us or between them that had him on the verge of compromising that relationship now? And how could I allow it after the hurt that had just been inflicted on me by Rory?

I conjured up the picture Carter carried of Meg Lindsey and wondered again if she were as severe and humorless as she had looked. But then, when had I ever seen one of those old tintype photographs in which the person looked anything but severe and humorless?

The puzzles were too complex for me to figure, so the following morning I called Madam Erika and set up an appointment with her for Carter and me. She said we were lucky; we could see her that very evening. She had to squeeze us in before Christmas, because after the holiday she would be busy with all the people who had received gift certificates for her services. That made me smile. I wondered what a gift certificate for Madam Erika would look like. And who would think of a gift certificate for a psychic as a Christmas present?

Carter met me at the store after work wearing a new shirt, a simple white cotton buttondown that complemented his naturally honey-colored complexion and looked great with the rapidly fading blue jeans. Mr. Malone, of Green Way Landscaping, was paying him daily, in cash, so neither of them would be obligated to pay taxes. This was fortunate, I thought, because Carter had no social security number and would thus be unemployable in any sort of regular position. With his newfound wealth Carter was careful but generous. The shirt was the first thing he'd bought for himself with the money.

"You're looking dapper." I smiled as he walked toward me in the back of the store.

"Just hoping to impress the gypsies," he said.

Sylvie's ears pricked at the sound of Carter's voice,

and her head whipped in his direction from where she stood at the shelves. "Hi!" she called, waving to him over a cart full of books.

Carter glanced at her and nodded once. "Hello," he said amiably. Sylvie waved again, blushed, and pushed the cart aside to come over.

I smiled grimly. I hadn't told Sylvie anything about the situation with Rory, nor how my relationship with Carter appeared to be changing. We talked a lot but weren't that close. In fact, if I could have gotten away with never mentioning Rory again to anyone, if he could have just melted soundlessly out of my life, I would have been happy. It was humiliating, and maddening, to have to think about it all again. And my emotions for Carter were too young and tender, too threatened by what might happen in the future, to bear talking about either.

So Sylvie had set her sights on Carter. Crazy or no, she found him attractive and didn't care who he thought he was. This was pretty much true of all the men Sylvie chose to pursue, and more often than not it was a policy that failed her.

I only had enough time to whisper, "Be careful," to Carter with a sly grin before Sylvie was upon us. Or rather, upon him. Carter had just turned a questioning gaze on me when she latched onto his arm.

"Hi! How are you feeling?" she asked buoyantly.

Carter stepped back self-consciously. "Fine. I'm doing fine. And you?"

"Oh just great. Hey, I missed you guys the other night. I heard you were at the Windsor Tavern!" she bubbled.

Carter tensed. "Last night."

"Was it only last night?" She giggled. "I guess it was! I had such a good time I don't even remember. Anyway, you guys were there, right? Rory told me I just missed you." Then she added more thoughtfully, "And boy, was he in a foul mood."

I felt a wicked smile creep across my lips as Carter shot me a quelling glance. He didn't like losing his temper and didn't want to be reminded of it now.

"We really don't have much time, Sylvie," I said, to stop her from getting on a roll. "We've got an appointment in fifteen minutes, so why don't you go ahead and pack up."

"Oh." Her face fell. "I was hoping maybe you guys were going out. But if you're busy, Shelby, maybe I could meet Carter somewhere later. Just a beer or two?" She looked pleadingly at Carter, and some evil being inside me kept quiet to give him either the chance to accept if he wanted to or the obligation to turn her down if he didn't.

He glanced at me, then narrowed his eyes. I should have known he'd see right through my little strategy. It wasn't that I thought he was gutless or anything; I just wanted to be sure that if he didn't want a female's attention, he knew what to do to be rid of it. I was doing this as much to be sure he actually wanted *my* attention as to know he didn't want *hers*.

"Thank you, no," he said flatly, with a calm, tempering smile.

I'd thought he might add an excuse or something to soften the blow, but he left it at that, and an awkward silence ensued.

Sylvie hesitated. "Well, maybe some other time," she said. "Tomorrow or after Christmas?"

"I think not," Carter said gently.

This was a bit much for me. I was the type to go on and on about how busy I was and how completely impossible it would be to get together however much I would like to, thus leaving the door wide open for the person to badger me into going out at some other time.

Carter's approach, while more effective, was distinctly uncomfortable.

Sylvie looked taken aback, then embarrassed, then annoyed.

"We'd really better go if we want to be there on time," I said into the silence. "Sylvie, would you mind locking up?"

She looked at me, eyes flashing, her face red. "No. That's fine." She walked back toward the stairs to the office. "I'll just get my things. You two have a nice time."

I watched her go, feeling guilty for something. "Yeah, thanks," I called to her retreating back. "See you tomorrow." There was no answer as we heard her clump up the back steps. I turned back to Carter. "Well, so much for that."

He lifted a brow. "Did you want to meet her?"

I grabbed my coat and purse from the counter and pulled on the coat. "No, no. I just—she seems lonely, that's all."

"You think she'll be less lonely with us?" he asked patiently, as if quizzing a small child.

I thought about this for a moment. Nothing was worse than being a third wheel. "I guess not. But I thought you could have been a little more gentle with her, instead of just shooting her down like that." We moved toward the front door.

Carter pulled the door open and stepped back for me to precede him. "That never works," he said dismissively.

I stepped out and stopped at the bottom of the stairs, looking up. "And how is it that you know so much about it?"

"Because I've been on both the giving and the receiving end of that sort of behavior, and it doesn't work for either. Where are we going?" he asked as he stood at the top of the stoop, gazing down the street.

"This way." I started up Caroline Street and he fell

in beside me. "I feel like I should warn you about this woman, the psychic. She's a little—strange. You may think she's just a nut, and maybe she is just a nut, but she has an aura about her that makes me want to believe her."

"An aura?"

"Yes, there's a feeling I get from her. She projects an air of knowledge, or perception." I waved to the shop-keeper of the place next to mine, which sold nothing but pigs—stuffed, ceramic, and papier-mâché, pig teapots, pig oven mitts, pig salt and pepper shakers . . . your basic pig paraphernalia store. "Anyway, it'll be interesting if nothing else."

I noticed Carter's eyes trailing the pig store as we passed. "Did you want something?" I asked dryly.

He shook his head. "I've never seen so much useless merchandise in my life as I have in this town. Do people really buy things like that?"

We cut up the alley across from the Ben Franklin five and dime. "They must. She's been in that shop longer than I've had mine. But this town isn't any worse than anywhere else for that sort of thing. In fact, it might be better than most places. It's just that we've become a very materialistic society. Something to do with capital-ism and the idea of money being synonymous with suc-cess."

"Is that true? Is that what people think now?" Carter asked in all seriousness.

I smiled wanly. "Oh, I don't know. That's what the cynics will tell you. I suppose a lot of people tend to equate wealth with greatness, but not everyone."

As we came into the part of the alley near the apart-ment building, I felt my stomach begin to curl. My eyes stole over to the door with the bright orange EXIT ONLY painted on it. It was closed, hiding its sleazy secrets be-hind a dirty gray exterior.

Carter's attention was centered on the neon hand in Madam Erika's window. "So we *are* to have our palms read!" He laughed. He opened his hands in front of him and looked at them. "I'm glad I washed them."

I shushed him and started up the stairs. Before we had made it halfway up the short flight, Madam Erika opened the door. I turned and whispered, wide-eyed, to Carter, "She *knew* we were here!"

"Of course," he murmured.

Madam Erika stood in the doorway wearing a floor-length black, kimonolike dress, with long gold earrings and many, many rings on her fingers. "Welcome," she said in her curiously accented voice, wiggling a jewel-laden hand for us to enter. "Do come in."

"Thank you," I said, and walked into the laundry room again. I stopped awkwardly next to the washer, thinking she would lead us into the other room, and we all found ourselves pushed into the little space between the door and the dryer as Carter entered and Madam Erika closed the back door.

"Go on, go on," she ordered brusquely, brushing us forward with her hands as the door slammed. "You know the way."

I moved forward into the dark red room with its black floor and lacquered table. This time the smell of incense was overwhelming, and I could see little chimneys of smoke curling upward from various spots around the room. Very soft, discordant music tinkled down from hidden speakers above our heads.

Carter gazed around himself with an expression on his face that was somewhere between skepticism and amusement.

"Sit, sit," Madam Erika chirped shrilly behind us. Carter pulled out a chair and sat, an educated Pennsylvania farmer in the den of an eccentric Czechoslovakian gypsy.

I sat beside him, and Madam Erika sat across from us. There was an awkward silence.

"We actually had some specific quest—"

She stopped me with a sharply raised hand. At first she studied us both, then she concentrated on Carter.

Then she extended a bony finger toward Carter, bangle bracelets jangling on her wrist, and said ominously, "YOU." Carter recoiled slightly. "You are very interesting to me." Her words were slow and deliberate, sending a chill up my spine. Then she added crisply, "Let me see your hand."

Carter unfolded his fingers and lay his hand flat on the table. She took it firmly in hers and pulled the fingers back gently, laying his palm open wide. Her brow puckered as she peered into it in a nearsighted way. Then she closed her eyes and placed her own palm on top of his.

He looked at me slyly out of the corner of his eye, his lips slightly quirked. I could tell he took none of it seriously, but her actions intrigued me. I had told her nothing of Carter's alleged past. In fact, I had not even told her his name—just that I wanted to see her again and to bring a friend who needed some advice.

Time lengthened as Madam Erika sat holding Carter's hand. The strange music seemed to get louder, or maybe it was just that we had become so still. I thought I heard a clock ticking somewhere and wondered what lay beyond the door partially covered by the hanging rug.

"Descend . . ." Madam Erika murmured into the spirit-filled air. "Your family is muddled and gray. . . . " Then she muttered, "Ignorant imposters."

I started at this. Was she saying Carter was an imposter? I glanced furtively at him; his brows were drawn together in a frown.

Madam Erika opened her eyes and took a moment to focus them. Then she peered again into his palm. "You see this," she poked him in the palm with a red nail.

"This line here where it is crossed by this one?"

Carter leaned forward and looked into his own hand.

"Here." Madam Erika stabbed again. "And here where this line starts again to go to . . . here." Her nail traced a path and punctuated it again with a poke.

"I see," Carter said.

"This is the life line. For you it is broken, and then it starts up again—here. *Very* unusual. Perhaps you will undergo a change, very significant, a trauma. Perhaps you will assume a new identity. You are not . . . in trouble with the law?" She raised a formidable brow.

Carter met her eyes. "No."

"Good. I don't like to help criminals escape." She patted his hand and held it. I could sense an anxiety in him to pull it back. "I am getting strong feeling from you. I feel there are others who share your name. Do you have children?"

Carter hesitated, and a strange expression crossed his features, one I could not read. "No, I don't."

Madam Erika's heavily madeup eyes narrowed. "Hmmmm. I feel someone close by. . . . Someone you would not think of, but who thinks of you." She closed her eyes again and tilted her head back. "You are far from home?"

"Yes." Carter's voice was short, choked with some emotion I could not name.

"Yes," she repeated slowly. "I feel that, a great distance." She opened her eyes, folded his fingers closed, and pushed the hand back toward him. "Now. We shall read your cards." She pulled a deck of tarot cards from a hidden drawer on her side of the table and pushed them toward him. "Shuffle until warm, then cut three times," she ordered.

He picked up the cards and shuffled them with surprising skill. Maybe he was a gambler to boot; the way he shuffled would have done any Vegas dealer proud. I wondered if there was such a thing as overheating the cards. Maybe Carter would burst into flame too.

He cut the cards and she picked them up. Laying them out in that strange pattern she had used with me, she nodded at some and murmured unintelligible words at others. Finally, she said, "Ahh, the Chariot. You are a very balanced person. You go into battle with the promise of victory."

Carter shot me a look, then glanced pointedly at the Chariot, shrugging. I held back a laugh.

"The Lovers," Madam Erika said then, shifting both of our attention immediately back to her. "This is a love between equals; it will bring much happiness and harmony to you." She passed a significant look from one to the other of us. I felt my face grow red. "This, with the cups, is a very good thing. But here I am concerned. You have these swords, a struggle. You must be careful." She shook her head. "I am surprised I don't see the Tower here. Because of your life line, you know. Perhaps you have already had this trauma in your life?" She raised questioning eyes to him.

"I have known change," Carter said guardedly. "And some tragedy, I suppose."

She studied him, leaning back in her chair. "This would be something very significant. You would know it as a defining moment, I believe. You have not felt this?"

Carter took a deep breath and studied her in return. "I have," he said finally.

She nodded in satisfaction. "This change," Madam Erika said darkly, "it affects not only you. Your life is drastically altered, altering many others in its path. You would do well to consider those others whose paths travel alongside yours."

"How many others?" he asked.

Madam Erika smiled with the confidence of one who

knows a secret. "More than you know, or would think of."

Carter's face took on a suddenly serious expression as something appeared to dawn on him. He leaned forward. "Madam," he said intently, with a great deal more seriousness than he'd demonstrated up to that point. He lay his hand open on the table between them. "Can you tell me, do you see children here? Is there a way you can tell me if this has happened to me?"

Madam Erika drew herself up in her chair and leaned over his hand again. "Yes. I see a child for you, *of you.*" She emphasized the last two words.

Carter drew his hand back and rolled it into a fist unconsciously. His face was an expressionless mask, drained of all color. "One last question," he said tightly. "Will I know this child? Will I be there to see it grow to adulthood?"

Madam Erika folded her bejeweled hands before her on the table. "You should, young man," she stated unequivocally. "You should."

"Carter, what is it?" I asked as we hastily left Madam Erika's. His face looked as if it had been set in stone, and he'd marched out of the room as if he'd just noticed the devil himself sitting in one of the armchairs. "What's the matter? I thought you weren't taking any of this seriously."

He stopped in the alley and turned to me. "Is there a way we can find out if I have any descendants?"

"Descendants?" I echoed hollowly. The thought hadn't occurred to me. But now, on the heels of his question about children, the whole picture dawned on me. I nearly groaned aloud. He'd left Meg pregnant.

I felt as if the wind had been knocked out of me. Madam Erika had said someone shared his name. Someone close by. The whole terrible truth seemed to hit me in waves. If he had descendants, he had to have had children. If he had children that he did not know about, then he must have left Meg pregnant. If he had left Meg pregnant, there was no way he could consider not going back, because a woman alone in the 1860s on a farm with an infant was as vulnerable as could be. Not to mention the fact that Carter would never abandon a child to grow up fatherless.

I felt my heart sink with a disappointment far greater than I would have anticipated, considering I still wasn't convinced I believed his story. "We could consult a genealogist," I said blankly. "Someone who traces family histories."

Carter nodded. "Could they tell us if there was someone nearby that I was related to?"

I shrugged, gazing at the ugly gray door. *Exit only.*

"I can look in the phone book to see if someone in town has your name," I said. It was something I'd planned all along and somehow kept forgetting to do. Maybe it had been some instinct on my part, some self-serving, self-preserving instinct that hadn't really wanted to find out where Carter belonged. I had the sinking feeling that the answers we sought weren't far beyond our reach. "We can go back to my shop and look at the phone book there right now."

As I opened the door to the darkened store I felt an ugly foreboding consume me. We would find his descendants and he would have to return. How, I did not know. But all his efforts would be concentrated on it, and my growing hopes of lasting happiness with Carter would be dashed.

We moved to the back of the store and I pulled out the phone book from beneath the counter. My hands shook as I flipped through the flimsy pages. *Lacey, Lederer, Lieberman, Linberg.* Carter leaned over my shoulder as my finger traced the column of names, finally coming to rest on *Lindsey, C. Bartlett*. There were two other entries, but both spelled their names *Lindsay*. There was no reason to believe that *C. Bartlett* was any relation to Carter, but I knew in my heart that he was.

I looked up at Carter's face to find him watching me. "Do you want me to call him?" I asked quietly.

Carter swallowed and nodded. "Yes," he answered firmly.

I hesitated for only an instant before pulling the phone toward me. I dialed the number. On the fourth ring a woman answered.

"Hello," I said, suddenly wishing I'd formulated a plan of what to say. "This might seem like a strange call, but, uh, my name is Shelby Manning and, um, and my— my husband and I were trying to trace his family history. We came upon your—I guess it would be your husband's name, in our studies, and then found him in the phone book. We wondered if he might be related. I don't know if he's into genealogy at all . . ."

I heard the woman shift the phone from one ear to the other as a baby cried in the background. "As a matter of fact," the woman said in a cheerful voice, "Bart's very interested in his family tree. He's had the whole thing done by a professional."

"Has he?" I tapped a pencil on the counter in front of me, avoiding Carter's eyes. "Well, we're just a couple of amateurs, but my husband has an old picture and a name he's been trying to trace back to—"

The baby cried louder, and the woman murmured something to it about knowing it was hungry. "I'm sorry," she said into the receiver. "I was just about to feed him, and he gets so angry when I'm distracted."

"I'm sorry. I don't want to interrupt," I said hastily.

"Nonsense! Bart's fascinated with this sort of thing. He'll be thrilled that you called." I heard the phone jostle against her shoulder as she moved, and a noise that sounded like a spoon against a bowl. "There now. His family was nothing if not a bunch of pack rats. He's got all sorts of junk up in the attic, family memorabilia and whatnot. I'm sure your husband would be interested in it. Something up there's bound to be able to help him trace his roots."

I felt my spirits sinking with every word that came out of her mouth. "You don't happen to know if your husband was related to a Carter Lindsey who fought in the Civil War, do you? We're mostly interested in that connection." I could feel Carter's eyes intent on my face, and I hoped he couldn't see the disappointment in me that grew with each word the woman spoke.

The woman chuckled. "I'd imagine so. Bart's first name is Carter."

My stomach dropped what had to be its final notch at those words. Couldn't she have been just a little *less* helpful? "How—how interesting," I said in a lackluster voice. "My husband's name is Carter Lindsey too."

That got her. I believe she actually stopped moving. "Good heavens, you're kidding. Right here in town?"

"Actually he's from Pennsylvania. Do—do you recall whether your husband's family came from Pennsylvania?"

"To tell you the truth, hon, I only listen to his ramblings on the subject with half an ear, but this is fascinating. I'd let you speak to him right now, but he's not home. Let me get your number so he can reach you." The baby squawked angrily.

I blinked rapidly to clear my welling eyes. I looked down at the counter so my hair would drape over my face, blocking any view Carter might have had of it. "Sure. Tell him we'd love to get together sometime and talk about it if he thinks he'd like to," I said, and gave her my phone number.

"I'm sure he'll be giving you a call," the woman said.

"He'd love to find some distant relative. He's an only child, you see, and always wished he had a brother or sister. I guess a cousin'd be almost the same thing."

"Almost," I echoed. But how would he feel about finding a great-grandfather?

Chapter Twelve

I had the creeps. For some indescribable reason, every bone in my body knew that C. Bartlett Lindsey would have some proof of Carter's existence in the past. In fact, C. Bartlett Lindsey's very existence proved that there had been a Carter Lindsey, and that he'd had a child. *A* Carter Lindsey, I groped, not necessarily mine. But I knew— and it was this knowledge that gave me the creeps—that we would find some proof, some confirmation of Carter's story that would seal our fates to live separately, in separate times.

Until that moment on the phone with Mrs. Lindsey, I don't think I realized how drastically confirmation of the time-travel idea might affect me, for I was sure I was being open-minded about the possibility. But after talking to Mrs. Lindsey and feeling that inexplicable wave of doom come over me, it was suddenly clear that I was clinging to the idea that Carter simply had some kind of delusionary amnesia, and that he would awaken from it at some point to clear up everything and make way for our lives to progress together. It would have been simpler even if he'd just had a wife and child somewhere in Pennsylvania that he couldn't remember. Instead, it seemed he remembered all too well that he had a wife somewhere in 1862. How much more insurmountable could circumstances have been?

I needed to learn how to take a hint—a large, cosmic hint, that is. I mean, if things happened for a reason, which most of the time I believed, I should have been ready to take this sign for what it was—a clearly negative answer to the question of a future with Carter. But if things happened for a reason, whether or not the impossible had taken place, the inevitable question remained: Why had he come, if we were not to be together? If this incredible, outlandish story turned out to be true, what was the point of this weird time displacement? And could I ever truly believe that he'd been transported through time?

I made a decision. The day before Christmas Eve, I gave myself a lunch hour and walked to the Rappahannock Regional Library. It was a huge collection, housed in an old, five-story brick schoolhouse, seven or eight blocks from my shop. The area being so rich in Civil War history, I was confident I could find materials on the battle of Fredericksburg.

Once inside, I stopped at the reference desk, was divested of my driver's license for security, and then directed to a back room and a spiral staircase. On the way down the perilously steep steps my purse caught on the railing and I tripped on the bottom step, stumbling awkwardly into the tiny, silent room, filled with yellowing books, pamphlets, papers, and bookish, irritated-looking people. I wondered if my sudden clumsiness might have been another one of those cosmic hints I was so good at ignoring—and I decided to ignore it.

After ambling gracefully to the back of the room I
turned to survey the shelves, not anxious to ask any of
the people I'd disturbed with my entrance, but unable to
fathom where to begin. In an effort to appear purposeful,
I studied some of the books on the nearest shelf. *The Life
and History of E. M. Spofford; Sociological Expression-
ism in the Early Colonies; Industrialism in the Mid-
Atlantic; Virginia: The Cotton Years.* I turned to look at
the shelves behind me. County journals for various years
lined the upper shelves, with the bottom ones loaded
down by a hodgepodge of yellowed papers, leatherbound books that said *Tax Records* in gold leaf, and
rolled, poster-sized documents that proved to be maps
upon further investigation. It was daunting.

One man, on whom I'd nearly landed when I arrived,
floated noiselessly toward me, his face a pinched mask
of disapproval partially obscured by thick, brown-rimmed
glasses. He had that kind of stringy, gray hair that's
parted way over on one side and drawn across the pate
to cover conspicuous baldness. He'd frowned in annoyance at me before, and I thought perhaps he was coming
to ask me my business, but he proceeded past me as if I
weren't even there. I had to step out of his way to avoid
being bumped. I turned to another set of shelves and tried
to appear engrossed in a study of the geographical terrain
of Virginia.

They were all so serious, all of the people in the room.
I couldn't possibly ask one of these scholars to help me
find proof of a man's existence in the 1860s because that
very man had mysteriously turned up in a park a couple
of weeks ago. Even if I didn't tell them the reason, my
own mind would rebel at the inquiry. Was I afraid of
proof that he *had* time-traveled, or proof that he hadn't?
I wasn't sure anymore.

I gazed at the shelves again. This was foolish. I looked
at my watch: forty-five minutes left before Sylvie and Ja-

ney called out the guard and had me dragged back by my hair. I had to ask someone. I weaved around the shelves and came to a broad table with microfiche monitors on it. This was even better. Seating myself at one of the monitors, I pulled out the translucent blue sheet of microfiche that would encompass the Civil War and inserted it, with some difficulty, onto the glass plate. I pushed gently on the handle to place it under the light, but it didn't budge. I pushed harder—it slid to the right. Gripping it with both hands, I pushed forward. With a loud *clap*, the glass shut and disappeared under the monitor. Words sprang onto the screen at the same moment that I craned my neck around quickly to see the stringy-haired man frowning at me again through the rim of his spectacles. I flushed and turned back to the screen.

The section on the Civil War was, predictably, huge. I located the Battle of Fredericksburg and wrote down some numbers on the scrap paper supplied. Then I stood and turned back to the shelves, prepared to ignore the stringy man, when my eye was caught by a rather large volume on the shelf in front of me, entitled *The Battle of Fredericksburg*. It was bound in leather and looked to be very old, with a cracked spine and frayed edges, but it clearly bore the number of one of the books I'd written down. I could have avoided the whole stupid microfiche machine if I'd just looked a little harder.

I pulled the book from the shelf and sat down again at the table. It was a very dry and technical account of the military maneuvers of the three-day campaign that took away much of the chilling horror and realism that came from hearing the same story as a personal account by one who'd lived through it. There was the occasional quote from an officer who'd been there, but even that was rendered so lifeless on paper that it hardly seemed the same event.

General James Longstreet purportedly said that the effects of the artillery "made gaps in the enemy's ranks that could be seen at the distance of a mile." This was direct confirmation of Carter's story, but it hardly conveyed the reality that living, breathing, flesh-and-blood men fell in shrieking anguish beside their friends, men who struggled hard to extinguish all feeling for life, and love, and humanity.

A Confederate officer named E. Porter Alexander had apparently boasted before the battle that, "A chicken could not live on that field when we open upon it." This bravado sickened me when I thought of Carter, his face tear-streaked and fierce, as he explained how he'd lain wounded just a short distance from a friend named Peterson and tried to gauge whether the blood his friend had lost was sufficient to kill him.

But those were the only two remotely interesting things I found in my casual glance through the text of the book. I continued to flip through the pages, past various charts, maps with large multicolored arrows, and lists of everything from previous battles to casualties, until I came to the end of the book, where I found the treasure I'd hoped for. There, in long columns of tiny print, were listed the troops, both North and South, that were present for the battle, along with the names of those who were captured, wounded, or killed. Jackpot.

I ran my finger down the pages until I found the Pennsylvania listings of troops present for the battle. My heart quickened in anticipation as I scanned the names. They were listed by brigade, a designation that meant nothing to me, so I went through each list individually. It wasn't until I was halfway through the extensive inventory that I remembered Carter had said he was with the 114th. I flipped two more pages.

He was there. Under *Regiments at the Battle of Fredericksburg.* The inside column on the left page. Lt. Carter Lindsey. Just below Lewis, just above Linwood. I ran my finger across the name. An odd chill ran down my spine. Lt. Carter Lindsey. He was real. He'd existed.

The odd feeling was ridiculous, I told myself, hugging my arms to my stomach and staring at the name. I already knew Carter Lindsey had existed from talking to Mrs. Lindsey. But somehow seeing the name in print was more affecting, more absolute.

I heaved a sigh and reasoned with myself. If I could research and find this information so easily, so could anyone. An overzealous reenactor could easily have picked the name Carter Lindsey, discovered his rank, and followed the troop movements for that regiment in an effort to be authentic. That's not to say my Carter was a liar, but if he had adopted a persona for the enactment, then suffered that blow to the head, he could have woken up believing he was actually that person. It was possible. I'd seen it happen in the movies.

I turned further back in the book and found a list of casualties at Fredericksburg. Again, it was an extensive list, with some names that were apparently unclear to the catalogers and typed merely as L—, or La—. These, I imagined, had come from identification tags that were illegible. I had read somewhere that before a battle men would scribble their names and addresses on slips of paper and pin them to the insides of their coats, to identify their bodies for their relatives in case they were killed. Many of these tags were undoubtedly ruined by whatever fatal wound had been inflicted.

Carter's name wasn't on that list. Unless he was one of the L—s, or one of the unknown men listed only by their rank, which could often be discerned by their uniform.

For some reason I was inordinately relieved that he wasn't listed among the dead. Why, I wasn't sure. It certainly wouldn't have changed the fact that he was here now.

I closed the book and leaned back in my chair. What else could I look for? He'd existed, but that proved nothing. Any pertinent, personal information probably wouldn't be available to me here in Virginia. Maybe I could drive up to Bucks County and look up family records; but even that would be information that anyone could have memorized.

As I rose with the book and returned it to the shelf, I saw the stringy-haired man staring at me. I frowned at him and gathered my purse. Did he think he owned the place? He was seated next to the spiral staircase, papers spread haphazardly across the tabletop, and I was determined to ignore him as I left, even though I had to pass right by him. But as I neared him he caught my eye with a gruesome smile. Thin, pointed lips spread across uneven teeth, revealing one in the front that was lined with silver.

I looked away quickly and trotted up the stairs. Why did people get those kinds of fillings for front teeth? I wondered. With all of the dental techniques on the market—

I stopped at the top of the stairs. Fillings! I could see if Carter had any fillings, or visible dental work of any kind. *That* would prove whether he was from the twentieth century. Elated at this thought, I tried to imagine other signs of the twentieth century that would have to be evident in him.

I already knew he hadn't had the benefit of any up-to-date surgery; the raw, uneven scars on his chest had testified to that. Other than that, though, the only things I could think of were so obvious as to be already eliminated—things such as glasses, contact lenses, and vaccination scars.

As I left the library and made my way down the steps to the sidewalk, I noticed a green van with large white lettering that said GREEN WAY LANDSCAPING parked across the street. It was beside the backyard of the house that Carter had called Mackey's Folly, a wide, terraced lawn that descended to the sidewalk on Caroline Street. Apparently the lawn had once swept all the way down to the river, which must have been a beautiful sight. Now it backed up to Caroline Street and the library.

Shading my eyes to the bright winter sunshine, I looked around the grounds for Carter, finally finding a knot of men around the base of a large tree on the far left side of the property. They all gazed up into the tree at another man, who stood far out on a thick branch with a saw on the end of a long pole. I knew at once that it was Carter. His gold hair shone in the sun and the strength of his posture, as he stood nimbly on the branch, was so distinct as to send a little thrill of pleasure down my spine. I crossed the street toward them.

"Up a little higher!" one of the men on the ground shouted up at him. "That's it, son. Just past that one with the squirreled end—yeah, right there."

Carter scooted slightly farther out on the branch and began to saw. He wore only a T-shirt on this chilly day, and I hoped it was because of the heat of exertion and not because it was all he could afford. The muscles in his arms stood out prominently as he strained upward with the pole. Strong shoulder and back muscles flexed as well as he deftly manipulated the saw, finally sending the offending branch down in a graceful spiral to the waiting men on the ground. Two of them took it to the shredder that stood nearby, while the third yelled further instructions up to Carter.

I turned and was about to continue on my way without disturbing him when I heard the familiar mellow voice call out my name.

I turned back to see him standing on the branch, waving the long pole in his right hand as though it weighed nothing. His grin was broad as he pushed his hair impatiently from his face.

"Come on up! I need some help!"

His companion on the ground grinned at me as well. "Naawww, she needs you to carry her up!" he contributed.

I smiled back and waved. "I'm a bit afraid of heights myself. But if you'd like to meet in a bush sometime, I'm available."

Carter and his companion laughed, the sound rich and harmonious. "That's an offer I'd take, son," the other man told Carter. "Unless you got one in the hand, a bird in the bush ain't so bad."

Carter pitched the saw down to the ground. "Hold up a minute, Shelby," he called, squatting on the branch to grasp it with his hands, then swinging deftly to the ground. "Be right back, Shaw."

He trotted toward me, slowing to a long-legged walk as he neared me, and his eyes smiled into mine. His face was lightly tanned from his outdoor work, even with the weak winter sun, and perspiration darkened the roots of his hair. But he smelled of clean, healthy sweat and his body exuded warmth the way a horse's does on a cold day. He looked very large, his muscled shoulders straining against the thin shirt, his lean forearms darkened by dirt and bark. It was hard to believe this hearty specimen had not long ago been felled by a gun. To a body not used to antibiotics, the drug had an amazingly speedy effect.

"I thought I'd make dinner tonight," he said. "So don't start anything when you get home."

I couldn't help but smile. This big, brawny man with the leaves in his hair and the dirt under his fingernails had climbed down a tree to tell me he was going to make dinner.

"No problem," I answered. "I'll just lounge around until you arrive."

He brushed futilely at the dirt on his arm. "I've an idea for something you've probably never had before. Bullock's heart and Saratoga chips."

"Heart?" I echoed.

"Bullock's heart," he repeated, gray eyes dancing with amusement. "A delicacy. I saw some in the butcher's on the way to work this morning. Some people like to stuff it, but I prefer it broiled."

I smiled weakly. "Sounds great. I'll try not to snack too heavily today." Starvation would be the only way to get a heart down my throat, I was sure.

"Good." He glanced quickly behind him at the waiting men and held up a hand. "I'd best mosey along. I'll see you about six."

"Okay," I said, but he had already run back to the men. Heart. Was this another one of those cosmic hints? Was I meant to be eating my heart out?

Even though it was outright sacrilege on my part, I didn't work the following day, which was Christmas Eve. Instead I left the shop in the questionably capable hands of Sylvie and Janey. It was bound to be mobbed with frantic last-minute shoppers, not the most friendly people, and I prayed that my loyal help wouldn't hate me for my desertion. But what I wanted to do was to prepare a fancy meal for Carter. Something French, perhaps, that he might never have had before. I wanted to make it a special occasion—one that he wouldn't forget even after he returned to his home, and her.

His dinner of Bullock's heart and Saratoga chips was one that I wouldn't soon forget. I had spent most of the evening trying to peer into his mouth every time he spoke or laughed in an effort to find a filling, but only managed to get a glimpse of his teeth by asking him about the dentists of his day. I was rewarded with an exaggerated grimace and a view of clean, white, fillingless teeth. So much for my detective work.

The food, however, had turned out to be an incredibly tasty meal of extremely tender meat that tasted of broiled beef, and homemade potato chips. He was stunned when I pulled out a bag of Lay's, but we both agreed that his ''Saratoga chips'' were superior. I'm still not sure if the meat he served was actual heart, or one of those tasty euphemisms some cookbooks like to use, but whatever it was, it tasted good.

We hadn't heard from the Lindseys yet, but I hadn't expected to. It was, after all, Christmas week, and people were busy. I think Carter was disappointed, however, and I was determined to take his mind off it. Hence, my dinner plans.

He was working Green Way's Christmas tree sales, which I was glad of because it gave me a chance to set things up as a surprise for dinner. As I spent the day cooking and cleaning, I tried to remember what my life had been like before he came into it, and how it would be after he left. Though I knew it was foolish to feel so attached after so little time, especially since I had known from the beginning that his existence in my life was temporary at best, it didn't stop me from wondering how things might have turned out, if only—what? If only everything had been completely different.

I hadn't gotten a Christmas tree—I almost never did because I had one at the shop—but I decided to get some greens to put on the mantel. The sharp, sweet scent filled the room as I toyed with them, setting them first all along the mantel, and then breaking up some of the smaller twigs to fill a bowl with their needles and some red Christmas balls. I placed candles around the room for atmosphere, then decided that I would use nothing but candles and oil lamps for the evening. Maybe Carter would feel more at home that way.

I decided to prepare Veal Oscar. The smell of hollandaise sauce, crabmeat, and baking onions laced the air, and I retrieved from the bottom of my wine rack a 1979 bottle of *Reserve de la Comtesse* red bordeaux that I'd been saving for just the right moment. I set the table with my best plates, my good wineglasses, and all the requisite silverware for the various courses I'd planned. I played classical Christmas carols on the stereo and stoked up the fire to make it snugly warm throughout the house.

I was ready. Where was Carter?

It was after six o'clock, and I couldn't imagine that Christmas tree sales would be particularly brisk on Christmas Eve; I would have thought most people bought them well in advance. But I decided to give it the benefit of the doubt and occupy myself with wrapping the last of my gifts instead of agonizing over Carter's lateness.

At seven o'clock I abandoned my attempts at distraction and gave in to wholehearted rampant paranoia that Carter had left. That was it. I knew it. The moment I felt confident enough to count on his return, he had gone. I paced around the living room, alternately calming myself enough to hum along with the carols, then losing all patience with the room and prowling from one window to the next to the front door to peer out into the darkness with a worried frown and twisting stomach.

How pitiful it would be, I thought, to be left like this— with a huge cut of veal and an open hundred-dollar bottle of wine. The house was dressed to a tee and clean as it hadn't been in months. I felt like a bride about to be left at the altar.

At seven-thirty I abandoned my post and fled to the bathroom, something I had been trying to put off so that I didn't miss a moment of sidewalk searching, and it was at that precise moment that Carter arrived. I heard him enter from my less-than-optimum vantage point at the back of the house with the toilet running and decided to maximize my position by brushing my hair while I was there. I took several deep breaths before leaving the tiny sanctuary in an effort to face the object of my agony with a face that spoke of nothing but the ecstasy of having a day off from work.

He was dirty and disheveled, his hair mussed and his face and clothing streaked with dirt. He looked as if he'd been beaten by an evergreen-wielding criminal. And he looked tired.

"Tough day at work?" I asked as he passed me on the way to the kitchen.

He dropped his coat on a chair and sniffed loudly as he passed. "I was balling trees."

I stared after him. "I beg your pardon?"

He reached the kitchen, opened the refrigerator door, and pulled from it a bottle of water that he tipped heartily into his mouth. He wiped his wet lips on the back of his arm and turned to me, his eyes appearing even more pale from the dark, dirt-stained skin of his face. "I was balling trees," he repeated. "For people who don't want a dead one in their parlor."

"Oh, you mean balling like making a root ball—burlap and all that."

He polished off the water and tossed the plastic jug into the recycling bin (which had been another interesting lesson in Carter's crash course on the 1990s). His lips curved into a smile that was mirrored in his eyes. "You see, you do know something about gardening."

"Well, I've seen them, you know." I leaned back against the table and watched him pull another bottle from the refrigerator. "So you must be tired. Sounds like hard work."

It was at that moment that he caught sight of the fancy table dressing behind me. He paused in the action of up-ending another bottle into his mouth and looked suddenly uncomfortable. "Are you having company?" He glanced quickly around, as if he might have overlooked someone on his single-minded trek to the refrigerator.

I smiled. "I was waiting for you. I've made dinner."

He looked disconcerted and glanced down at his hands, the nails black with soil. "I'm sorry. I'm a mess. And—" He glanced at the clock on the wall. "I'm late, too."

"It's okay," I lied. The fact that I panicked every time he didn't show up when I thought he would wasn't his problem, it was mine. It was definitely mine. "I can wait. Why don't you clean up and I'll pour you a drink. What would you like to start? I've got some eggnog. It's Christmas Eve, after all."

He carefully replaced the top on the water bottle and put it back in the refrigerator. "Nothing just yet, if it's all the same to you. I'll just go bathe. I shouldn't be long." He looked uncomfortably at the table again. "I'm sorry about being late," he repeated. "You should have told me. I hadn't thought of doing anything special tonight."

Perhaps he was not in the mood for festivities. Perhaps I should have asked him first. "Oh, it's nothing that special," I said airily, turning to the table and toying with one of the multiple forks. "It was just a last-minute idea."

His shrewd eyes scanned the kitchen, the pile of dirty pots and pans, the up-ended Kitchen Aid mixer, the onion skins and lemon rinds, the corkscrew with its impaled cork still attached, and then he turned back to me with a small smile and a heavy-lidded gaze. "Last minute," he repeated.

I flushed. "Well, what do you normally do on Christmas Eve?"

His face closed up. "Nothing." Bad question. I mentally kicked myself. I should have known it would be.

Perhaps the whole scenario reminded him too acutely of home. But his next statement refuted that naive idea.

"My family didn't celebrate holidays. And Meg and I haven't either, not for a while now." His voice was terse, his eyes avoiding mine. "I'll just get cleaned up." He moved past me toward the stairs, and I watched him go, perplexed.

His family didn't celebrate holidays. He was upset because it was so different from home, not because it reminded him of it. I shook my head. This constant juxtaposition of here and there, of now and then, was dizzying, especially since I had no idea what there and then was like. It was all guesswork, and more often than not I guessed wrong.

Carter reappeared twenty minutes later, wet hair combed back, with a crisp white shirt tucked into the dark gray chinos he had bought with one of his overtime payments. He smelled of soap and clean cotton, and his gray eyes looked all the more brilliant for his wet lashes and freshly shaved face.

He smiled ruefully. "I hope I'm not underdressed."

Would that he were, I thought shamelessly. After seeing him yesterday with his strong arms bared to the winter sun, I could think of nothing but the feel of those arms around me when we'd kissed that night by the train station.

"You look very nice," I said sincerely.

Carter shoved his hands into his pockets and looked around. We stood there awkwardly, like two teenagers on a first date.

I asked, "Do you want something to drink now? How about a beer to start?"

Carter nodded. "Fine. A beer would be good."

I moved to the refrigerator and wondered how one simple little Christmas Eve dinner could create such awkwardness between us. But I knew it wasn't just that. It might have been my imagination, but ever since the conversation with Mrs. Bartlett Lindsey we both seemed to be feeling a renewed polarization. Even last night, during Carter's dinner, there had been a strain between us that had not been there for several days—since we'd acknowledged our mutual attraction with that kiss at the train station.

As I pulled out a beer, I mused briefly about dropping some kind of drug into it, some kind of truth serum that might open the reticent man up. Maybe then he would tell me what kind of family wouldn't celebrate holidays; what kind of wife he would not want to talk about; what sort of life would make such a gentle person so obviously unhappy.

I thought about the fact that last night Carter had cooked dinner, and cooked it very well. Wouldn't it be strange for a nineteenth-century man to be able to cook for himself? Maybe that ability said something about his wife. Maybe he had an unhappy marriage. Maybe he was a twentieth-century man who knew how to cook.

Carter had seated himself at the table when I returned. He looked distinctly uncomfortable gazing at the multitude of forks and spoons, the shiny clean plates, and the spotless glasses. Wordlessly, I handed him the beer. I longed to be able to reach out, take his hand, and make him talk about what must be an astonishingly confusing array of thoughts. As I had been since we'd talked to Mrs. Lindsey, I was sure he was thinking about whether he'd fathered a child. A child who, as we sat toasty warm in my house in winter 1996, would have to be long dead and buried.

I had made Oysters Rockefeller as an appetizer, so I excused myself once again to retrieve them from the oven. They lay on the tray, spread across the rock salt like a flag, looking conspicuously fancy. I shrugged. In for a penny, in for a pound, I thought.

I breezed out of the kitchen to the table and set the hot plate down on a trivet in the center. Carter's eyes widened and he leaned forward to inspect it.

"Oysters Rockefeller," I announced, thinking he probably had no idea who Rockefeller was. A chef, perhaps, to him.

"Hmm. They look good."

I served him and then myself. Then I sat, taking a hearty swig of my white wine aperitif. Without conversation, other than *very good* and *thank you*, we consumed the appetizer.

Carter finally broke the silence. "I thought you were to go to your brother's tonight."

"No, he called to say, what with the weather and all, maybe it would be best to cancel."

"What weather?"

"They're predicting snow," I said, refilling my wine. "And freezing rain."

He nodded and drank his beer. I fidgeted with my glass. Finally, taking a deep breath, I said, "What's wrong, Carter? Are you okay?"

With a slight jerk, his head came up, and his gray gaze pierced mine. He wore such an intense expression that I felt I should somehow know what he was going to say. I held my breath.

He opened his mouth and inhaled, as though he was about to speak, then let the breath out slowly, his eyes not leaving mine. Finally, with an almost unbearable slowness, his gaze traveled down and away from me, and he picked up his glass, twirling the liquid around and around with hypnotizing deliberateness.

I felt the way a fisherman must when he senses the Big One he's been reeling in getting away, kind of frantic and helpless at the same time.

"There are some things, Shelby," Carter said in a calm, clear voice, "that we ought not to speak about."

He continued to watch the swirling amber liquid, eyes veiled, countenance stern. "Even though I'm finding it increasingly difficult to do so."

I looked from him to the swirling glass and back again. He was slipping away. He'd made a decision to separate himself from me. We were no longer in this together.

Was this how it would be, then? Was I to step gracefully out of the picture now that we'd determined that Carter had a child and had to return? My spoiled, selfish mind recoiled at the thought. As long as he was here, he was mine. If he had to return, she could have him back then.

"I'm in love with you," I blurted, then stared at him in shock.

I had said it. I had never even allowed myself to think it, but here I'd gone and said it. The words, and the way they burst forth, startled both of us, perhaps me even more than him. His eyes shot back to mine.

I expelled the breath I'd been holding, looked frantically around the table, picked up my glass and drained it. "I'm sorry," I said quickly. "I didn't mean to say that. I didn't mean to make you uncomfortable. I don't want to burden you. It's not your problem, really. It's not a problem. I just wanted—I just—I don't know—I don't know why I said that." The sentences tumbled from my mouth and my face flamed almost painfully hot.

Carter reached over and grabbed my forearm in a hard grip. I looked at his hand, then his face. He wore an expression of—was it fear?

"Shelby," he said low. His eyes held mine for a long, intense minute, during which I could think of absolutely nothing to say. His expression softened somewhat and a sort of laugh escaped him, quietly short and despairing. "That's just the sort of thing I thought we ought not speak about." A sad smile reached his eyes and his grip loosened, though he did not move his hand.

I licked my suddenly dry lips. "Tell me about Meg," I said quietly.

He removed his hand from my arm while his expression changed subtly, his eyes becoming dark and guarded.

"I really want to know—" I hesitated. "I think I really *need* to know what she was like."

He sighed and looked at the table. His hand rested on the white tablecloth, fingering the edge of his plate. If I could have, I would have liked to sculpt that hand, so perfectly shaped did it seem to me at that moment, expressing all of Carter's control and vulnerability in its intricately strong form. With a courage I did not know I possessed, I took the hand in mine and placed it firmly between both of my palms.

His eyes met mine and we shared the moment of illicit physical contact.

He took a deep breath. "I grew up in a very strange household," he began. His fingers tightened on my hand and he gazed at our clasped fingers, dark skin against pale. "My parents married because of me." He looked at me significantly, and it took me a moment to realize that he meant his mother had been pregnant—that he was the product of a shotgun wedding. "They never really cared for each other. Although I guess they must have at some point—in some way." His lips curved upward without humor.

"My father'd always been a drifter, though he was the only son of a respectable farmer in Pennsylvania, and when he drifted to Virginia he met my mother. Her parents were against the marriage, but what could they do? There I was, already started. So my mother and father married and moved to his house in Pennsylvania, away from her disapproving family.

"My father was rarely around after I was about five or six years old. My mother worked hard, but she was bitter about the life she'd stumbled into. She wasn't in touch with her siblings, and her own parents had disowned her because she had so disgraced them by her marriage. Though they eventually acknowledged me, they never forgave her.''

He was silent for a moment, remembering. ''In any event, I grew up with a very serious, hard-working, embittered woman who, I am sure, loved me intensely, if in a strangely unfriendly way. My life was fine—good, even, compared to those who were not fortunate enough to work their own land—but there was never much joy in the house. No laughter, ever, and no special . . . happinesses. No birthdays, no holidays, nothing like that.''

I watched his face as he spoke. The burnished lashes that shadowed his eyes when he looked down framed them with unbearable tenderness when he glanced up to the ceiling and around the room. He did not look at me. His voice did not change from that mellow softness, but I could tell by the way his hand gripped mine that the story he told came from deep within, perhaps spoken aloud for the first time.

''Meg,'' he continued, ''lived nearby. And she was so lighthearted and full of life that sometimes I felt that if I could only get close to her it would have to rub off on me. All of that laughter I'd squelched as a child would come spilling out of me if I could just figure out her secret, her carefree way of looking at the world. My whole dreary existence inside that old broken-down house would be magically forgotten if I could just spend time with her, learn to be like her.

''She was pretty, so of course all the young swains in the area wanted her. And she'd already given the mitten to quite a few of them, so she was starting to look like quite a prize to those of us watching from afar.'' His glance finally landed on me and he smiled wryly. ''But I had no idea what to do. I was such a greenhorn that I hadn't the foggiest notion what to do to gain her attention. And I was scared to death of being the next one all the untried lads would openly pity and privately scorn. So I didn't do anything. I just watched her, trying to figure out how she did it, all that laughing and light-heartedness.

"It was after my mother died—I was about twenty or so—when Meg approached me at a church social. I was tongue-tied and stupid, but she managed to make me laugh. So I courted her for a while." Here he looked down again and frowned. "I was in no hurry to get married, which I guess was unfair to her, so we just went on like that for a while until Meg got frustrated and we parted. I went back to my farming and she went back to her flirting, trying to make me jealous." He smiled a little. "And maybe it worked, or maybe I was just lonely out there on the farm all alone. In any case, after a few months of her running around we started stepping out together again."

"Were you in love with her?" I asked.

He did not look up, but he shook his head very slowly. "No. I was never in love with her. In fact, after a while I was fairly certain I didn't want to marry her. But then I did a very stupid thing." He looked up at me, his eyes cynical, his lips twisted into a rueful smile. "It was after a dance where we'd been drinking a good bit of hard cider, and Meg—clever Meg," he snorted a very cynical laugh and tilted his head, looking down, "she decided what she had to do. And it worked. Like father, like son—bad blood, I suppose. He rolled his eyes to the ceiling and clenched his jaw. "Right behind the church, it was." He shook his head again, his face clearly disgusted with the memory, and stared at a spot beyond and above me. "We were married in that church two months later, two weeks after which she lost the baby."

I held his hand tightly in mine, stroking the back of it

with the fingers of my other hand, tracing the lines of his veins. I was unsure of what to say. He hadn't loved her, didn't love her, and to me that was a profound relief. But the disgust he had for himself, for the way in which he'd been caught, was clear.

"Everyone does something they regret," I said softly.

He laughed, a short, hard sound. "Yes. Some people invest badly, some people say things they shouldn't, some even marry the wrong person. But they don't regret it the way I do. They don't become as cruel with remorse as I have. For I've been cruel to her. Despicably cruel. And all because of a mistake that I made."

"She made it too," I said.

He shook his head. "No, she didn't. She was in love with me once. She did what she had to do, to get what she wanted. I didn't have to go along with that. In fact," he squinted his eyes and looked back into the past, "in the back of my mind I knew what I was doing. I knew that I was somehow sealing my fate that night behind the church, but I did it anyway. Something inside me figured, what the hell—life wasn't getting any better all alone." He pressed his lips together. "What I didn't know was that it could get worse."

I felt the weight of his sadness, the burden of his regret. "How did it get worse?"

He shook his head. "I don't know. The guilt, I guess. I didn't love her and after a time I wanted nothing to do with her. Oh, I tried to hide it, to act as if everything was fine, but it got harder and harder. She was carefree, all right, but that was because she took nothing seriously. What I noticed, after a while, was that we never had a conversation. We were either in bed or apart. When I tried to point this out to her, she told me she did not like to think about things all the time the way I did. She didn't want to become as stodgy and serious as I was. In fact, she hated that part of me, she said." He stopped there, staring thoughtfully at, but not seeing, our two hands clasped together.

They were either in bed or apart, I thought. That statement could as easily have been said about Rory and me. And it was only by the good fortune of being born in a time when sex did not naturally lead to marriage that I had not followed a similar path and married Rory.

Carter's thumb rubbed mine with a pressure that spoke of wanting to erase all that he was saying, but he continued.

"She was very young when we married and I suppose I got irritated with some of the things she did. It wasn't fair, but it bothered me that the most important things to her were socials and dances. She loved to visit her friends and I felt—slighted, I guess. But she was just being young. We had different ideas about married life. She was *determined* to maintain her life the way it had been before we married, and that was not the way I thought things would be. As for me, she couldn't understand that I had to work the farm constantly, every day, or we could lose everything. She'd been brought up in town, you see, so the constant demands of a farm were unfamiliar to her. But even after a couple of years, she still thought I worked too much. I tried to explain to her that I *had* to do those things, that I *had* to be the serious one, but she thought I was doing it to keep her down, to ruin any chance she had of having a good time. And maybe I was. I was pretty disillusioned about the whole thing after the first year or so. I had thought that a good marriage should be a partnership."

He extricated his hand from mine, placed both of his flat on the table and rose, walking to the window and looking out.

"But I don't know why I thought I knew anything about it," Carter said. "Marriage, that is." He sighed heavily. "After a while she started—behaving indiscreetly, flirting with every man who passed her by, one time taking it so far as a stolen kiss at a party. And the thing that bothered me most about it was that I didn't care. And that made me angry. I saw us behaving with each other exactly the way I remembered my parents acting. They didn't speak, they weren't close, but they would step into the bedroom at any moment and be gone for hours. I knew what that led to. It led to the same sort of screaming unhappiness my parents had at the end, before my father left for the last time. They hated each other, but they didn't realize it until they no longer wanted each other physically. Mine was every bit as bad a marriage as theirs, and I hated myself for getting into it. But I didn't know how to fix it. I had no idea how to undo what I'd done. Our personalities were too different.

"Naturally, after a time, I noticed her happiness ebbing away, being replaced by a kind of forced, unpleasant gaiety. And I found myself angry with her for that too, for losing that happiness, for *abandoning* it when it was the only thing I needed from her. And I knew it was my fault. It was all my fault because I should have known. *I should have known the marriage was wrong, because I'd seen it all before.*" As he said this he pressed white-knuckled fists onto the windowsill, his jaw clenched, obviously despising the mistake he thought he should have avoided.

"You know," I said thoughtfully, "these days when couples make that discovery, they divorce. No stigma, no social outcasting. They realize they made a mistake and they divorce. One out of every two marriages ends in divorce nowadays. That's how many people make that mistake, Carter."

He expelled a deep breath and threw his head back. "It doesn't help me to know that others have been as stupid as I have been. I only know that because of my thoughtlessness, I have left behind a wife who is with child. And I must go back to her.'' He turned to face me, his expression set. ''I must go back to her—*somehow, some way.*''

I felt my breath catch against the lump in my throat. ''Must you, Carter?'' I asked, my voice low and intense. ''Must you *really?*''

For a long moment Carter stared at me, hard. Then, without a word, he turned his gaze back out the window.

Chapter Thirteen

Carter was able, after a time, to shake off the melancholy that had consumed him upon telling his story. I brought out dinner, and we both made a concerted effort to relax. Carter seemed to feel better for the telling of the story, and I was glad to know that he wasn't pining for his wife, even if he had made it abundantly clear that he had to return to her, so it was easier to force ourselves into a happier mood.

Just after we finished eating it began to snow. Big, downy flakes at first, then more furiously, tiny pinpoints of white that crackled softly as they hit the windowpanes. Carter poured two brandies, one of them very small for me to try, and we stood palming the large glasses as we watched the snow coat the ground.

I sipped the brandy slowly, being careful not to breathe in at the same time because the strong fumes made my eyes water. Tendrils of fire scorched my throat as I swallowed, sending a thick heat tingling through my veins. I found myself enjoying the lethal liquid, if not for the flavor exactly, then for the living, burning sensation it created within me. I did not feel drunk or tipsy, just warm from the inside out, and relaxed in a deep, languorous way.

"Do you think they'll contact us?" Carter asked, his voice a rich, low sound in the silence of the candlelit house.

I watched the rosebush by the back porch slowly become covered with white. "Who?"

"My relatives." His breath made a brief, shadowy fog on the windowpane in front of him.

It took my food-and-drink-saturated mind a moment to remember who he meant. "Oh, them. If they don't we can call them back."

"I'm curious to know," he said slowly, "what sort of life they're leading."

I turned my head to look at him. "What do you mean?"

He hesitated. "If they're doing well, what sort of house they live in, that kind of thing." Another moment of silence passed before he added, "It was rumored, back in my time, that my mother was hording a fortune. People in the town, perhaps because she was not the most personable of their neighbors, speculated that she had stolen a great sum of money from her parents and that was why they had disowned her, not because of her marrying my father."

"Why in the world would they say something like that? Honestly, I don't understand where gossip comes from. Someone somewhere manufactures it for public consumption and, sure enough, people eat it up." I shook my head and looked back out the window.

From the reflection I saw Carter take a healthy swig of his brandy, gently rocking the glass in his hand afterward. "I believe my father started the rumor. He apparently believed it himself. My mother told me that was the reason he married her, not because of me. He believed her to be rich.''

His mother told him that? How could she had said something like that? *Your father didn't give a damn that you were on the way, but he believed I had some money, so he married me.* Had everyone he'd known been cruel?

''Maybe he just believed her family would eventually forgive her. You did say they had money, didn't you?'' I asked.

Carter's face wore a small, enigmatic smile. ''Yes.''

I turned to look at the real face instead of the reflection. An involuntary smile tugged at my own lips in response. ''What? Why do you look so smug?''

Carter shrugged.

I studied him. ''She *did* have money . . . didn't she?'' I guessed. His smile grew, though he obviously tried to stop it. ''She had money and you knew it!''

Carter turned to look at me and laughed out loud at the expression on my face. ''You do love a mystery, don't you?'' One raised eyebrow teased me for my curiosity before he continued. ''She had some jewelry, just a small pouch, that she hid from my father. Before I left for the war I hid it myself, from Meg, in a hollowed-out book . . . a place I knew she'd never look,'' he added wryly.

''What sort of things were in this pouch?'' I asked. ''Jewels with enough value to make a difference to descendants living now? Is that why you want to know how well off they are?''

Carter pursed his lips and narrowed his eyes, thinking. ''I don't know,'' he said slowly. ''But I believe if Meg were to have found the jewels, she could have set herself up quite nicely. Seems to me, if she handled it well, it could have made a difference to our descendants.''

This confused me. ''Then why didn't you sell the jewels when you were working so hard on the farm? Then you could have worked less and Meg might not have been so unhappy.''

Carter eyed me narrowly. ''Are you asking why I didn't sell my mother's heirlooms to buy an easier life?''

I thought about this carefully. The brandy was having some effect on my logic, I imagined, but even yet the question didn't seem unreasonable. ''Yes, I guess that's what I mean.''

''And then what?'' He regarded me steadily.

I couldn't help feeling that I was missing something. ''I don't know—enjoy life? Travel? Do something other than work all the time?''

Carter looked out the window again. ''The only way I would sell those jewels,'' he said in a quiet but firm voice, ''is if we had a plan, a way to put the money to work. The idea of selling them just to fritter the money away until it was gone is abhorrent to me. That's why I hid them from Meg.''

This shut me up for a time. It certainly was the virtuous, responsible answer. ''Well, they're gone now, one way or another,'' I said. ''What were they?''

He shot me an inscrutable look. ''There were various unset stones. A large diamond, flawless, four carats, in a heavy gold setting. A painted miniature of some ancestor in England was framed in gold and hung on a gold-link chain. And there was a ruby and diamond brooch. Those were the most valuable things. There were also some earrings and a couple of rings, but they probably wouldn't amount to much, monetarily.''

''Sounds pretty valuable, all together.'' I didn't know the first thing about jewelry.

''It would be enough to keep Meg in crinolines for a goodly time to come,'' he said dryly. ''Or to pay for an Oxford education for my sons.''

''Your sons,'' I repeated.

He turned to me, amused. "And daughters," he added. "Intelligence is important in both the sexes."

This attitude shone a new light on Carter, one that seemed now to be inherently obvious. But having never heard him talk about himself before, it struck me as a revelation, one that made perfect sense. "Education is important to you," I stated.

"Paramount," he said, draining his glass.

I nodded, understanding a part of him for the first time. Carter turned from the window and moved to the liquor shelf to refill his glass. Then he threw another log into the stove and gazed moodily at the fire as the flames devoured the dry wood.

"I'll call the Lindseys after Christmas," I told his back. "We can see what sort of legacy you left."

I saw him nod slowly. "Good."

"Carter?"

He turned from the fire, his eyes glittering in the flame light.

"May I see your photo of Meg?" I asked.

He hesitated. "My photo?"

"I know you have a picture of her—because I saw it that day I thought you were never coming back. I went to your room and looked at your things. I hope you don't mind." A little late, now, if he did.

He shook his head. "Why do you want to see it again?"

I rolled my glass between my palms and tried to articulate it. "Well, I didn't know anything about her then. Now that I do, I think I'd look at her differently."

Carter placed his glass on the coffee table and strode up the stairs. He retrieved the picture and I sat on the couch with it. As I opened the little leather box, I felt Carter sit down beside me. Inside was the oddly angelic face with the clear, hard eyes. She was just as I remembered her. And the impressions I'd had then, that first time I saw her, fit with all that he'd told me tonight: She was calculating, manipulative, and a spoiled brat. He had not said as much, but between the lines of his story I saw a woman who sold her virginity for marriage, and quite possibly lied about a pregnancy to force the issue. Carter blamed himself, and he certainly was somewhat to blame, but I knew in my heart that this woman had planned the whole thing.

I ran my finger along the red velvet interior of the box. On the left-hand side, scratched rather crudely into the velvet, were the initials WV FW.

"Whose initials are these?" I asked, looking up at Carter. I was startled to find him as close as he was, but mostly because of the intense look in his narrowed eyes as he stared at me.

He did not answer immediately, but searched my face with his eyes. Finally, in a quiet voice, he asked, "You don't know?"

I drew back, surprised. "Should I?" I looked back down at the initials. Had anyone he'd told me about tonight had those initials? Not his mother or father. Not Meg. Did he think that I had put them there when I'd looked through his things? "I don't know. I don't know what they mean. Weren't they there when you—when you left—home?" I stumbled over the question. It felt awkward to ask if they were there when he left 1862.

"Yes, they were." He seemed to relax beside me. "A woman—I believe she might not have been in her right mind—scratched them into the case just before I left home. She was uncommon strange and uttered some nonsense about those letters being a key to my future." He laughed. "It's amazing how gullible one becomes in a time of war. The very fact that she intimated I *had* a future became important to me later, in the midst of heavy fighting."

I stared at the initials, puzzled. *WV FW*. They did not

look even remotely familiar to me. "Why did you think I would know about them?"

"I don't know," he said dismissively. "Maybe because you have been part of that future that she predicted. Of course, she might have mentioned something about traveling through time; *that* would have been helpful. But all she talked about were those initials."

I smiled. "And you would have believed her if she had mentioned the time travel? I don't think so."

He laughed then. "You think you know me well, don't you?"

"I know you wouldn't believe me if I told you that tomorrow aliens from outer space would come pick you up and take you to Mars."

He laughed and ran a hand over his eyes, rubbing them tiredly. "I might now. The way things have gone lately, I might truly believe it now."

The following morning I awoke early. It was Christmas, and we were to go to my parents' house in Washington. The snow had been heavy, but I believed we would not have a lot of trouble getting there, especially since the plows would have been out all night, and because it was Christmas the traffic would probably be light.

I was up before Carter, so I made some coffee and started to read the newspaper. The coffee was rich and strong, the aroma almost enough to wake me even without drinking it, and it warmed the chill atmosphere of the overcast day. A thick ceiling of clouds hung low outside, promising more snow, but also making for a close, cozy feeling inside the house. It was perfect Christmas weather.

I was poring over the Outlook section of the *Washington Post* when I noticed an article about the Northern Lights. Curious to see if they'd mention anything about that night back in 1862 when the meteoric display had been seen this far south, I started to read the article. It was a little more scientific than I was prepared to absorb, and I was about to turn the page when I noticed, blocked off toward the bottom of the page, a little blurb about the possibility of being able to see the Aurora Borealis in our area again in about a week's time.

I ripped out the blurb, planning to show it to Carter when he arose. Then the idea struck me that maybe, as long as we were humoring the occult and the idea that spiritual forces might be at work where we could not see them, this reappearance could have something to do with Carter's time travel. Granted, I felt I was starting to believe his wild story about coming from the Civil War, in part because of my growing emotion for him and also because of the convincing tales of his family and childhood; but here it was, just two days after he told me about his experience possibly being linked to the Northern Lights and I read about their imminent reappearance. I had the odd conviction that this was not a coincidence.

Suppose he were to go back to that spot on the battlefield and lie down beneath the Northern Lights. Would he disappear back to his own time? Just disappear, slowly, like a mist that the sun burns off? Or would it happen in the blink of an eye? How did this madness work? And suppose I were to go lie with him. Could I go too? *Would* I go?

While the rational part of my mind told me I was crazy to even consider the possibility, the part of me ruled by emotion looked around my house, at the walls that I'd painstakingly painted and stenciled, at the furniture I'd collected through the years, at all the familiar knick-knacks. My glance fell on Steve, curled in a ball by the back door. I wouldn't want to leave her, I thought. But everything else could as easily exist in another time as now.

I realized that when I had asked Carter if he must go back, to whatever or *whenever* he had left, what I was really asking him was to give up everything he knew—*everyone* he knew—to stay here, in this place, this unfamiliar future, with me. Would I be able to do the same thing if offered the opportunity to go with him? Could I leave everything behind for the love of Carter Lindsey?

I thought about my family—my parents so happy in retirement together, James and his girlfriend Michelle— how happy they were, and how often I'd felt jealous of their easy camaraderie, their passion without strife. I thought about my friends, Jerry, Sylvie, Janey—Rory . . .

Then I thought about the anger Carter had shown the night Rory had tried to explain himself to me, when he'd lied through his teeth about sleeping with that girl. Unbidden, on the heels of that came the remembrance of the kiss Carter and I had shared, and the feel of his callused hand in mine. I thought about the look in his eyes when he'd warned me we shouldn't talk about some things and the soft, knowing smile he wore when he saw right through me.

Could I leave everything behind for the love of Carter Lindsey?

Yes, I decided. I could.

The drive to Washington, fifty miles straight up route 95, is a boring one unless you happen to be someone unused to traveling at high speeds in an automobile. Even though I was driving well below the speed limit because of the snow, Carter's hands clenched reflexively on the seat cushion and the muscles in his jaw stood out clearly.

In an effort to calm him, I began to talk about my family, describing for him my mother and father, and the unusual aspect of growing up with a deaf brother. He seemed to realize what I was trying to do—to distract him from what he perceived to be imminent peril on a snowy road at fifty miles per hour—and participated in the conversation eagerly. He was quite taken with my description of sign language, and my assertion that it was not, as so many people thought, simply "painting pictures in the air," but an actual language with a grammar and syntax all its own. He asked me to show him this language sometime and I proceeded, with a zeal I could never disguise when asked to teach, to demonstrate various signs. This, however, resulted in an increased nervousness in him as my hands occasionally left the steering wheel, so I contented myself with teaching him the signed alphabet with one hand.

"You see, you can say anything if you know the alphabet. It'll take forever, but you can say it." I watched him from the corner of my eye as he actually let go of the seat cushion with one hand and practiced the letters.

He was an amazingly quick study, which impressed but should not have surprised me. He was quick to pick up everything, especially that which was most unfamiliar, it seemed.

"And he can read this, from my hand?" Carter asked, painstakingly spelling out the word *ice* and then *slow* to himself.

"He can read faster than that," I said, indulging in a little cockiness. Within a second I spelled a word with my right hand.

He frowned and gazed at me through heavy-lidded eyes. "All right. What was it?"

I smirked. "Shall I do it again?"

He crossed his arms over his chest. "If it amuses you."

It did. I spelled it again. " 'Relax,' " I said, then smiled and nodded at him, "Relax."

My parents' house was situated on a one-way street with very little traffic. The houses were old, solid, and replete with quirky, character-building details that enthralled the eye. My parents' house actually had two stone gargoyles carved into the eaves on either corner, where they were now barely visible because of the huge trees that had grown up against them. But Carter picked them out almost immediately.

"That one's name is Laurel, and the other is Hardy," I explained, pointing, "because as children they frightened James and me so badly we sometimes couldn't sleep."

Carter turned to me in incomprehension. "What do those names signify that they would chase away childish nightmares?"

Though I had long since given up trying to trick Carter into betraying at least a rudimentary knowledge of the twentieth century, it continued to impress me that he didn't seem to know even the most basic cultural commonalities.

I opened the back door of the car, and Steve bounced out, sniffing along the barren flower beds as if tracking a known criminal.

"Laurel and Hardy were a comedy team in the movies. One was very fat and the other very thin. They're pretty corny, but I liked them as a kid." I shrugged and started to grab packages from the back of the car.

I could sense Carter's pensiveness next to me as I passed him boxes to set on the curb. After a moment, as if he'd tried to figure it out without asking and couldn't, he asked, "What are 'the movies'?"

I backed out of the car and stood, placing a few packages on the roof and arching my back a little to loosen it up. It was so easy to forget which references he wouldn't understand, especially if one lost all semblance of concentration when one was looking at him in his new shirt and tie.

"Moving pictures. Photographs that move and look like real life. Like plays, you know."

He nodded solemnly, and I turned away again to bustle around in the back seat. I felt suddenly anxious to get inside the house; the wind was kicking up and blowing through my very bones.

"I'd like to see the movies sometime," Carter persisted, with more direct curiosity than I'd seen in him so far. "Where do you go to see them?"

I reemerged with a bag and smiled at him. "I'll show them to you today, if you want. You can watch some television. No doubt Dad will have a football game on anyway."

Carter's brow furrowed and I laughed. Life took on an unaccustomed richness with Carter. There was always some new wonder to introduce him to, some new concept, new people, new life. Everything was new with him, even to me, and I reveled in a complete lack of boredom when he was around.

That would wear off, I told myself. Once the novelty of having a time-traveler around the house went away, that excitement would, too. But I didn't believe it, as much as I wanted to; I didn't believe that it was just his displacement that was so appealing. It was the positive things that I loved, the things that would not go away: Carter's curious nature; his calm acceptance of change, odd situations, technology; his ability to cope with anything thrown at him; his warmth and protectiveness of me . . .

As the regret for what might have been bubbled once again to the forefront of my mind, I slammed the car door shut and pasted a smile on my face.

"So, are you ready to meet the family?" I asked.

Carter began to pull packages from the roof of the car, tucking a flat one under his arm and stacking several larger ones to carry in his hands. "As ready as I'll ever be," he said. "Are they much like you?"

I laughed at his tone as I filled my own arms with

gifts. "Would that help or hurt the situation?"

He smiled and did not answer that question. "I'm just curious," he said, as we headed up the sidewalk to the house, "how would James speak in a situation like this?"

I glanced at him, unsure of what he meant, and he made an obvious gesture with the boxes in his arms, his hands completely occupied.

"Oh! Well, it's tough. That's one of the odd trade-offs of sign language: You can't talk with your hands full, but you can with your mouth full." Carter smiled politely at the old joke. "Actually, he would have to speak and rely on me to either recognize the word or read his lips. Otherwise, he'd have to put everything down."

We made it to the stoop and I bent my knees to push the bell with one free finger.

"It's interesting," Carter murmured. "I'm very curious what his world must be like."

I laughed quite genuinely at that. "Well, the feeling is definitely mutual."

We were greeted with enthusiasm by my parents, professional hosts that they are. While I had told my mother about Carter, I thought it best to tell my father that he was a friend of a friend and was staying with me while he was in town for various Civil War reenactments. This would appeal to my father, I knew, as he was something of an amateur historian, and my suspicions that my mother would like him were immediately confirmed upon our arrival when she whispered conspiratorially to me, "You might have *mentioned* he was so good-looking."

As usual, the house looked wonderful and the tree was gorgeous, just skimming the fourteen-foot ceiling and gilded with every sort of tinsel and ornament imaginable. A fire blazed in the living room grate and the curtains were drawn against the cold gray sky. It might have been a snowy midnight for all the room projected, and I loved it that way.

With a single backwards glance, Carter disappeared with my father for some warm wassail. I stood by the hearth, letting my cold bones absorb the heat and thinking of all the Christmases I'd spent in this house. From the ones of my youth, when I was too small to reach the hook on which my stocking hung from the carved mantelpiece, to just last year, when Rory had made the evening toast with sparkling champagne and that devilish aplomb that had everyone thinking he was going to make an announcement of some import—only to wish everyone their own dreams come true and that they stop second-guessing ours. I had laughed—his delivery had been truly superb—but in the back of my mind I'd wondered how it would have felt to have made an engagement announcement, to have basked in the happiness I was sure would have emanated from everyone there.

But now, with Carter in the next room casually conversing with my father, I was intensely happy that Rory had never made that speech. Knowing how I felt now, with Carter, I realized how lonely I'd always been with Rory. Not lonely in the way of needing someone to talk to, but lonely on a much deeper, emotional level. I'd never felt understood by Rory, only tolerated. I'd never felt appreciated, only amusing.

I imagined the emotional battle with which I would now be struggling if I had been married to Rory when I found Carter. But I wouldn't have been fighting it, I thought wryly; Rory would never have allowed him in the house, and Carter would have had to wander the empty streets of Fredericksburg alone. Or worse, he would have brought his strange blend of disorientation and calm, of impossibility and opportunity, to some other household, to some unknown, lucky soul with the sense to keep him, if they could.

The sound of approaching footsteps roused me from my reverie, staving off what would inevitably have become melancholy ruminations on how empty life would be after Carter left. I turned to see Carter and my father enter the room, both armed with steaming mugs of wassail.

"There she is!" my father declared, as if I'd been hiding for some great length of time. "We've just been getting acquainted, Carter and I."

Carter carried two glasses and extended one to me with such unconscious consideration that it struck me as exceptionally generous. Perhaps it was because I'd just been reminiscing about Rory, who would no sooner have thought to bring me a drink than he would have thought to stand on his head and whistle "Dixie," but Carter's constant awareness of me was one of the things I was rapidly starting to feel I could not do without.

"I hope you don't mind my asking—you may be sick to death of talking about it—but I've always been curious about the war," Dad said to Carter. My father is a big man, with thick white hair that had once been a fiery red, who loved the art of conversation more than anything. "The *Civil* War, that is, though a more curious name for an armed dispute I can't imagine."

My father chuckled at the irony and I glanced at Carter. After his impassioned speech on Sunken Road I wasn't sure he'd be able to approach the topic of that war from the scholarly standpoint that 130 years of distance makes for, but he took it in stride. Why I even questioned such things after seeing him take virtually everything in stride, I wasn't sure.

"To be honest, I believe as wars go it had some quite civil moments," Carter replied amiably.

"Is that right?" my father asked. "In what way?"

Carter thought for a moment, then continued in his quiet voice, "I don't know if you've ever been in the situation, sir, but during warfare there can be many days of boredom between battles—days when you feel even fighting would be better than sitting around waiting. Some people don't believe that—they think it must be a relief not to be involved in bloodshed—but that's frequently not the case. At least, not when you know a battle is coming and you just don't know when. Anyway, during one of those times, just before Fredericksburg, in fact, our band—the Union, that is—was playing—loudly—along the shores of the Rappahannock. Such songs as the 'Star Spangled Banner' and 'Hail Columbia,' well known to all of us on both sides, and well within hearing of the southern troops just across the river. In fact, the goal was to get the southern troops involved.''

My father looked at Carter speculatively, but with great interest. Perhaps he thought it was just some reenactor "thing" that had him speaking as if he had been there. "And did they get involved?"

Carter's smile broadened. "Not until we played 'Dixie.' And then they created quite a ruckus. Rather sporting of us to play it, though, don't you think?''

That did it; he'd won my father over. Anyone who knew more than he did on a subject, and particularly if they knew amusing anecdotes, would be grilled until my father could claim that knowledge also. The two continued on in that vein for the next hour, until enough guests arrived that my mother had to drag my father away to play host.

Throughout the day Carter met and spoke easily with everyone he was introduced to, never betraying any nervousness, nor any trepidation that someone might "discover" his story. I was the only one in the room who knew the truth—my mother believed him still deluded from the blow to his head—and once the guests began to show, history ceased to be the topic of conversation.

As evening descended and the hearty smells of roast

turkey filled the house, my mother drew me aside to ask about Rory. I tried to brush her off with a vague comment about his work schedule, but she wouldn't let it go.

"It's him, isn't it?" she said certainly. "Rory's upset about him." She inclined her elf-tasseled head toward Carter, where he stood conversing with Dr. Shrewsbury. He still looked as fresh as he had that morning in his crisp white shirt and perfectly knotted tie. (I'd shown him how to tie it the modern way and, with the same dexterity with which he adopted the manual alphabet, he tied it perfectly the first time.)

I shifted uncomfortably under my mother's intense gaze and sipped what had to be my tenth eggnog. I tried evasion one more time. "He was at first, but now I don't think he's upset with Carter."

Mother shook her head, as if I'd confessed something to her. "You've had a fight. I knew it. I could tell the moment you said he wasn't coming. And right before Christmas! Should we send his gifts home with you, or do you think it would be better to wait?"

I sighed heavily. "Better to wait, Mom. I'm not going to be seeing him any time soon, I don't think."

Mother smiled through pursed lips. "Now, now. Surely you two will straighten it out; you always do. You've been together so long, it would be a shame to let it all go to waste."

I knew what she was saying. After so much time, how could she ever hope for a wedding if we broke up now? It would take me another ten years with someone to get to the point that she could hope for an engagement again.

I scowled and ignored the hollowness in my stomach, which had nothing to do with hunger. "I hate to disappoint you, Mother, but it's all gone to waste already. I'm tired of 'straightening things out' again and again. Besides, it's different this time." I swigged my eggnog and thought that if I took one more sip of the milky stuff I would dissolve into a chalk-white pool of it. "But anyway, if you don't mind, I'd really rather not talk about it right now."

I gazed at Carter as I said it, thinking that all I wanted to do was sit in an empty room and talk to him. He made me forget about Rory and all my feelings of inadequacy. He had no expectations of me, or of anything, and he knew my situation without my having to detail it in words. For some reason at that moment I felt as if he understood me better than anyone else in the room. How that had happened in such a short time I wasn't sure, but when I was with him I felt supported on the most basic of levels, as if the most tender part of my soul were enveloped by a soft, resilient cushion of protection.

"He's not a bad consolation prize," my mother said dryly, following my gaze, and suddenly the comment stung.

I turned to her. "Rory's not even in the same league with him," I said vehemently. Then, turning back to look at him again, I added more calmly, "He's different. He's—he's an amazing person."

There was no way I could tell her, no way I could define the many facets I'd seen of Carter's personality. Unless she'd seen him as I had—in utter despair and confusion, as on that first night I'd found him—in impassioned abandon as he'd described the scene he'd left on Sunken Road in 1862, reliving gruesome memories of unspeakable horrors in an appeal to have me believe his incredible story—and then resisting a dangerous desire with tender control as he kissed me that night by the train station—unless she'd seen him in all those lights she would never understand the depth of his strength, the quality of his soul.

I glanced back at my mother to find her watching me shrewdly. She nodded slowly, a small, funny smile on her lips.

"What?" I asked defensively. It was a strange look she had given me.

She just continued to nod until someone started tapping a spoon against a glass: the toast. I looked at my watch. Good Lord, it was seven-thirty already and time for the toast. One of the caterers was making the rounds with a tray of champagne, and I grabbed two glasses. My mother winked, then made her way through the crowd to my father, and I went to rescue Carter from the clutches of Dr. Shrewsbury.

"What's happening?" Carter asked me quietly as I reached his side.

I handed him the champagne. "It's our annual Christmas toast," I explained. "Somehow, over the course of the years my parents have thrown this party, it's become a tradition for one of the family members or a close friend to make a toast before dinner. Looks like James is going to make it this year." I had finally located the source of the noise and it was James, standing by the tree with his girlfriend Michelle next to him. A strange, sinking feeling crept into my stomach at the sight of them, unnerving me because I was unsure of the reason.

Michelle interpreted for James. "For those of you who don't know my friend," he signed, indicating Michelle, who bowed lightly, "this is Michelle Johnson. She will, obviously, be interpreting for me, but you must remember that these are my words."

The crowd noise died down until a final quiet descended. James went on to explain how they'd met, occasionally stopping to look at her and share between them a look I recognized as a lovers' gaze, the kind that makes bystanders feel embarrassed in a jealous sort of way.

"Michelle and I have been together for almost a year now," James continued, "and we have decided that before 1996 disappeared we wanted to be sure to mark it with its proper significance in our lives. It was the year in which we met.'' James raised his champagne glass, and the others followed suit. ''And we want it to be the year in which we announce our commitment to spend the rest of our lives together. We plan to be married in June.'' The crowd gasped dramatically, and a collective murmur shot through it. ''So Merry Christmas, everyone! We wish for you all the happiness that we have found.''

The party erupted into applause and a waving of hands, the deaf way to applaud, as well as the clinking of fifty-some champagne glasses. I felt my eyes sting with tears of poignancy: happiness for James and a selfish, unwelcome pity for myself. Carter touched his glass to mine and I turned to him.

''To love,'' he said quietly, his lips curved in that serious half smile I was coming to know very well.

I swallowed over the lump in my throat and smiled back. ''Yes.'' We touched glasses again and sipped, our eyes in silent communication. He knew how I felt; he could see it in my face. Did he feel the same regret I did—the regret for what might have been between us? Or was that just a hope of mine alone?

Chapter Fourteen

Late that night, after the guests had left and my parents had gone to bed, Carter and I sat alone in the living room. The lights were all extinguished except for the ones on the tree, and the room was cozy in the dimness of their red and green pinpoints and the glow from the fire.

Carter cradled a Wedgwood brandy snifter in his palm and gently rocked the amber liquid with an unconscious motion that caused it to coat the sides of the glass. He stood with his back to the fire, surveying the darkened room, while I sat on the sofa, leafing through a book I'd given my mother on cottage gardens.

"Your parents are wealthy," he said pensively. It wasn't exactly a question.

I looked up, then followed his gaze around the room, seeing what he saw. "I suppose so," I answered. It wasn't something I thought about often, but money had never been an issue in our family. It was for me somewhat, now that I was trying to make it on my own in the book business; but I never had the fear that many people did of failure and a complete loss of livelihood.

His eyes rested on the now-opened packages that lay stacked in neat piles under the tree. "You're lucky. They're very generous."

I knew he was thinking about the boxes of clothes they'd given him. (I'd made the mistake of ad-libbing the reason he'd had to stay at my house as being one of acute poverty. He was only a gardener, I'd said, who happened to have a zealous interest in history. He couldn't even afford a suit to wear to Christmas dinner, I'd wailed. I guess I got carried away with my story and represented him as nearly homeless.) They'd given him nice cotton pleated pants, dress shirts, more jeans and socks and running shoes. It had made him extremely uncomfortable, I knew, but in his incredibly astute way he'd seen how uncomfortable it would have made my parents if he were to have refused it all. And besides, it was nothing compared to what they'd lavished on James and Michelle and me.

Carter had brought them some plants from Green Way Landscaping to go with the book on cottage gardens that I'd bought. And he'd been quite proud of them, I thought, when he'd gotten the idea and brought them home. But I could tell when we'd arrived that he thought them thoroughly inadequate and slightly embarrassing next to the showy display of packages heaped under the tree.

"Mother loved the plants," I said. "Really. The garden is one of the few things she does alone, without hired help."

Carter nodded vaguely, then turned his contemplative gaze on me. I returned the look without any discomfort at the silence. I almost felt that we communicated best that way, by watching each other's faces and reading each other's eyes. It was an odd, comforting realization.

"I've got something for you," he said. "I don't know

that you'll like it, but I want you to have it.''

I felt a thrill of uncertainty at what he might have gotten for me. A souvenir, I thought, something I could have to remind myself of him after he was gone. Something tangible I could believe in, long after this strange story became a dream I might have made up.

He moved slowly through the darkness to sit beside me on the couch, pulling from his pocket a small rectangular package wrapped in a piece of gold wrapping paper. He turned it in his long fingers, gazing at it, the firelight silhouetting his profile, gilding his pale lashes.

"It was the only thing of value I had with me, and I considered selling it—to pay you back for all you've done for me." He looked up. "But I'd rather give it to you. You may sell it if you wish."

With that he handed it to me, extending it on an open palm. "Thank you, Shelby. I shall remember you always. And—I hope," he took a short breath and expelled it, "I hope you shall remember me too."

I reached out a hand to grip his forearm. "Carter, I could never forget you—even if I wanted to," I said firmly. Then, "Thank you."

I gingerly took the package from him and set about opening it with trembling fingers. It was heavy for something so small, and I couldn't for the life of me fathom what it might be. As I pulled off the thick paper, a glint of silver sparked bright in the dim firelight, and the lighter that Carter had had in his pocket that very first night appeared in my hand. The heavy metal warmed immediately to my touch and I noticed for the first time that it was engraved, rather ornately, with many swirls and initials that I couldn't read.

"My father gave it to me," Carter explained in a low voice, his breath warm on my shoulder as he leaned toward me. One long finger traced the flat side of the lighter. "It was one of the only things he had, and the only thing he left when he disappeared for the last time. These are his initials, ABL. Ambrose Bernard Lindsey. I believe it is valuable, although I'm not sure now. I saw some larger and of a more classic form in a shop window downtown one day.''

It was one of those moments when emotion hit so powerfully that I was unable to speak. I clasped the lighter in both hands and closed my eyes.

''Open it,'' Carter said.

I opened my hands and looked for the top, but it appeared to be a solid piece of metal. Perhaps it wasn't a lighter at all. Did they even have lighters back then? What would they have put in them, butane?

He took it gently from me and pressed a tiny button to open it lengthwise, revealing a long, oyster-colored clock face with delicate little hands and fine Roman numerals.

''Oh, it's a clock!'' I exclaimed. ''A pocket watch!''

Carter smiled ruefully. ''Well, not exactly. I'm afraid the design is a little impractical. You see, it has no place to be attached to a chain, and it's a bit small to be considered a table clock. That's why I thought you might wish to sell it. Perhaps a dealer might think it of value because of its oddity.'' He handed it back to me.

I nearly snatched it away from him. ''I would *never* sell it!'' I protested passionately. ''It's the most beautiful thing I've ever seen.''

He looked pleased and slightly embarrassed. ''Well, it is rather distinct.''

''It's beautiful,'' I insisted. ''And it's from you,'' I added more quietly. ''I'll cherish it.''

I gently snapped the lid shut and studied the tiny button on the edge that released the clasp. It really was the most unusual thing I'd ever seen, and beautiful in its delicate antiquity. But, to be perfectly honest, it could have been a shoelace and I couldn't have valued it more.

"I'm glad," he murmured beside me, leaning back on the couch.

I rubbed the clock lightly in my palms and wondered at his generosity. The one thing of value he owned and he'd given it to me, offering to let me sell it despite the fact that it had been given to him by his father.

"But perhaps you'll want this, when you—when you get back." I didn't want to bring up the dreaded possibility of the child, but it seemed too pressing to ignore. "When you get back there might be someone to whom you'd rather give such a valuable gift, someone with whom the connection to your father would be more significant."

Carter looked at me solemnly. "There is no one else I'd rather give it to." Then his eyebrows raised slightly, and he shrugged. "Besides, there are plenty of other heirlooms at home to be passed out, if Meg hasn't found them already."

I rubbed my fingertips along the lid of the clock, pressing the graven initials into my skin.

"That reminds me," I said hesitantly. "I was reading in the newspaper this morning that scientists believe that we might be able to see the Northern Lights next week." I concentrated on looking at the tree across the room. "I thought—and maybe we can ask Madame Erika about it too—that their appearance might have had something to do with your time travel. Maybe you could get back the same way."

I felt Carter sit forward beside me. "Are you sure of this? That they'll return—the Northern Lights?"

I shrugged and studied the clock in my hands. "As sure as they ever are, I guess. Unless it's a cloudy night or something, we should be able to see them."

He said very quietly, "The witch spoke of a fire. . . . ."

"Well, I thought we could call her with the idea, and

maybe she could tell us if it's possible. She seemed to know quite a lot.''

''Yes,'' he said quietly.

''And I know you must get back, so I thought . . . well, I thought of it immediately when I read the article. And I meant to tell you this morning, but what with one thing and another . . .'' I was babbling, but I couldn't stop myself. ''I know it must be hard for you to be here. Separated from her and everyone you know. I know this place must seem so alien, so cold and unfriendly, but—well, no 'buts,' really—it's just that I've grown so used to your company—''

I felt his hand take my elbow. ''Shelby,'' he said quietly.

''Oh, I know, I know,'' I said, my voice rising as I lost control of the direction of my own thoughts. ''You don't need to tell me. She's alone there without you. And I'll help you, really I will. But I don't—I can't—I don't have to like it, do I?''

I turned my face to his and he pulled me into his arms. I wrapped my fingers around the watch and let my arms cross in front of my chest as he held me, letting him cradle me as I hugged my emotions to myself. I *would not* cry, I told myself; I simply could not keep crying every time we had a conversation about his real life. I buried my face in his neck, the fingers of my other hand grasping his shirt and knotting it in my hand.

''She is alone,'' he said into my hair. ''I don't like it either, but she's all alone. If only she weren't so—helpless.''

I nodded, not needing to hear the reasons. It was not to be, Carter and me. He had to go. I'd known it all along. Even if he had turned out to be an amnesiac, he'd have had to go. But at least then I could have known him; I could have visited him.

It struck me then for the first time that if he did make

it back to his own time, he'd be dead. To me, in 1996, he would be dead, a hundred years dead, and nothing more than one of the weathered tombstones I used to like to study, to see if I could still read the dates and names.

I felt the terrible well of realization rise up inside of me and burst forth. "Carter, you *can't* go! You can't die; I couldn't bear it," I protested, pushing slightly back from his chest to look him in the face and demand that he not ask it of me.

But his arms tightened around me and he levelled stern, almost angry, eyes at me. "I won't die, Shelby. That's the one lesson we should have learned from this. Time is parallel somehow. It must be, if I was alive enough to travel to you when I did."

There was no possibility of my being able to analyze the point at that moment. None of it made sense to me, and I was incapable of considering it with any logic. "Oh I don't know, I don't know. All I know is that you'll be gone and I'll have this watch that's a hundred and thirty years old, and somewhere there'll be a headstone with your name on it, and Meg's, and everyone in between you and that stupid man with your name in Fredericksburg—oh, and I *hate* him. I just *hate* him for even existing!" I clutched his shirt even harder and pushed my fist into his chest. He pulled me closer and I could smell his clean, warm scent, feel his cheek against my hair.

His arms held me tightly, a hand rubbing my back comfortingly from my hair and down my spine.

"It's an odd thing for me to say, I guess, considering the possible relationship," he said, "but I do too, Shelby." I could feel his fist clench in my hair as he spoke, and he pressed his lips roughly to the top of my head. "I hate him too."

"Merry Christmas, Shel." It was Rory's voice. I had an instant image of him sitting in his tiny, dim studio apartment outside town. He'd have the curtains drawn and there'd be dirty dishes strewn about, waiting as vainly for soap as sunlight.

I sat at the kitchen table. It was only the day after Christmas, but for some reason it felt like weeks since I'd spoken to him. And it was strange, considering I'd spent the last ten years of my life talking to him daily on the phone, but I found my heart actually hammering with the surprise of hearing his voice. "Merry Christmas, Rory," I answered evenly.

I heard him shift in his seat, and something tapped in the background—a pencil against the counter, perhaps. "How was yesterday?" he asked finally.

"Fine. It was nice." I wondered if I should elaborate—tell him people had asked about him, that my parents had gifts for him—but I didn't want to. I didn't want to say anything that he could construe as an invitation back into my life.

I heard him breath deeply and felt a pang of pity for him. His own family had moved to Texas after Rory'd finished high school, and he wasn't close to them anyway. For the past nine years Rory had been a part of my family.

"What did you do?" I asked reluctantly. Phone silences always made me uncomfortable.

"I worked. Flanagan's was short a waiter, so I volunteered. I hadn't heard from you, so . . ." His voice trailed off.

This struck me as a really inane thing for him to say. Inane, but typical. "Of course you hadn't heard from me, Rory. Did you think I was going to call you up and invite you for Christmas dinner after what you did?"

He expelled a blast of air on the word, "*God.*"

I uttered a short laugh in disbelief. "What, did you think I'd just forget all about that?" I rolled my eyes and shook my head, as if he was there to see me. I knew that was just what he'd thought—that this would blow over like all of our other fights. "You really are something else." It was all I could think to say.

"Shelby, are you going to hold this against me forever?" he asked, anger in his voice. But I could tell it was forced anger; the best defense is a good offense and all that.

I ran my had through my hair, then rested my forehead on my open palm, an elbow on the table. "No, I'm not," I said firmly. "Someday I'll get over the anger, and the humiliation, and then it will just be one of those things that happened in my past. *You* will just be one of those things that happened in my past."

"Shelby—"

"No. Listen to me, Rory. You're going to have to do better than this if you even want to have a conversation with me. Why did you call today? Did you think I'd swoon at the sound of your voice and forgive everything?" I could feel my face heat up with my anger. "Well, guess again. I learned something about you that I will *never* unlearn. Maybe someday I won't be mad about it, but it won't change what's happened because of it."

"Shelby, I told you I was sorry. And I *am* sorry— more than you'll ever realize, probably. I just want to get past it. I want to know what I have to do to make you forget about it." He paused. "Please, Shelby."

I felt pity rise again and squelched it. "I'll never forget about it," I said in a hard voice. "You should have thought of that before."

He muttered an expletive. "Sometimes you are so *damned* bullheaded," he said, true anger in his voice, along with an obvious effort to control it. "I know I should have thought of it before. I know that now. And I'm sorry. I'm very truly sorry. How can I make you understand that? I just feel—I felt hurt, and angry that you'd taken in that—that *psycho* and stopped—"

"Don't you *dare* use Carter as an excuse," I interrupted, hissing the words. "And I do understand. I understand you're sorry, *truly sorry* you got caught." I scoffed. "Can you honestly tell me that that girl was the first time you ever cheated on me? Can you?" I didn't give him the chance to answer—I didn't want to know how long I'd been a dupe. "I don't think so, Rory. I may have been a fool for a long time, but I'm not now. My eyes are open."

Rory laughed harshly. "And who opened them? *Carter?*" he blasted into the phone, a sneer in his voice. "Now that you've gotten rid of me, are you two through playing footsie under the table? Have you just moved right into the bedroom—"

I slammed the receiver into the cradle. The bulletin board trembled on the wall. I wanted to strike him—smack that dirty, slimy, gutter-dwelling mind of his. All he could think of—*still*—was whether Carter had gotten me into bed. I wondered if he would even have made this effort to explain if Carter hadn't been on the scene. He probably would have thought I'd come around in time, as I always did after a fight. He just couldn't grasp the humiliation, the gross betrayal I felt at the discovery of his infidelity. And how he could not grasp that, while at the same time getting so incensed at the idea of me sleeping with Carter, was beyond me.

I thought about calling him back and screaming this at him. Screaming that he was a hopelessly self-centered egotist who understood *nothing* about me, *nothing* about relationships. But I knew it would be useless. Rory was only aware of what Rory wanted to be aware of. Anything I told him that didn't mesh with what he wanted to think he would ignore, or twist to suit his own purposes.

I squeezed my eyes shut and rubbed my hands over

my face. I knew he would be sitting there at that very moment, justifying and rationalizing away all that I'd said. He would tell himself that I betrayed him first—that by trying to help a poor soul in trouble I'd been rejecting him. He'd tell himself that I was being unreasonable to take his one small mistake and make a major issue out of it, that I was rigid, unbending and unsympathetic. He'd tell himself that there were plenty of women out there who would forgive him—especially after he'd made what he would consider such a humble apology. I dropped a fist, hard, to the table and felt angrily gratified by the accompanying rattle of the salt and pepper shakers. *God,* it made me so mad to think of him over there, actually *believing* he was right. He was probably, even now, calling up some sympathetic girl or other to complain about his small-minded girlfriend.

I swept the salt shaker up in a tense fist and hurled it toward the wall. It flew crazily from my hand and shattered the glass of a framed etching. I seethed at the picture, glad of the sharp shards of glass that poked from the carpeting like some kind of modern art sculpture. I picked up the pepper shaker, ready to do more damage, when a noise from behind me caused me to whirl in surprise.

Carter stood in the doorway, surveying the scene. One hand thoughtfully rubbed the side of his unshaven face. He was home early from work.

I felt color flood my cheeks as I carefully replaced the pepper shaker on the table. Carter's eyes moved from the table to the floor, from the spikes of glass in the carpet, to the picture hanging askew on the wall. His heavy-lidded gaze came to rest on me.

"Something wrong?" he asked.

I pressed my lips together. "I just talked to Rory."

He nodded slowly. "I take it the conversation didn't go well."

The phone rang again. I stood frozen, glaring at the offending lump of plastic. It rang again. Again.

Carter looked from me to the phone and back again. After the fourth ring he moved casually to the instrument and, as if he'd been doing it all his life, picked up the receiver and said hello. He didn't say it as a question, as I did, but as a solemn word to let the other person know he was there.

I watched him as if he might actually do something physical to Rory, for I was sure that was who it was.

"Yes," he said. "Yes, that's right." His eyes met mine with an inscrutable look. He actually appeared somewhat concerned, and I wondered what in the world Rory had said to him.

"Yes, I know. Very interesting." He took a deep breath. "That would be acceptable to me. Let me confer with—yes. With my wife." His lips curved into a small, wry smile with the words, his eyes lingering warmly on my face.

I was very confused. It couldn't possibly be Rory.

"She's beside me," Carter continued. "I'll ask her. Please wait." He took the phone from his ear and held it awkwardly in the air, as if unsure what to do with it when one was not speaking into it.

"Who is it?" I asked.

He said, "It's Mr. Lindsey."

I felt my stomach drop. "Mr. Lindsey," I repeated. The phone was still in the air, in Carter's outstretched hand.

I took it. "Hello, Mr. Lindsey. How are you?"

"You can call me Bart," a nasal voice said in a dry tone. "I've just asked your husband if you would be interested in coming to the house on Thursday. I'm most interested in our connection. I wasn't aware of another line coming from Carter Lindsey the First."

Carter Lindsey the First watched me like a hawk as I

shifted the phone between my ear and shoulder. With my hands I grabbed notepaper and pencil, wrote *Thursday?* and turned it to Carter. He shrugged and nodded.

"Of course we would love to come," I answered. My stomach was actually trembling at this point with adrenaline and anxiety.

"Good," the nasal voice continued unemotionally. "I have a lot of information about the family tree; I'm sure your husband will be interested. Let me give you the address."

He gave me an address in a new subdivision at the edge of town. So much for him occupying the ancestral home, I thought. I guess the Carters never completely forgave their daughter for running off with a renegade, though Carter's descendants must have come back to Virginia for some reason.

"Come about six o'clock," Bart said. "My wife will cook dinner."

"Great," I said. "Great. Should we bring anything?" He paused. "Like what?"

"Oh, I don't know. Wine? Dessert?"

"We don't drink," he said bluntly. "And my wife will cook dinner, as I said."

I felt chastened by the words. "Okay. We'll see you Thursday, then." I hated to think it, but I already didn't like him.

"Six o'clock," he repeated.

"Okay, thanks." We finally hung up.

I met Carter's eyes and sighed. "Looks like we're dining with your grandson on Thursday."

Chapter Fifteen

I dressed carefully for the Lindseys. For some unknown reason I had a strong desire to impress them. It wasn't as if they were going to know that the Carter Lindsey they were about to meet was *the* Carter Lindsey, but all the same I wanted to convey to them that he was doing well, and had an attractive, or at least clean, 'wife.'

As I fussed around my room, trading in one set of earrings for another, then swapping bracelets and donning and removing a vest, I heard Carter emerge from the bathroom and enter his own room. Two minutes later, while I was trying on another pair of shoes, I heard him leave his bedroom and go downstairs. He, apparently, wasn't suffering from the same clothing conundrum that I was.

When I finally made it downstairs myself it was five-thirty. I had drawn my unruly curls back loosely to the nape of my neck and tied them with a black scarf. Loose russet tendrils framed my face and I wore simple gold earrings. I had finally decided on a long black silk skirt with a short matching jacket and a deep purple silk blouse. I looked, for once, classy instead of wild.

Carter turned from the woodstove as I descended the stairs. He wore trousers and a blazer my parents had given him for Christmas, complete with a pale gray tie that exactly matched the color of his eyes. He looked fantastic, and the expression he assumed upon seeing me was more gratifying than any verbal compliment could have been. The fact that he followed this up with a verbal compliment was a bonus.

"You never cease to make me glad I'm here," he said softly, with a smile that was much more relaxed than I felt.

My heart swelled with his words. "Oh, Carter, do you mean it?" It wasn't the classic rejoinder my outfit might have deserved, but it meant so much to me that I had to know if he meant it.

He moved toward me and took my hand in his. "You must know that I do," he said, stroking my fingers with his thumb. His eyes searched my face while his other hand rose and cupped my chin. "For tonight," he said quietly, "you are my wife."

With that he bent forward and caught my lips with his for a long moment.

When he pulled back his hand still held mine. "Mr. and Mrs. Carter Lindsey," I said and smiled. "The First."

He laughed easily. "The First," he repeated and nodded once, definitively.

The game promised to be fun, I thought, as my heart tripped gaily at the idea of being Mrs. Carter Lindsey for a night. I wondered just how far beyond the dinner the game would go but wouldn't let myself contemplate what I'd like to have happen.

He helped me with my cape and escorted me out to

the car with my arm pulled chivalrously through his; then he opened the car door with a short bow and flipped the tail of my coat inside before closing it. I leaned over and unlocked his side, then started the car.

We sat for a moment as the engine warmed up and the frost slowly melted from the windshield.

"Are you nervous?" I asked.

He shook his head. "Curious, mostly. I can't imagine what they would have to say that would help me, unless they reveal that they're related to some other Lindsey." He pushed down between the fingers of his gloves to make them fit better.

"That would help you?" I asked.

"It would help me to know that I did not father a child with Meg," he said.

"In case you can't get back?" I wasn't sure what I was groping for.

Carter looked over at me. "Among other reasons," he said cryptically.

I eased the car into gear. The neighborhood where the Lindseys lived wasn't far away, and before long we were parking in front of their house. It was a low brick rambler with two Ford Escorts parked in the driveway, one a station wagon, the other an older, beat-up hatchback. Carter once again opened the door for me and helped me to my feet on the icy street. There was a moment by the car when I slipped and he caught me to his chest. My hand gripped the lapel of his coat, a loaner from my father, and I gazed up into his face. It was all I could do to stop myself from wrapping my arm around his neck and pulling his face to mine, but he only gave me a small smile and righted me on my feet. Then we turned to the house.

I rang the bell, pulling nervously at my gloves and trying not to drop the small clutch purse I held at the same time. After a moment the door opened.

As light pitched out into the darkness, I had to swallow

a gasp at the sight of the man before me. Encased in a polyester suit of dark blue, with a wrinkled yellow tie and a pale blue shirt, his tall, skinny, pooch-bellied frame filled the doorway. It was the stringy-haired man from the library.

I was immeasurably glad we were still in the darkness outside the door so that my undoubtedly horrified expression couldn't be seen, but I could tell by the tightening of Carter's hand on my elbow that he sensed something strange in my reaction.

"Good evening, Mr. Lindsey," Carter said, his subdued, mellow tones sounding as comfortable as could be. "Carter Lindsey." He released my elbow and extended his hand. Bart took it cordially enough and shook it. "And this is my wife, Shelby."

I felt my hand shoot out from beneath my cape automatically; it couldn't have been stiffer if it had belonged to a corpse. Of all the images I'd conjured of this moment, from meeting a Carter look-alike to seeing Meg's face mirrored in the despised descendant, not one of them could compare to the shock of seeing this strange and unpleasant figure before me.

His hand closed on mine, but his gaze remained pinned on Carter.

A plump, kind-faced woman emerged behind the man who could only be Bart, and her beaming countenance took away some of the chill I was feeling, which had nothing to do with the cold.

"Come in, come in," she sang merrily. "Bart, don't leave 'em standing out there in the cold." She had a country accent and a warmth of manner that I was drawn to immediately, though to be honest it could have been a direct result of the repulsion I felt for Bart.

Bart moved back and I stepped into the light of the foyer. "So nice to meet you, Mrs. Lindsey," I said to Bart's wife, but both she and her husband were concentrating on Carter as he followed me into the hall.

They turned to each other with a strange look, and Bart raised his eyebrows in an odd way. "Remarkable," he murmured.

I couldn't hear her reply, but Mrs. Lindsey recovered herself first. She turned to me with a warm smile. "Please, call me Carol. And it's delightful to meet you too. Can I take your coat?"

We were relieved of our winter gear and ushered up a short flight of stairs to the family room. It was just as I would have pictured it from the outside, with orange shag carpeting, brown plaid furniture, and photographs lining the mantel. Hanging on the wall was a framed poem with the image of a cross and a dove printed on the paper under the words.

"Can I get y'all somethin' to drink?" Carol asked. "Somethin' warm? We've got hot cider. Or hot tea, if you'd rather."

"Cider sounds wonderful," I said, trying not to look at the stringy man and hoping fervently that he didn't recognize me. I racked my brain to remember if I'd given him a dirty look or done anything else at the library that I would now have to be ashamed of.

"The same for me," Carter said.

We sat on the couch, and even our close proximity— Carter's leg pressed along mine for the length of the cushion—couldn't shake my preoccupation with the fact that this weird man had turned out to be Carter's relative.

Carol returned with our drinks, and we indulged in some awkward small-talk. Carter took my hand in his after shooting me a perplexed look, and I found myself wishing the Lindseys weren't teetotalers; I could have used several shots of something very strong at that moment.

"So, are you two newlyweds?" Carol asked with a benevolent smile.

Carter and I answered at the same time—me with an exaggerated "Oh nooo" and Carter with a curt, "Yes."

We looked at each other awkwardly until Carter nodded at me to continue. "Well, Carter's right, really," I added quickly. "It's just that we've lived together for several years, so I don't really consider us 'newlyweds.'" Congratulating myself on this effective ad-libbing, I looked up at Carter in triumph. His face, suffused with red, wore an appalled expression.

I frowned at him. He didn't realize how accepted living together was these days, I thought—until I turned back to the Lindseys. They, too, wore duplicate expressions of disapproval. Was I the alien here?

"Well, not exactly *together* together," I continued. "You know, we, uh, lived in the same apartment building. Just down the hall, you know. So close as to be, you know—"

Carter's hand tightened significantly on mine. "Shelby's making a mess of this," he said with an indulgent smile and a bone-cracking grip. "The truth is that we did live in the same, ah, apartment building until just before our wedding, when we stayed with her family while we built our house."

Carol nodded her approval, and I wondered how long we'd have to continue this conversation-making before dinner was served. Then how long after that before we could get down to what we were really here for—that is, the genealogical charts.

"I thought you lived in the old town," Bart intoned nasally. "You built your own house there?

Carter said, "Yes."

I said, "Well, not *built* really, like from the ground up. More like *remodeled*." I glanced at Carter and, at his frown, added, "Extensively. Gutted it, really."

Bart patted one long, gray strand of hair into place on

the top of his head and said, "That must have been quite costly."

I said, "Oh yes."

Carter said, "Not really."

I began to get the feeling that I should shut up and let Carter do the talking. He definitely had a better feel for what these people wanted to hear than I did.

"But I don't handle the finances," I said, sinking into the couch a little deeper. I pulled Carter's hand into my lap and held it with both of mine. "You tell them about it, honey." I smiled at him sweetly and nodded.

Bart looked at both of us with a sour expression. He thought we were weird. I nearly laughed out loud at that realization, though I guess we were weird—weirder than they could imagine.

"Portions of the frame were rotten, so the whole endeavor was rather extensive, requiring a complete overhaul." Carter turned to me with a quelling look. "I provided most of the labor, so we saved a considerable sum."

"You do that for a living?" Bart asked him. "You a builder?"

"Precisely," Carter said. He calmly sipped his cider.

Before Bart could continue his interview, I interjected, "What is it that you do, Bart?"

"I work at the college," he said. "I'm a historian."

That explained his presence in the reference room at the library.

"How convenient for you," I said with great animation. "You can almost walk to work. And is that how you became interested in your family tree?"

"Actually the *genealogy* is why I became a historian." Bart played with his hair again. For someone who was so condescending, he certainly seemed nervous when speaking. I would have thought he'd have made more of an effort to be genial in conversation. "My family has always been interested in their ancestry. I grew up having memorized the family tree from 1798 on down. That's why I was so surprised when my wife told me you called. I don't see how we could be related to the same Carter Lindsey. You did say you were interested in the one who died in the Civil War?''

I felt Carter stiffen beside me. ''Oh, did he die in the war?'' I asked. ''We only knew that he lived during that period.''

Bart cleared his throat with a self-important air. ''He was presumed dead. They never identified a body, but that was not unusual. He was involved in the slaughter on Sunken Road in town here, so there was very little chance he survived it. Though I suppose it's possible that he took the opportunity to desert. Some of the more cowardly sorts did.''

''I'm certain he was not a coward,'' Carter said rigidly.

The stringy man eyed Carter. ''Well, your presence would certainly point to the conclusion that he was. If he deserted, then he could have gone on to have more children, rather than just the one that I'm related to; the one we could trace through marital and birth records. It's a direct line from him to me, with all in between accounted for. So unless you're related to a different man . . .'' He let the words trail off.

The air in the room bristled with tension between the two men. Glancing at one and then the other, it was almost laughable. The idea of the strong, handsome man beside me being remotely related to the sour, stringy creature across from me was ludicrous.

''I'd doubt that,'' Carol said, venturing into the conversation for the first time. She gave her husband a significant look. ''Maybe your chart's wrong, hon. In any case, let's eat before we go poring over them old moldy papers.'' She rose with a smile and led us into the dining room.

After we were seated and served a salad I asked, "When I called I thought I heard a baby in the background. Do you have children?"

Carol smiled with motherly pride. "Yes, three sons. You heard the baby, Nelson. He's eight months. He's with my sister tonight. And the other two, Bartlett Jr. and Devin, are ten and eight. They're on a sleepover at a friend's house. We thought it'd be nice to have a quiet evening with y'all." She picked up a knife and began to carve the roast in front of her. "Do you two plan on having kids?"

It always amazed me when people felt at liberty to ask a question like that of people they didn't even know. Suppose I was unable to have children? Suppose it was a point of argument between us? Suppose we weren't really married and he was a man from the 1800s? Some people just never thought before asking personal questions.

I was about to answer vaguely when Carter chimed in, with a sly smile at me, "Yes, we intend to. As many as possible."

Carol laughed with approval. "Easy for the man to say, don't you think, Shelby? Just wait until you've got a couple, Carter; a passel of 'em won't look so attractive after that."

"Damn right," Bart muttered under his breath, then stuffed a large lettuce leaf into his mouth.

As far as I was concerned, it was the wrong Lindsey who was reproducing.

"We'll just take it one at a time, though, won't we, darling," I said.

Carter smiled across the table. "You remember, we did agree on at least four. Don't go changing your mind now," he said, and turned graciously to Carol. "After that she said we'd have to see."

I bit my lip to keep from laughing.

The roast was dry, the vegetables overcooked, and the badly needed wine nonexistent. We were just making our way through an impossibly heavy chocolate cheesecake when Bart, pushing his empty plate away from him, rose with a remark about getting to the point.

"I'll just get the papers and meet you all in the family room." He made his lanky way out of the room, leaving the three of us to choke down dessert alone.

"He's always so anxious to talk business," Carol said. "Once you get him on the subject of his family it's hard to get him off."

"I know what you mean," I said shaking my head, thinking Carter deserved a little of his own medicine. "My Carter's the same way. Sometimes I wonder if he'll ever shut up about it." It was lucky I wasn't drunk, or I'm sure the boredom produced by these people would have driven me to some further extreme. As it was, I took pity on Carter and toned down my revenge. "He just goes on and on and on about it. That's why he wants so many kids, you know. I used to say, 'How about one or two, sweetie? Wouldn't that be enough?' But he wants to name one for each and every relative." I turned to Carter with a chastising finger raised. "But we'd better start soon, honey, if you really want four. I'm not getting any younger!"

Carter's face flushed scarlet and I smiled into my iced tea. After a moment, into the ensuing silence, I added, "You know, men just have no conception of how long these things take. Four kids; that's practically four years of my life right there just having them! And then raising them is a whole other issue. I mean, Carter's good with cows and pigs, you know, but babies—I don't know. I told him we shouldn't even go out anymore until we'd started one, just to see what it was like. Almost stayed home tonight to work on it."

Carter looked to be in the throes of apoplexy. "All right, Shelby," he warned.

Carol rose to her feet and began collecting plates. "Let me just clean up a little and then we can join Bart."

"Here, let me help you," I offered.

"No, no!" She filled her arms with plates. "You two just finish your conversation. Don't mind me. I'll just see you in the other room in a minute."

Carol backed uncomfortably from the room.

I looked innocently at Carter, who began to regain his normal color. "Sorry," I said lightly. "But you asked for it."

He glared at me and said nothing.

"Conversation was just getting a little . . . dull," I said. "Besides, when people ask a personal question like that, they deserve a personal answer that makes them very uncomfortable." Carter's mouth twitched at the corners and I smiled tentatively. "Forgive me?"

His eyes narrowed. "I'm not sure." He stood and pushed back his chair. A definite smile lurked near his mouth. "I'm not sure you're truly repentant."

I rose and moved around the table toward him and the door. "Oh, but I am. You just married a tactless woman," I teased.

His arm slid comfortably around my shoulders as we walked toward the family room. I nearly preened like a cat at the contact, so gratifyingly right did it feel.

"And I'd do it all over again," he said, and smiled for our hosts as we entered the room.

Bart sat on the couch, smack in the center, with piles of yellowed papers and books spread out before him on the coffee table. Carol sat in an armchair across the room, pulling a wad of pale blue yarn and a crochet hook from a bag next to it. Carter and I were left with no choice but to sit one on either side of Bart.

Bart pulled a sheaf of papers from the pile before him

and handed it to Carter. He virtually ignored me, turning halfway in his seat to face Carter, presenting me with his wrinkled polyester back.

"That's the family tree, starting in the late 1700s." Bart leaned close to Carter. "As you can see, I'm related to Benjamin Franklin through his aunt by marriage." He paused to give Carter a chance to be impressed with that little pretentious piece of genealogy. "The area you're interested in is just here." He flipped some pages for Carter as he sat helplessly holding the bottom sheets. I could tell he longed to shove Bart out of the way and go through the stuff himself, but he sat politely silent.

Bart stopped flipping and poked a crooked finger into the pages in Carter's hands. "Here. Carter Lindsey, son of Ambrose B. Lindsey and Madeleine A. Carter, born August 10, 1837."

August 10, I thought. A Leo. Carter bent close to read.

"As you can see," Bart continued, "the date of death has been listed as December 13, 1862, but as I told you, a body was never recovered." He flipped another page. "And here, Carter Lindsey married Margaret G. Gilley on June 5, 1858. Margaret gave birth to Carter D. Lindsey on April 3, 1863."

I taxed my mathematically challenged mind to come up with a July 1862 date of conception. Hadn't Carter joined the army by then? Hope sprang eternal.

"Carter D. married June Bartlett—so you can see I came by my names honestly—" he wheezed out a laugh, revealing the bad teeth with the silver lining, "on September 14, 1888. They had three children, Sarah L., Joseph C., and Martha S. I came down from Joseph C., who married . . ." He droned on some more, reading off dates that Carter could easily, and more quickly, have read to himself.

After a moment more of this Carter gently moved the papers from Bart's grasp and gave him a curt smile. "If you don't mind, I'm particularly interested," he flipped back several pages, "in *this* Carter Lindsey."

Bart cleared his throat as Carter studied the dates and leaned back with a self-important air. "Well, you can see that there are precious few direct lines back to him. He had one son, who had one son, who had two, only one of whom had children. I'm curious to know where you think you fit into this. Unless you were somehow—conceived out of the bounds of a study of this sort."

Carol gasped and shot her husband a stern look. "Bart, *no.*"

"It's a perfectly valid question, Carol," he replied calmly. "And I'd also like to know why you're so interested in that particular man."

I glanced apprehensively at Carter. We hadn't rehearsed any sort of genealogical connection, and I wondered how he could justify his interest without it. Without, that is, implicating himself in illegitimacy, or even adultery. Amusing as that might have been to me, I knew it would have gone severely against the grain in Carter.

Carter gave Bart a shrewd look and let the silence lengthen until Carol, who appeared to be as uncomfortable as I was, piped in with, "Show him the picture, Bart. I think you're being ridiculous. You should've shown it to him the second he walked in the door!"

I looked from Carol to Bart, who made no effort to conceal a very ugly expression directed at her.

"What picture is that?" Carter asked mildly.

Bart shuffled through the piles on the table, and I took the opportunity to study Carter's expression, to try to discern if he was surprised or disbelieving of the information we'd garnered so far. But when I glanced from the mess on the coffee table to Carter's face, I found him watching me, not Bart, with a strangely concerned expression. I raised my eyebrows in a silent question. Carter shook his head with a barely discernible motion but continued to watch me. I felt he was trying to communicate something, but I had no idea what.

''Here,'' Bart said grumpily.

I looked down to see him pull from the mess a small leather box. It was the exact size and shape as the one in which Carter carried his picture of Meg. I felt my chest tighten with apprehension, and breathing suddenly became something I had to concentrate on to accomplish. I glanced back up at Carter, but he was watching Bart's bony hands on the worn leather—leather considerably more abused than that which covered the box that Carter carried.

I took a deep breath and swallowed with some effort. It seemed an eternity before Bart got the thing opened, and when he did, he extended it toward Carter. Unable to control myself, and moving as if some other being suddenly inhabited my body, my hand reached out and pulled Bart's arm toward me.

Inside the box, staring out across the years in eerily sharp detail, was the face of Carter Lindsey.

271

Chapter Sixteen

"Excuse me." I rose clumsily, bumping my knees into the coffee table and overturning Bart's tea. My stomach rose to my chest and I thought I might hyperventilate.

"*Sweet Jesus,*" Bart muttered, grabbing the cup and blotting some nearby papers with the tail of his shirt.

I walked swiftly to the door before realizing I had no idea where the bathroom was. I looked desperately at Carol, who pointed to the hall. "Around the corner, first door on your left."

"Thank you," I murmured. I could actually feel the blood leaving my face and knew with absolute certainty that I was white as a sheet.

Why was I so shocked? I had thought I believed Carter's story.

I made it to the bathroom, a ridiculously cheerful affair that even in a normal state of mind I would have found excessive, and slammed the door behind me. Blackness threatened the edges of my vision as I dropped the toilet cover down and sat.

It was really him. It was Carter. It was *my* Carter in nineteenth century garb, looking every bit as serious and humorless as every other nineteenth-century photograph I'd ever seen. It was authentic. It was 130 years old. And it was my Carter Lindsey.

Had I really not believed it before? Why else would I feel so completely astonished? That tingling I'd felt along my spine at the library, when I'd found Carter's name among the troops, was nothing compared to this. My God, it was a *photograph*. It was the ultimate proof. In all my imaginings of what would actually *prove* it to me, I hadn't even considered the existence of a *photograph,* for God's sake. Or a tintype, daguerreotype, whatever the heck they were called back then. Even looking at the picture of Meg, it had not occurred to me that one might have been made of Carter.

Why? Why hadn't I thought of that? Because I hadn't believed him. It was as simple as that. Until this moment I had not been absolutely certain that he'd been telling the truth, or even whether he knew if he was telling the truth at all. It was, I thought, like the difference between being told someone is dead and actually seeing the body. Whether or not you believed what you were told, a dead body is horrifying.

I put my head between my knees and breathed deeply. My God, I was going to faint. I'd never fainted in my life, but here I was with my head between my knees and my sight blacking out in a strange bathroom with green daisies and yellow butterflies on the wall. How stupid I would look in my classy black silk passed out in the cheeriness of this little room.

After a moment I became aware of a knocking on the door. I tried raising my head but felt nauseated. I'd had the feeling all through the roast that dinner wasn't going to sit well with me. Little had I known the reason . . .

"Shelby." It was Carter's voice, low and discreet. "Are you all right?"

I reached for the knob and opened the door a crack without raising my head. I saw his shoes beneath my eyes, then his knees as he knelt. He laid one hand on my back and rubbed lightly, laying the back of his other hand against my forehead.

I grabbed his hand and held it to my cheek, which I was shocked to find was wet with tears.

He pulled the door shut behind him. "Shelby, look at me. Come on," he coaxed gently, raising my chin with his fingers. "Please, look at me. You're making me feel like a freak."

I looked up at him through tear-filled eyes. "You're a ghost," I squeaked. "I'm in love with a ghost. You might as well be dead."

He looked wounded at that, but continued to stroke my back, whispering, "Shhhh." I closed my eyes.

"I had the feeling he might have that," he continued, "when he looked at me so strangely when we arrived. I was afraid it would shock you."

I emitted a watery laugh.

"I had thought you believed it all before this," he said quietly. "Or I might have thought to mention that the picture existed." His voice held no accusation, no blame, but I was sure he was hurt by my reaction.

"I *did* believe you, Carter. Or at least I thought I did." I sniffed loudly, and he handed me a tissue from the top of the toilet behind me. "It's just that theorizing about something is so different from having proof—irrevocable proof."

He smiled dryly. "It could just be a relative, some fluke of nature that made me look just like an ancestor."

The fact that the very same thought had flitted through my head seconds before upset me again and tears dripped onto the mint green tile floor. "I'm not going to get over this. Even if you stay forever I'll always wonder—I'll never know. How did this happen? Is he real? What *is* it and which day will I wake up to find him gone?"

Carter's palm cupped my cheek and his thumb rubbed at the wetness of my skin. "Shhhh," he said again and kissed my cheek.

"Oh, *why* couldn't it have just been amnesia?" I wailed.

"Shhhh." He kissed my closed eyes, moved his hand to the nape of my neck, and kissed my other cheek. He kissed my mouth, lightly twice, then lingeringly. "I'm real, Shelby," he said against my lips, his breath brushing my face. He kissed me again, and I felt the panicked thudding of my heart give way to the steady acceleration of arousal. "I'm very real."

I leaned into his kiss, grasping his sleeves and raising my head. Our lips opened in unison and our tongues met. I thought, with split-second clarity, that *this* was why the ancient Greeks thought that breath was the soul of man. That the essence of this kiss, the power, came from the mingling of our souls as his breath mingled with my own.

His hand on my neck entwined with my hair as my hands rose to his chest. I wanted to tear his clothes from him to be as close to his whole body as I felt I was to his soul.

A sharp knock resounded through the tiny room. "Shelby? Carter? Is Shelby okay?" Carol called.

My breath came in rasps as we separated.

"She'll be all right," Carter answered. "Could we possibly get something to drink?"

"A Coke," I whispered. Cokes were always good for upset stomachs. Surely they'd believe it if I'd had a bad reaction to the food or something.

"Perhaps a cocoa?" he asked.

275

I had to smile. He was so *sincere.* "I love you," I said, again.

He smiled back, as warmly as I'd ever seen, sleepy gray eyes crinkled at the corners. Then, softly, "I love you, Shelby Manning."

There, in that hideous green and yellow bathroom, I was happier than I'd ever been.

We left the Lindseys shortly thereafter. From them, we had discovered what we'd needed to know: that Meg Lindsey had borne a son and that the date of conception was within the realm of possibility, as far as Carter could remember. I contended that men never kept track of those things, however, clinging to whatever morsel of hope I could invent for myself; but, of course, we would never know for sure if that was the case. Not until it was too late for him to come back, anyway.

And I'd established what I'd needed to, namely that Carter was, in fact, a traveler from the past. There was no longer any doubt in my mind, nor any hope that he'd magically regain his memory and we could proceed to lead a normal life. This situation was as bizarre and impossible as my worst imaginings. And though for the moment I was riding a cloud of ecstasy because of Carter's feelings for me, I knew that soon I would sink into the desolation of losing the man I was desperately in love with.

The Lindseys had been understanding about my "illness," or at least Carol had been. Bart had actually looked happy that we were leaving. He had been overtly suspicious the whole time we were there, and, upon reflection, I thought it was odd that he should have been so contentious. I mean, after retrieving that picture of Carter and comparing it to the real thing, he had to have known we weren't lying about an association with the man. Why had he been so anxious to prove we were?

Why had he made such a point of being the only living, legitimate descendant? It wasn't as if we threatened a vast inheritance. In fact, when Carter asked if they knew anything about the house in Pennsylvania, whether it still stood or had been torn down, Bart made rather a large point of saying that they'd tracked down the property and, while the land was still used for farming, the only thing left standing of the house was the chimney, and even that was crumbling and barely distinguishable.

On the way home I asked Carter if he was disappointed by that fact.

"No. It was never a happy home," he replied evenly. "It's probably best that it's in ruins. Now it accurately reflects the lives that were led there."

I didn't respond to that. I couldn't think of one phrase, one platitude even, to diffuse such bitterness.

He looked over at me and smiled grimly. "Don't look so stricken, Shelby." The resolution in his eyes was far older than his years. "It's not so bad for me; I didn't grow up in a family like yours. It's not as if something's been taken from me. The home that I go back to will be the same as the one I grew up in. No better, no worse."

I nodded halfheartedly. But it *was* as if something had been taken from him, I thought to myself. His ability to comfort me, to laugh with me, to see happiness when it was in front of him, proved that he did, indeed, know what was missing from his life. Whether he'd grown up with happiness or not, without it he was being robbed.

"What strikes me as odd, though," Carter continued in that clinically detached voice, "is that *he* was so interested in *me*."

It took me a moment to figure out that he was talking about Bart again. "But wouldn't you be interested if some unknown relative suddenly popped up? Especially one who was the spitting image of an ancestor's picture?"

Carter shook his head. "That's not what I mean. In fact, just the opposite. He wasn't interested in me, the me that was sitting in his parlor. He was interested—and apparently has been interested for a while—in the Carter Lindsey in the picture, the one from a hundred and thirty years ago. For an ancestor who was historically insignificant, he's unusually taken with me. He tracked down my *house*, Shelby. Why do you suppose he did that?"

I hadn't thought of that. He was right, of course. As far as being a relative of note, Carter was insignificant. A twenty-five year old man killed in the Civil War wouldn't have had time to accomplish much. As far as Bart was concerned, the only thing he could have done of any interest would have been to father a child. The only thing we could see, anyway.

"Do you think he could know about the jewels you hid?" I asked, the memory of them suddenly hitting me. "Do you think he might have suspected they were still in the house?"

Carter frowned. "Maybe. But I don't know how he would know about them. They were hidden in a book and must be long gone now. Either someone, somewhere along the way, must have discovered them already, or they were thrown out with the books."

"Unless there's a Carter Lindsey Memorial Library somewhere," I volunteered, half-jokingly. "What book was it? Maybe we could find it, if we scoured the antique bookshops in the area."

Carter scoffed. "Not anything anyone would save, I don't think. It was a book on phrenology."

"Phrenology? What's that?"

He chuckled. "The science of reading one's personality by the bumps on one's skull. Very popular in my mother's time."

I laughed. "The bumps on your skull? That's hilarious."

"Yes, it was quite popular at parties, I understand."

"Instead of a clown, or a magician, or a band, they invited some guy over to feel everyone's heads?"

"A phrenologist, yes." He laughed at my amusement.

We pulled up in front of the house. "And have you had your head read?" I asked, giggling at the terminology.

"No. Sorry." He raised an eyebrow at me. "You're welcome to do it, if you want." His lips curved in a reluctant smirk.

I shook my head and opened the car door. "I don't know. It could be dangerous having your head read by an amateur."

He got out of the car and waited while I walked around to his side to proceed up the walk to the house. "In any case, Bartlett Lindsey knows something we don't about me. Or suspects something. And I can't imagine what it might be that would hold someone's interest a hundred and thirty years into the future."

"It must be the jewels," I said decisively. "Did you have anything else of value?"

"Only the land."

"And ownership of that's apparently not in question," I said. "Bart said it was owned by Agritech. That's a pretty huge agricultural company. It has to be for me to have heard of it. And I have to believe even Bart wouldn't take them on for some wild idea of reclaiming an old inheritance. He doesn't exactly strike me as the farming type."

I unlocked the door, and Steve wound herself around our legs in paroxysms of joy. Carter knelt to her level to rub behind her ears and she licked his face in ecstasy.

"Do you have a dog?" I asked, watching his contented face as she basked in his attention.

"No. I always wanted one, though," he said. And from the tone of his voice I knew it was another one of those happinesses he'd resigned himself to never having.

"In any case, perhaps he's given up on whatever it was, now that he's discovered the house is gone."

"You know, I'm surprised he didn't ask you more questions." I flipped on lights as I made my way into the house. "It seems to me, you being so obviously related to the object of his interest, that he would have asked more about your relationship. Why wouldn't it have been possible that you knew about whatever it is he's looking to find?"

Carter started up the stairs, his voice coming to me after bouncing hollowly off the hall walls. "He did ask why I was so interested in that particular man, and how I thought I fit into the family tree."

I heard his steps echo up the stairs, then stop on the landing near the top. "Uh, Shelby?" His voice was odd, and not just from the hollowness of distance. "Shelby, could you come here? Now."

I felt my blood quicken. "What is it?" I asked, moving through the living room toward the stairs. From the bottom of the stairs I could see his feet take the last two steps very slowly. "What is it?" I asked again, reluctant to follow him up. I was never one to investigate strange noises in the night, nor to venture through graveyards at midnight in search of ghosts, and Carter's tone gave me the same chilly, cowardly feeling those other prospects did. I took one step up, straining to see to the top. "Carter?"

His next words did nothing to propel me any farther. "I think someone's been up here."

Carter's room had been trashed. His meager store of clothing was scattered around the room, the bed stripped and the mattress turned over. The drawer that housed his few belongings, the buttons, the string, all the things he'd had in his pockets, was turned over in the middle of the floor. One of the buttons looked as if it had been stepped on, its little round eyelet flattened onto its back. Eerily, the picture of Meg was left intact and stood, propped open like a folding frame, on the desk, the hard, pale eyes staring coldly out at the disaster.

My room, as well, had been ransacked, the drawers emptied and the bed stripped; but it was the strange way Meg's picture had been left standing that gave me the biggest concern. After discovering Carter's story to be true I had all sorts of visions of other ghosts coming forward—Meg to exact revenge for Carter's desertion, Carter's son searching for his father, messengers from the past seeking to pull him back to them.

I found myself shaking violently as I stood in the middle of my room, trying to survey the damage but unable to stop the twisted wanderings of my imagination. It could have been someone Bart had sent, knowing we wouldn't be at home. He was searching for something; he thought we knew something. But he didn't know where we lived. I hadn't even told him my last name, had I? He thought I was married to Carter. But I couldn't remember exactly what I'd said. I only knew he had the phone number, and perhaps he could have traced the address that way.

But if it had been someone sent by Bart, wouldn't they have taken the picture of Meg? Why would they have propped it up like that? In the chaos of overturned bookcases and upset mattresses, why would anyone leave that picture of Meg standing open so pointedly? Unless it was Meg herself . . .

Carter entered the room behind me. "Does it look like they've taken anything?" he asked.

I turned slowly and watched as he explored my room, moving aside articles of clothing from my chest of drawers and checking the window locks.

"It's odd that they only did this to the upstairs." He turned and saw my face. "Shelby, are you all right?" He moved through the mess to my side. "Come here, sit down," he ordered, pushing aside the debris from the bed and seating me on its edge.

"We should call the police," I said in a shaking voice.

He took my hand, smoothing it flat on his open palm. "Have you noticed anything missing?"

I shook my head. Through the open door between our bedrooms I could just see the picture of Meg staring coolly at us. I felt my limbs begin their involuntary shaking again. "Carter, what if it was Meg?" I asked in a small voice.

He started next to me. "Meg?" he said with undisguised doubt and surprise. "How could it be Meg?"

"How could it be you, here in this room? Maybe she could have come here and done this the same way you came here."

He shook his head with absolute, and comforting, certainty. "Shelby, you know how I felt when I arrived; you know it was nothing I *planned,* for God's sake. It was nothing I could even have *imagined* happening before it actually did. For Meg to conceive of such a thing, let alone determine how to do it, and then to come here only to *mess up our rooms* . . . Well, it seems a little ludicrous to me." I heard the laughter in his voice and looked up gratefully.

"You're right," I said, my shoulders slumping. It had been an emotional evening and I suddenly felt completely exhausted. "Of course you're right. It's ridiculous." I caught Meg's eye again. "It's just so odd that the picture is the one thing left standing in that room."

"Yes, it's all very odd," Carter admitted. "And nothing downstairs appears to have been touched. Only the bedrooms."

I looked around the room. It was impossible to tell for sure, but it seemed that nothing had been taken. Everything had just been dumped onto the floor. My jewelry box, which contained nothing of much value anyway, was overturned on the floor, but the couple of rings I had that were semiexpensive I could see from where I sat.

"You don't think Bart had anything to do with it, do you?" I asked.

Carter shrugged but did not look at me. "If he did, he didn't find what he was looking for."

I heard Steve's nails click up the stairs then, hesitantly, her face peering around the door. "And here's our valiant protector now," I said, patting my leg for her to come forward. She appeared disconcerted by the unaccustomed chaos of the room and slunk in to sit docilely next to me. "Did you do this, Steve?" I asked facetiously. "Who did this? And why didn't we find him cornered in a room with you snarling viciously?"

The tip of her tail flapped hesitantly on the floor and she looked up at me with a worried expression. "Just teasing, sport," I said, ruffling her ears and bending down to lay my cheek on the top of her head. Carter got up and began putting drawers back into the furniture.

"For some reason I always thought she'd be a better watchdog than this," I said, glancing back into his room and meeting the eyes of the picture again.

Unable to stand Meg's stare any longer, I rose and crossed the threshold into Carter's room. I picked up the picture and studied it again. She looked small and powerless there in her little leather frame. How silly to think that she'd passed through time to claim her husband by messing up our rooms. I looked again at the initials scratched into the side of the case. WV FW. Maybe it was some kind of Latin phrase or symbol. In any event, Meg was light years away from us now. I closed the case soundly, righted the bedside table, and stuck her back in the drawer.

Chapter Seventeen

The police came, looked around, brushed for fingerprints, made a report, and left. Nothing had been taken and the house showed no sign of forced entry, so they could do nothing further. They said they'd let us know if the fingerprints turned up anything; but they doubted it, it was obvious. It was probably an unfair interpretation of their attitudes, but the whole thing, their skepticism about a break-in along with the lack of theft, just reinforced my underlying fear that mystical elements were at work.

Carter showed no such trepidation about The Unknown, but when pressed about his opinion on the Bart Lindsey theory he could not offer a convincing denial of his suspicions. This idea, while in keeping with my desire to frighten myself, had less of a basis in reality than in paranoia, I thought. After all, we'd only just met the man, and until we'd shown up at his door he'd had no idea who we were. The fact that I had seen him at the library just days before our meeting I kept to myself. There was no way Bart could have known I was researching his relatives. I hadn't asked anyone at the library for help, so unless he'd been reading over my shoulder he wouldn't have been able to tell whose name I sought. So even if Bart had gotten anxious about our designs on his name or inheritance, whatever that might have been, he wouldn't have had time while we were at dinner to arrange this sort of break-in. That, as far as I was concerned, eliminated him from the list of suspects. Of course, without him my list of suspects consisted solely of ghosts and time travelers, neither of which I could report to the police.

While we were caught up in theories about the break-in, Carter and I did not talk—at all—about that which we were both most aware, and that was his assignation with the Northern Lights. Monday was the dreaded day, about an hour before midnight the time. Another reason to hate Monday, I thought cynically.

Carter continued to work at Green Way Friday and Saturday, though I wasn't sure why. Perhaps it was to keep his mind from his impending departure; perhaps it was to keep him from seeing too much of me. Both of us tried valiantly to avoid speaking about our feelings, strong and futile as they were, but whenever we were together the tension was thick. At one point during the weekend I asked him if he wanted to travel to Philadelphia to see what was left of his house, but he declined. He'd see it soon enough, he'd said dryly.

At night, over dinner, I continued to teach him sign language as much as a way of avoiding dangerous conversation as to give him something to take back to his time with him. Granted, it wasn't nuclear physics or a revolutionary twentieth-century farming technique, but Carter said there was a boy on a farm near the school he ran in wintertime whom he believed might be hearing impaired. Many people thought the boy was mentally retarded, but since coming here and learning a little about deafness from me Carter thought perhaps the boy simply couldn't hear. If he could take even the basics back with him, he reasoned, perhaps this bizarre trip to the future would help at least one person. In any case, my knowledge of sign language was the only thing I had to offer.

I enjoyed the teaching immensely. Maybe because I had a student of above-average intelligence and aptitude, the process of instruction filled me with a kind of purpose I missed in my everyday life. Carter, having taught for many years, instructed me in basic methods of teaching as I instructed him in the basics of American Sign Language. It was fun. And it took our minds off the fact that soon he would be gone.

Even after fighting the urge to pray for cloudy weather, I was nonetheless disappointed when Monday dawned clear and cold, with more of the same in the forecast for the entire week. Conditions would be perfect for seeing the Northern Lights, the meteorologist on the radio announced with glee.

Carter and I both went to work on Monday, by unspoken agreement, and though I couldn't speak for him, I could say without qualification that I was beyond useless the whole day. Several times Sylvie asked me what was wrong, only to receive a sharp look and a curt, "Nothing" in reply. One time she even went so far as to ask if something was wrong with Carter, but she backed off when I glared at her. I stayed, for the most part, in the little office at the top of the stairs, trying to do some of the paperwork that had accumulated since Carter's arrival. Normally, I stayed late to do such things, but since he'd been here I hadn't wanted to miss a single moment we could spend together, as tantalizingly frustrating as that had become.

It was dark at six o'clock when we locked up the shop. I apologized to Sylvie for my snippy behavior as we stood on the stoop and I fumbled with the deadbolt. The bolt never did fit quite right in the hole and always required some jiggling.

"It's okay," Sylvie said buoyantly, relieved. I got the feeling that she thought I'd been mad at her. "I just hope whatever's eating you isn't too serious."

I turned from the door and stepped down to the sidewalk. "Not too," I lied, feeling my heart quiver as I mentally projected what tomorrow morning would feel like, and the one after that, and the one after that—all those mornings after Carter had gone.

"Well, that's good," Sylvie said with a sigh. "You know," she continued hesitantly, "I don't know if I'm out of place saying this or anything, but if it has to do with Rory, he's pretty miserable too."

I turned to look at her. Had she become the sympathetic girl to whom Rory confided his problems? I laughed shortly. How simple it would be if Rory was the source of my unhappiness. "No, it's not Rory," I said with a somber smile. "I'm sorry he's unhappy, but my mood has nothing to do with him."

If Sylvie had become his sounding board, the last thing I wanted her to do was carry back to him tales of my sadness over our breakup. In fact, I couldn't think of anything that would depress me more than reuniting with Rory after losing Carter.

Sylvie nodded sagely. "I didn't think so, but I wanted to let you know anyway. You've seemed pretty happy lately with your soldier." She smiled encouragingly. I'm sure she wanted the whole scoop on my relationship with Carter, but she wasn't going to get it. Since my feelings for Carter had intensified, I'd been pretty reticent on the subject, and she'd asked on numerous occasions very thinly veiled questions about his status, whether or not he'd remembered who he was, if we'd found his home, etc. But other than telling her small things, like when we'd gone out for dinner and had a good meal, I revealed nothing.

As I walked toward home I indulged in fantasies about our last night together. Some of them involved stirring, heart-wrenching scenes of good-bye, and others descended into pure Hollywood-style sex scenes, complete with professional lighting and dramatic music. Though sleeping with Carter was something I'd often fantasized about, it was never something I realistically contemplated. He was married, and he took that fact rather more seriously than most of his modern-day counterparts did. After what Rory had done to me I had to respect that, even if I longed for Carter's touch more than anything I'd ever wanted in my life.

I arrived home first and changed my clothes. I wondered what it would be like up there, on that familiar battlefield, watching Carter disappear. Would it happen with me there? The whole idea was too weird to try to figure out. Suppose it didn't work—what would Carter do? Would he be happy, or disappointed? Sometimes it seemed to me he wanted to stay, but he'd never said anything except that he needed to leave; he needed to return to Meg and, now, their son.

After donning some jeans and a sweater, I went downstairs to the kitchen. Because I couldn't decide what to cook, I'd bought enough food to feed thirty people. Perusing the refrigerator, I finally settled on filets of lamb in a rosemary sauce with baby vegetables to complement. I'd bought a good bottle of wine and had every intention of making this a Last Supper he would never forget; but as I pulled each ingredient from the refrigerator, my energy left me. By the time I reached for the lamb I felt physically ill, my arms weak and my head swimming with unwanted thoughts.

Was this how people felt before assisting a loved one to suicide? For all intents and purposes, after I brought

Carter to the battlefield tonight he would be gone, dead—
to me, anyway. But would he be gone in his own time?
Bart had said he'd been presumed dead on the battlefield.
If Carter made it back, would all of that history be suddenly wrong? Would Bart suddenly know something
else? Would the books and papers, records of the Union
dead, be somehow magically changed? How would this
work?

Maybe everything would stay the same and Carter
would go back to inhabit a corpse. Maybe what history
wanted was for Carter to be spared, but that could only
happen by traveling to the future. Perhaps he was supposed to accomplish something here. Oh, how in the
world could I figure this out? I pleaded to the Powers
That Be. It was impossible.

Slowly, I placed the food back in the refrigerator. I
couldn't cook now. I'd start it after Carter came home,
when I'd be able to think straight. Wiping stray tears
from my cheeks, I returned to the living room and lay
on the couch. How had my life gotten so mixed up? I
thought pitifully. What would have been wrong with me
finding some nice guy who wasn't involved in a cosmic
scenario over which he had no control?

I'm not sure how it happened, but I think I actually
fell asleep. Maybe it was because I hadn't slept at all the
night before, listening as I was for any stray sound Carter
might make and reluctantly counting the hours we had
left together. And maybe it was because I expected him
to be with me at any moment that my mind let down its
guard and I drifted into unconsciousness.

But some time later I awoke to the feel of his lips on
mine. Opening my eyes, I could see in the darkness the
outline of his face as he pulled back from me. I was slow
to take things in, but after a moment I noticed that he
wore his uniform and carried the pistol he'd had with
him when he arrived. I didn't have to search his pockets

to know he had everything there with which he had arrived. He was ready to leave.

I jerked to a sitting position and fumbled vainly for my watch. It was too dark to see.

"What time is it?" I whispered, my voice sleep-filled and harsh.

He sat on the edge of the couch next to me. "It's ten-thirty," he said quietly. "I have to leave. I was hoping you wouldn't awaken."

I felt panic surge to the surface of my emotions. "But I was going to cook dinner!" I wailed inanely. "I have plans; you can't go yet." I started to swing my feet off the couch, but he stayed me with one hand. "No," I protested, "let me go—surely we have time—we can at least have some wine—" Food as a replacement for sex, I'm sure.

He took my hands in his very firm grip and pinned me with a sharp look. "We don't have time, Shelby," he said. "I'm leaving and you must stay here."

"No!" I gasped. "I'm coming with you. You can't go without me; I won't let you. Surely you don't expect me to just wait here while you—while you go and—just— *go!* Tell me you want me with you, *please.*"

"You can't come with me," he said in that infuriatingly calm voice. "I've spoken with Madame Erika. You can't come with me. I want you to stay here and do everything the way you normally would. Cook dinner, call your parents, listen to music. I want to know that you and this house are just the way I remember them. I want to know that you're all right, Shelby. Can you do that for me?"

For the first time I noticed that the calm, hard voice he used was employed with great effort. He was torn by this decision, this necessity of leaving, as much as I was; but he knew he had to go. Slowly, through my sleep-fogged brain, I realized that he was in pain, too, and that all my ranting was only making it harder for him.

He hadn't come home tonight because it would have been too painful. The more I woke up, even I could see that it would have been bad. It wouldn't have been a Last Supper to remember; it would have been a strange, strained evening that had nothing to do with the friendship we'd forged.

I sniffed and tried to nod, but my neck was wooden. My whole body felt frozen by our impending parting, but he seemed to sense my acquiescence.

"Good," he said huskily. "Just do everything as you normally would."

I reached up to finger the torn spot in the shirt where he'd been shot. The little nurse at the hospital had sewn it up and washed it, but the rent fabric was still a testimony to what he would be returning to—the bloodiest war in American history. A sob caught in my throat, and his hand reached up to clasp mine to his chest. My eyes raised to his, meeting the clear gray gaze in the darkness.

"I love you," I said. "I don't want you to go. I know you have to, but I don't want you to. I just want you to know that."

Carter nodded. Then his other hand came up and touched my cheek. "You're so beautiful," he whispered. "I'll miss you—very much."

He slid his hand to the nape of my neck and pulled my face to his. Our lips met, and whatever it was we'd been holding back for weeks threatened to overpower both of us. My arms wrapped around his neck and his slid around my waist. We merged together like pieces of a puzzle, our kisses frantic, our hearts thudding wildly against each other.

His lips pressed mine, then my eyes, my cheeks, my neck. I felt chills of sheer pleasure as his tongue traced my collarbone. My fingers twined through the thick softness of his hair, willing him to go further, to descend to those parts of my body that were racked with a longing as potent as pain.

Just when I was ready to rip all the clothing from his body, he pulled back and we sat gasping at each other, unnerved by the passion we'd unleashed. His hands ran the length of my sides and back up again, his thumbs subtly caressing the swell of my breasts. He sighed and shook his head.

"How can I leave you?" he asked, in a voice so soft I barely heard it.

Like Eve grasping the apple, I clutched at this statement. "*Don't* go," I said fervently. "Don't leave me. Stay, Carter; we could be like this always. Please stay. *Make love to me*," I whispered.

Carter's eyes glittered in the darkness, their expression unfathomable. "There is *nothing* I want more," he said. But the tone of his voice said it all. He was leaving anyway.

Disappointment made my words sound harsh. "Apparently there is," I said.

He shook his head again. "Please don't be bitter," he said firmly. "I wouldn't be able to stand thinking of you bitter."

I lay my forehead on his shoulder. What I couldn't say was that he probably wouldn't be doing too much thinking about me anyway. Though I couldn't pretend to understand what had happened to bring him to my time, I didn't think that history would be rewritten if he went back. Carter Lindsey would die in the Battle of Fredericksburg and no body would be recovered. I wouldn't even be able to visit his remains, morbid as that seemed.

"I can't believe fate brought you to me only to take you away," I said in a small voice.

"We make our own fate, Shelby," he said. "Somehow I got myself here, and now it's time to go back. I must go back."

I sighed and threw in my last chip. "What about Meg's fate, Carter? Doesn't she make her own, too? Why isn't she responsible for herself?"

"Because I chose to be responsible for her," he stated. "By my own actions my fate is entwined with hers. The child is proof of that. And I must do right by her."

I forced myself to change into my nightshirt and brush my teeth. *Do everything the way you normally would,* my mind chanted, over and over again. It was the same as a death, I thought between chants. I was a widow with no right to grieve. Carter would be dead and there was no one I could tell. No one who would believe it, anyway.

Do everything the way you normally would, I said again to myself. I stoked the fire, fed the dog, tried to read the newspaper even though it was one-thirty in the morning and the dog wouldn't eat. I climbed the stairs and brushed my hair, settling myself into bed to lie, stiff as a board, in the dark. I wasn't going to sleep. *Do everything the way you normally would,* traipsed unheeded through my mind.

He was gone, I knew. If it hadn't worked he would have been back well before now. I'd stayed up, waiting, but now it was time to face facts. He was gone. I was alone.

I lay in bed for what seemed like hours, studying the ceiling and letting my mind go blank, when it would, otherwise going over and over every moment I could recall with Carter, from the first time I saw him to this evening's passion-filled kiss on the couch.

I don't know if I completely fell asleep, or if I was simply in that dream state that restless exhaustion and emotional turmoil creates, but I had a most peculiar dream. I was walking on a lawn, a beautifully kept and manicured lawn. I marveled over the fine edging and emerald consistency of it, the graceful, rolling swells, the way you could see for acres and acres without anything interrupting the flow of your vision over the uniform blades of grass.

Then, at some point during the dream, I began to feel panic at the unending perfection of the lawn. I became disoriented and lost. I longed to see a path, a wood through which to forge my way, a weedy tangle of uncut growth, anything to move through, or against, or even around if need be. The pure perfection of the lawn frightened me, caused my breath to catch, made my eyes ache in their sockets as they searched for distance, for depth, for definition.

I awoke with a start to the pitch blackness of my room. Loneliness enveloped me in the dark like the uninterrupted flow of the pure green lawn. With energy borne of panic, I sat bolt upright in bed and took deep, gulping breaths of air. I clutched the sheets around me in tight fists and tried to make sense of the shapes of my furniture in the dark. Just when I thought my overwhelming confusion might swallow me whole, I heard a noise from downstairs.

I froze, breath halfway down my throat, fists clenched on twisted sheets, eyes bulging in the darkness. My panic crystallized into a laserlike focus on the noise. It was the front door. I heard the knob jiggle as it was grasped, then the distinct sound of wood against metal as the warped door was pushed past the point in the frame where it always stuck. The hinge creaked its familiar two-note tune, then swung back with a nearly silent push of air against the storm door, as it always did.

Visions of my overturned bedroom flashed through my brain. Carter's mattress, the flattened button on the floor. Carter had thought it was Bart who'd been responsible. Bart wouldn't have known that Carter was gone, that all hope of discovering whatever it was he sought had left with him. Whoever was downstairs now had come to finish the job they'd started four days ago.

My eyes flicked to the red glow of the digital clock: 4:32 A.M. Wasn't that the time that most burglaries occurred, in the hours just before dawn? Was that something I'd read, or just something I'd always thought? I didn't know, it didn't matter, I didn't know what to do.

I sat frozen, hearing nothing. Whoever it was was waiting to see if I'd heard them enter. They'd made some noise, and now they waited to see if I'd heard and gotten up. I strained my ears, reaching out mentally in the darkness for any stray perception I could pick up.

Finally, as slowly as I could, I moved my legs under the covers, inch by inch so they wouldn't make a sound, toward the side of the mattress. My eyes scoured the darkness for something I could use as a weapon. At this point, with the adrenaline flowing and terror fueling my muscles, I felt I could pick up the desk and hurl it at the intruder with very little trouble.

My feet made it to the carpet and I stood, raising myself slowly. My anklebone cracked, as it usually did in the morning, and the sound echoed through the room. I listened. I thought I heard a footstep on the stairs and waited to hear whether the fourth step from the top creaked.

Where in the world was Steve? I thought frantically. At least I should have heard her collar. Surely she'd heard the front door as clearly as I had.

I realized with a jolt of dread that I had never let her back inside after feeding her. I'd been so distraught before going to sleep that I'd left her outside. I left her out every once in a while, so she didn't complain. It was as if this whole evening had been orchestrated by the intruder.

Had this happened last night, I would have felt perfectly safe with Carter in the house. Even the night of the break-in, I'd had no trouble getting to sleep because of the security I felt in his presence. But now he was gone, and this ugly incident was going to be just one more reason to lament that fact—if I came out of it alive.

I took a deep breath. *No need to be melodramatic,* I told myself. *Perhaps whoever it is just wants to steal something and leave. Perhaps they have no intention of doing anything to me at all. Maybe they came back to do the downstairs, since last time they only did the bedrooms.* Then I heard the fourth step creak.

I swooped up the closest thing to me, which was the telephone. I could club the thief in the head with the receiver. As soon as I'd yanked the wire off the back so I could carry it with me, rational thought returned and I realized the enormity of what I'd done. I'd just cut myself off from communication with the outside world unless I could somehow make it downstairs to the kitchen phone. What an idiot! I wanted to club myself in the head with the receiver—but then I saw the knob on my bedroom door turn.

Chapter Eighteen

Clutching the phone to my chest like a child with a favorite blanket, I watched in horror as the knob slowly turned. There was no mistaking the movement in the dark; I could hear the gentle click of the tumblers at the same time.

In an effort to get out of the first line of sight of the opening door, I slid one foot to the left, shifted my weight, then slid the other over. With an effort I raised the receiver above my head, ready to attack. But even then, in the throes of terror, I was unsure if I could actually do it. I tried to envision myself beating a human being in the head with a phone and couldn't do it. At the last minute I had the belated thought that it would have been wiser to stay in bed and feign sleep.

Too late. I'd held my breath so long, my head felt light. I wondered briefly if I would pass out before this slow-motion horror scene played itself out, and I half hoped that I would.

A moment later a man's broad frame rounded the edge of the door. Too terrified to scream, I gasped and silently hurled the phone at him, stumbling backwards over the bedside table as I did so and landing with a *thud* on the bed. He'd been facing in my direction as he entered, so he caught the phone with the ease of natural coordination, but he was unable to stop the receiver as it bounced wildly on its accordion cord and knocked him in the shins.

I heard him grunt as I scrambled to push myself back up to my knees on the bed. It wasn't until he bent to pick up the receiver from the floor that I caught a glimpse of the lightness of his hair and the glint of a gold military button. I stopped.

"Carter?" I gasped the name.

Peering through the darkness, I could tell by his careful movements and the quiet way he replaced the receiver on the phone that it was him.

He straightened. "I know. I should have called."

I bounded across the bed on my hands and knees. Before he even had a chance to place the phone on the table I threw myself at his chest, my arms around his neck. The phone clattered to the floor and his arms embraced me, as much to keep us both from falling as to hold me. The momentum I'd gathered propelled us toward the wall where, with a gentle expulsion of air, Carter's back hit and sustained us.

My lips found his and were met with equal passion. My hands buried themselves in his hair, while one of his ran up my back and the other down to my hips, pressing me into him.

"You came back," I murmured between kisses. "Thank God, you came back."

Carter straightened himself against the wall and, in a graceful motion, picked me up and carried me toward the bed. My lips not leaving his, my hands cradled his face, smoothing his hair back and tracing the bones of his face from his temples to the high cheekbones, from cheekbones to jaw.

Our breathing came fast and furious. "We'll marry," he said in a voice husky with passion. "And we'll live our lives here, like normal people."

My eyes widened in disbelief. Was I dreaming? "*Yes,*" I answered quickly.

Without losing the contact of our lips, he lay me gently on the bed and stretched out next to me. "I've figured it—all out." He kissed me again as his fingers found the tiny buttons of my nightshirt and hurriedly made their way down the line. "I can continue to work for Mr. Malone until I have some money. Then I can teach school, maybe, or start a landscaping company of my own."

"I can help you," I volunteered, working at the belt and strange button fly of his pants. "I know people who work for the college."

After he'd reached the last button of my shirt he spread the cotton from my shoulders and, raising me up slightly, smoothed the fabric down my arms and away from me. I lay back as he gazed at me, running his hands from the base of my neck, over my breasts to my waist.

"You're perfect," he whispered. "More perfect than I imagined."

His head descended to my breast, where his lips closed on one pink tip and pulled gently. My back arched involuntarily and a sound of perfect contentment came from my throat. His lips moved to my other breast, then up to my neck as he pushed his loosened pants over his hips. I fumbled with the buttons of his shirt until his deft fingers made short work of that and the rest of his clothing. I pushed my own shirt from my arms.

He was perfect. Though I'd seen him shirtless before, it was with the distraction of a bloody gunshot wound at his shoulder. But now, despite the assortment of scars,

299

the flawless symmetry of his chest took my breath away. The firm, well-muscled biceps were defined enough for the dim light of an outside street lamp to cast crescent shadows in the hollows, and his flat stomach tapered to tight, strong hips. The golden hair on his chest darkened below his navel to a line that pointed tantalizingly to the hardening I could feel against my leg.

Shed of our clothing, we came together chest to chest, skin to skin, and the feeling was as delicious as pure silk on naked flesh. One of his hands ran up my side to my breast while the other pulled my hips into his in a slow, compelling rhythm. Both of my hands traveled down his arms, feeling the hard, flexed muscle. He was so solid and real, so strong. I felt like a plaything in his arms; it was as if he could pick me up and turn me, twist me any way he liked with those broad hands and powerful shoulders.

He raised himself over me and brushed his chest along mine, his hardened manhood teasing me, touching my hot, pulsing center. My hands gripped his shoulders and felt them flex as he lowered himself into me.

My breath came in desperate rasps and my legs opened to encircle his waist. And though I could not be said to have heard anything too clearly, I could have sworn that the moment he slid into me—that moment when desire explodes and the body's primal certainty of what to do next takes over with irresistible force—I could have sworn at that moment I heard thunder. Distant, but distinct. A low rumbling from the farthest horizon. And upon that impression, swirling through my mind with the complete conviction of our action, came the sudden, clear thought: *This man was born in 1837.*

I threw my head back and groaned as he thrust deeper, his own breathing ragged and his muscles straining with the exertion.

I thought, *If he was to plant his seed inside me, what*

would that do to time, to the logic of progression, to parents and grandparents, uncles and brothers? With that thought came a desire so intense, it felt like an alien possession of my soul. I wanted Carter's child, wanted it with an instinctive fervor that seemed to come from my soul. I couldn't have said so at that moment, but I wanted it so that if he ever disappeared forever, I would have that piece of him. I would have from him what Meg would never have: a child conceived in love.

Carter pulled me up and sat back on his heels, our bodies still joined, my legs around his waist. We were face to face and we did not kiss, but maintained an intense look between us that spoke far more than words. It was as if we both knew we engaged in something momentous. Whether or not I had actually heard thunder, I knew with certainty that Carter's thoughts traveled the same determined path as mine: *We could defy time.*

Our bodies moved together fluidly, following an age-old rhythm of their own. Pleasure coursed through me the likes of which I had never known, ever. This was right—that was all I could think. Our bodies created perfection together: That which God intended, Nature demanded.

His hand wound itself through my hair and supported my shoulders as I came to the brink of fulfillment. His other arm was positioned securely around the small of my back as I arched toward him with an explosion of pleasure that rocked me from my toes to the top of my head. I could feel myself contract around him when his own eyes closed and he lay me back on the pillows. Neck muscles taut, stomach tight as a washboard, he thrust once, twice, then a final time as he tilted his head back and expelled a long, sated breath of air.

It's done, I thought exultantly. *We have done it.* I clasped him tightly to me, as if I could pull him inside my body the same way I had his life-giving seed. I had him now, forever; I was sure of it. As sure as I was that he had me—forever.

I awoke the next morning to the feeling of Carter's fingers in my hair, combing it between them, then rubbing the strands between his fingers. His gaze was so intent on my hair in his hand that he didn't immediately realize my eyes had opened. He was thinking about something, hard, and it wasn't difficult to imagine what it was.

I lay on my back and watched him silently. His hair was mussed and his face looked rugged with stubble. His eyes, clear and intense, were framed by those thick wheat lashes that tangled gently at the corners. After a moment his gaze moved to my face, and I watched as his pensive expression changed, with the focus of his eyes, to awareness.

His lips curved into a quiet smile and his heavy-lidded gaze made his expression decidedly sultry.

I felt unusually awake for having just opened my eyes, and it stemmed from a fear that Carter already regretted his decision. The look on his face before he'd noticed I'd awakened had been too odd, too intensely absorbed.

In a voice hoarse from sleeping, I asked, "Why did you come back?"

His fingers didn't stop their gentle combing of my locks, but he waited a long moment before answering. "It didn't work," he said finally.

I studied him. "You waited there all that time, until four-thirty in the morning?" How desperate he must have been to return. But, of course, I knew that.

He shook his head slightly and sighed, looking away. "No. I gave it about half an hour." Then he smiled wryly out of the corners of his eyes at my expression.

"Half an hour!" I turned on my side to face him. "What do you mean?"

He moved his hand from my hair and began tracing small circles on my skin, up my shoulder and along my collarbone, then to my jaw. He took a deep breath. "I—I suppose I didn't want it to work . . . so, it didn't."

His expression was dark, closed, frightening me more than anything.

He continued, "I decided to walk a little, just around the town, and I thought about—about everything. About you. Then I came back here. And it was very late."

I eyed him skeptically. "You're not telling me everything," I accused, fear making me stiff beside him.

"No. I'm not." He looked at me and raised one eyebrow, as if challenging me to ask again.

I did. "Did you see the Northern Lights?"

He nodded. "They were faint. More so than the last time I saw them."

"Did you lie on the grass where you were that first night?"

He hesitated. "I sat. Near there."

Disturbed by his reticence, I sat up and leaned back on a pillow. He drew back at my sudden move and looked up at me, his gray eyes knowing and determined to keep things to himself.

"Did you actually try to go back? Or did you change your mind before that?" These were things I needed to know.

He bunched a pillow under his head and positioned it so he could look at me. I found it hard to keep my fingers from the muscular expanse of chest, but I was determined to know how paranoid I needed to be about his decision not to go home.

Eyes narrowing, he asked, "Are you sorry I didn't go?"

I expelled a breath of air. "God, no! I just want to know how you made the decision. You were so determined to go back! Are you sure you won't regret it?"

He laughed once, without humor, and looked away. "It's a little late for that now, isn't it?"

"Carter," I said seriously, apprehension making the blood thunder in my ears. "I need to know why you stayed. Maybe you think it's something I can't handle hearing, but not hearing it is worse. Trust me on this; I can't spend the rest of my life worrying that you blew your chance and you're sorry."

He looked up at me, and the expression in his eyes wasn't reassuring. His mouth set in a solemn line, he inhaled deeply. "I may have 'blown my chance,' " he said slowly, "I'm not really sure. I—I went there. I—" He swallowed hard and paused. "I thought hard about—about Meg." He glanced up at me, and I held his gaze. "Shelby," he said softly, "I just didn't want to go."

I expelled the breath I'd been holding.

"I may regret it," he continued, studying the sheet and tracing part of the floral pattern with a finger. "I may live to hate myself for the guilt. But God help me," his hand stopped and squeezed into a fist, "I couldn't make myself go."

I trembled now, but from what emotion I couldn't say. "You were there, though, on the battlefield. The Northern Lights shone. What more could you have done?"

He shrugged and shook his head. "I don't know. I don't know." He looked up at me. "I could have wanted to go. I could have wanted to do the right thing."

"God, Carter. You tried. You did more—much more—than I would have."

He smiled, a sad smile, I thought, and pushed himself up to kiss me, slowly.

"Are you going to marry me?" he murmured.

I hesitated, kissing him back. "Carter, there's nothing I want more. But . . ."

He pulled back onto his haunches and stared at me. "But?" he asked quietly.

"But I can't marry you until you're sure you've done the right thing by staying."

He frowned and dropped his eyes.

"Don't you see?" I asked. "I can't—I don't want to be the one responsible for your guilt—your regret."

"But you're not responsible. It's me—"

"It's the same thing, Carter. I want you," I said with a longing I couldn't hide, "but I want *all* of you."

That night, in an attempt to avoid the awkwardness that now existed between Carter and myself, and to give him a chance to think about all I had said, I returned to the bookstore to finish the paperwork I'd botched the night before. I'd been so distraught about his leaving that my orders and check-ins were completely mixed up.

Carter had made dinner, the lamb with rosemary that I'd intended to make as his farewell dinner, and I can say without equivocation that despite our tension it tasted far better as a welcome meal than it would have as a farewell. But we didn't drink the wine because the celebratory mood had dimmed with my refusal to marry him.

I was sitting in the little upstairs office, trying to keep my mind on the work at hand, instead of the memory of Carter's lovemaking and the guilt of stealing a man from his wife and child, when I heard the bells on the front door chime. It wasn't a doorbell, but a string of jingle bells on a leather thong that clapped against the door when it was opened, so it could only mean that someone had entered.

I was sure I'd locked that door after coming back, so I called Sylvie's name. Perhaps she'd forgotten something and had come back to get it. She had a key and so could have let herself in.

There was no reply to my call. "Sylvie?" I tried again, louder. Nothing.

Then I heard footfalls on the old wooden steps. A man's tread, heavy and sure. My heart began to accelerate.

He wasn't trying very hard to be quiet, the rational part of my brain acknowledged. But still I was frozen in my chair, my pen poised to check *A Natural History of the Senses* on my "in" list.

If it wasn't Sylvie, who could it be? The only other person with a key would be—

The footsteps reached the landing and strode the two lengths to the door of my office.

Rory.

I heaved a sigh of relief. I guess the burglary really had gotten to me. Last night, it was Carter. Tonight, Rory. Both times I was sure I was about to die.

He stood in the doorway, his familiar face covered with a five o'clock shadow, that same old lock of hair loose on his brow. His pale blue eyes raked me from head to waist, which was as much as he could see from the other side of the desk, then looked around the room.

"What are you doing here?" I asked, my voice less than hospitable. But, after all, he could have announced himself when he heard me call for Sylvie.

He gave a short laugh. "Nice to see you, too, Shel," he said, nodding. He walked lazily into the tiny room and sprawled on the chair across from me.

"I wanted to talk to you," he said then, more seriously, and he let those piercing blue eyes command my attention.

But he'd forgotten how well I knew him, and how well I knew his plots and ploys. He had used his good looks with success on every female I'd ever seen him near, but over the years I had become invincible. "Go ahead," I said mildly, leaning back.

He bent forward and rested his elbows on his knees. "You're determined not to make this easy, aren't you?"

"Since I don't know what *this* is, I don't know how to make it easy. Why don't you just say what's on your mind, instead of playing these games of intimidation you like so much?"

He shook his head in disbelief and gazed heavenward. "My God, you're hard," he whispered.

"Rory, have you forgotten who you're talking to?" I asked incredulously. "This is quite a performance, but I can assure you, you're getting nowhere. Now what's on your mind?"

He seemed to deflate at that comment and rested his head in his hands. "I don't know what to say to you," he said to the floor. He looked up. "You're so—different. I wanted to apologize—*again*. I wanted to see if you're okay. I just wanted to see you, Shelby. I miss you."

I really had no idea what to say to that. In fact, as I sat watching his mixture of part real, part feigned anguish, I marveled at how little I felt for him. I didn't feel coldness, or hate, or even anger; what I felt was fatigue, mostly. And an irritated desire to be done with this interview so I could finish my work.

I took a deep breath and slowly let it out, looking away from him. "Look, I don't know what to say, Rory," I said. At my gentler tone of voice, he looked up hopefully. "I don't want to seem heartless, but I think it's best that you know. It's over between us."

He looked confused. "Between us? You and me?"

"Well, yes," I said, confused myself. "Who else?"

His eyes hardened to twin shards of ice. "I thought maybe you'd finished with that *nut* you've taken up with and come to your senses."

My own face hardened. "I refuse to take part in this conversation if you intend to denigrate Carter."

"*Carter,*" he breathed sarcastically. "That's him. Isn't he married, Shelby? And doesn't that seem a little—*hypocritical* to you?"

I felt a flush sail to the roots of my hair. ''What are you talking about?'' I asked weakly.

He couldn't completely conceal his smile of triumph. ''He's married, isn't he? Can you deny it?''

I tried to regulate my breathing. ''I can.'' He was, technically, a widower.

Rory scoffed. ''Then who's the broad in the picture? The pretty blonde? You don't even seem to be his type.''

I glared at him, my eyes wide, and my mouth dropped open in shock. ''It was *you,* wasn't it!'' I gasped. ''It was *you* who broke into my house and messed everything up!'' I shook my head at the unreality of it all. ''No wonder Steve didn't do anything,'' I murmured in amazement.

He looked angry and wary, but a good distance from remorseful. ''It was hardly a *break-in,* Shelby. I have a key, remember? And most of my stuff is there. In fact, I could probably argue that I have spousal rights, in a court of law. Ten years is a long time, Shel.''

I laughed incredulously. ''Are you threatening me with common-law marriage? You *are* desperate.'' My laughter was a very angry-sounding thing. ''What was it you hoped to find? I can tell you that your things are in a box in the basement, along with every memory I have of you. You are *out* of my life, and if I ever catch you anywhere near *my house* again, I'll call the police!'' My voice had risen an octave and my muscles fairly twitched with the anger that coursed through my veins.

Rory sat back, looking amused at my histrionics.

''I could press charges, Rory,'' I hissed. ''I could call the police right now and have you brought up on charges of breaking and entering. They've already made a report; all they need is a name.''

His eyes narrowed and time drew long before he answered. ''So you've slept with him, haven't you?'' he said with quiet certainty.

I stood bolt upright, knocking over the chair behind

me. "*Get out of my office.*" I pointed dramatically to the door. "No: First give me the keys—to the house *and* the shop—then get the hell out of my life."

Rory stood slowly, anger oozing from every pore. "My God, it's like you're a different person." He shook his head at me in disgust. "I came here to apologize, to figure out what we need to do to get back on track, and you treat me like a goddamned criminal!"

"You broke into my house," I ground out between clenched teeth.

"I was hoping to find you there. I was hoping to talk some sense into you. When I found you gone, and my things gone, and *his* things still there, I guess I got a little angry, yes. I'm sorry. But all I wanted to do was talk."

I fired a shot in the dark and hit a bull's-eye. "No, you didn't. You knew I wouldn't be home. You knew from Sylvie that we were going out for dinner."

Rory's well-trained, deceitful face couldn't hide his surprise at the accuracy of my bullet.

"You're *despicable,*" I spat. "A sorry, drunken, lying, pitiful, cheating—*lump* of a man. And I'm glad to be rid of you."

"*You bitch,*" Rory growled, lunging across the desk. I moved far enough out of the way that his fingers only brushed the front of my sweater. For the first time in my. life I was actually afraid of him.

I grabbed the phone to my chest and started punching numbers. "I'm calling the police, Rory! This, on top of breaking and entering, and you'll be in jail before the night's over!"

That stopped him. He stood glaring at me, nostrils flaring and eyes wild. One hand still rested on the scattered papers on my desk.

"Get out!" I repeated, the phone raised. For the second time in twenty-four hours I was about to beat someone with a telephone.

Elaine Fox

With a barely contained burst of anger, he ripped the cord from the phone in my arms and threw it on the ground. Then he spun on his heel and left the room, slamming the office door behind him. I heard him clatter noisily down the steps, then stride across the raised platform where the counter stood. There was a moment of silence while he descended to the carpeted main floor, and then a second later I heard what could only have been the large shelf containing women's studies thunder to the floor. Then the bells jangled frantically and the front door slammed shut.

I sat at my desk and took a deep breath. With trembling hands I replaced the phone on the table, having to take two tries to put back the receiver.

I shivered. It wasn't that the room was cold, which it always was; it was how close this person I thought I knew so well had come to physically hurting me. He had never, in all our years together, come anywhere near the level of anger he had tonight. Of course, neither had I—but the way he'd *lunged* at me . . .

I crossed my arms and lay my head on them. I took some deep, calming breaths and closed my eyes. *Thank God for Carter,* was all I could think, over and over again. As soon as I could calm myself I would go to him, let him take me in his arms, and make love to him. He would cleanse away this dirty, unwashed feeling I had from the encounter with Rory. He would erase all memory of Rory's scathing voice saying, *"You slept with him, didn't you?"* As if that was all there was to it. He just didn't know. He would probably never know.

Then I remembered the strain that lay between Carter and me, and fatigue washed over me. I wasn't used to so much emotional upheaval. I might have even slept, considering the little amount of sleep I'd had the night before and the strange, careless jumbling of my thoughts. In any case, I'm not sure how long it was that I sat there, alternately thinking of Rory and then Carter. I had just caved in with worry over the precariousness of my life with Carter when I thought I smelled smoke. I raised my head and looked at the door. Was it my imagination or was the room slightly foggy?

I stood up behind the desk and looked at the crack beneath the door. To my complete horror, I saw fine tendrils of smoke curling up from beneath the gap. As if in immediate response to the sight, I coughed, then forcibly stopped it. No, this was not real. I shouldn't have coughed. I could somehow stop the fingers of smoke from being real if I didn't cough.

I stood motionless, watching. *Rory—the bookshelf—women's studies—the kerosene heater was on the other side.* The thoughts flashed through my head in an instant and I knew exactly what had happened.

On shaking legs, I made my way around the desk to the door and placed my hand on the knob. Searing heat singed my palm and I whipped back my hand, clasping it in terror. The building's on fire, I thought incredulously. *If I open that door, flames will come roaring in just like in the movies.* I backed away from the door and coughed again. How quickly the air became thick. Feeling the desk behind me, I rounded it, eyes still glued to the smoke that drifted ominously up from the floor. *In the event of fire, never open a window and always keep the doors shut . . . always keep the doors shut and never open a window in the event of fire.* I must have learned it in school, because the phrase echoed through my head in the bored, nasal tones of a grade-school teacher. I backed farther away from the door in complete confusion.

The office was tiny. There was just enough room for my desk, a chair, and one set of bookcases. Off to the left was a small crawlspace without a door, but it was crammed full of old file cabinets and junk.

There was no window.

There was no other door.

There was no way out.

There was no way out.

I gasped and reeled against the back wall, steadying myself with my burnt hand and then jerking it back in pain and falling on my shoulder against the wall. Was I light-headed from the smoke? Or had I just, in my terror, forgotten to breathe?

Frantically, I grabbed the phone off the desk. Dead: Rory had pulled the cord. I thought I heard, through the thundering of my own heart, the faint rustling of the fire—the sound of a sheet being swept open, a sail catching the wind.

What was going to become of me? Rory was gone. It was night. No one was around. Unless someone noticed the fire from outside . . .

I curled myself under the desk, in the tight spot that had only, until then, seen my legs. *Idiot,* I told myself, *this is what you do in an earthquake.*

My whole body shook and I closed my eyes, hoping that when I opened them I would awaken from this nightmare. After a moment I found I could not open them at all. My terror was so complete, I couldn't even open my eyes. I was going to die there, that night, in a fire. I was going to be the next heartrending story of loss in the Metro section of the paper. I was going to die the most hideous death imaginable.

Coughing, I lay my head back against the desk and prayed. I prayed to God, my parents, and Carter. I prayed to Allah and Buddha and anyone else I could think of. I prayed to Lucifer when I felt the heat on my cheek where it lay against the wooden desk.

I noticed myself getting hotter, but I wasn't sure if it was fear or that the fire was that much closer. I saw flashes of light and shapes against my closed eyelids, and for a moment I actually forgot about the fire and thought what a strange creature it was that inhabited the inside of my eyelids. When I noticed how deviant it was to have a thought like that at a time like this, a new terror hit me. I was losing cognizance. I was passing out. I tried to open my eyes and succeeded, only to close them against the stinging gray fog that enveloped me.

I was wrong, I thought to myself; I always thought I liked heat better than cold, that if I was to have the choice of the world burning up from the greenhouse effect or slowly freezing into a second ice age, I would have chosen the greenhouse. But at that moment I couldn't think of anything worse than flames charring my tender flesh, of heat curling my hair into ashes, of life being taken from me layer by layer. The palm of my hand stung, and I realized that that pain would be nothing compared to what was to come. How long would it take? How bad would it be?

Just when I felt my neck losing the strength to hold up my head, I heard something pounding at a wall. Or was that my heart beating against my rib cage? No, it was definitely pounding. Had someone said my name? Was that Carter's voice? He was calling my name! Wasn't he?

Or was I losing my mind? I tried to raise my head and couldn't.

"Carter?" I tried to speak, but it was like one of those awful nightmares where you try desperately to scream and can't. Nothing came out but a thick, smothering silence. A wild panic threatened to consume me. As if from a distance, I heard someone coughing . . . then realized with a bottomless horror that it was myself.

"Shelby?" My name again. It was Lucifer, answering my prayers with a mirage.

I opened my eyes to see that the lights had gone out. The room was black as pitch and ominously silent. And then I passed out.

Chapter Nineteen

I awoke in a field of tall grasses on what appeared to be a warm, sunny afternoon. I must have been carried from the burning building, but I couldn't conceive of a place nearby with green grass in January, nor could I comprehend the daylight and warm weather.

I sat up slowly, nauseously, evaluating the stiffness of my back and chest, cautiously examining my soot-blackened hands and arms. My chest ached from the inside out and I coughed, sending a spasm of pain through the cavern of my body.

Other than a grove of trees to my right, there was nothing around except rolling hills and more grass. It was a beautiful sight, and I thought I must be dreaming, except that I had never felt so lucid in a dream. I raised my eyes to the sky and had to brace myself against the ensuing dizziness.

Standing was an exercise in pain, my rigid muscles stretching as if I'd been asleep for twenty years. The horizon rocked crazily so that I stumbled and closed my eyes, but I maintained my awkward rise. I opened my eyes slowly against the bright sunlight and gazed about. In the afternoon silence I thought I heard voices from the grove of trees. I started toward them. Maybe they could tell me where I was and how I had gotten here.

As I walked, I awoke more fully and began to feel the magnitude of my disorientation. I knew I was awake now, feeling ill but definitely myself, and I had *no idea* where I was or how I'd gotten there. My mind spun as if in rutted grooves to figure out what this place was and what had happened to my office, my shop, to Fredericksburg itself. I scanned the horizon back and forth, over and over, anxious to see anything familiar, but my mind only returned again and again to total confusion. The environment was beautifully benign, yet utterly terrifying in its unexpectedness. Where was I? Had I blacked out for six months?

I concentrated my efforts on walking without falling. The dizziness threatened to overwhelm me, but I plodded forward stubbornly, as if my feet carried lead weights that I must move in order to avoid sinking. If I didn't keep going, I was sure I would lose myself in mindless screaming, so deep was my derangement.

As I neared the trees I heard a woman's low laughter. Not a flighty giggle, but a soft, voluptuous sound. I hesitated. Here was something other than terror on which to concentrate. Next, I heard a man's low tones and then the woman's voice, still soft but clear, and teasing, "I tell you it's so, Dev. I don't know why you question me."

There was laughter in her voice, so I proceeded another few steps. Even in my foggy stupor there was something about the secluded spot and the fact that the two people were so carefully hidden from prying eyes that made me suspect that perhaps I shouldn't barge in and demand to know where I was. Instead, I proceeded to a point where I could push aside a low branch and look through the trees. I was rewarded with an eyeful.

There, in a glade on the pine-needle-and-moss-covered ground, were a man and a woman, stark naked, engaged in rhythmic and enthusiastic sex.

I stood uncomprehendingly for a moment, while the woman, with milk white skin and pale hair, gently pushed the man over so that she was on top. The man, darkly tanned and leanly handsome in a slick kind of way, grinned up at her and kneaded her breasts. Pine needles stuck to his hair.

She had her back to me so I couldn't see her face, but the woman's hips moved methodically, skillfully, and as to the sheer mechanics of the thing, I was impressed. This wasn't the first time these two had made love; even I could tell that.

"You know what I want, Dev?" the woman's low voice asked. She had a decidedly sexy voice, husky and teasing, promising far more than the words she uttered.

Dev's hands roamed the length of her and returned to her breasts. "Anything, darlin'. Just you tell old Dev what you want. I'll give it to you."

"I want to do this in the house, in a bed, just once."

Dev's expression altered at this sentiment, and he looked suddenly wary, an expression that seemed considerably more at home on his guileful face than the smile had. "I don't—"

The woman's hip movements became visibly more active.

"Don't say no, Dev. I'll tell you when it's safe; you just come." She nuzzled his neck and he groaned.

"All right?" she insisted.

He moaned again, reluctantly.

Uncomfortable, I started to turn away from the private display, when the woman stopped the motion of her hips and sat up. I could almost see her face, just the curve of a pale cheek and the jut of a strong jaw.

"Dev?" she said in a voice one might use with a recalcitrant child.

"Come on, darlin'," Dev groaned.

She didn't move. I found myself frozen, wishing I could see her face. There was something about her that niggled at the back of my mind.

Dev's fingers squeezed her hips nervously, trying to pull her forward, back into the motion. "All right," he said finally. "You tell me when, and I'll come."

The woman's hips began to move again, and Dev joined back in, closing his eyes and moaning his pleasure.

I backed away from the scene. I shouldn't have watched for so long, but it was a strange conversation for two people so obviously familiar with each other to have. In my half-alert state, I had felt as if I should stay and see how the conversation worked out, but good sense finally won out and I knew I should leave. I attempted to back up as quietly as I could, but because of my nearly overwhelming dizziness, when my heel caught on an old branch I sprawled backward into the brush with a crackling *whoosh*.

"Someone's here," the woman said in a loud whisper.

"Forget it. It's jest a animal or somethin'," Dev said breathlessly, urgently. "C'mon, hon, I'm near to bustin'."

There were the sounds of a slight scuffle, and I used the noise to hide my rising. Once on my feet, I didn't look back but ran, like an unsteady drunk, across the field. I don't know why I felt so sure, but something told me it would be worse than awkward if those two caught me watching them.

I crested a hill and glanced back at the wood. I could just see a flash of white disappear back into the green of the trees as I looked. My head swam from the exertion

317

of running, and as I moved to wipe my forehead I realized that my hair, normally wildly in the way, was nowhere to be found. My hands flew to my head, feeling only short stubble, and came back blackened. My hair had burned off! I felt the nape of my neck. There was a thick short knot in the back, but the front was completely gone. Nausea threatened to overwhelm me and I clasped my hands together in front of my mouth. No, my overtaxed mind protested, none of this could be true. It was just too weird to awaken to such unfamiliarity.

I turned back to the scene in front of me and was rewarded with a view of a farmhouse and some men working in an open field of grass just over the hill. Nearby, an old-fashioned flatbed wagon stood with a horse hitched in front, drooping in its harness.

It was odd, the feeling that crept up my spine, but the scene was too pastoral, like something out of an old Wyeth painting. Tall grass gave way to plowed land, men with pitchforks, scythes, and suspenders, the horse in the harness and the flatbed wagon. I felt my breath become labored. I scanned the horizon for another building, for a tractor, a road. My eyes swept skyward, searching for the white path of a jet. My ears strained for the sound of a nearby highway, a road with a car on it, anything. Nothing but the sound of birds and the clean sweep of the scythes greeted my ears.

I looked back at the men in the field with dread. One of them stared up at me, his hand shading his face. Then, calling to one of the others, he stretched out a finger toward where I stood. I tried to walk down the hill, but one foot stumbled into a hole, and I toppled over like an aging wino.

I refused to believe it. It couldn't be what I thought. But as I raised myself up feebly, I could conjure no other explanation for the strangeness of things. The sky was a stark, unmarred blue, the fields stretched as far as the eye could see, and the men making their unhurried way toward me through thigh-high grass wore britches and suspenders. I looked down at my clothing, my jeans and sweater, all charred and black. I felt again my hair, the unfamiliar stubble offensive. My lungs clogged again and I coughed.

It was frighteningly clear to me what had happened. I had traveled backwards through time as surely as Carter had traveled forward.

I must have lost consciousness for a moment, for when I came to strong arms were picking me up. My head lolled backwards, but I was unable to control it. Whoever it was who carried me adjusted his arm to hold up my head and began walking. Voices swirled around me like the ones in half-remembered dreams, conversational tones clear but words indistinct. It seemed we walked a long way while my mind absorbed what my feeble senses conveyed to it. I couldn't open my eyes, didn't really feel the desire to, and my ears took in everything as if from very far away.

It was as he lay me down on a bed that my heavy eyelids opened. Carter leaned over me, his face concerned.

"Thank God," I whispered, my voice a croak. "Carter—thank God."

He started and drew back from me. His face was suddenly unfamiliar with its distant expression.

"How do you know me?" He peered into my face as if trying to make it out through a fog.

I closed my eyes, willing my roiling stomach to settle. Panic threatened, and I pleaded with him silently. *Don't do this to me; don't be part of this nightmare.* But all I could voice were stupid, obvious questions, questions that had nothing to do with the abject fear and desolation I felt. "Where am I?" I asked weakly. Tears stung my eyes. "What's happened?" With that I gave in to unconsciousness.

I awoke sometime later to the sound of voices raised in anger. Startled at first, I thought they were quite close, but a quick glance told me I was alone in the austere little bedroom. An argument, my foggy brain surmised, from somewhere below. There must have been a heat vent in the room, one of those holes in the floor for heat from the fire to drift through, because I could hear the voices with some clarity. I lay still in my bed and listened, ignoring the way my chest burned with every indrawn breath and my head pounded incessantly.

"I don't know how you can talk that way," said a woman's voice, indignation, hardness, and desperation warring for supremacy in the tone. "How am I supposed to carry on? I can't run this place—not alone! While you're off trying to be a hero." The last was said with undisguised scorn.

I heard a chair scrape, as if someone had pulled it from beneath the table to sit. "You're not as helpless as you like to think," said Carter's voice, dry and unfeeling.

"It doesn't matter what I think! A woman can't run a farm alone. Everyone knows that. I would think even a high-minded *intellectual* such as yourself would know that much." Pots and pans clanked.

"You won't be alone," Carter said calmly. "You'll have Jackson and Smitty. And Devin, of course."

A pot clanged down on an iron surface. "Why do you say it like that? 'And *Devin*, of course,' " she mimicked.

"Because he trails after you like a dog sniffing up your skirts. You won't be rid of him until you smack him smartly across the snout. Maybe not even then. And something tells me you're not going to do that." No anger, just a wry, cynical, knowing tone.

"*Christ Almighty—*"

"Meg," a gentle chiding from Carter.

"I'm sorry, but the way you talk! Is it my fault if he follows me around? He thinks I'm pretty! I'm sure you can't understand *that,* but am I wrong to like a little flattery every now and again? Lord knows, I'm never going to get it from you."

Carter said something unintelligible.

"No, you do not. Besides, he's a help around here."

"When he's in the mood to be. Couldn't find him for love nor money today, though, with all that mowing to be done."

Plates were placed on a wooden table. Metal silverware chimed. It was amazing, I thought with detachment, how much one could tell from simple sounds.

"Well, I can't say *nothing* about that. I was here all day scrubbing these damned floors."

Carter must have looked down because she hastened to add, "Oh, you can't tell because they were *such* a mess, I'm going to have to do them all again tomorrow! I tell you, I just don't know what I'll do if you leave and I have to take on even more." Another chair was pulled out. Meg must have sat.

"I don't know who you're trying to fool, Meg, me or yourself. You don't give a damn if I'm here or not." This time I could make out the anger in Carter's voice.

Meg's voice softened, and I could just hear the placating tones, not her words. Carter's voice was quiet as well, but after a moment I heard Meg's sharply indrawn breath.

"How can you *say* that?" she gasped. This time the emotion sounded real.

A chair moved again, this time with the occupant in it. Carter's voice rose from a different area of the kitchen. "Don't be stupid, Meg. We both know this is a lie—this *life.*" Hard, heartless words.

"Carter, honey..." That sultry, pleading tone gave

her away, and I realized with a shock that this was the
same woman I'd seen making love in the glade that
afternoon—with a man who was definitely *not* Carter.
Her voice neared the spot where Carter's had come from.
"Honey, can't we make it better? I miss you. I miss you
in my bed."

"Don't even try it, Meg."

A slight shuffling. "Oh, *why* won't you ever just let
go? I tell you, I do miss you. My body misses you." The
voice dropped in timbre to a low, husky purr. "These
miss you, Carter. Don't you miss them?"

For the second time that day I'd become an unwitting
voyeur. I heard more shuffling, the sound of clothing being manipulated, a wet smack as if a kiss had ended.

"You do want me; you can't deny it," her voice continued, smug. "It's been so long . . . so long."

Carter's voice was still angry, but breathless too.
"Yes. I'm no better than the rest of the rutting pigs."

I tried to rise up in bed. Carter was downstairs, about
to make love to another woman, and every fiber of my
being demanded that I stop it. Granted, it was his wife
and he didn't even know me, but if this was not just some
smoke-induced nightmare, then Meg could easily have
been pregnant with this Devin's child already. And Carter's making love to her now would only muddy the waters, so to speak.

I heard a thump on the floor and the rustle of petticoats
as I struggled to my feet. I noticed, through the wave of
dizziness that engulfed me, that there was, in fact, an
open heat vent in the floor of the room. I held on to the
bedpost to get my bearings.

"Oh, yes, honey, yes," Meg's voice said, gasping.
"You are so ready for me. After all this time . . . you
need it, hon. I need it, too. The way I need you. Here,
let me help you with those."

I thought briefly of looking through the vent, but the

idea of seeing Carter making love to another woman was enough to make me want to throw up. If I clambered down the stairs, it would probably be enough to stop them. And stop them I must, I thought. For some reason I knew it was imperative that Carter not make love to his wife.

I opened the door, hoping it would squeak, but this was Carter Lindsey's house. What it lacked in decor it made up for in solidity. The door opened soundlessly.

Another feminine gasp. "Oh! Yes, come on, honey, *please.* I'm dying for you! Oh!"

I squelched a wave of disgust. Carter had married a sex kitten.

I was three noisy steps down the stairs when I realized I had very little on. Granted, it was a floor-length gown, but the light, gauzy material hid very little from anyone's view. However, my footfalls on the bare stairway had the desired effect. I could hear bodies rising rapidly and clothing rustling as it was readjusted over heated skin.

"Is anyone there?" I called out in a quavering voice.

"*Dammit!*" I heard Meg hiss.

"Get up," Carter said softly. "It's just as well. It wouldn't have solved anything, anyway."

I rounded the corner at the bottom of the stairs to a sight that would have broken my heart had the situation been anything other than what it was. Carter, disheveled and devastatingly handsome, leaned arrogantly against the back of a chair, looking at me with cool, disinterested eyes. Meg's pale blond bun was askew, her skirt hitched up in the back. With a familiarity that was painful to watch, Carter leaned over and carelessly snapped the fabric down over her petticoats. They were married. They were obviously, familiarly, comfortably man and wife— argument or no—and I had no right to do what I was doing.

Meg glared at me with undisguised loathing as I stood swaying in the doorway.

"Where am I?" I quailed at her look.

I began, genuinely, to lose my balance, and Carter strode forward, taking my arm in his work-hardened hands. I had to concentrate in order to keep from grabbing them, pulling them to my face, and pleading with him to remember me, to comfort me.

"Steady," he said. "You shouldn't be out of bed. We've sent for the doctor."

"No!" I protested. I had heard enough about the doctors of the day from Carter to know that treatment was the last thing I needed. "No, I'll be fine. You're right; I just need rest." I tried to turn and head back up the stairs, but Meg's cold voice stopped me.

"Ask her who she is, Carter," she said. She obviously didn't feel obligated to hide the resentment she felt about my interrupting their little scene.

Carter shot her a narrow look of disgust, then turned back to me solicitously. "We'd like to notify your family. Is there someone we can send for?"

I looked at him blankly.

"What's your name?" he prompted gently. I gazed into his warm gray eyes, achingly dear but heartbreaking now without the light of recognition. I wanted to reach out and stroke his cheek, but the slight swell of a red bite mark on his neck stopped me cold.

"My family's dead," I said suddenly. "There was an accident." One hand rose to my burned scalp.

I looked around the room in only half-faked panic. The floor was bare, the furniture threadbare. It was neat, clutter-free, but there was no warmth, no comfort.

"I have no one," I said, the truth of the words hitting me with a crippling fear.

Meg scoffed openly and Carter's eyes narrowed. "Earlier you called me by name. Do you know who I am?"

"I—" This stumped me for a moment. "Your name is Carter."

"She heard me," Meg said. "She's just saying what I said. She's crazy, Carter; don't listen to her. Where'd you come from?" she asked me aggressively. "Why were you in our field? Why were you dressed so odd?"

I looked at her, and in the moment our eyes met she knew I knew. She knew it had been me who'd seen her in that copse of trees, and she knew I had the power to destroy her.

"I don't know," I said weakly, into those cold blue eyes. "There was an accident . . . I don't remember anything."

"Nothing?" she pushed. I could see what she was getting at.

I glanced back at Carter, who had let go of my arm as I'd steadied myself against the door jamb. "You look familiar to me," I said softly. "Don't you know me?"

Eerily, I had a sudden memory of Carter's face in the odd green glow of the safety lights in my shop. The night that Sylvie had turned the lights off early, accidently putting us in the dark when Carter had first come to visit my store. "Don't you know me?" he'd asked then. I'd looked familiar to him. He'd already met me. *This was his past.*

The thought gave me a chill and I shuddered with the strength of it. This Carter gave me a stern look. "No, I don't know who you are. But you should be in bed." I swallowed back tears and looked away from him. This was too weird. "Don't worry," he continued more gently. "We'll take care of you for now. You must have family somewhere. Once you're feeling better we'll find them. But now you should rest."

I nodded mutely. Raising my foot to ascend the stairs, I felt a wave of fatigue hit me. I did not really faint, but knowing that Carter would catch me gave me all the reason I needed to give in to the weak feeling in my knees. As I collapsed he swung me neatly into his arms.

"I'm sorry," I murmured as we ascended the stairs.

Carter shook his head. "Not your fault."

I heard Meg's footsteps on the stairs behind us. Carter turned into the hall and took the first door. All the other doors on the hall were closed, as if hiding dark secrets.

He lay me gently on the bed and I leaned back on the pillows gratefully. He lingered for a minute after laying me down, studying my face.

"What happened to you?" he asked quietly. "Was there a fire? Your clothes were all sooty. And your hair . . ." He trailed off with a slight movement of his hand toward my head.

"Yes, a fire," I said. My fingers touched my face. Even my eyebrows were gone.

"Where?" Meg demanded from behind Carter. She nearly cowered back there, like a cat beneath a chair, as if I might reach out and grab her by the nape of the neck.

I sighed defeatedly. "I don't know."

"I haven't heard of any fire around here," Meg said.

"*Meg,*" Carter rebuked her. "Don't be rude." He turned his gaze back to mine and then gave me a half smile. "You rest now. We'll figure it out later."

As he rose to leave I instinctively reached for his arm. Something inside me hoped that he would turn and be my Carter, the one who knew me, the one who looked at me through those heavy-lidded eyes with amusement, understanding, and love. Instead, he turned in surprise.

"Carter," I said in a whisper. I clutched his callused hand, turning it over in mine. I remembered those strong, graceful fingers forming letters, spelling words to me. How do you tell the difference between a V and a two? he'd asked, those dear, gray eyes open and questioning. Context, I'd said; everything is context.

His gaze was intense now, confident and sure, as his brows drew together. He extricated his hand from mine. "What is it?"

I swallowed convulsively. "Join the army. You must—join the army and fight, fight for your beliefs." He looked at me then as if I truly were crazy. But I felt the need so strongly, as he regarded me like a stranger, to somehow direct him back to me. I had to make sure he still came to my time. I was in the past now. Could things change?

Suppose he didn't join the army? Suppose Meg's wiles worked and he never came forward in time? If it had truly been Carter's voice I'd heard in the burning bookstore, I could die in that blaze. Or I'd be stuck here. Trapped in a time where my love was married to another—and had no idea who I was. "Please, Carter," I said pitifully, withdrawing my empty hand and hiding it under the covers. "You have no idea how important it is. Please, please, please . . ." My eyes closed under a new wave of exhaustion. It was all too much. *Context,* I thought. My context was gone—everything was strange—and there was no way to figure it out.

When I opened my eyes again he was gone. They were both gone. I was alone.

Chapter Twenty

I heard them the next morning, arguing about me, about the doctor who couldn't come until tomorrow, and about Carter's decision to join the army. Though I was panicked about Carter's leaving me here, regardless of the fact that he did not recognize me, I was relieved at knowing that he was doing what he had to do to ensure our future.

I listened to them bickering—or rather, Meg's bickering and Carter's calm, dry, no doubt infuriating, answers—and I could understand why Carter hadn't wanted to come back. Listening to some of the awful things Meg said, it was amazing to me that Carter had even contemplated it, even believing he'd fathered a child. But if he left now, today, from all I'd gleaned, he would have to know the child was not his. From the way that Meg said it had been such a long time since she'd been with Carter, from the way that Meg and Devin had made love so familiarly, and from some of the things she said in this

328

morning's argument, I was positive they hadn't slept together for several months.

I drifted and dozed throughout the day, wondering what was to become of me and whether this sick, dizzy feeling was from the fire at the shop or the travel through time. If it was the time travel, it had either not happened to Carter, or he had hidden it extremely well. Thinking about it, I decided that he had probably experienced it and hidden it well. All in all, he had dealt with his displacement far better than I had mine. No whining, no whimpering. I was a little disgusted with the way I'd handled myself so far. Carter had let his curiosity go; he'd asked questions, he'd investigated technology. All I'd done was cower in my room and try not to cry when I saw Carter.

It was late afternoon when I awoke again, and this time it was to the sound of heavy footsteps on the wooden stairs outside my door. From the sound of them, I was fairly certain it was not Meg, and very hopeful that it was Carter.

He knocked on the door.

"Come in," I called in as strong a voice as I could muster. I struggled to sit up in bed. Though it was useless, my fingers attempted to comb through my hair, but the nonexistent locks surprised me yet again. I dropped my hands, depressed.

He opened the door slowly and entered. It was Carter. He was dressed in what looked to me like traveling clothes, with boots and a light, sacklike coat over his white cotton shirt and baggy trousers. He entered politely—not hesitantly as he might have in my house—the host entering a room in his own house.

"I've come to inform you of my departure. My wife will take care of you until your relations can be found."

I looked at him steadily. "You're going to join the army, aren't you?"

He nodded. "That's right. It's something I've planned on for some time. I was simply waiting on my orders, and I received them today. I'll be leaving forthwith."

I closed my eyes. "Oh, thank God," I breathed. "I have something I need to tell you."

His eyes narrowed skeptically. "Yes? Have you remembered something?"

I chewed my lower lip for a minute. "No, actually, I wanted to warn you about something—sort of a premonition I had. I know, that is, I believe I've always had a—a *sense* of things. I remember that I always, sort of, *know* what's going to happen."

He smiled dryly. "Are you telling me you've remembered you're a witch?"

Immediately I remembered my conversation with Carter near the train station and the problem he seemed to have with Madame Erika's being something of a witch. I wasn't sure how to answer. Being a witch would certainly have been the easiest way to promote what I had to say, but my history was so bad, I couldn't recall when they stopped burning people for that. "I wouldn't say a *witch,* necessarily," I hedged. "But I do know things that other people don't." His eyes were laughing at me. "I know things about *you,*" I said firmly.

He sighed. "What is it you feel the need to tell me?"

"Come here," I said. This was serious stuff, and he wasn't yet in the proper frame of mind to heed what I said. There was a straight-backed chair in the corner, and I motioned him to it. "Come here and sit a minute."

He inclined his head. "Begging your pardon, ma'am, and with all due respect," his lips were curved slightly but his eyes betrayed his irritation, "but I need to be leaving. I have many miles to go before dusk. Perhaps my wife can help you."

"Carter Lindsey, come here and sit down," I said in a strong voice, willing myself not to cough and drawing myself up as straight as I could. "I have something very important to tell you about your future." Even I could hear how stupid this sounded. Coming from a strange woman found in a field, it would sound completely ridiculous. "Let me tell you this: Your mother married your father because she was pregnant with you. Your father was a drifter from whom your mother withheld her only legacy from her wealthy family: a bag of valuable jewelry."

Carter's jaw actually slacked open at this, and his wide eyes now held open hostility. I looked at him smugly. He snapped his jaw shut. "Who told you that? Where did you learn such things?" he demanded.

I leaned back against the pillows. "I told you. I know things. Are you going to sit down?"

He stood motionless for a moment; then he strode angrily across the room. Just before he sat I said, "You might want to close the door."

He raised his eyebrows at the suggestion.

"I only mean that Meg should not hear all this," I said.

He laughed lightly, derisively. "She already knows my sordid past."

I gave him a condescending look. "But she does not know your future."

He shrugged in annoyance, strode back across the room, and closed the door with a quiet *click*. He did it with enough care to be silent that it was obvious that he knew Meg was capable of pounding up those stairs and scratching my eyes out in a jealous fit. What he didn't know was that she had more reason to worry about us speaking privately than mere jealousy, and I wondered if perhaps she was unaware that he was up here speaking to me now.

Once he was seated, I began, "Since you don't appear to be convinced yet, I'll tell you a bit more. I know that you and Meg married for the same reason your parents did.'' His eyes bored into me, twin shards of flinty steel. ''I know your marriage is not a happy one. I would advise you—that is, I think it best to tell you, that you should not, under any circumstances, um, try to *reconcile* things before you go.'' Whether or not he understood what I was saying, I wasn't sure. All I knew was that it would be impossible for me to tell him, this strange, unknown Carter, not to sleep with his wife before he leaves.

He crossed his arms over his chest. ''And why is that?''

Should I tell him his wife's been unfaithful? Should I warn him that she will try to pass another man's child off as his own? If I say those things, will he listen, or will he write me off as crazy? Looking at his hard face and angry eyes, I knew he wouldn't listen. He would also consider my words an open act of hostility and possibly throw me out of his house. After all, he had taken me in as a kindness. To cast blatant aspersions on his wife would look like the grossest ingratitude.

The only course open to me was to tell him that he would meet someone in the future who could explain more to him. I needed to tell him something that would convince the Carter in my time that it was, in fact, *me* here in his time. Something that made sense with the fact that I hadn't recognized him the first time I saw him. That way he would believe what I had to tell him about Meg and Devin. Because right now—or rather, when I left my time—he was convinced that Shelby Manning was not the woman he'd met in his time.

But what could I tell him? If I told him I remembered my name, he would have me out of the house in a flash, especially now, to go home to my own people. And who knew how long it would take me to get back to my own time? No, I needed to stay in this house. Besides, there were more things I could possibly discover even after

Carter left . . . like what became of the jewelry. And anything I *told* him would most likely be forgotten, or misinterpreted, or remembered incorrectly. No, I needed to give him something.

I strained my mind for an answer, feeling as if there was one just below the surface that I was overlooking.

Carter, tiring of my silence, rose and moved toward the door.

"No, wait!" I cried.

He spun to face me. "I don't know how you know these things, but I would appreciate it if you said no more. There is no use in dredging up the past in this ugly way. Now, we've said we will help you and we shall. The doctor will be here tomorrow, and then Meg will help you find your family."

I started to rise to follow but was consumed by a fit of coughing. Carter hesitated, his hand on the doorknob.

"Are you all right?" he asked mildly when I'd stopped.

I brushed my hands across my tearing eyes and stared at that familiar hand on the doorknob. "Please, give me one more minute." Then it hit me. *That hand!* "Wait!" I insisted.

My mind spun. The way the answer came to me, in a flash, blinding in its brilliance, was amazing in its symmetry. A trembling began deep in my chest and spread throughout my body.

"You and Meg had portraits—no, tintypes!—done of each other. Isn't that right?"

He looked irritated and confused, and not a little bit frightened. "Yes."

"Do you have one with you?" I asked urgently.

Slowly, he put his hand in his pocket and drew out the perfect leather case. Chills raced up my spine at seeing it so new. "Let me have it," I demanded. "Just for a moment."

He walked back over to the bed and handed it to me. I opened it nervously.

As I'd suspected, the inside cover was blank; smooth, unmarred red velvet lined the interior. My breath caught in my throat. It was too strange, this sudden clarity; but the answer was too unique to be mistaken. I looked around myself for something with a point. A hairpin lay in a dish by the bed. With shaking hands, I took it up. Then I scratched into the velvet as neatly as I could, *WV FW.*

The initials looked just as I remembered them. Not like my writing, because the instrument was so crude and my hands were shaking violently with the enormity of what I'd done. WV FW. Had I figured out what they meant—or had I made up what they meant? One thing was certain—it could not be coincidence. Beginnings and endings blurred. Who had thought of it if I hadn't? But which had come first, the answer or the question? My head was spinning before I realized I had been holding my breath. Gulping in a breath of air, I handed the picture back to Carter.

"There'll be a fire," I told him. Something about the look in my eyes, probably, held his undivided attention. "A serious fire, a deadly fire, and in it there'll be a woman who looks much like me. Ask her what this means; she'll be able to tell you. Ask her, also, about this time now, and about me and what I know, and she'll tell you. She'll answer *all* your questions."

Carter drew back a little after I handed him the box and eyed me warily. "You are uncommon strange," he said quietly, half fearfully.

"I know it." I laughed, a high, almost hysterical sound, at the understatement. *Everything* was strange; he didn't even know the half of it yet. "I know it; I really am strange."

* * *

I watched Carter leave the house from my upstairs bed-room window. I'd heard them talking in hushed tones, presumably about me, and then I'd heard the door shut. He walked with a sack on his back and a strong, pur-poseful stride.

He was only about twenty yards from the house, just beyond the barn where the door stood open, when Meg, her face tear-streaked and her hair loose, came dashing from the house. She threw herself into his arms and be-gan kissing him, his face, his neck, frantically.

Carter caught her with his one free arm, holding her securely around the waist, and, as far as I could tell, returned the kisses. Perhaps it had something to do with the drama of leaving for the war, but Meg's emotions struck me as sincere. And Carter responded to them.

He dropped his sack and held her in both arms. Her hands cupped his face as her body leaned into his. His arms clutched her tightly and they spoke a few words, then kissed again. Before I knew what was happening, Carter had lifted her into his arms and was heading for the open barn door.

I watched in disbelief as they disappeared inside. "No," I murmured to myself. This couldn't be. She couldn't succeed now, at the last minute. "No!" I said again louder, though the window was closed and they were much too far away to hear.

This was it! They were making love and this was what Carter would point to and say, *But there, that time, I could be the child's father.* I pounded my fist against the window, as if the noise would distract them. But they were too far away, and my pounding was a feeble weapon against fate.

I whirled toward the door, lost my balance, and fell back onto the window ledge. Gasping, I closed my eyes and leaned my head on the glass. Even if I could dash down the stairs and out the door, rush across the yard to the barn—and I envisioned myself doing it—I knew it would be too late. They weren't going to linger over this act. Their embrace had been too frantic, a need borne of absence and estrangement.

Sure enough, shortly after despair hit me in full force and I had to sit in the chair that Carter had vacated not a half hour since, they emerged from the barn. First Carter, buttoning his shirt and shrugging into the jacket; then Meg, her lovely pale hair like an aura around her flushed face, her skirts crumpled. I wanted to weep with the frustration of it, and for the sadness of it. Whatever feelings Meg had for Carter—and I did believe she had some— she was willing to go to any length to save her own skin. And Carter, unhappy and dissatisfied, still clung to the idea, no, the vow, of the fealty of man and wife.

As I watched Carter walk away from the house, with long, sure strides, the wind lifting his hair and the bag shifting as he walked, the seeds of an idea came to me. The Carter that I knew in my time had told me that before he had left to join the army he had hidden the pouch of jewels in a book. If I could find them, perhaps I could bring them back with me. My mind raced back to the conversation to recall exactly which book he'd said he'd put them in. Knowing Carter, he probably had more books than it would be practical to search through, particularly with Meg in the house. And something told me now that Carter had gone, Meg wasn't even going to try to keep up the guise of hospitality.

I remembered it was a book about feeling the bumps on people's heads to discern their personalities, but I couldn't remember the name of the science. Some long word, beginning with *ph*, I was pretty sure. In any case, it was something to go on, and all I needed was some time alone in the house. I determined that I would try to sleep less and concentrate on the goings-on of the house, now that Carter was gone. If I could figure out Meg's routine, surely there would be lengths of time when she wasn't in the house.

Now that the coast was clear, so to speak, I wondered if Meg would dare to bring Devin here to the house, to fulfill the desire of making love in a bed that she'd expressed that day I'd spied on them. She knew, I was sure, that I was the one who had seen them together, and I was hoping that the fact of my not spilling the beans to Carter would stand me in a little better stead with her now that he was gone. Besides, she'd gotten what she'd wanted: the viability to claim her child was Carter's. Maybe she'd be a little more hospitable now that she could relax about that. But I doubted it. And I felt a churning pool of resentment for her bubble in my stomach.

She had no idea how many lives she was playing with. Had she told Devin about the child? Did he know he would have a son? Did she realize the implications of bringing a child into the world who would never know his real parentage? I knew I was thinking in twentieth-century terms, but it didn't make me hate her any less. And hate her I did. She was chaining Carter to herself in ways that she couldn't even imagine. And if she could imagine them, I knew she wouldn't care. She was one of those people who cared only for solving the problem for herself. She wanted, needed, Carter beside her, no matter what. And I think part of her wanted him just to have him, the same way Carter had said she wanted the jewels.

Would I change history if I took the jewelry? I didn't care. I was here now, through no fault of my own, and my actions would have to be reflected, no matter what I did. I thought about the initials. I had written them. By the time Carter had gotten to me, I'd already been part of his life. I was part of history now as surely as I was in my own time. And even if I never figured out why this had happened, it would still be true.

I slept fitfully that night, which turned out to be a good thing because I was awake when Meg rose early, before dawn, to go to the barn. The only thing I could think was that she had to milk some cows or gather some eggs, or whatever one did before dawn on a farm; but it gave me the opportunity to search the house for the book of jewels, and whatever else of interest I might find.

I rose in the chill morning air and crept to the bedroom door. I opened it swiftly, knowing it wouldn't creak, and stepped out into the hall. The house wasn't big, but it was one of those old-fashioned farmhouses with lots of nooks and crannies. I felt pretty sure the books would be downstairs, so I snuck down the steps in my bare feet, feeling the smooth wood beneath my toes and the chill drafts that wafted along the floors.

The first room I came to was the one in which I'd interrupted Carter and Meg. As I'd noted before, it was quite bare, and this time I saw that it was devoid of books. The major piece of furniture in the room was the heavy black woodstove, which stood unlit as I passed through.

On my way I paused and glanced out the window toward the barn. The door was still open, so it was obvious she was still inside. I moved through the room to another, smaller, but equally bookless room, then on to the dining room, which was quite obviously never used and certainly housed no books.

The next room was the kitchen and, as might have been anticipated, it held no books either. It had a slightly more lived-in feel, though, than the other rooms, with its worn sawbuck table, rough-hewn and marred with circular burns as from pots and pans, and a large cast-iron cookstove, bubbling now with something that smelled like chicken broth. But it still gave no hint as to the character of the people who lived there, other than that they were not particularly adept at making things homey.

Overall, I was impressed with how simple and spare the furnishings were throughout the house, and I wondered if this was due to monetary constraints or a lack of imagination. But the absence of even small touches, such as cut flowers or simple stenciling on the cabinets, pointed to the latter. There was no woman's touch in this unhappy home. From what I knew of Carter, I had the feeling the house might have had a completely different—warmer—feel if Meg moved out and Carter lived here alone.

The next room after that was the one in which I'd started. Where in the world were the books? I knew he had them; he'd spoken of them often.

From outside I could hear the barn door rumble and then close with a smack of wood against wood. I pranced on cold bare feet to the window to see Meg striding, quicker than I'd imagined, toward the house with a bucket in each hand. They were heavy, I could tell, and I had the thought that if we were men involved in the same situation, I would have had to be very nervous that she could beat the tar out of me.

I turned quickly and raced up the stairs, stopping to pant hoarsely at the top. My head spun dizzily with the unaccustomed exertion as the door opened downstairs. Her feet clattered heavily on the bare wood floors; then I heard her drop the buckets on the table in the kitchen with a grunt.

I felt exhausted. From just that short trip downstairs and the quick, panicked run back up, my muscles and lungs protested as if I'd just run a marathon. Was this how heavy smokers felt?

I crept quietly back into my room when I heard a brisk knock on the downstairs door. I tiptoed to the window and looked out. Below me was the roof of a porch that shielded my view of the front door. I looked around and saw no horse tied out front, and the barn door was still shut; but I was unsure if people necessarily traveled that way in this time and part of the country, or if that was just an idea I'd gotten from "Gunsmoke." I tried to figure out who it might be, but I had no idea how the Lindseys lived, whom they knew, or how much they socialized. Then the thought struck me that it might be the doctor, and visions of leeches drove me to the heat vent to eavesdrop. The prospect of crawling out onto the porch roof and running hell-for-leather away from the house was a decidedly attractive alternative to having slugs placed on my skin in an attempt to promote health.

"That was fast," I heard Meg's sultry voice say.

"News travels quick," Devin's voice purred in return. "Teddy Maxwell saw him pass by last night, before dark, he said. When was you plannin' on lettin' me know he'd gone?"

Water sloshed into a bowl. "Eventually," Meg said carelessly.

Devin was silent for a moment after that. Then, almost whining, he said, "I came by like you asked, Meg. You wanted to do it in the house. Now we can do it whenever we want."

More water sounds. Meg was keeping herself occupied, perhaps washing something. "I'm gonna be busy here, now, runnin' this place all by myself. I can't just be poppin' off with you any time I please." Her voice was insolent.

Something clattered to the floor. "Hey, what is this?" Devin's voice, angry. "You was all hot for me while he was around. Now he's gone, you don't seem so hot. Were you jest usin' me? Tryin' to make him jealous?"

If I expected fear in her voice, as if he'd grabbed her or struck her in anger, I was to be disappointed. "Of course not," she scoffed. "And let go of me, you big lout! The last thing on earth I wanted was for him to find out, and he didn't. How could I make him jealous if he never knew? Huh? How?''

It sounded like Devin's feet actually shuffled. "I don't know," he sulked. "How come you don't want to do it, then? I run right over when I heard, knowin' you and me can be together. Hard as a bull, I was, when I heard it.''

"And about as thick-headed as one, too," Meg said, her anger diminishing. "Don't you think it's gonna look mighty peculiar, you comin' over here first thing in the morning after he's gone?''

"Who's gonna know, huh?" he asked, his confidence returning. I could hear the cajoling note in his voice. "We could jest trot right upstairs now and—''

"No, we couldn't either," Meg snapped. "Stop it! *She's* up there, that strange girl we saw.''

"What girl?''

"The one who saw us in the woods. Carter took her in, the soft-hearted fool. She's up there now, waitin' on the doctor.''

Devin sucked in his breath. "Do you think she told him? Told Carter 'bout you an' me?" His voice held undisguised fear.

Meg made a sound of disgust. "Do you think you'd be standin' there alive if she had?''

Devin sniffed loudly. "That don't make me feel any easier," he said in a flat voice.

"I think she's crazy; that's what I think. She claims she don't remember who she is, and I'm sure I never saw her before," Meg complained. Then she added thoughtfully, "But she knew Carter, for some reason.''

Devin laughed. "Maybe Carter beat you to it, and brung her into your house before you could bring me into his.''

Meg's response was scathing and quick. "You shut your cowardly mouth, Devin Mackenzie," she hissed. "Carter'd never do a thing like that to me! He's got

341

honor. Something you'd know nothin' about!''

''Yeah, an' he talks like a goddamn book. So what're you out there in the woods with me for?'' Devin asked angrily, his pride obviously stung. ''I've half a mind to tell him myself what you been doin'. We'll see how far that *honor* goes in stoppin' him from beatin' your pretty face!''

''Don't be silly,'' Meg said mildly. ''He wouldn't beat me and he'll never find out. Besides,'' her voice took on that sultry coo I recognized, ''he's gone now.''

There was a conspicuous silence; then Devin said, ''That's better. C'mon, let's go upstairs.''

''We can't. I told you, *she's* up there. Let's go out to the barn; then she'll think you're just helpin' me.''

I watched them go. Disgust welled up inside me like a sudden case of indigestion. I saw them enter the barn and close the heavy door before I realized what this little tête-à-tête afforded me: time to search the upstairs for the book.

Turning my back on the barn and the sordid activity it housed, I quickly stole out the door and into the room next to it. Immediately upon opening the door, however, I was completely taken aback. Like a physical slap, the smell of brine and sour meat nearly knocked me over. Huge slabs of meat hung from hooks in the ceiling, and scattered over the floor were what looked to be charred chips of wood, smelling strongly of hickory. I retreated quickly back out the door and closed it firmly. *Good Lord, they had their meat smoking right in the house?* The small room was right next to the big chimney in the kitchen, and I imagined that must have been part of the plan. In any case, I was pretty sure there would be no books in there.

I decided to try the bedroom, half because it made the most sense to me, and half because I was morbidly curious about the personal life Carter shared with his wife.

I was pretty sure the room they shared was the one straight down the hall, so I moved directly to that door. Opening it, I was rewarded with the sight of a large four-poster bed, two armoires, a dressing mirror, and a long wall of bookshelves. The room was bigger than any of the others, which perhaps explained the presence of the books here rather than downstairs, and had a worn but comfortable-looking armchair in the corner. Did Carter sit and read there at night? I could almost picture him with a lamp on the tiny table next to the chair, golden hair glowing in the lamplight, only it was myself waiting in the high, soft bed and not the surly Meg.

Snapping out of my reverie, I felt the guilty urgency that comes with creeping through someone else's bedroom and, like a seasoned criminal, I quickly scanned the room for anything of interest. But other than the books and the cozy armchair, the room had the same dry, impersonal feel as the rooms downstairs. I moved toward the books and let my eyes scan the shelves for what I needed. It was there, on the top shelf, the fifth book I looked at. *The Science of Phrenology* by Emmett Stone.

I had to jump, twice, before I could accurately hook my finger over the top and pull it from the shelf, but I finally managed to jar it loose and pull it down. It was a thick book, heavy, and when I opened it, it was clear the center had been hollowed out to hold something. But the book was empty, the hole gaping. Carter had been gone less than twenty-four hours, and Meg had already found the jewels.

Chapter Twenty-one

I slammed the book shut and sat holding it for a minute. If she had taken the bag from the book last night, then she hadn't yet had time to do anything with it other than to hide it somewhere else. By my calculations it was now about 6:30 a.m. The sun was just peeking over the hills outside the windows and birds were chirping with the wild abandon of a cool summer morning.

I gazed around the room, trying to gauge where someone like Meg would hide a bag of jewels. She had no one here to hide them from, really, now that Carter was gone, unless she suspected me. And she had no reason to think I'd know about such unexpected wealth in this obviously struggling household.

Upon opening the armoires, I found the one that was hers. A selection of seven or eight dresses hung there, with petticoats hooked on a nail at the back. There was a section of three drawers on the left, which I proceeded to open, but other than a small cache of cheap jewelry I found nothing of any value. I closed the armoire with a frustrated sweep of my hand.

I turned around and leaned against the mirrored front of the wardrobe, scanning the room. My eyes returned again and again to the bed, large and imposing, covered with several quilts on top of a thick down mattress. I gazed at the mattress contemplatively. The first place a burglar will look, echoed through my head. Would she really hide something so valuable in a place as obvious as under the mattress? But perhaps it wasn't so obvious. After all, as far as I could tell it was 1862. Something that was cliché to me might be new to these people.

I moved to the bed and hastily threw back the covers. I would never have thought feathers could be so heavy, but after a moment or two of thoroughly unladylike heaving and hefting I could see underneath. And there, to my wondering eyes, was a leather pouch a little smaller than your average sandwich bag, and a small, leatherbound book. I grabbed both things and let the mattress drop solidly back into place.

Though I knew the bag contained what I sought, I went to the chair in the corner, sat, and pulled open the leather pouch, just to be sure. The muted wink of a red stone in gold confirmed that it was. Feeling through the bag with my fingers, I could tell it contained quite a few pieces, as well as a number of individual stones. I stashed the bag up the long sleeve of the nightgown I wore and turned to the book. As soon as I opened it my heart tripped and I knew I'd found the real treasure. It was Meg's diary.

I opened the book to a middle page. Dense rows of loopy, childlike script lined the paper, but the obviously uneducated scrawl was at least easy to read. I flipped through it.

14th December 1861
Carol Nelson tole me today what Really happened

to Cora and it was Just Exacly as I suspected. Her husband didnt know Nothing about it until he arrived home after the Deed was done.

29th December 1861
Liddy says the Johnson boy was kilt by a black bear yesteday night. He was just out working in his Field when the animal attacked. Werent nothing left of him but his Arms and his Head.

3rd February 1862
If Liddy tries One More Time telling me what to do Im going to scream in her face. She tries telling me she knows just what Im feeling but she dont. Same time Momma come by and tole Liddy to Keep Away from me. Momma knows Liddy makes me crazy. I wish Momma would come by more often but now shes got the Gout making her so she cant walk very good. Carter said hed go get her but she dont like riding in that wagon neither.

10th February 1862
Theres no telling Cora whats right and what aint. She wont listen to me At All. I tole her I Know how to handle her Husband, but she just keeps claiming hes going to hate her forever because of that Damm Cow.

I leafed through a few more pages of such gossip until I reached a time closer to the present, or whatever. It was also the first time I saw Carter's name mentioned in any way other than as an aside.

24th March 1862
Devin Mackenzie come round again this morning. I dont trust him but he sure does talk nice to me.

Carter has Nothing but sour looks for him but he needs the help for the Farm and Devin said he will work for Cheap. I think he said such just to be Close to Me. Hes always giving me Looks and touching my Hand whenever Carter aint looking and it kind of makes me excited and kind of makes me mad. I might let him kiss me just for fun if Carter stays mad about the Party. He just dont know what hes got and I wish he would Notice more the Way Devin looks at me.

I flipped further ahead.

6th June 1862
Times running out and Carter wont hardly even Speak to me. I just know hes going to join the Army specially now hes so mad about Devin's kiss. He wanted to send him off again but I tole him Devin feels Real bad about it all and wont hardly even talk to Me at all anymore. At least I think Carter dont still think I Wanted Devins kiss but he dont want to let Devin stay on but that I insisted. But I'm afraid because my monthly is late and Carter would never Ever forgive me if he knew I been Lying to him and that Devin got more than just that kiss. I knew I should never of gotten involved with him but now he will tell Carter if I tell him no.

16th June 1862
I know that jewelry is here someplace and hes hidden it. Carter says he wont tell me where it is because hes not sure yet what to do with it. He dont want it Squandered he said and I tole him Id never do such a thing. But its all worth Alot of Money because I Saw it one time when Miz Lindsey

showed it to Me when I was a kid long before I married Carter. She tole me anyoned be Lucky to get her boy even without it but that he would be a Rich Man. I know Ill find it and then Ill show him how much Good can be done with such a sum and he will be happy I did what I did. Cora just ordered a rug almost the size of her sitting room and was quite Huffy when I told her wed be getting the same Thing before long.

22nd June 1862
Carter almost gave in today but for that Witch he found. I just know I can get him to do it before he goes if she dont interfear Again. If hed just do it Once with Me then I wont have to worry about Devin any more because I know he cant say for sure its his even if he wanted to which I surely doubt. Devins a Wastrel but he can keep me from being Lonely here specially with Carter off winning the War. Maybe a few months without a woman will make him want me again and after I give him this Baby maybe he will think more Im a better Wife. I dont want Devin thinking its his in case he comes back and says something to Carter about it. I'm going to tell him Carter and I had relations before he left for the War even if it never happens because I dont want Dev thinking Nothing about this baby. I can run him off before Carter comes home but he can be good help here until Carter comes home. Specially now I can write and tell Carter about the Baby and he will come home for me quick but I better wait until its not so obvious when I got this child. He cant know Devins fathered this Babe or he will kill him for sure and leave me alone and Devin wouldnt help me even if he knew

*everything about the baby being his and he lived
through Carters—*

"Just *what* in Sweet Jesus's name do you think you're
doing?!" The screech hurt my ears, made the hair on the
back of my neck stand on end, and caused me to jump
so violently, I dropped the book. I looked up to see Meg
tearing across the room toward me, her face flushed purple and murder in her eyes.

She grabbed my arm in a bruising grip and dragged
me to a standing position. We were about the same
height, but as I'd noticed before, she was considerably
more muscular. She hauled her arm back and slapped me
a stinging blow across the face.

Stunned by both the blow and her sudden appearance,
I could do little more than stumble backward, tripping
over the leg of the chair and crashing into the table next
to it. The oil lamp teetered, then dropped, shattering on
the floor, as I caught myself against the wall.

"You lying little *trollop!* Did Carter set you up here?
Did he? Are you spyin' on me?" Her pale blue eyes spat
hatred and her mouth twisted with the force of her rage.
"How *dare* you read my private, personal writin's!"

She had a point there. I'd had no right to read her
diary. But what it contained was the key to my future
with Carter, and I couldn't feel anything but elated about
that.

"I can see that you wouldn't want anybody reading it,
especially since it says in plain words that the child
you're carrying has nothing to do with Carter," I shot
back. "Do you think it's fair to him or the child to pull
such a trick?"

For a moment I thought she might explode like the girl
who turned into a blueberry in *Willy Wonka and the
Chocolate Factory*. She was almost as purple, and mad-
der than I'd ever seen anyone. It was a little intimidating.

"How *dare* you say such a thing! You got *nothin'* to do with this situation. I took you in and did you a kindness, and this is the thanks I get?" She moved closer to me and I flattened myself against the wall.

"Why don't you just tell Carter about the child? He'd probably support it anyway, and it's better that he knows it's not his," I said, bracing myself for whatever she might dish out.

She laughed scornfully. "Better for who? You stupid bitch, do you think I'm going to admit it to Carter because of anything you say? How big a fool do you think I am? Besides, you got no proof." She bent and picked up the book with a cold, evil smile. "And anyway, Carter'd never believe *you*, a tramp he found in the field."

This was probably true. The Carter she knew wouldn't believe me, but the Carter *I* knew would. I smiled back, an angry, powerful smile. "I don't need proof, Meg," I said quietly. "You're going to lose Carter and I'm going to have him. Mark my words. That child you're carrying will not have Carter Lindsey for a father."

Her nostrils flared as she took a deep, enraged breath. "Get out of here," she said in a low, quaking voice. "Get out of my house. Now!"

"Fine," I said as calmly as I could, and started to skirt around her.

"You're nothing but a *freak!*" she screamed after me. "Look at yourself! Carter could never love *you!* Not when he's got me!"

I slipped through the door, pulled it shut behind me, and hoped she wouldn't think of the jewels until I could put them someplace safe. I was sure it wouldn't be long before she missed them. I could hide them myself, I thought quickly; then I could sneak back in the house and get them after she kicked me out.

I heard her banging around in her room as I quickly opened the door to the smoke room. Between its rank odor and messy floor, I figured it would be the last place she'd look. As I pulled the bag from my sleeve, however, I heard her angry footsteps head for her door. I tossed the bag across the floor, hoping it would bury itself amid the wood shavings, then watched in horror as it slid easily through the shavings and into what must have been a smoke hole in the chimney.

There was no time to investigate. I stepped back out the door, closed it as quietly as I could, and slipped into the guest room next door, flipping the door shut behind me just as Meg's bedroom door slammed open down the hall.

I had just made it to the window, in an effort to appear as nonchalant as possible, when the door to my room banged open behind me. I whirled as Meg appeared in the doorway, for all the world like the sheriff in a western standing imperiously in the saloon doorway. The breath left my body as she swung the long barrel of a shotgun up toward my chest.

"Where are they?" she demanded, her eyes every bit as steely as the gun she held.

"What?" I asked feebly, already feeling weak from the stress of the morning, not to mention the large breath of fetid air I'd gotten from the smoke room.

"You know what," she said, deadly calm. "The bag, the stones. I know you've got them. Where are they?"

I pulled myself up straighter. "I don't know what you're talking about."

"*Bitch!*" she snapped. "Take off that nightshirt."

I hesitated, and she cocked the gun. Thank God I had thrown the jewels aside, I thought fervently, pulling the filmy material over my head. Even if I never found them, at least she wouldn't have them. And I'd already found all the treasure I wanted: the proof that Carter had not fathered a child.

I tossed the gown on the bed and stood stark naked

351

before her. "Nothing up my sleeve," I quipped with a superior, if exhausted, expression. It was certainly obvious I didn't have the jewels on me.

She inched her way to a chest of drawers along the wall and yanked open the top drawer with one hand. Without taking her eyes from my face, she reached in and pulled out my burned jeans. She flung them at me across the room. "Go back to where you came from," she snarled, hurling the rest of my tattered clothing at me piece by piece. "Get out of my house and don't you *ever* come back here again or I'll have the law on you."

She watched as I pulled first the T-shirt and then my sweater over my head. "You're going to lose, Meg. Better to confess now. Maybe Devin would be happy about the baby," I said, halfheartedly, pulling on my underwear and jeans.

One of my shoes hit me in the face.

"Fine," I snapped. I could feel a trickle of blood inch down my cheek from where the heel had struck me. "Thank God I know you'll get what you deserve."

I had only one shoe on when she smacked me in the arm with the barrel of the gun. "Get out now," she said. "I ain't waitin' any longer."

"Don't forget the doctor's coming," I said, just to give her something else to think about.

"I'll tell him you run off. And you'd better do just that." She poked me down the stairs with the gun.

When we emerged from the house into the bright summer sun I gazed around myself in bewilderment. Where would I go? Had I been a fool to make an enemy of Meg? I was already sweating in the heavy sweater, and the thought of leaving Carter's land filled me with trepidation. Suppose I had to be here, in the same area, for the magic to take me back to my own time? I remembered the story in Meg's diary about the Johnson boy. Were there really bears here?

I glanced back at Meg, who watched me with cold, shrewd eyes. How like her picture she looked, standing there in the summer sun, with her hair a soft, feminine halo and her eyes of bone-chilling steel.

Then she surprised me. "You can sleep in the barn tonight if you want," she capitulated. "Then I want you gone, understand?"

Where had this sudden magnanimity come from? Did she feel sorry for me, with my odd, ugly clothes and my shorn hair? A softness of that sort in her would be incongruous; though I didn't trust her, I felt I had no other choice but to take her up on the offer. I nodded mutely.

She continued in a flat, unreadable voice. "I know it was you saw me and Dev in the woods, and you kept your mouth shut about it. One night in the barn ought to be thanks enough." She inclined her head curtly, once.

I nodded again. "I appreciate it," I murmured. Whatever her real reason, I was glad for the temporary respite. At least this way I could regroup a little, and try to figure out how to get home. As far as I knew, the Northern Lights hadn't appeared again the night I was transported, and other than that natural phenomenon I had no idea how this might have happened.

I was feeling extremely weak at this point and made my feeble way across the yard to the barn. I had only one shoe on as I limped away, but I was sure Meg would do nothing further for me. Retrieving my missing shoe from the room where she'd hurled the other one at me seemed among the least likely possibilities, so I continued.

I had to wrestle with the heavy barn door, and I thought again of Meg's strength as I recalled her comparatively effortless maneuvering of the thing. Finally I got it open a short way and squeezed in. The barn was empty of animals, but their thick, musty smell remained, along with the dry scent of hay and the peculiarly sweet organic scent of manure. Parked to one side was the flat-bed wagon that had been in the field with Carter, as well as a wooden plough and a few other implements whose uses I couldn't fathom.

I searched through the stalls for a clean one in vain. All had hay-strewn floors complete with dried manure and other unidentifiable substances. I couldn't imagine getting much sleep on them, wondering what lay just beneath the surface, even though I felt so tired I thought I might just drop where I stood. So I started up the ladder to the loft. There was plenty of hay there, and it all looked clean. Several uncut bales lined one wall and provided a corner that looked almost cozy.

I proceeded to that corner and collapsed. My eyes closed instantly, like one of those baby dolls whose eyes shut automatically the moment they're horizontal. But sleep did not come. Instead, I found myself pondering all the imponderables that had led me to this point. How had this happened? How was I to get home? What would I do tomorrow, when Meg kicked me off the property and I had nowhere else to turn?

The *why* of my voyage seemed clear enough. I had traced the mystery of Carter's descendants and I had proven it was me who had scratched the initials. I'd even seen proof of Meg's infidelity, and if I ever got back it surely would be as obvious to Carter as it would to me that we were meant to be together. But until I got back nothing was obvious. For as long as I was stuck here I'd wonder what else I was to learn, what else I was to do, what else had to happen for history to be complete.

As I lay thinking, I realized that the probable reason Bart Lindsey had been so suspicious and secretive could well be because he had Meg's diary. If he did, it would explain a lot about him. If Meg had written that the jewelry had disappeared somewhere in the house, it would explain why he'd gone looking for Carter's home. If she'd written about their purported worth, which I'd no doubt she had even in the portion she'd already written when I saw it, it would explain why Bart had insisted that he was the only rightful heir. And as far as explaining Bart's surly and defensive behavior when confronted with Carter's obvious relationship to the man in the tintype, Bart would have known from Meg's diary that he himself was in no way related to Carter Lindsey the First. And this man, my Carter, who was the spitting image of that distant relative, was most conspicuously an heir.

It was at once gratifying and frustrating to finally have the answers to all of those questions; satisfying to know and to be able to explain all the connections, and frustrating to have no one to whom to explain them. If I ever did get back, it would set Carter's mind at ease to know he'd not left Meg to fend for herself and his child, though how he could ever think that that manipulating woman wouldn't be able to fend for herself I couldn't imagine. And it would certainly set my mind at rest to know, *really know,* that he'd left nothing he really cared for behind. That had been my one trepidation, the one stumbling block to complete happiness upon Carter's decision to stay with me: the fear that he'd always regret, always struggle with guilt over leaving her alone.

I felt my eyes drooping and didn't stop them. The intricacies of the mysteries solved could be figured out in the morning. Even the memory that Bart had said the chimney—perhaps the chimney wherein lay the jewels—was all they'd found of the house wasn't enough to keep me awake. My body felt so fragile and weak that even a mere hour's exertion exhausted me as nothing else ever had. Slowly, with the blissful satisfaction that comes from indulging an all-consuming fatigue, I slid into sleep.

I awoke choking. My eyes stung even before I opened them, and an ominous crackling was suddenly quite loud.

I shoved myself to a sitting position and struggled with disorientation. The loft was thick with smoke. It rose from the hay like steam off hot, wet asphalt. I bolted to my feet and searched frantically through the fog for the ladder. It was to the left, I was pretty sure, so I shuffled slowly toward the place where I remembered ascending. I was nervous that the fire below might have weakened the loft, that the whole thing would go crashing to the ground, but when I made it to the edge I could see the real danger lay below. The ladder glowed like a red-hot coal, the bottom half submerged in flames.

I whirled around to look for a window, or one of those hayloft doors—anything through which to jump—but there was nothing but smoke and tinder-dry plank walls. Below me the fire raged uncontrolled. The whole floor of the barn was engulfed and flames ran up the walls with such hungry intensity that I feared the whole building might collapse as it ate the foundations.

I coughed and choked again, my lungs protesting the harsh spasms, still sore from the first fire. I wondered frantically if I had come to the past only to die here, my questions answered, my secrets silenced. My eyes teared with smoke and fear. Panic rose within me and I screamed, a horrifying, bloodcurdling sound. My own terror frightened me, and I screamed again, feeling rationality take flight like a frightened bird.

I ran to the wall of the barn behind me and clawed at it with my fingers. Surely someone would hear me. Meg? Would Meg help me?

Then the truth hit me. Meg hadn't been generous with her offer to let me stay in the barn; she'd planned this. This fire had started with a match, and it had been her milk-white fingers that had struck it.

Whirling, I searched the piled straw for anything that resembled a tool. These planks were breakable, weren't they? Surely I could ram through one of them a hole big enough to squeeze through. I found a pole about the width of a broom handle and as long as a jousting sword and tried stabbing at the walls. But the pole only bounced off the wood, threatening to toss me into the flames below.

I heard myself whimpering with fear and impotence. I turned again and again, quarter turns, around and around, my eyes searching the empty straw for something to help me, for some way out.

It was then that I noticed a knothole in the far wall. I stumbled through the hay to see if I could look out, find someone within earshot, then scream bloody murder through it for help. But when I staggered to the wall, lurching to a halt in front of it, I discovered it was too high.

"*Help!*" I screamed up at it, but the cry was cut short by more coughing. I swayed on my feet from lack of oxygen, then caught myself against the wall. I hung my head between my arms, gasping, when I noticed another, smaller hole, near my feet. I dropped to my knees, falling onto my hands, and pressed my eye so hard to the hole, I could feel the wood scrape my cheek and forehead. There, in the pretty green yard between the house and the barn, stood Meg. Watching.

My God, she means to kill me, I realized anew. My throat swelled shut with panic. Someone joined her— Devin—and the two of them looked up at the barn. Meg said something, gestured to the cows in the field, and shrugged. She was telling him the barn was empty. There was no use trying to save it. She'd *shrugged.* The true extent of her malevolence struck me like a blow.

I was going to die in this fire.

Chapter Twenty-two

Strong arms lifted me, but I couldn't stop screaming. I gasped for air as we descended through murky smoke, flinging my shattered fear outward with weakening cries and sobs. My skin was seared, my closed eyelids hot against my eyes. I was afraid to open them for fear it was Devin, come to throw me directly to the flames.

It wasn't until cool air hit me in the face and my tortured lungs got their first gasp of oxygen that my eyes flew open. Carter's face, soot-blackened and pinched with anxiety, floated over mine. Those clear gray eyes, arrestingly vivid in contrast to the dark soot, looked at me with an agonized relief.

"You're all right, Shelby," he said in a rasping voice. "*Thank God,* you're all right." He clutched me to him, his cheek against my forehead, cool and smooth, wet with perspiration.

He carried me away from the flames, away from the blinding brightness that darkened my eyes to all around me. *It was Carter. Carter had saved me.* My arms encircled his neck and I squeezed with all my might. "Carter," I squeaked, so softly I wasn't sure he could hear me.

But he replied, "Shhh," and knelt with me on the sidewalk, his hand cupping my face. We were instantly surrounded by more people. Medical people. People in uniforms. *Paramedics!*

My gaze shifted quickly to the building from whence we'd come and I saw, with complete shock and indescribable relief, the brick facade of my bookshop with flames licking out of the windows. *My shop!* I looked around me. *Fredericksburg! A sidewalk, for crying out loud!* I heard my own hysterical laughter and knew I sounded insane, but I was *home!* I'd made it back; somehow I'd made it back.

"Carter!" I called, panicked, lest it should all turn out to be a dream. He was suddenly gone and I hadn't even felt him move.

"I'm right here," his rich voice came from behind me, soothing as balm. He knelt again and I leaned against his chest, his arm cradling my shoulders. "You'll be all right," he murmured near my ear.

"No! I have to tell you—" A paramedic who'd knelt beside me started to strap an oxygen mask over my face, but I grabbed it with my hand. "It was me, Carter! The witch you met; it was me!"

Carter looked at me with real anxiety, then nodded to the paramedics. They once again offered the mask, succeeding this time in putting it on me as I was seized by a fit of coughing. I breathed deeply of the fresh, cool air, my eyes closing in dizzy gratification. No drug could have given me the rush that oxygen did.

After a moment I pulled the mask off again. "I have to tell you," I gasped. "No!" I held up a hand to the paramedics. "Please, give me a minute; then you can do

359

whatever you want.'' At Carter's brief nod they backed off.

The facts, the questions, the answers, all rushed into my head at the same time. Where to begin? How to tell him all I now knew?

''The initials,'' I began, ''you once asked me if I knew what they meant.''

''What initials?'' Carter asked, his eyes confused and concerned. His fingers stroked my face in an effort to calm my hysterical speech.

''In your frame, the picture of Meg,'' I insisted, so anxious to make him understand, I could hardly control my voice. ''*I* did them. *I* was the witch you met—I just went back in time, in the fire—I was at your house!''

He looked afraid. ''Shelby—''

''No, listen! I know now why you thought I looked so familiar. Look at me now!'' My hands reached up and knew before feeling the confirmation that my hair had burned off. ''Look at me!'' Tears stung my eyes and rolled down my cheeks. But they were tears of happiness. ''Oh, Carter, I thought I'd never see you again, not *my* Carter.''

He held me tightly. ''What do the initials mean, Shelby?'' he asked, uncertain if I was dreaming or if he was, I'm sure.

''Sign them,'' I said urgently. ''You know, with the alphabet for the deaf that I showed you; sign them. They're not letters, Carter, *they're numbers!* Look at that; the 'W' is almost exactly like a six. And the 'F' like a nine. Remember when you asked me how to tell the difference between a 'V' and a two? Context, I said. Look! WV FW—it's just like saying sixty-two, ninety-six! Sixty-two, the year you left, 1862, and ninety-six, the year you appeared to me! 1996! *I wrote the initials,* Carter. And I told you you'd meet me after a fire and I'd explain them to you. Do you remember?''

Carter's face had gone from skeptical to stunned in a matter of moments. "The fire," he repeated. "I thought she meant the battle, the fire in the heavens . . ."

My own eyes widened. Of course; that was why he'd given up on the idea that I was the same woman as the witch. The night we met he'd looked terrified to see me. He knew it was me, the witch from his house. But when I'd been so ignorant, and so different from that woman, he'd decided he was wrong. I hadn't even thought of the Northern Lights, the fire in the heavens, when I'd described to the Carter in the past what would happen. No wonder he was confused. My God, no wonder we were all confused.

"Don't you see, Carter? We were meant to be together! I didn't make up those letters; someone or something else did. But when I went back, and the picture frame was blank, I scratched them into it. Suddenly, *somehow,* I knew what they meant! It was as if some higher power was at work and planned the whole thing! Don't you see? And the child, Carter—it's not yours. It's Devin Mackenzie's. I saw them together, Devin and Meg. And she wrote in her diary about it. The child isn't yours, Carter, and Bart Lindsey can go jump in a lake!" I began coughing again, but through it I could hear Carter's low laughter, relieved and amazed. His chest shook against me and I leaned into it in sudden exhaustion.

He was here. I was back. We were meant to be together; I was sure of it.

He kissed the top of my head. "God, I love you, Shelby," he murmured against what was left of my hair.

"And the jewels—they're in the chimney," I continued in a voice that was losing considerable steam. "I put them there by accident. But remember, Bart said only the chimney was left of your house."

"Shhh," Carter murmured. "We'll figure it all out later."

"There's so much more to tell you," I wailed feebly. "But I'm tired. I'm just so tired." I felt my heavy eyelids droop over my hot, dry eyes.

His broad hand cupped my head against his shoulder and he rocked me in his arms, so sure, so safe, so permanent. "There's just one thing I want to know, Shelby," he said against my temple. "*Now* will you marry me?"

Despite overwhelming fatigue, laughter bubbled to my lips. "Oh, Carter," I said. "*Yes*. A thousand times, yes."

I felt his smile. "Then it can wait," he whispered. "It can all wait. We have all the time in the world."

A Glimpse of Forever

LINDA O. JOHNSTON

Her wagon train stranded on the Spanish Trail, pioneer Abby Wynne searches the heavens for rain. Gifted with the visionary powers, Abby senses a man in another time gazing at the same night sky. But even she cannot foresee that she will journey to the future and into the arms of her soul mate.

Widower Mike Danziger has escaped the L.A. lights for the Painted Desert, but nothing prepares him for a beauty as radiant as the doe-eyed woman he finds. His intellect can't accept her incredible story, but her warm kisses ease the longing in his heart.

Caught between two eras bridged only by their love, Mike and Abby fight to stay together, even as the past beckons Abby back to save those trapped on the trail. Is their passion a destiny written in the stars, or only a fleeting glimpse of paradise?

_52070-2 $4.99 US/$6.99 CAN

Dorchester Publishing Co., Inc.
65 Commerce Road
Stamford, CT 06902

Please add $1.75 for shipping and handling for the first book and $.50 for each book thereafter. NY, NYC, PA and CT residents, please add appropriate sales tax. No cash, stamps, or C.O.D.s. All orders shipped within 6 weeks via postal service book rate. Canadian orders require $2.00 extra postage and must be paid in U.S. dollars through a U.S. banking facility.

Name _____

Address _____

City _____ State _____ Zip _____

I have enclosed $_____ in payment for the checked book(s).
Payment <u>must</u> accompany all orders.☐ Please send a free catalog.

A Time to Love Again by Flora Speer. When India Baldwin goes to work one Saturday to update her computer skills, she has no idea she will end up backdating herself! But one slip on the keyboard and the lovely young widow is transported back to the time of Charlemagne. Before she knows it, India finds herself merrily munching on boar and quaffing ale, holding her own during a dangerous journey, and yearning for the nights when a warrior's masterful touch leaves her wondering if she ever wants to return to her own time.

__51900-3 $4.99 US/$5.99 CAN

Time Remembered by Elizabeth Crane. Among the ruins of an antebellum mansion, young architect Jody Farnell discovers the diary of a man from another century and a voodoo doll whose ancient spell whisks her back one hundred years to his time. Micah Deveroux yearns for someone he can love above all others, and he thinks he has found that woman until Jody mysteriously appears in his own bedroom. Enchanted by Jody, betrothed to another, Micah fears he has lost his one chance at happiness—unless the same black magic that has brought Jody into his life can work its charms again.

__51904-6 $4.99 US/$5.99 CAN

Dorchester Publishing Co., Inc.
65 Commerce Road
Stamford, CT 06902

Please add $1.75 for shipping and handling for the first book and $.50 for each book thereafter. NY, NYC, PA and CT residents, please add appropriate sales tax. No cash, stamps, or C.O.D.s. All orders shipped within 6 weeks via postal service book rate. Canadian orders require $2.00 extra postage and must be paid in U.S. dollars through a U.S. banking facility.

Name _____

Address _____

City _____ State _____ Zip _____

I have enclosed $_____ in payment for the checked book(s).
Payment <u>must</u> accompany all orders.☐ Please send a free catalog.

TIMESWEPT

Promises From The Past by Victoria Bruce. On a quest to discover answers about her missing father, lovely Maggie Westshire finds herself on a journey that begins in Hot Springs, Arkansas, and leads her back through the years into the strong arms of Shea Younger. And while Maggie is determined to continue the search for her father, she doesn't know how much longer she can resist Shea's considerable charms, or the sweet ecstasy she finds in his timeless embrace.

_52064-8 $4.99 US/$6.99 CAN

Yesterday & Forever by Victoria Alexander. When a carriage ride on a foggy night sweeps artist Margaret Masterson back to Regency London, she finds the picture-perfect nobleman she's always yearned for. But Adam Coleridge is more preoccupied with marrying off his rebellious sister than finding a wife of his own. Soon, however, Maggie and the handsome earl discover a desire that they are powerless to resist. But with time fighting against them, they fear that nothing can keep Maggie in the past—or prevent their love from becoming a passionate memory.

_52060-5 $4.99 US/$6.99 CAN

Dorchester Publishing Co., Inc.
65 Commerce Road
Stamford, CT 06902

Please add $1.75 for shipping and handling for the first book and $.50 for each book thereafter. NY, NYC, PA and CT residents, please add appropriate sales tax. No cash, stamps, or C.O.D.s All orders shipped within 6 weeks via postal service book rate. Canadian orders require $2.00 extra postage and must be paid in U.S. dollars through a U.S. banking facility.

Name_____
Address_____
City _____ State _____ Zip _____
I have enclosed $_____in payment for the checked book(s).
Payment <u>must</u> accompany all orders.□ Please send a free catalog.

EUGENIA RILEY

Devastated by her brother's death in Vietnam, Sarah Jennings retreats to a crumbling Civil War plantation house, where a dark-eyed lover calls to her from across the years. Damien too has lost a brother to war—the War Between the States—yet in Sarah's embrace he finds a sweet ecstasy that makes life worth living. But if Sarah and Damien cannot unravel the secret of her mysterious arrival at Belle Fontaine, their brief tryst in time will end forever.

_52052-4 $5.50 US/$7.50 CAN